38 Roads

Gene Lee

ISBN: 9798991537254

Library of Congress Control Number: 2025935677

Cover Design by All Things that Matter Press

Cover photo from Unsplash

Published in 2025 by All Things that Matter Press

This book is for Bob and Gabe, both of whom chased me down those
38 Roads back in the day.

Acknowledgments

A sincere thanks goes out to Phil and Deb Harris at All Things That Matter Press for publishing my work over the last seven years, as well as for putting up with me. That same sort of thanks goes out to Suzanne Fox who has worked closely with me since 2012 to bring my writing into a semblance of order, as well as to carefully point out where I have made the wrong turn, or missed the point of the story entirely. I also want to thank Leslie Lynch Archer for being the best reader a writer could ever wish to have in his corner.

Epigram: *"A young man ain't got nothing in the world these days"* Mose Allison

Part 1: Gainesville & Beyond

~1~ University Drive

"Stop the War," Sean Morgan yelled out with the rest of the throng as they marched down University Drive. "Stop the freakin' war now." Sean had promised his pal Chuck in the Gainesville chapter of the Vietnam Vets Against the War that he'd be at the protest. It was a promise he had forgotten all the way up to the weird, yet fortuitous, moment that brought him there on that Friday night in early May doing what he had said he would.

A restless sense of unease hung like a pall over Gainesville that spring of 1972—maybe over the entire state of Florida as far as Sean knew. Recently turned twenty-one, he had six credit hours left to finish his first two years of higher education. He was unsure if another two were needed. Nixon was gearing up to run for re-election with the war in Vietnam blazing away at high speed. His girlfriend Luellen had gone off to pursue a dream that Sean couldn't pursue with her. So yeah, when he thought about it there were reasons for him to be uneasy.

Like most of his friends, once the summer after his high school graduation was over Sean had made a beeline for college. In his case, the junior college in Gainesville where he arrived in the fall of 1969. He had one break from his tenure at Santa Fe, caused by a love affair that didn't turn out the way he would have liked. That found him, along with his pal Bob Wilcox, or Boober, stranded in western Mass as another fall was coming on. With Boober staring down the draft, and Sean missing the easy money from his dead father's Social Security benefits, the two of them hitchhiked back to Florida. Gainesville, or G'ville as students called it, where they re-enrolled in the junior college. Sean was planning to stay enrolled come hell or high water. As for Boober? He wandered off after one semester and Sean hadn't heard from him since.

Now another spring was in the air and Sean was still faced with many of the same issues he'd had to deal with after graduating high school. When not in class, which was often, he spent his time loafing around the campus, enjoying the warm days, sneaking a joint in the sunshine while watching the hippie girls going to class—girls enjoying the warm weather in shorts, halter tops, or thin tee shirts. If he had them on hand, Sean would hawk Sopers—that wonderful new addition to the Quaalude family—to his fellow students. Sometimes, during the process of hawking his wares, Sean was offered an invite to partake of them with the buyer. If the buyer was female, these were invites he didn't hesitate to jump on.

In this way April of 1972 had passed, the new month finding Sean strangely alone one Friday night, and suddenly aware of the unease that he had been trying to ignore.

The war, whether or not to continue his education, the creepy president, these were only minor factors behind Sean's unease. Other than having long blond hair the army would immediately cut off, and being nearsighted, which the army had no problems with, he was a prime candidate for cannon fodder. Fortunately, courtesy of the recent draft lottery and the high number his birthday earned him, going to Vietnam was no longer an issue in his life.

As for his education? The truth of it was he didn't really care—he was just passing the time as pleasantly as he could. He didn't care about the upcoming presidential election either. And Luellen? Yes, he missed her. But he had won and lost at love before, sometimes his fault, most times if he were to be brutally honest, and sometimes the girl's fault. There would be another. And that *another* might just be the One.

What he really cared about most on that first Friday night in May as he sat stoned in the house he shared with Will and Tommy, were the FDLE agents swarming their sleepy little college town. In the process. said agents were busily arresting people Sean knew and had done business with. This is what he was contemplating on that Friday night when there came a rude and unexpected knocking on the front door.

The house—the Cave they had named it after moving in—sat at the very end of a dirt road off of Route 20. The nearest neighbor was halfway between it and the highway, and across the street stretched nothing but pine trees and scrub. The concrete block construction kept it nice and cool, while the oak trees all draped with Spanish moss surrounding the structure, made it very dark and cold inside. Hence the name. But it was cheap. Better even than the low rent? The house was remote, a remoteness providing a sense of security when Sean and his roommates were off loading or sending the bales of reefer that paid for the place.

Will was off that night with the Tampa boys lining up a shipment of the Michoacán they had a steady line on. Tommy had borrowed Sean's old Ford pickup for a dope mission of his own. The Johnny Winter band was coming to town and Tommy, their local man, had to line up some smack. Through his efforts, whenever the band came around, Tommy earned both cash and smack for his own use. If Sean felt the need to go anywhere that night, Tommy had left his 650 Bonneville behind for him. It was a better than even trade. The bike was not only faster than his Ford, but a lot more fun to wheel around on.

Not that Sean had any pressing place to be that night. Instead, he was quite happy to roll up a joint, put Jethro Tull's *Aqualung* on the stereo, get high, drink a cold one while grooving to the tunes, and try not to ponder what possibly lay ahead. All of which he was doing when that loud knocking on the front door made its way through the music into his stoned synapses.

What the hell? He pulled himself out of the plushy old recliner that came with the place, stopping to check himself out first in the wall mirror by the door. He brushed his hair back from his forehead and tilted his glasses up his to see how red his eyes might be from the weed in case it was the law at the door. Then satisfied all was cool, he opened the door to find, not the furious agents from the FDLE who wouldn't have knocked anyway, but Pinko.

What the hell, he asked himself—but aloud he said, "Hey man. Where'd you come from?" A legitimate question since he hadn't seen Pinko in months.

"C'mon, man." Pinko was dressed pretty much the same as he'd been when Sean last saw him: jeans, a Stone's tee shirt under a faded army jacket, and ratty old Keds on his feet. He bobbed back and forth on the doorstep waiting for Sean to open the door all the way. "Let me in, will you? I'm coming back from Jax. Fucking hitchhiking, man, trying to get into town."

"Well that sucks," Sean said as he relented and opened the door for his unexpected guest.

"Tell me about it. Some ol' redneck picked me up in Hawthorne. All the way in he kept saying how my long hair looked so sexy. Gave me the creeps, man, let me tell you. The fucker pulled over at the end of your road, grabbed a gun out from under the seat and told me he was either gonna fuck me or kill me, my choice. I jumped, man, ran all the way down here hoping you were here and that sicko didn't follow me."

"Did he?"

"No, man. But I could hear him laughing as he roared off."

"Lucky for you, then."

Sean couldn't help but think the redneck had to be one horny dude to want to fuck Pinko. Tall, thin, Pinko possessed a scraggly face, usually hidden by a mop of untended black hair, that bore a slight resemblance to Mick Jagger's. Someone must have told him this once because Dave, Pinko's real name, did his best to cultivate both Jagger's look and his mannerisms. But looks like Mick's, copied mannerisms, or not, Pinko was one ugly cat—in Sean's eyes at any rate.

Legend had it that Dave was first called "Pinko" by Abbie Hoffman who had been in town with his attorney two years before to give a speech at the university commons. Sean had been there, it was a great speech, the crowd going absolutely wild when a hippie stepped out of the crowd and tossed a handful of Orange Sunshine tabs on the stage. Abbie, never missing a beat, scooped two of the tabs up, popped them in his mouth, offered some to the lawyer who shook his head, no, and then pointing to the hippie said, "Yeah, man, now here's a real honest-to-God pinko for sure, doing his God loving best to corrupt the minds and souls of America's youth." The crowd exploded, the hippie took a bow and then faded away. A year later, at a friend's apartment where Sean had gone to cop some weed, this same cat was, lounging on the sofa like he owned the place. Getting up to greet Sean, he said, "Hey man, I'm Dave." Sean had replied, "No you're not. Word on the street is you're Pinko."

It wasn't that the two of them became fast buddies after that. In fact, Sean had a tough time spending any time with him at all. But the occasions had come and gone, when the two of them could be of mutual benefit to one another. Apparently, this Friday night when Sean was comfortably stoned and minding his own business, was going to be one of them.

The next words out of Pinko's mouth were, "Listen, man, if you give me a ride into town I'll turn you onto something that'll blow your freaking mind."

"Really?" Sean was curious. "Tell me more."

Sean's "more" turned out be a plastic baggie a quarter full with a white powder that Pinko explained was, "Crystal meth, Seano, this shit'll take your head off'"

After getting a glass of water from the kitchen, Pinko took a set of works out of his jean's pocket and laid them on the cable spool that served as a coffee table in the sparsely furnished living room. After carefully tapping some of the powder into the spoon, he filled the syringe with water, squirted the water into the spoon, heated it up with his Zippo until the powder melted into the water, drew the mixture up into the syringe, tapped the barrel twice with his finger to get rid of air bubbles, and then satisfied all was well with both needle and empty spoon, looked up at Sean.

"Ready, Seano?"

Sean supposed he was. Adverse to needles for the most part, he had shot meth once before, a few years back when he was visiting some pals at State College, PA. The trip had included two firsts for Sean: seeing and playing in snow, and shooting up. He had enjoyed the rush from the meth and though the next day he was plenty ragged around the edges, he hadn't ruled out doing it again if offered. Now, here that offer was. Rolling up his flannel shirt sleeve Sean held his arm out.

"Tie me off, partner," Sean said. "I'm as ready I'll ever be."

By the time Pinko pulled the empty syringe from Sean's arm and began the process of cooking up his own shot ,Sean's head was indeed exploding. All of his senses seemed to have jumped alive, the laid back high from the Michoacán a thing of the past as the dull colors of the otherwise stark living room started to shimmer. The music on the stereo, Tull singing, "Snot is running down his nose," drummed into his head as his knees, legs, and feet suddenly propelled him out of the recliner to pace the floor in time to the beat. Pinko, having plunged his own hit home, jerked his head back as the meth raced through his system, and then just like that, was up with Sean pacing the floor, repeating over and over, "Now you dig it, right, Seano? Now you dig it?"

"Oh yes, my man, dig it I do."

Time melded into a rush of vibrating sensations as Sean paced the terrazzo floor, into the kitchen, back into the living room, around the recliner, and the spool in the middle of the floor. Pinko did the same while asking over and over if Sean dug it? Until finally assured that Sean did indeed dig it, Pinko switched to another issue, the substance of which was lost to Sean, wrapped up in his own speeding shimmering thoughts of what came next? An answer to this question seemed out of reach for him until suddenly, something changed in the room.

The music was what changed. It stopped, actually, replaced by the sound of the stylus scratching as the album side came to an end. Above this insistent scratching there was something else, heard when Sean lifted the needle and turned the album over. Just as he was letting the needle down on the first track—there it was. Outside, a car went slowly by, stopping for just a second before continuing down the road, turning around in the cul-de-sac, coming back to stop again in front of the Cave, and then taking off to disappear in the night—all of this happening in the speedy tempo of the meth Sean and Pinko had ingested into their veins.

A car, just a car, Sean thought, as the music once again filled the room. Only a car. Not the law ready to burst in with guns drawn. Whoever was in the car probably just looking for an address, and not finding it, moving on. Just as Sean's brain was moving on with the music. Moving with that, and something else, too. But what was it? Yes, a solution. And remembering this Sean grabbed Pinko by the arm as he came mumbling around the spool and jerked him around so they were face to face, Sean asking as he did so, "Tuscaloosa? What about Tuscaloosa, man?"

"The Stones, man." Sweat streamed down Pinko's face, his eyes. Even in the dim light of the room, his eyes were constricted slits. "The fucking Rolling Stones, man. That's what I said." Pinko smiled as he wiped the sweat away from his face. "The Satanic Majesties themselves. Mick and Keith, coming to Tuscaloosa. Can you dig it, Seano? Fucking Alabama, man. Gonna burn that redneck town down."

"When?"

"July 6th, man. The sixth and seventh. Right after all that fucked up American Independence Day shit. Fuck that. We'll be celebrating our own independence. In our own way. With the freaking Rolling Stones!"

And there it was. The key. Not even really about the Stones or Tuscaloosa. In that never ending rush of speed insight, there was suddenly a destination. A reason to go. To just go. Throw his stuff into the truck and go. And after the Stones? After whatever went down in Tuscaloosa? He would keep on going, all the way west to San Francisco. The Pacific Ocean. That magical coast where every scene had originated. A place where finally he could be free of the cloying academia and endless dope runarounds holding him down. And who knows? Maybe somewhere on that unwinding road he'd find a woman. That tall, blonde, willowy, faceless vision of, *Hey? Someone who knows me. Really knows me. Someone who wants to see and feel it all. Just like I do. With me. Right now. And always. Wild and free like it's supposed to be.* And with this sudden vision reeling in his head, Sean grabbed Pinko's arm again.

"Let's hit it." Sean snatched the keys to the bike off of the cable spool and headed for the door. "Time to go."

"Huh?" Pinko was right behind him, even if he didn't quite understand. "It's still two months away, man."

"Town, buddy. You said you needed a ride into town. Let's go."

And they did.

***

Sean had no idea what time it was as he ripped west on Route 20 towards town with Pinko on the back of the bike muttering a stream of words Sean couldn't catch. Once in town he figured to drop Pinko off wherever it was he'd been headed before making the unexpected pit stop at the Cave and be free of him. That late spring evening the 650 Bonneville moved through was dark, quiet, and cool, the wind on Sean's face a relief from the heat of the methamphetamine racing through his system. Scattered lights from the homes set off from the two-lane highway, flickered, and then faded away as they roared by.

Quickly lost in the enveloping darkness, the disappearing lights reminded Sean that as much as he felt all alone on the planet, he was not.

The normal fifteen minute ride from the Cave into downtown Gainesville seemed to take only seconds. Suddenly, instead of the steady wind in his face, Pinko's nonstop talking behind him, and the thumping growl of the motorcycle's engine between his thighs, they were on University Drive, rumbling past the bars, the record store, and the diner that seemed to have been there for as long as the university had.

Stopped at the traffic light past the railroad tracks that had once marked the eastern boundary of the town, Sean wondered, *What the fuck?*

Down the street, at the intersection of University and Main, more lights were working than just the traffic ones overhead. Blue lights, from at least one cop car parked beneath the traffic lights, revolved around and around, flashing off of the buildings and street lights on the four corners of the intersection. *An accident?* Sean wondered. A big-time traffic stop? He had no idea.

When the light he was waiting at turned green, Sean eased off the clutch and started forward, curious about how close he could get to this new wonderment. He wanted to make sure he'd be safe if it were some kind of police action, but he couldn't pinpoint why he felt driven to know what was going on. He didn't have to wait long to find out. A block later, wooden police barricades closed off traffic going both ways. Standing in front of the barricades, officers were directing traffic to either the right or the left, blowing their whistles as they waved their arms in one direction or the other..

Sean went to the left, rumbling his way down the street until he came to where it intersected with SW 4th Ave. An apartment building fronted the corner of this intersection and seeing an empty parking space, Sean pulled the 650 into it. With the bike's engine idling in neutral, he turned to get his companion's opinion on what was happening. But before he could even ask, Pinko hopped off the back and without a word took off running, up the street, head down and arms pumping as if he were in the Boston Marathon.

Well yeah, Sean thought. *Kind of makes sense. The kid was holding a sizeable amount of dope on him. Between that and the meth they had shot up, anyone could be overly paranoid.* But Pinko's sudden bolt for cover, wherever that might be, was actually one of those so-called blessings. Absent of both Pinko's company, and the bag of crystal he was carrying, Sean was now free to find out just what exactly was happening on University Drive .

After putting the bike up on the kickstand, he was cutting through the side yard of the apartment building to University Drive when the explanation he was seeking came loud and clear.

"STOP THE WAR!" many voices together were yelling. "END THE BOMBING! NO MORE WAR!" Overriding these voices could be heard, "CEASE AND DESIST IMMEDIATELY! THIS IS AN UNLAWFUL ASSEMBLY AND MUST END NOW!"

Oh yeah, Sean thought as he pushed through the hedge bordering the back yard of the apartment building and onto the sidewalk off of the main drag. The anti-war rally. He had completely forgotten. Well, there was nothing to be done for that now. Cosmic circumstance had brought him there, and by god, he was going to do his part. Stepping off of the sidewalk, Sean immediately became one of the throng marching up toward the police road block at the intersection, "Stop the war! Stop the freakin' war now," he shouted.

Between the air conditioned confines of the Cave and the cool wind on his face as he sat astride the Bonneville, Sean hadn't felt the heat of the early the May evening. Caught up in the marching throng, the force of the heat was brought quickly home to him. Crowded together as they walked down University Avenue, the combined body heat of so many only added to the already hot night. The flannel shirt he was wearing quickly became soaked with sweat that began to drip down the legs and into the snakeskin boots, turning the socks into a soggy mess.

As the protestors in front burst into a loud, off key, and to Sean's mind, totally inappropriate rendition of "We Shall Overcome," Sean realized he was actually having fun. Rid of Pinko, he was out and about in the world. Not only that, but he was also doing something important: protesting against that fucked up war in the rice paddies, and doing so with his brothers and sisters of the Resistance. All of them marching together: white and black, straight or freaks, returned vets in their army fatigues, some still with their military crew cuts, others wearing their hair long and girls from Sorority Row wearing dresses, hippie chicks in jeans and tee shirts, and flower dresses that had become the thing. They might disagree on everything else, but they were together on this.

Some guys, jerks from Fraternity Row in their Arrow shirts and pressed slacks, were jeering at the protestors, waving American flags, and tossing beer cans. One of the cans bounced off someone Sean guessed was a returning vet, who broke ranks to smash the asshole to the ground. That act of violence clearly freaked the other frat jerks out totally—for instead of retaliating, they turned and fled. So that that night Sean was with his true people. Up in arms—well, sort of arms, if one counted the signs and banners they carried—all of them in revolt against the fucked up established order. An order that without conscience was blithely sending some of them to an early grave far from home.

All of this newly found insight ripped through his meth fueled head, and when the crowd segued into, "Where Have All the Flowers Gone," Sean raised his voice with theirs and sang.

Pinko showing up at the Cave and the rally were two complete surprises for him that night. But there was one more coming his way. For apparently, one of this *legion of unknown brothers and sisters* in Resistance, *did* know him.

"Sean?"

The soft question, barely registering above the yelling and singing, came from behind him. This was followed by someone taking his hand and yelling, "Sean."

"Poco?"

Yes indeed, it was Poco the Witch Girl. At least that's how Sean thought of her. Always dressed in black, with jet black hair, and deep dark eyes, she wasn't anything close to that willowy blonde vision he imagined waiting for him somewhere out in the void. But she was damned attractive, friendly, fun to be with, and available. Unlike his vision.

He'd gotten the idea she was a witch one night when they were listening to King Crimson and getting high at her place. "I've cast a spell on you," she told him as *In the Court of the Crimson King,* came to an end.

"A spell?" Sean didn't really believe in witches—even so, he figured a certain amount of caution was in order. "What kind of spell?" He was damn sure it wasn't a love spell, seeing as how she had yet to allow him into her bed.

"A good spell, silly," she laughed, moving over closer to him on the sofa. "One that will make you drive me home to Key West with all my stuff at the end of the semester."

"Will that be on my magic carpet?"

"No, you goof. With your truck. It'll be fun." She leaned in then and kissed him, her tongue going deep into his surprised mouth as she placed one of his hands on her breast—a breast, sad to say, fully covered by the black shawl draped over her shoulders. "Once we get there, I promise you will be greatly rewarded, my Prince."

He eased her down on the sofa, thinking a taste of his reward might be in the offing. "What happens if something interferes? You know? And breaks the spell?"

"That would not be good." She levered them both back upright on the sofa. "No, it would not. Never a wise thing to disappoint a witch. Or break one of my spells."

"Well that's good to know, then," he said, disengaging himself from her arms enough that he could fish another joint out of his jean jacket. "I'll make sure that doesn't happen."

She had ruined the flow of the evening for him with her dead serious stuff about her so-called spell. He left shortly after, thinking on the ride back to the Cave that Key West with Poco could be cool. A blast actually. And she pretty much said that once he got her there she'd give it up. So where was the harm in humoring her silly witch act? A chill ran through his body though with his next thought: *But what if it's no act? What if I break the spell?*

Sean hadn't seen her since that night, putting her off with an occasional phone call to say how busy he was. *You know, school stuff, and other crap. Once that's wrapped up we'll get together. I promise.*

But now, here she was at the protest march, looking up into his eyes with her witchy deep dark ones as she asked, "You haven't forgotten about my spell, have you?"

He didn't have a chance to answer. Hearing a loud commotion in front of them Sean witnessed how quickly a night can change. Under the street lamps and flashing red and blue beacons, a shadowy figure ran out ahead of the marchers and tossed something up in the air. He thought at first it was a lit torch but realized in the next moment he was wrong. *Holy shit! A Molotov cocktail? Here? In peaceful Gainesville?* The fiery bottle crashed against the roof of a police car and burst into flames, and Sean's questions were answered for him in what seemed less than a heartbeat.

An angry roar went up from the marchers, a roar that echoed off the walls of the university and apartment buildings. The protestors seemed at first to back away from the police and the burning roof of the cruiser. Then the police closed ranks and began to launch their own projectiles into the crowd of demonstrators. Tear gas exploded in a thick white cloud, enveloping the scene in a haze as those up front reeled back from the line of cops, coughing, clutching at their eyes, and trying to get away from the stinging cloud.

"Jesus," Sean whispered to Poco. "We've got to get out of here. Before it gets any worse!"

But it was too late. Just as Sean was turning away from the crowd to steer the two of them to some semblance of safety, another shadowy figure darted out in front of the police, Molotov cocktail in hand. Before he could toss it at the cops one of the officers drew his handgun and shot him down. The Molotov cocktail smashed against the pavement and an explosion of red hot flame quickly spread over the wounded protestor. In the brilliant flashing light and just before the raging fire consumed the fallen figure, Sean saw that the burning man was Pinko.

The whole scene burst into chaos as the protestors swarmed the police, the cops adding to the chaos with their billy clubs and guns—all of it a madness Sean only wanted to get himself and Poco away from and find a place where they could regroup and come to grips with the insanity that had erupted on University Drive and Main Street.

Yelling, "C'mon. Let's go," Sean did his best to steer her out of the crowd. Most of the protestors were retreating from the pitched battle in front of them—a current of humans so strong it swept Poco up in its stream, out of Sean's grasp, and down the street. He lost her.

It wasn't that he didn't look for her after she disappeared into that raging current of people. He did. But after pushing his way through the herd rushing away from the conflict and with Poco nowhere to be found, Sean finally gave up to focus on his own escape. As he finally reached the sidewalk, and from there into the relative safety of someone's backyard, two thoughts crossed his mind. One—that Pinko couldn't possibly have died, burned to cinders courtesy of the police. They hadn't been the best of buds, true. But still, Sean knew Pinko. Had done dope with him just that night.. So no way he could be dead. Burned to a crisp at the hands of the Gainesville police. Maybe, just maybe, that whole blazing scene had been a hallucination. One caused by the drug Pinko had shot into Sean's veins. Maybe, Sean found himself hoping.

His second thought was about Poco. Maybe she hadn't really been there at all. She was a witch girl, right? Perhaps her in his arms, looking up into his eyes as she asked if he remembered the spell she had cast over him—perhaps none of that had been real. But her doing some sort of astral projection thing, or whatever. Best he let it all go. Best to find the 650 and get his young ass back to the Cave, and away from the madness still going on up the street. A madness, judging by the freaked out looks on the faces of the hippies, vets, and other protestors streaming by, still going on full bore.

Finding the bike being right where he had left it gave him a rush of relief. Yanking the keys out of his jean's pocket, he pushed the kickstand up. In another rumbling moment he blew past the stop sign at the end of the street and headed east and out of town as fast as he could go. Wanting only to get back to the recliner in the Cave where he could sit back, fire up another joint, and feel all right again as he let the night go. Tomorrow he could reassess the situation with a clear mind. Maybe hear something on the TV news about the protest. Maybe find out that the Molotov cocktail throwing nut shot down by the cops wasn't Pinko. Maybe give Poco a call—or better yet, swing by her place and see if she was all right. Tell her he hadn't forgotten her spell, before asking her nicely not to do that astral projection thing on him ever again. It was just too freaky.

Above all, as he roared out of town on Rt. 20, the rumbling beneath him was a reassurance he sorely needed, he wanted desperately to get back to the safety of the Cave.

But when he turned off on the dirt road leading to his sanctuary, he once again saw the flashing blue and red lights of police cruisers in front of where he and his roommates lived. It had to be. There was no other house down there. The fucking cops were at the Cave. And if he continued he would fall right into their fucking hands.

And that, Sean wasn't willing to do. Not that night. Not ever if he had anything to say about it.

Shutting the bike down, after pushing it into the pines off the side of the road, Sean went deeper into the woods, working his way to a position across from the Cave. Concealed behind some palmettos and gull berry bushes, he had a clear view of what was happening where he lived.

What he saw wasn't good. Sean's old Ford pickup was parked haphazardly in the front yard, both doors wide open while two officers rooted through the cab searching for contraband. Knowing Tommy as he did, Sean didn't think it would be long before the cops found what they were looking for. Sure enough, the cop on the driver's side of the truck backed away and held up in the air for his fellow officer to see, a plastic baggie, plainly visible in the glaring light of the cruisers. The baggie looked to be half full—a lot of smack, was Sean's thought. Smack the Johnny Winter's band would be sadly missing for their concert that weekend.

As for Tommy, short and lithe, a star on his high school wrestling team who took them to the State Finals his senior year, he was up against one of the cruisers, hands cuffed behind his back, shaking his head back and forth as if he couldn't understand how he had gotten himself into such a dire position.

Will, like his brother Tommy, now being led out of the wide-open front door of the Cave, hands cuffed behind while other cops ransacked his Volkswagen van parked in front of the Ford pickup. This sort of thing wasn't supposed to happen. Not to them. Young, invincible, just doing their thing, making a little cash, getting high, digging the scene, not hurting anybody. It just wasn't right.

But right, or not it was happening and even Sean could see there wasn't a damn thing he could do about his roommates' fate. As quietly as he could he snaked his way back the way he had come, found the Bonneville, pushed it out of the trees onto the dirt road, and walked it back up to the paved road. Feeling that he was far enough away from the Cave to start it safely, he hopped aboard, revved it up, and headed back toward town.

When he came to the business by-pass on the edge of Gainesville, he turned south. He had no real idea of where he was going or what he was going to do. But halfway between Rt.20 and 441, Sean knew what he had to do.

He had two twenty dollar bills in his jean's pocket, the clothes on his back, and a motorcycle in good condition, though admittedly one he didn't own. He hadn't been shot down in the street like Pinko. Wasn't in handcuffs like Will and Tommy. Nope. None of the above applied to Sean Morgan.

In fact, he was free. Twenty-one and in good health. Everything still out there in front of him, just waiting for him to find it. Close to two months lay between him and the Stones concert in Tuscaloosa. Plenty of time for him to regroup. Scrounge up some cash. And then make his way there. And from there? After the concert? West, of course. All the way to the golden city on the hill and the vast ocean beyond its shore.

He turned south at the light on 441, heading, as much as he hated to admit it, back to Fort Lauderdale, his hometown. Probably to his mother's house if he were to be brutally honest. At least it would be safe there. He could clear his mind a little, set up some action, make his nut, and be ready to haul when the time was right. Yep. He was going home. Just for a bit. Just long enough to get ready for the next run.

Once south of Ocala, Sean finally settled into the ride, his hair blowing out behind him. All the bad stuff that had happened that night was gone in the breeze, his plan, vague as it was, felt as firm in his mind as his two hands on the throttle and the clutch of the motorcycle. No sweat moving forward. All would be revealed, in time, but revealed—all of it good until out of nowhere he remembered—Poco

What about Poco? And that spell of hers? And how she'd said it wasn't wise to break one of her spells. To disappoint a witch. Oh no, she'd said. Not wise at all.

It didn't look like he was going to be moving Poco and her stuff down to Key West anytime soon—that was for sure. Was there a clause anywhere in her spell for situations beyond the control of the person the spell was cast on? A good question, Sean thought as he passed a slow-moving truck in the right lane. One he didn't have an answer for, other than to just keep moving.

And that was all there was to it. *Just keep moving and see what happens,* he told himself. Let the rest of it work out as best it could. With any luck he would come out clean on the other side. He always had. With any luck at all, that might happen for him one more time.

~2~ US 27

He rolled into Lauderdale shortly after three in the morning. It was a long, slow ride, through every small, quiet town in between Gainesville and Fort Lauderdale. Sean minded the speed limits, and the traffic lights; the idea of dealing with another police situation the last thing he wanted any more of in the immediate future.

As Sean turned east on State Road 84 off of 27 west of Fort Lauderdale and was finally on the home stretch, the idea of actually going to his mother's house suddenly struck him as very unappealing. Considering the long day and night he had been through, he was amazed he was even capable of coming up with an alternative. But he did, just as the light turned green at the first intersection. He would go to Dewey's. The Party Palace as it was locally known. Even more surprising than the fact he'd come up with a better plan was that Dewey answered the door at four o'clock in the morning. And instead of telling Sean to go fuck himself, said, "Hey man, the other bedroom's empty so go ahead and make yourself at home. I'll see you tomorrow afternoon at Mary & Charlies when I get off work," before blearily heading back to his room—and that was that.

***

Sean had no idea how long he would stay at Dewey's. If asked during the first few days he was there, he probably would have said something along the lines of, "Oh you know, maybe a week but that's it." But that "maybe a week" turned into over a month, what with summer coming on, and the warm breezes blowing in off the Gulf Stream melting away the cold days and nights at the Cave in Gainesville.

Dewey didn't mind the company. There was always room for one more at the Party Palace. Sean was lucky he arrived when he did—no one other than Dewey was there, and Sean was able to claim the second bedroom for his own. Not that he would have minded sleeping on the floor. He certainly had in the past when his weed-bearing travels brought him to town.

Besides all of that, Sean was happy to see his longtime pal again. The two of them had grown up together, being pretty much inseparable when they were kids. Both of them lean and tow haired, they did all the boy kid's things: swimming at the rock pit, shooting their BB guns at inappropriate targets, riding their bikes to the beach with their skim boards—all of it a magical time in Sean's life he realized, whenever he bothered to look back that far.

By the time high school rolled around, though, they had drifted apart. Dewey went one way—football team and jock pals. Sean another—smoking dope with the hippie kids starting to come out of the dark. By a strange quirk of fate, just before senior year of high school started, Sean found himself living catty corner to where Dewey still lived with his mom and older brother. This quirk of fate occurred when Sean's mom—on the advice of her psychiatrist—kicked him out of the house and set him up in an efficiency apartment on the corner of 17th street.

One Saturday night not long after Sean had moved in, Dewey came over to say *Hey*. The next thing Sean knew they were dropping some tabs of Blue Barrel acid he'd been keeping on hand for the perfect occasion. Just like that, their vanished childhood friendship was back; renewed all over again on that strange tripping evening in Sean's apartment as they listened to The Beatles White Album over, and over. The *Big Realization* of the night was that some things, despite plenty of evidence to the contrary, did last.

Lulled by the warm days, the ocean breezes, and with no pressing place he had to be, Sean spent his days tooling out to the beach on the 650 to go for a swim, soak up some rays and check out the girls in their bikinis. When he tired of this, he would mosey down to the Parrot Lounge on the corner of A1A and Sunrise Boulevard to partake of their famous special: seven drafts for one dollar. The only catch with this beer special, was that the seven drafts were presented all at the same time. Because of this, invariably the last two or three drafts were fairly warm and flat by the time it came to drink them—for the price, a minor catch and one Sean had no problems with.

But the money thing, when he was forced to think about it, was getting close to being an issue. As it neared the end of May cheap drafts, and a diet of Royal Castle burgers, the two twenties he had rolled into town with were shrinking—a factor he brought up one afternoon while shooting pool with Dewey at Mary & Charlies.

"Fuck, man," Sean said as he sank the eight ball prematurely, losing the third game in a row. "Something's got to change here. How're you at darts?"

It was a Wednesday afternoon, "Hump Day Specials" day at Mary & Charlies where from 4 PM to 7 PM the normal fifteen cent Budweiser drafters were only a dime, and fat and juicy cheeseburger with fries, cost a buck.

"Now don't take it so hard, Seano, it's only a game." Dewey chalked the tip of his pool cue, a big grin spread across his face. "One you suck at, it's true. I hate darts, by the way. So in the meantime rack 'em."

"It's not really that," Sean replied as he plunked another quarter into the slot. "The sad truth is I'm running low on bucks." After setting the pool balls in place he waited for Dewey to break. "If I don't do something soon, I'll be flat broke. I damn sure won't make the Stones gig in Tuscaloosa at the rate I'm going. And one way or the other I've got to get there. Flat broke isn't how I envision my arrival there, is all. If you can relate."

"They're looking for some guys at the shop. Need a couple more to man the tar kettles."

"Yeah?"

"Yeah. I could put in a good word for you."

"You're kidding, right? You see me manning a tar kettle?"

Sean certainly didn't see himself doing such a thing—figured he'd rather die than do such a thing.

"Nope," Dewey said as he broke the rack, sinking one high and one low ball. "I'll take low balls. And no, I can't imagine the Sean Morgan I know getting his hands all dirty doing something like manual labor."

"Jesus, Dewey."

After high school, Dewey followed his older brother into the roofing trade. The fact that he was good with his hands and a pair of tin snips got him a place in the sheet metal part of the shop—but not before a tour of duty manning those tar kettles had to be suffered through. Meanwhile, Sean had been doing the college thing in Gainesville and the perks that came with it: money every month from the social security administration, plenty of good weed, and the chance to get down with cute hippie chicks—a resentment-causing situation that one drunken night during Sean's first visit home, Dewey spilled out, and that Sean had not forgotten.

"You know, bud," Sean continued, "That's not what I meant."

"It's cool, man, no sweat." Dewey flipped him a quarter. "I'm just fucking with you. Go get us a couple of fresh beers while I'm busy running the table. I might have a solution for you. We'll see what you think about it when you get back with the beers."

Dewey's prediction about running the table came close to being fulfilled. When Sean came back with the beers he was only able to make one shot—which he missed—and then Dewey finished him off.

"That's enough pool for one day." Dewey put his cue stick in the rack on the wall. "Seeing as how the competition ain't that much. Let's have another cold one and I'll tell you about something I overheard at the shop. It just might work for you."

What Dewey had for him was for sure more to Sean's liking. A Cuban guy by the name of Hector, who worked at the sheet metal shop with Dewey, had a cousin down in Homestead with a line on some quality smack. Hector knew people in his neighborhood who would love to partake, and that Hector could sell to. With another kid on the way, Hector was desperate for extra income. The problem was that working six days a week and Sunday being his only day off, Sunday, being for church and family, he had no way to go down to Homestead and cop. In light of that he was willing to pay someone decent bucks to make the run for him. Hearing this Dewey had immediately thought of Sean, being at loose ends like he was.

"Smack, huh?" Sean replied, after a minute or two of thinking this opportunity over. "Not really my thing you know."

"Hey, man." Dewey said. "I hear you. No big deal. Just thought you might be interested, is all."

Sean finished his beer, but while on the way to the bar to get two, he made a decision. "Not my thing or not, I can use the money," he said when he returned with the fresh drafts. But remembering something as he set the beers down Sean brightened up. "But hey, if smack was good enough for Captain America and Billy, who am I to turn a golden goose away?"

"Now that's the Sean Morgan I know!"

"Only thing is, how am I going to carry it on my bike? Not real comfortable cruising with an ounce of smack in my pocket."

"You have a point there." Then it was Dewey's turn to brighten up. "But like you said, if it was good enough for those dudes in "Easy Rider …" Dewey's smile grew even bigger. "We'll borrow a trick from their scene."

"I'm listening."

"No sweat. Tomorrow after work I'll whip up an airtight, waterproof, metal container. One that'll easily hold an ounce of smack. Make it so it fits right nicely inside the gas tank of your bike. I 'm a sheet metal man after all."

"You're not only a sheet metal man," Sean said as he toasted Dewey with his half full draft. "You're a fucking genius too. Tell your man I'm in. And what the fuck, on that happy note I'll even let you beat me in another game of pool."

On the next Wednesday morning, and for the next two after that, Sean met Hector at his house before Hector had to go to work. Out on the front porch, while Hector's wife was inside the house getting the kids ready for school, Hector handed Sean an envelope with five grand inside. Also inside the envelope were a crude map drawn on one of the kid's school notebook pages, a telephone number penciled in below the map in case of trouble, and that was that. When Hector got off work that afternoon at 4.30, Sean, having been and back from Homestead, met him again at his house and handed over the plastic baggie full of smack safely retrieved from the gas tank of the 650. For his efforts, Sean received another envelope from Hector, this one containing five one-hundred-dollar bills.

"Decent bucks," Dewey told Sean at Mary & Charlies later that afternoon—and decent bucks it was indeed.

By the middle of June, because of Hector, Sean was able to beef up his wardrobe. This was a much-needed beefing up, too, since he left G'ville with literally just the clothes on his back. He bought another pair of Levis, a couple more tee shirts, some of them in different colors and two long sleeved Western shirts. On a mad whim, and despite the heat of the summer, he also bought a leather fringe jacket, the total coolness of which was simply too much to pass up. Besides, he reasoned as he laid the cash down on the counter, *Won't I be looking so totally cool sporting it at the Stones concert, fuck the heat besides?* Not only that, seeing as how Dewey hadn't hit him up for any rent, for his part Sean kept the ice box loaded with grub and beer. So all in all, things were looking up in Sean Morgan's world. About damn time too was the way he saw it.

Except—on the Tuesday evening before Sean was to do his thing with Hector the next morning, Dewey, after gratefully pulling the ring tab off the can of Budweiser Sean handed him, he dropped the hammer.

"Bad news, Seano. Hector says to tell you it's all done."

"Done? Damn, I was hoping to make one more run before heading to Tuscaloosa."

"Aint gonna happen. Seems the Feds took down Hector's cousin."

"Fuck." But Sean couldn't help wondering, *Why oh why, were all his good money making schemes being put to an early rest by the law lately?* "What about Hector? Shit, what about me? Should I be booking out of here now?"

Dewey started laughing. "Oh man, you should see the look on your face, buster. I can't believe it—Sean Morgan, the King of Cool is worried about something!"

"It's not all that humorous, man. Sorry to disappoint but it seems to me my concerns here are legit."

But Dewey told Sean not to sweat it. "Hector says Raul is a standup guy. He told me to thank you for helping him out—his exact words actually being, 'Tell Seano mucha gracias from me.' He also said that if something else comes along he'll be sure to let you know. So relax King of Cool. And consider yourself lucky."

So there it was, and that was just fine. *Bummer about Raul,* Sean thought. *But hey, bummer for Will and Tommy too—the one common denominator being that Sean Morgan's luck was holding up.* Holding up pretty well, actually. Courtesy of Hector, Sean had close to a thousand bucks to head to Alabama in two weeks, a motorcycle, and new duds to wear for the event. In the meantime, all he had to do was lay back, dig the beach, the sunshine, whatever else good to dig that came his way, and *voila!* Next stop? The Rolling Stones concert in Tuscaloosa. And after that? The plan was still the same. Like the famous man said: Go west young man.

Except—on one of those warm, humid mornings as Sean was debating the beach, or fuck it, just go right to the Parrot for seven drafts, he heard a knock on the front door. *Well it damn sure won't be Pinko standing there will it?* Pinko or not, Sean got up to answer the knock. *Pinko's ghost maybe*, which made Sean sort of sad, and surprisingly so. But it wasn't Pinko, or his ghost, at the door.

But Boober—and unknown to Sean, the beginning of the end of his Tuscaloosa plan.

~3~ SR 84

It was Boober all right, still looking pretty much the same despite the interval of time since Sean had seen him last. He was dressed pretty much the same as back then: faded jeans, loose Hawaiian shirt covering his lanky torso, and a pair of beat up boots on his big feet. Also the same? The sardonic grin splitting his thin lips, the Camel hanging from his mouth, and the long black hair falling down the back of his neck completed the picture. The Budweiser in his right hand, a six pack dangling from his left hand only added to his image.

"Boober?"

Sean knew it wasn't much of a g greeting to his old pal, a result from the Quaaludes, and beer, he consumed the night before with Dewey while listening to the Derek and the Dominos record Dewey brought home after work. They had copped a good buzz while listening to the record and passing the time. Enough of a buzz that come morning Sean was grateful, that unlike Dewey, he didn't have to go to work, but instead could loaf on the sofa.

"That's right, it's me, Boober. You gonna let me in or what?" Not waiting for an answer Boober pushed into the apartment, pausing only to hand Sean a beer. "Here, drink this. You look like you need it." He plopped down in the recliner in the corner. "You look like shit, by the way. Got any reef?"

"Yeah, we've got some lying around here somewhere. And thanks for the compliment. Don't know what you expect, though. Don't hear or see from you in more than a year and here you are at the doorstep like it was just yesterday, man."

"I've been keeping a low profile, man." Boober put his empty beer can on the coffee table. "I had to split from Gainesville. Been down here with the old man, since. Working with him at the airport trying to put together some cash for a plan I have."

"Man, you sure left me and Curly hanging." Sean had found the bag of Jamaican Dewey stashed under the sofa before they crashed the night before and got busy rolling a joint. "You know, at Ol' Yeller?"

Fortunately for his hangover, Sean was thinking, it was comfortably dim in the apartment because of the shadows created by the light coming through the closed Venetian blinds. Playing off Boober in his Hawaiian shirt, and the wooden coffee table stacked high with empty beer cans, the shadows gave the room an eerie 1940's black and white feel—a cozy one at that.

He snapped out of this hangover created reverie, though, when Boober passed him the lit joint. He took a good hit, letting the smoke drift off into the shadows, the cozy 1940's black and white haze that made him feel like, *Hey, it's going to be all right. It's all going to be all right.*

"So yeah," as Sean suddenly remembered what he had been talking about. "What was the deal with that, you know? Curly and I come in from morning class and you and your stuff are gone, man. Just like that, not a fuck you, or nothing. Rude, buddy. Pretty damn rude." And then, because he didn't really mean any of it. He was suddenly stoned and happy to see his old pal again, Sean couldn't help but laugh.

"Ah man." Boober let his own toke from the joint seep out from his lungs. "You remember those dudes and the smack they had up at that fucking Hippie House on the corner? That freaking George and his trust fund paying for it making it so I couldn't say no?"

"I remember."

"I woke up that morning you're talking about, and my immediate thought was to go find George, head up to the corner, and well, shit, Sean, all of a sudden that scared the shit out of me, you know. I realized I had to split. Just get out and change it all up. So that's what I did. It's been working, too. And now I have a better plan."

"I'm a fan of better plans." Sean added his empty beer can to the pile on the coffee table, took another hit off the joint, before passing it back to Boober. "Give me another one of those beers you're packing and tell me about this plan of yours."

The Jamaican bud they were smoking was okay, though nowhere close to the Michoacán Sean and the Tampa boys had been floating around Gainesville. Still, it was good enough to keep Sean elevated in that black and white 1940's type groove while he waited to hear what Boober had to say. There was something to do first, though. Something to keep the groove stable. Rooting through the albums stacked by the turntable he found a Boz Scagg's album and slipped it onto the turn table. As Boz began to sing about how he was going to get up and make his life shine, Sean had to agree. *Oh yeah, me and Boober, man, we're gonna get up and make our lives shine all right. Just like they're starting to shine right now.*

"Ready, partner," Sean said as he settled back on the sofa. "Let's hear it."

"I'm off to Canada." Boober's usual sardonic grin was gone, replaced by a tight look Sean couldn't recall seeing before. "I have to. No choice."

"Yeah. I hear you. But you don't need me for that."

"I know. But some of us aren't' as lucky as you."

"I *have* been lucky on occasion." Sean didn't want to smile, considering how his luck of late hadn't included Will and Tommy in G'ville. Or for that matter, Poco, when one got right down to it. "But like I said, you don't need me for that."

"Yeah, you're right. I don't. But there is something you *can* do."

What Sean could do went like this: Boober had a friend up in Amherst going to school there. A guy Boober had grown up with in Bramford, Mass. Red being this guy's name, happened to know some guys who had set up a colony of draft dodgers—or exiles as they liked to call themselves—in Montreal. Red was more than happy to get Boober an invite to the colony, but Boober had to do something in return. And here was where Sean came in.

"They're dying for weed up there. Going crazy about the drought, as Red put it."

"I'll run anything state side." A statement made true by Sean's recent partnership with Hector. "But I'm not crossing any international borders. Sorry, pal."

"Not into Canada, jackass. To Red in Amherst, which last I looked, was still a part of the United States."

"You're a funny guy, all right. I'll give you that." Boz Scaggs, as Sean had hoped, was doing a good job of keeping that 1940's feel going. *You know, those old Bogart flicks? Gun runners, the black bird, stuff like that?* Which brought up another question. "Where we going to get the weed? I'm pretty much tapped down here."

"What about G'ville?"

"Yeah, I don't know." Not with Will and Tommy, and from what he'd heard, the Tampa boys, all locked up awaiting trial—until, just like in one of those 1940's Bogie gangster flicks, a possible solution appeared. "You know, I might have a connection. Can't swear to it. but I might. Will require a phone call and some luck."

This possible connection centered on a chick from Englewood by the name of Kat. She , and her wacked out roommate, were always peddling some sort of dope around G'ville; the last crop being powdered THC. When Sean ingested some with those girls—just like Kat said it would— it took him to another planet. If anyone knew where to cop some weight in G'ville right then it was probably her.

"Make the call."

"Let's not get pushy, partner. Give me a second or two. I might come up with another question."

Which he did, almost in less than a second it seemed, though it could have been longer, what with the stoned groove he was drifting in.

"How're we going to get to Amherst? I don't see us packing the dope, you, and me, all of us, on my bike. I don't even know how you got here this morning, come to think of it." And added, remembering Pinko and the horny redneck in Gainesville, "You didn't hitchhike did you? The last guy who used his thumb to come hang with me ended up dead. Well … maybe dead."

"Huh? What the fuck're you babbling about?" Sean had to admit that he liked the quizzical look on Boober's face. "No, don't tell me. And no, I didn't hitchhike. My sister dropped me off on her way to work at the diner. Don't ever eat there by the way. Not unless you're into a cockroach or two sharing your grub. But yeah, that wheels thing? That's a problem for sure."

They were quiet then as the album played out, both of them, or at least Sean, contemplating the transportation issue necessary to the plan.

Like Sean's sudden inspiration about Kat in G'ville, it was Boober's turn to come up with the solution. "Got it, buster! A drive-away car. There's an office by the port on US1. It's easy, man. We'll find someone who needs their car driven to Boston. Red can pick us up when we get there, and bingo, done deal."

"I like it." And he did—suddenly Sean liked it very much. What was not to like? A road trip north with an old pal he hadn't run with in a while. The chance to make some bucks, and what with the Tuscaloosa thing looming on the horizon, the more money he carried with him the better. But—and just like that, there was another snag.

"Only thing is, man, I'm out of here in like two weeks. Going to Tuscaloosa for the Stones gig right after the 4th of July. I'm not missing that, pal, no way, no how."

"No issue there. I don't see it taking more than a week, tops, to line up car, weed, and book. You'll be back in plenty of time to hop on that 650 and make like Easy Rider to redneck country and the Stones. No problem at all." Boober suddenly realized they were out of beer. "We've run dry here. Want to hit Mary & Charlies for a couple? My treat."

"You're on, partner." Sean hated to leave the Bogie, 1940's, Boz Scagg"s *Loan Me a Dime* groove they had going. But Boober was right— another couple of cold beers were in order to celebrate Boober's plan. To celebrate Sean's next move in whatever the grand scheme of things was to be. "Let's hit it," he said. "And yes indeed sir, the beers are on you."

~4~ Florida Turnpike

Two days later it was a warm and humid morning in June. Actually, by the time they left the Party Palace in the drive-away 1970 Oldsmobile Cutlass, , it was no longer morning, but early afternoon as duly noted by the noon horn at the port, when Sean and Boober made tracks for the turnpike entrance west of town. From there, next stop, other than for gas and beer if needed, Gainesville.

Boober was at the wheel, which was just fine with Sean, slightly hung-over as he was from the going away party the night before. It wasn't much of a sendoff, really—just Dewey, Boober, and Sean, the three of them smoking Jamaican bud, tossing down beers, and bullshitting about what they saw coming in their immediate futures. It was enough of a party, though, to leave Sean queasy and his nerves ends slightly rattled. But Boober, who had drunk and smoked as much, if not more, seemed perfectly content behind the wheel as he threaded his way through State Road 84's Friday noontime traffic. Puffing away at a Camel, sardonic grin back in place, his boot heel on the gas pedal tapped to the beat of the tunes coming out of the car radio. The songs were mainly AM hits from WQAM out of Miami with the occasional Beatles, Rolling Stones, yeah baby, the Stones! Be seeing you soon, or Cream song thrown in. Though the good songs were few and far between, when they arrived they helped to clear Sean's brain of the disgust brought on by the Top 40 stuff the station had to play for the record companies paying the tab.

Just after getting the toll ticket at the turnpike entrance Boober turned to Sean—semi-nodding, and tapped him on the shoulder. "How about making yourself useful and hand me a beer. Roll a joint, too, while you're at."

"It's a little early for beer, isn't it?" In fact, the thought of drinking a beer—cold Buds Boober had lovingly nestled on a bed of ice in a cooler, was just about enough to make Sean gag.

"You heard the noon horn just like I did. It's time."

Well, there you have it, was Sean's thought. After retrieving beers for the both of them he rolled a fatty out of the bag Dewey had given him as a going away present the night before. Just as he fired it up, *surprise, surprise,* Spirit's *Trucking* came blasting out of the car radio. Boober and Sean in synch looked at one another, with Boober the first to break the spell. "Fucking A, man. Let's get it!"

Ramping the Olds up to 85 mph, Boober kept it there until they stopped for gas at the Orlando Plaza. By then they had made a dent in the case of the beer and their travel buzz also supplemented by another joint smoked along the way. By the time they stopped for gas at the plaza, the afternoon had turned into sort of rolling dream. A dream marked by the mile posts on the side of the road, and his faint reflection in the window glass adding to the illusion of the day.

They rolled into Gainesville later that afternoon, the clock on the university tower reading just past six. They would have arrived a little earlier, but Boober had suggested a rest stop at Payne's Prairie. At a pull off on 441where they sat in the comfort of the air-conditioned Olds drinking beer, smoking another fat splif, and digging the good tunes from the universities' FM. The sun's fading light shafted through the thunderheads building up over Payne's Prairie, the wire grass covering the prairie waving in the wind blowing out from these thunderheads.

It was a mellow scene— one that turned not so mellow when they entered the city limits and the events of his recent past in Gainesville began to wash over him. Flashing in his head from that TV show, Lost in Space, he couldn't help but blurt out, "Danger Will Robinson! Danger!"

"What the fuck are you babbling about now, amigo?" Boober pushed his black hair away from his forehead, a look of concern crossing his face. "You okay?"

"Aw man, it's this fucking town. Suddenly I'm not sure this is such a good idea. Dig?"

And he *wasn't* sure—was wary in fact about any potentially bad spell Poco might have cast his way when she realized, on the agreed upon morning to head together down to Key West that he wasn't going to show. Good spells, bad spells, real or not, he didn't know and didn't want to find out. And there was that other reason for him to be suddenly wary: the possible presence of FDLE agents still around, just waiting to fuck with Sean Morgan now that he was back on their turf.

"Paranoia strikes deep," Boober said, Buffalo Springfield's song, *For What It's Worth*, playing on the radio. "You're just stoned is all. I'm hungry. Let's hit In & Out before we show up at your girlfriend's place."

"She's not my girlfriend, but yeah, burgers and fries might help. Cut the freaky edge a little."

Waiting on the light at University and Main, proof positive that he was indeed back in G'ville, appeared. For there on the corner, bobbing up and down on his feet as he waited for the light to change, still skinny, still long-bearded with greasy hair hanging down past his shoulders, wearing a ratty pair of cut-offs and equally ratty tee shirt, and sandals, was another local legend, still alive, still the same.

"Look, Bobby," Sean said, pointing at the G'ville denizen on the corner. "It's Whacko, man. Fucking Whacko."

"Jaysus!" Boober was laughing as the light changed and he made the turn on to Main Street. "That's fucking amazing, man. He's still alive? Doesn't seem possible."

Also still the same? Two frat guys coming out of the bar on the corner, where Whacko was anxiously waiting, and starting up with their crap, insults, jokes, and other crap. Sean thought, *Whacko's a nut job, no doubt*. But he doesn't deserve that crap from those guys.

"Remember that night, Bobby, at the Florida Theater? When they were showing that fucked up Stone's *Gimme Shelter* flick? And all of a sudden Whacko goes running up in front of the screen, jumping up and down and singing along with *Gimme Shelter* and trying to get us all to join in?"

"Burned into my memory, sad to say. Fuck it. Let's grab a bite and go cop."

Well, Boober was right, Sean supposed. Still, he couldn't help feeling a little sorry for Whacko. Just another burn out, yes, but it wasn't right he should suffer abuse at the hands of assholes that would never walk in his shoes. Or sandals, as the case might be. On the bright side, Whacko was still alive. Unlike Pinko, possibly. So who knows? Perhaps hope, for him and others like him, might still spring eternal. A weighty question indeed. But then Boober was pulling the Olds into the drive-up lane at In & Out, and Sean's sympathy for Whacko and those others like him was smoothed away by the smell of greasy burgers and fries.

The hot food, consumed inside the car and washed down with a thick chocolate shake as opposed to Boober's Budweiser, were as good as ever. Much needed too, after the long drive, beers, and reefer. Fed, and somewhat back to normal, they started for Kat's place. Boober turned down Sorority Row so they could gawk at the potential debs with their out-of-date hairdos. Seeing quickly how nothing there had changed, Boober swung the Olds around and headed for Kat's. Just as they were coming up on her street Sean grabbed Boober by the shoulder.

"Listen, Bobby, let's not hang any longer than necessary." As usual, Boober's sardonic grin revealed all of nothing. "I mean it, man. Once we cop let's split. Drive all freaking night if we have to. I just don't like it, man. This place, dig? It's just one big drag."

"Yeah." Boober sounded mellow and worn out, wrung empty perhaps by the beer, the reefer, and the five hour drive. "I hear you."

For Sean knew as well as Boober did how Boober's college time demons from his tour of duty in G'ville still haunted him. The nights spent working at the local taco stand while his more affluent roommates were downing brews and getting stoned. His parents cutting off pocket money until he brought up his grades. Other nights, ones spent after skipping the day's classes to float around Gainesville, further ensuing low grades and no pocket money from home. Thus mandating more shifts at the taco joint, all of this a vicious cycle with no end in sight. A cycle that came to an end when George, a trust fund kid, turned Boober onto the smack scene at the Hippie House. Finally, after months of nodding out every chance he could, Boober woke up one morning and realized the only way he could save himself was to run.

So yeah, Sean was thinking, Boober had bad memories of his own concerning Gainesville. But the good news right then was no FDLE agents anywhere in sight when Kat opened the door. Just a big hug from her and a "Good to see you again." Followed by a, "Nice to meet you," when Sean introduced her to Boober. And then they were inside her place, her strange roommate nowhere around. What *was* around, were the ten keys of commercial grade Colombian Sean had requested over the phone two days before, all wrapped up in plastic bundles, stacked neatly in a large duffel bag, and looking pretty much like manna from heaven.

Sean had met Kat through Luellen when both his girlfriend and Kat were taking an anthropology class together. In fact, Kat had been chosen for the Egypt dig back in January, instead of Luellen. Unfortunately, for both Sean and Kat, Kat had to bow out due to some family issues back home. Chances were, Sean believed, that he and Luellen might still be together if Kat hadn't had to bail on the Egypt thing.

Not that he harbored any grudge against Kat. She was cool, perhaps considered homely by those who didn't know her, being tall, thin, with long straight brown hair, and just a hint of boobs underneath the tee shirts she usually wore. Sean pegged her as being a tomboy, a chick ready to do whatever the guys were doing. If competition was involved—ingesting drugs, grades in school, being up on the latest music, cool movies, cool scenes— Kat wanted to be on top.

She had also been there to comfort Sean after Luellen left—friendly comfort only. Luellen was her best friend after all. As for Sean, he just wasn't interested at the time. But now, *Well hey, that Kat's looking pretty good these day.*

For not only had it been a long, tiring, day, it had been a long time, too, for Sean. A shudder rippled through him suddenly at the thought of the Witch Girl. A shudder he was able to shove aside when Kat stood up from the couch as the The Doors, *The End*, one of Sean's favorite songs, filled the air.

"I'm hitting the rack, guys," she told them, a sleepy smile on her face. "Early class in the a.m. Get up whenever you want, just lock the door behind you when you split."

"Will do," Sean and Boober echoed, and then Kat was gone, disappearing behind her bedroom door. Sean kicked his boots off and stretched out on the couch, Boober and he having flipped a coin for the honors. Boober, took the blankets Kat had put out, and made a bed for himself on the floor, muttering loud enough for Sean to hear, "I should have taken a look at that coin before we flipped." Sean's last thought, *Come morning? On the road. Out of here. And not a freaking moment too soon.*

Then he was asleep, deeply, dreaming, most of which he couldn't quite make out. There was one dream he *could* make out, of Pinko at the protest march, Pinko, turning as he was lifting his arm to toss the Molotov cocktail, and winking at him. Except it wasn't Pinko, but Boober. Sean jerked awake then, but only for a moment before he drifted off once more, to wake, finally, to gray light filtering in through the blinds on the living room window. But it wasn't the early morning light that woke him. But a sound. Raising his head, he discovered that the unknown sound came from Boober as he closed the door to Kat's bedroom. *Now what the fuck is that all about?*

A question left unanswered when Boober shook Sean by the shoulder. "You awake buster?" he whispered. "It's time to hit it."

Sean didn't see the need for such urgency, but Boober was the wheelman. If the wheelman said it was time to go, he couldn't say no.

"Right behind you, Bobby." Sitting up on the couch, his head spinning with this sudden movement, Sean repeated, "Right behind you."

After leaving a note on the kitchen table for Kat—Sean's aside to Boober as he was scrawling a goodbye on the napkin they were using for paper, "Maybe you oughta tell her you love her, or something?" A small joke, true, but one, even that early in the day, that raised a twinge of a grin on Boober's face. And then it was out the front door, an hour before dawn, the big eights of the Olds reverberating off the silent street, the two travelers comfortably ensconced in the front seat, everything fine and dandy—except for one thing.

"I'm hungry, buddy. Too many hours between In & Out last night, and now. How about Hap's on the way out?"

"Krispy Kreme not good enough for you?"

"Only good when you're tripping," Sean said, remembering how late at night, or very early morning, that donut shop crawled with every freak in town stoned on whatever it was they were stoned on.

"Was it good even then?"

"I suppose that would depend on one's take at the time."

"Yeah," Boober said. "Pretty much how I remember it, too. Hap's is it then."

***

Hap's, a long room with small sets of table and chairs on one side, a counter running the length of the place on the other, was just like any other time Sean had been there: most of the stools occupied by an assortment of workers eating before punching the clock, as well as students grabbing a bite before class. Two fat waitresses were busy as all get out; one manning the tables, the other behind the counter taking orders, while the smell of eggs and meat being fried wafted out from the kitchen in the rear of the building. The food—grits, two eggs, bacon, and white toast for Sean, Boober opting for an omelet—the food was pretty good.

The most interesting thing in the whole place was the front page of the *Gainesville Sun*. Sean was casually looking at it as he ate, when a small story at the bottom of the page got his attention. This story was about five men getting arrested for breaking into the Democratic Party headquarters at the Watergate complex in D.C.

With breakfast over Boober paid the tab and headed out the door, Sean right behind him, both of them into the early summer heat of a Gainesville morning. Boston and Amherst were in front of them. Everything else was safely in the past.

~5~ Highway 301 North

Coming up on Waldo on 301north some ten miles or so out of G'ville, Boober pulled a crumpled pack of Camels from the pocket of his Hawaiian shirt and frowned. "Damn, my last smoke." He lit up anyway, a grin of satisfaction on his angular face as he exhaled a thick stream of Turkish tobacco smoke that filled the Olds—his grin quickly replaced by one of concern. "No beer, either. Not good Tonto, not good at all."

"Now why is it I have to be the Indian here?" Sean, all the way awake, fueled by the breakfast at Hap's, was feeling good to be in the fast moving car, out of Gainesville, away from the paranoia washing over him while there—despite his efforts to keep it at bay.

"It's obvious," Boober said. "I'm sure time will prove me right."

"You're an asshole, I know that." Laughing at his own little joke he added, "And time has certainly proved me right on that." Seeing the city limits sign for Waldo, Sean offered a word of advice. "Better slow it down, bub, or cowboy, Indian, whatever, if you don't we could wind up in a world of shit."

The sun was well up over the pine trees, palmettos, and scraggly oaks scattered through the wiregrass fields lining both sides of the highway. Waldo's only purpose, appearing out of nowhere like it always seemed to do—to Sean anyways—to break up the monotonous experience of driving Highway 301. The little country town did have a train station, though, a feature of the redneck burg Sean had used in the past. It was also a notorious speed trap. A place where one mile over the posted 25mph was good for a ticket from the cops, armed with radar guns, and stationed out of sight on both ends of the town to nail speeders coming and going—hence Sean's warning.

When Boober went to pull into the only convenience store in the town to re-up on smokes and beer, Sean found it necessary to warn him again.

"Not here, Kemosabe. If one of the two local cops spot a couple of longhairs like you and me coming out of the store packing beers, their curiosity might get the better of them."

"You're just a big wad of paranoia today, Tonto," Boober said as he kept on going. "Lighten up buster. It's not a good look for you."

"Cautious is all. That's the word I'd use. There's bound to be another store up the road."

"You better pray this 'bound to be store' has Humps and Budweiser."

"It's fucking redneck central from here to Jacksonville, Bobby. They'll have what you're looking for. Not to worry."

"Oh, I worry. Riding with you I have to."

After barking out a snort of a laugh, Boober fell silent, his eyes on the road, one hand on the wheel, the other fiddling with the radio dial searching for decent tunes. All he could find was annoying chatter about the U of F's football team on the one station that came in clearly—keeping that station tuned in, until finally he'd had enough, of both chatter and the silence.

Rolling down the window Boober yelled out to the world they were rushing past, "Fuck the goddamn Gators, I say! Fuck them and the goddamn reptile."

"That's right, Bobby. Let 'em have it." Suddenly, Sean's curiosity from earlier was back. "So tell me, Kemosabe, how was she?"

Boober, his face, shrouded in a cloud of smoke, showed no sign of hearing the question.

"Who?"

"Okay." Sean laughed as he got busy rolling up the first joint of the day from the travel bag of buds he'd carefully skimmed off one of the kilos. "If that's how you want to play it."

It was quiet again in the Olds, other than for the sound made as they smoked, and passed the joint between them. Silent until a few miles later they rolled into Starke where Boober suddenly perked up, having spied an open package store; well, a bar, actually, along with a package store. Both bar, and package store, were housed in a ramshackle stucco building with that stone Alamo kind of false front popular in buildings in Florida in the 20's and 30's. The marquee atop the doorway still had its neon lights on announcing, "The Stoned Cowboys." This band, according to the sign, had played a gig there the night before. *The night before?* Hell, it could have been ten years ago, Sean thought, for judging by the faded looks of the town it was like it was stuck in some kind of time warp.

"It's about freaking time." Boober slammed on the brakes as he ripped into a parking space in front of the bar/packy store, that sardonic grin of his gone all maniacal as he turned the engine off. "And that's all I've got to say."

"Huh?"

It was the only response Sean could come up with, still wondering as he was, if time warp enveloping Starke was—*what? Good? Or bad?* He had no idea.

"You heard me, Tonto. It's well past 7a.m. I've had coffee, breakfast, smoked a J, covered plenty of miles behind this wheel, and now I'm ready—no, not ready, but deserving of a beer. Out!"

Though Sean heartedly agreed with all of the above, there was still some unfinished business. While opening the rear passenger side door to grab the cooler from the back seat, as innocently as he could muster, Sean asked, "So tell me, Kemosabe. How was she?"

"Sweet," Boober answered—but only later, after they completed their mission in the packy store and he popped the top of a cold can of Bud and took a long pull. "Sweet. That's how she was."

"Sweet?"

"Yes, Kat's a very sweet girl—what with the way she came out and tried to wake you on the couch. But sadly, very sadly, you were dead to the world. Unlike Yours Truly. Who Kat, seeing that I was awake and you were not, told me, 'There's plenty of room in my bed, Bob, if you don't want to crash on the floor.' And Tonto, who was I to argue with her? Especially after she told me smoking pot always made her horny— well there you have it. I had to help that sweet girl out. All I could do."

"Fuck." If the cold beer was taking away the sting away from Boober's revelation, it was too early to tell.

"Exactly Tonto, old pal. Fuck."

"Yeah," Sean whispered. *"Fuck."*

Followed by, and again, to himself, *Good for Bobby. Good for him. It doesn't matter who gets the girl, who will save the day. We're on the road. Like Sherlock said: the game is afoot. So fuck.* Smiling, Sean finished his beer, chucked the empty on the floor, and looked at Boober. "Ready for another?"

"Fucking A." Boober chucked his own empty can into the back as well. "Fucking A buster."

~6~ I-95

The Cutlass topped the crest of the high I-95 bridge just north of Jacksonville a little past nine that morning. The bridge, a mass of concrete and steel cables spanning the St. Mary's river, had been like a sparkling beacon in the early morning sun when they approached. As they rolled across it Sean looked down to see the vast river, all brown in the early light, slowly moving from the west to the east on its journey to the sea. With his window down, the morning air flooding into the car was warm, but happily, nowhere near the suffocating heat of the July, August, and September days to come. The flood of air just warm enough to dry up the fine sheen of sweat on his forehead.

Being that he was on his second beer of the day, not to mention the fat bomber they had just finished before reaching the bridge, Sean was feeling no pain. In fact, he felt rather fine, grooving along with *"Sympathy for the Devil"* blasting on the radio, thinking, *That's right, man, pretty soon I'll be there with you guys, Tuscaloosa, yeah, not that far away.* Just as "Pleased to meet you," belted out through the radio speakers, Sean beating time on the dashboard, Boober joined in with him, "... guess my name." while down below, sea birds wheeled in the blue sky over the banks of the river, the boats, big and small, moving on that big water, lit up and shining in the morning sun.

Then, just like that, they were back to sea level, the Cutlass whipping past the "Welcome to Georgia" sign at its steady 75 miles per, the Wheelman unwilling to push it, especially in Georgia. Much like Waldo, the whole state of Georgia was a freaking speed trap, with State troopers hiding behind trees or hunkered down off to the side below a dip in the road. As every hippie knew, these troopers possessed keen eyes, well trained to spot any longhair traveling through their state and up to no good; those good old boys in their buttoned up uniforms and flat brim hats, very much aware that hippies were going to be the ruination of the good old US-of-A, what with all that dope smoking, loud music and naked dancing they liked to do.

But Florida was behind them now. What lay ahead? *Unknown—but hopefully about to go according to plan.* In the meantime; Boober and he were in Georgia, suddenly awakening in Sean a memory of another crossing of that same bridge.

When he was fifteen, a year or so after his father died in the accident. Accident yes, but as Sean knew, along with everyone who knew his father, Sean's mother included, the accident wouldn't have happened if his father hadn't been drunk, coming home late at night from what he'd told his wife was a business meeting, but God knows where Sean, Sr. had really been. It was on an October morning cool, crisp, and heavy with portents of a future to come, when Sean crossed that bridge—this time on the back of Cal's Honda Dream 150, destination New York City. *The Big Apple, yeah.* Where women, and plenty of good kicks awaited them. Both Cal and he had just read "On the Road," a paperback copy of which Sean had liberated from his local drug store, both title and author's name catching his attention. The fifteen year old boys figured anything had to be better than what they were living in their respective homes and high school hell. So instead of going to school that morning, they headed north. Their grand adventure ground to a halt the very next morning after crossing the river, at the hands of a deputy sheriff in the little town of Folkston, GA. The next thing Sean knew, he was on his way back to Lauderdale in his mother's Chrysler, and she, madder than hell.

From there, 10th grade turned into a revolving door of juvenile detentions. Most of the charges that landed him in Juvie were minor ones: shoplifting, public drunkenness at the Armory one night, and so on. Finally, that Christmas holiday, he and an older pal of his were nabbed for grand theft auto. While waiting in the tank at the Lauderdale police station, Sean's pal, Frank, told him, "No more Juvie for me, I guess. It's off to Mariana from here."

Sean's reply? "That sounds cool," wrapped up as he was in some fantasy world of being just a young jail kid like his hero from the Kerouac book, Dean Moriarty.

"Not cool at all," Frank informed him. "My brother did a year there and it fucked him all up."

This struck a nerve in Sean, wondering as he was just what the fuck they could have done to Frank's brother in the reform school to change him so much—thoughts that stayed with him as he went before the juvenile judge the next morning. His mom was there in the courtroom, weeping so hard that for once Sean felt sorry for her. What he was thinking, though, as court came to session was, *Please, dear God, don't send me to Mariana.* A plea, much to Sean's shock, granted by the stern looking man in his black robes seated up on the bench, gavel in hand as he pored over Sean's charge sheets.

"Well, young man," the judge said, "From reading your history here it's apparent that you're one troubled boy, one who has been up to a lot of funny business."

Sean wasn't sure if he was supposed to say something, thought maybe it best if he just stayed quiet, but then blurted out, "Yes sir."

"I was good friends with your father, you know." This took Sean completely by surprise. According to his own estimate of his drunken father, there was no way he could have had any friends. "So in light of that," the judge continued. "I am going to give you one more chance. But if you come before me again, I'll have no choice but to send you to the school for troubled boys in Marianna. Are we clear?"

"Yes sir." And then realizing the magnitude of the gift just extended him, Sean added, "Thank you, Your Honor."

He was placed on juvenile probation until he was eighteen, or graduated from high school, whichever came first, Sean's plan to drop out of school when he turned sixteen, dashed just like that. But as he walked out of the courtroom with his sobbing mother, he thought of Frank's brother—of what had happened to him at the school for troubled boys. Sean decided then and there, What the hell, guess I'll give it a try.

Which turned out all right. At the beginning of 11th grade he met Will in his English class, became pals with him and his older brother, Tommy, who introduced Sean and Will to the joys of marijuana, and from there, LSD, the hippies, love-ins at Grenolds Park, the cool head shop in Ojus, the new music, …. All of which eventually led Sean to where he was right then: with his good pal Boober. In a fast moving Oldsmobile, its big eights growling as they sped north. Not to NYC, maybe, but to another plenty cool town, Boston, where if everything went okay, both he and Boober would have a wad of cash they could use to further their separate goals.

So yes, , Sean was thinking as they were coming up on the Brunswick exit, life was one rolling trip all right—currently one enhanced by the beers they'd been drinking, and the good reef they'd smoked. And so far?

But right there, on the side of the highway where the interstate bled into the exit ramp, stood a figure. A guy, maybe a little younger than Sean and Boober, looking all forlorn with a battered suitcase at his feet, thumb stuck out in that universal pleading gesture of *help*—not even thinking about it, Sean yelled out, "Stop."

~7~ Dwight

"We're not stopping." Whether Boober's feigned indifference to Sean's sudden request was real, or just a goof, Sean couldn't tell—until Boober repeated, "We're not stopping."

"C'mon, man. Let's give the kid a ride."

"Screw that. We're making good time here."

"I'm telling you; we need to stop for him."

Airplane's *"Got a Revolution,"* courtesy of a FM station out of Savannah, blasting through the speakers of the Cutlass, drove home the point he wanted to make to his indifferent pal at the wheel. They were well past the hitch hiker by then, but his imploring look as they rushed by stuck in Sean's mind—the waggling of the kid's outstretched thumb bringing up memories of some of his own travels by thumb.

"It's all about karma, man, I'm telling you. Don't fool yourself, partner. Me and you may be out there in that kid's place before this trip's all over."

"Yeah, yeah, I hear you." The sardonic smile was back, though, stretched across Boober's face. "I don't like it, is all. Not one bit."

With a soft, "Ah fuck," Boober brought the Olds to a screeching stop on the shoulder of the highway. Smoldering Camel hanging from his lips, slamming the car into reverse, he began backing up—at a faster clip, too, than the car's transmission might have preferred, judging by the whining coming through the floorboards.

Whining transmission, Boober's lack of enthusiasm, it didn't matter—the kid on the side of the road was obviously happy about the sudden change in his affairs. Proof of this lay in the big smile on his face Sean could see as the kid ran for the Olds, his long hair streaming out behind him, battered suitcase banging at his thighs, the old Army jacket he was wearing flapping as he ran. In another second, car and running hitch hiker, converged. The kid grabbed for the rear door handle, but Sean beat him to it, opening the door for the kid who flung his suitcase in on the seat and quickly followed behind it. And then, just as quickly, Boober pushed the gear shift into drive and they were off, back up to 75 mph—leaving a shower of dirt and torn grass in their wake as if nothing different had happened to intrude on their forward progress.

Sean had referred to the hitch hiker as a kid—and kid he was, Sean could see, now that he could inspect him up close. Seventeen or eighteen was Sean's guess, medium height and thin, with long, brown hair dropping down on his shoulders. A hungry kid, too, Sean figured. But hungry or not, the green eyes, looking out from a somewhat pockmarked face, lit up once he was settled in the back seat of the Cutlass and said, "Thank's guys. For the ride."

"Thank him." Boober jerked a finger towards Sean.

"Yeah." Apparently, the kid hadn't paid attention to what Boober had said. "You guys are the greatest, man, I gotta tell you. I've been out there for quite a while now. A State Pig came by not long ago and hassled me big time. Told me I better not be there when he came back. Pretty much freaked me out, I gotta tell you. Wow." He stopped, his eyes glued on what lay ahead.

Just then, Boober tromped on the gas at the last possible second and wrenched the Cutlass into the left lane to pass, the sudden acceleration slamming the kid backwards.

"Wow," the kid said again when they were back in the right lane, a slow moving semi left behind. "Either you dudes are in a major hurry, or you just like to fly."

"A little bit of both," Boober replied, Sean happy to see his wheelman smiling again, "Yes sir mister, I'd say it's a little bit of both."

"My partner here's right," Sean said. Reaching for Boober's pack of Camels on the dashboard, he offered a smoke to the kid, who readily accepted it. "And you're right about Georgia cops. They're pigs all right. Pigs that don't fuck around." He nodded at Boober. "Something our wheelman should keep in mind."

'Yeah, yeah." But Boober let off on the gas, bringing the Olds back down to the respectable 75 he'd been holding it at.

Though he couldn't see it, the Atlantic Ocean, Sean knew it was there, the interstate following the coastline as it did. But he could picture it in his mind's eye: an ocean stretching out to Africa and beyond. The paper mill outside of Brunswick's city limits, its smokestacks belching fumes over the salt marsh surrounding it.

The cold facts were these: there were three of them in the car now. Said car barreling along towards Savannah. Where, by Sean's rough calculations, the car would need gas and Boober and he would need to re-up on ice and beer. Chow might enter into the equation. But seeing as how Savannah was still seventy some miles away, Sean dragged the traveling bag out from beneath the seat and began rolling a slim Jim—a little taste, he figured, a solid way to keep the morning buzz going.

Sean said over his shoulder to the new guy in the back, "How about making yourself useful amigo, and pass me and my partner a beer out of that cooler?" Remembering his manners he added, "Help yourself if you want one."

After Boober took a turn on the joint Sean handed it over the back seat to the kid. Without a word the kid smoked nearly half of the joint in one drag. Holding the smoke deep in his lungs his face began turning a light shade of blue, until suddenly the kid exploded in a loud and violent coughing frenzy, spewing smoke and spittle all over the back of the Olds.

"Jesus!" Sean laughed as he took back what was left of the joint, barely even a proper roach after the kid was done with it. "What the hell's wrong with you?"

"Sorry, man." The red-faced kid was still hacking. "It's been awhile since I smoked any decent weed."

Rolling down the window the kid hacked again one more time, the end result a huge lunger he launched out the window.

"Yeah man, that's the way." Boober turned from the wheel just in time to see the wad of mucous sailing out the window to disappear somewhere on the edge of the highway. "Good one."

Boober's comment cracked the kid up, sending him into a gut-wrenching laughter that doubled him over in the back seat—laughter that became contagious. Soon, all of them were enveloped in uncontrollable guffaws. Sean clutched his stomach as he laughed, while Boober held tight to the steering wheel as he did, and meanwhile, everything a hazy blur in Sean's tear-filled eyes.

"Listen pal," Sean managed after settling down a little. "My friend's little joke wasn't that funny."

"I know, man." The kid, half stretched out across the back seat, was struggling to sit upright as he wiped his eyes. "It just kinda hit me, you know?"

"Screw that." Boober lit up a Camel. "It was very funny. Just like all of my jokes."

"That's right," Sean agreed. "I forgot. You're a regular freaking Bob Hope."

"Exactly."

Other than the static from the radio's faded signal, it was quiet in the car until Sean suddenly thought of something.

"Where you headed, amigo? Might help if we knew that."

"Boston." The kid's face went serious as he slumped back in the seat. "I guess. I don't have anywhere else to go."

Sean looked over at Boober, who just shrugged his shoulders, staring straight ahead.

"I don't give a damn." The wheelman exhaled a stream of Camel smoke out the window. "I got my seat. One more won't crowd my scene any."

Sean, who had been busy fiddling with the radio tuner, finally found a station— a Rockabilly AM, out of Savannah, the DJ laying out a steady supply of Country blues and rock, hot guitar licks, pounding drums, and mournful lyrics, replacing the crackling static with a driving beat, instead.

"Well ain't you jest the lucky one, today," Sean said. "As ol' Boston happens to be where we're a headin'."

Where his sudden Southern drawl had come from Sean had no idea. But he kind of liked it. It most definitely fit in with the Rockabilly blowing out of the radio. He figured it fit in, too, with the beer, the reefer, and the blue sky above. All of it seemed so right: the music, being stoned, digging the breeze, digging the way his hair blew out behind him in that breeze, Sean himself—all of it joined in with the warm summer day. So yeah, a southern drawl for the time being seemed just the way to go.

"So lissen up, partner. If yore gonna be ridin' wit us, smokin' this c'here dope of our'n, and drinkin' our cold beer, it strikes me you mite better tell us yore giv'n Christian name, son."

"It's Dwight," the kid answered, not blinking an eye at the change in Sean. "Dwight. That's my name."

"Well now, yes sir, 'at shorely is a rite fine name, son." Sean tossed his empty beer can out of the car window as he turned to face the kid in the back seat. "Now shet th' fuck up and han' me 'nother one of thos' col' Budweezers. By th' way," and he jerked his thumb at the wheel man. "At ther's Boober. An' they call me, Sean."

~8~ Highway 204

"Can that hillbilly shit, Tonto." Boober flipped his cigarette butt out the window, chasing the dead cigarette with his empty beer can. "Find some real music on the radio, while you're at it. I hear any more of that love sick crap I'm liable to barf."

"Right away, Kemosabe." Sean began fiddling again with the radio dial, sadly with no success, other than Top 40 stuff he didn't want to listen to—couldn't imagine anyone else in the car wanting to either. "Should I lick your boots while I'm at it?"

"Yeah." Boober's usual grin was back on his face, instead of the snarl concerning the tunes they'd been subjected to. "That'd be a nice gesture of friendship, come to think of it."

"In your dreams pal," Sean said, finally giving up on finding any decent music left the radio station where it was. "In your dreams."

"You sure you guys're friends?" Dwight piped up from the back as he handed over two cans of Bud.

"Yep, we're friends." Sean opened one of the beers for Boober, and then opened his own. "Just goofing around is all."

"Cool. I had to deal with enough mean shit in Miami. Ain't looking for anymore, if you can dig that. Why I had to hit the road."

"I can dig it," Sean nodded. And he could, in a general way; though he wondered what exactly it was Dwight had against Miami—but figured given enough time on the road with the kid he might find out. "Can dig it completely, amigo."

The Rockabilly music continued to wail out of the radio, suddenly interrupted for a few minutes by a pleasant DJ surprise: Led Zeppelin's *"Good Times, Bad Times."* The DJ's intro into the song being, "Here's a little something to wake y'all up on this sleepy June morning." Both Boober and Sean joined in on Plant's drawn out, "Ohhhh suck," when the time came. Just below the music, the steady growl of the Old's big eights as Boober pushed hard for Savannah, filled in for ambiance.

The whole state of Georgia could just as well have been a dream. One only made real by the exit signs on the highway for unheard-of-before towns; signs that vanished as quickly as they appeared; signs for towns with names like Woodbine, Waverly, Darien, and Midway—towns where people actually lived. Not only lived but grew old and died. Lives and deaths unknown to him. Never to be a part of his life, but still … well, they were real. But perhaps their lives were only a dream—something to hold onto.

"Oh yeah, now you're talking." Boober had seen the sign as well. "Man, do I ever have to take a leak."

"I hear you, partner." Sean turned to share the good news of a rest break coming their way with Dwight. But the new guy was sound asleep, his head lolled back against the seat. "Check it out Bobby." Sean nudged Boober on the shoulder. "The kid's either super beat, or he can't handle weed. Gotta be one or the other, wouldn't you think?"

"Hopefully it's the weed." Boober did that wheel shrug thing of his. "That way we don't have to waste it on him."

"What about our Southern hospitality and all?"

"Screw that." They were coming up on the red light at the end of the exit ramp. "I'm a Yankee, remember? And we won." The light turned green, and Boober turned the Olds to head east on Highway 204, next stop the heart of Old Savannah. "What's important right now is finding a bar & grill where I can take a piss, and then dig into a burger and some cold beer. Especially the beer, dig? A real cold draft in one of those tall Pilsner glasses, all frothy like, you know? Just the way suave cats like me and you should be drinking out of."

Boober didn't have to twist Sean's arm over the merits of what he was suggesting—that was for sure. He was tired suddenly of being in the car and wanted to feel that old Terra Firma beneath his feet again. A Terra Firma that wasn't moving. The idea of burgers and beer out of tall Pilsner glasses sounded like just the thing. Boober, wheelman that he was, must have realized suddenly that the needs of the Cutlass were of importance, as well, for he whipped them into a *Raceway* station just past the exit ramp.

Once they were stopped Sean jumped out, grabbed the Hi-Test nozzle from the pump, stuck it into the tank, and flipped the handle up, just as the attendant came running out of the office. The attendant, an official *Raceway* cap tilted at a jaunty angle, was just a kid, maybe fifteen or sixteen, his uniform a freshly starched white that shone in the late morning sunlight. Probably working the gas station for his summer job, Sean thought as he waved the attendant off—but he kept on coming.

Yep, that's it. Doing a little pump jockeying to make some coin. Maybe saving up his cash for his own set of wheels. And who knows? Yeah man, next summer it'll be that kid making the cruise, heading out to see just what the heck life was really about.

"Can I do the windshield for you, sir?"

The attendant had made it to the car, where up close like he was, Sean could see the marks of acne running down one cheek—proof indeed he was just a kid. His eyes, though, staring out from under the brim of the Raceway cap, got Sean's attention. Dark, and intense as he hailed the new customer, the look was a good indication he was well aware the new customer was no more a 'sir' than he was.

"That's all right, bud. I got it. You've probably got plenty to do around here as it is." Remembering his own days pumping gas, Sean added, "You probably get some real beauts in here on occasion, huh?"

"Yeah, that we do." The kid took a long look at the black Cutlass. "Boy, that's a nice ride y'all got. Bet she gets up and goes."

"She gets, all right."

And there it was: the kid's bright look, his eager admiration of the Cutlass with its chrome grill shining; the car sitting low and mean on the gas station tarmac, ready, as the kid had said, to get up and go.

After dipping the squeegee into the bucket next to the pump Sean started on the windshield. For indeed he could, ex-pump jockey that he was, having done his own tour of duty manning gas pumps a few years back. Fortunately, that tour of duty had been a short one. After four months of ten-hour shifts, six days a week, he walked off one morning, stuck his thumb out, and was on his way to meet Boober up in Massachusetts.

But that was then. The windshield was clean, the gas tank filled, and there was Boober coming back from the men's room, drying his hands on a paper towel before lighting up a smoke and sliding into the driver's seat.

"You coming with me or not, Tonto?"

"Yeah, in a minute. Gotta use the head first." A shudder went through him, when turning for the restrooms on the side of the gas station he caught sight of a billboard rising up behind the station—a re-elect Nixon billboard with a picture of Mr. Creepy flashing his V for Victory sign under a brightly colored American flag. The thought of four more years of that used car salesman made Sean feel like gagging. Pointing at the billboard, Sean said over his shoulder to Boober, "You going to salute your Fearless Leader up there?"

"Not my leader," Boober said as he cranked the engine. "Motherfucker wants to kill me."

"That's right, Kemosabe. He's no friend to the Indians, either."

It was a much-needed piss all right, and afterwards, as he was splashing cold water on his face and retying the ponytail, he took the opportunity in the dim light of the restroom to check out the face staring back at him from the cracked mirror above the restroom sink. Not only did he look pretty good, he thought, he was feeling pretty damn good too, buzzed as he was. And though he was sort of stationary at the moment, he was still on the move with his good friend, traveling toward whatever it was awaiting them. These reassuring thoughts were interrupted when Dwight came stumbling into the bathroom.

Dwight looked to still be half asleep as he mumbled, "Where we at, man?"

"Savannah, man." Sean splashed water from the sink at the kid. "Lunchtime, partner so wake your ass up."

In short time the three of them were back in the car, Boober wheeling the Olds into downtown Savannah. The tires of the big car clacked on the cobblestones as they drove past the red brick buildings rising up from the streets of the old Southern town. A residual from the weed they'd been smoking all morning, perhaps, but the cobblestone streets, the red brick structures built when cotton was still king, and Mr. Lincoln's war yet to explode, seemed to create another of those time warp things in Sean's—the warp abruptly vanishing when Boober turned into an alley off of the main drag and came to a stop in front of one of those red brick buildings, whose sign above the doorway proclaimed in bold black letters: **MICKEY'S BACK ALLEY PUB. COLD BEER! THE BEST BURGERS IN THE SOUTH!**

"Yeah?" Sean looked at Boober, then back up at the sign. "Sounds like advertising bullshit to me."

"I guess we'll just have to find out." Boober got out of the car, his lanky frame uncoiling in the glare of the daylight streaming into the alley between the buildings on both sides. Leaning down to look at Sean, still sitting inside, he added, "Won't we, Tonto?" The wheel man's smirk spread a little wider. "Unless, of course, you're not interested? Maybe you just want to hang out here, maybe beat off or something while Dwight and me get our fill of that cold beer and best burgers they're bragging about."

The glare of the noonday sun flowed into the dim light of *"Mickey's Back Alley Pub."* As Sean's eyes slowly adjusted to the gloomy light of the place, the first discovery he made was that there were no big-breasted barmaids to serve their every whim. A wizened old redneck type behind the bar, an Atlanta Braves ball cap tilted back on his balding head, appeared to be the only one on duty.

Besides the bartender, and the three travelers, there were two working men types hunkered over the pool table in the back corner, the pool table light overhead creating shadows where there should have been faces beneath their caps. Across from the pool table a bandstand occupied another corner, the speakers, mikes, and lonely looking drum kit, seemingly waiting for someone to come and set them alive. Topping off the bar's décor were several of those old style pictures of nude women. The same velvet nudes, Sean was willing to bet, gracing the walls of countless bars, ancient men's clubs, and pool halls across the south—if not indeed the whole country.

Sean no longer had any qualms about trying one of Mickey's famous burgers—indeed it was burgers all around for the three of them and the cold beer the sign outside promised. Even if the bartender looked suspiciously at Dwight before going ahead and pouring a draft just as Boober had wanted: in tall Pilsner glasses. After a couple of sips Dwight sauntered over to the pool table and plunked a quarter down on the side rail. The working men looked up warily from their game at the long hair challenging the table but didn't say anything. As for the burgers, when they came? They tasted as good, if not better, than they had smelled while cooking on the grill behind the bar: thick, still steaming patties, done medium rare, topped off with a slice of raw Vidalia onion on a potato bread roll.

By the time he was halfway done with his, Sean went ahead and answered Boober's questioning look across the table. "I retract my earlier comment about the truthfulness of Mickey's advertising."

"Good boy," was all Boober said, before diving back into his burger.

Dwight, in the meantime, was looking cool, calm, and very much at home as he waited for the winner of the previous game to break. When his turn came Dwight ran the table, banking the eight ball into the corner pocket. He won the next game, as well, leaving his challenger with five balls resting quietly on the green. To their credit, the local boys took it all in stride, shaking their heads a little at the kid's expertise, shaking his hand afterwards as well. Dwight finally declined offers of a rematch and went back to the bar to finish his burger, a slight smile of success cracking his pockmarked face.

"Hey, man." And Sean just had to ask when he sat down next to the kid. "Where'd you learn to play like that?"

"Hanging with my old man, I guess." The kid nodded, kind of embarrassed as he worked on his burger. "I used to watch him play when I was a kid. Until he ran off."

"Oh." Sean knew about losing dads. "That sucks. My dad kicked a few years back."

"Yeah, it sucks for sure." Dwight finished his burger, finished off his draft as well, signaling to Mickey for another before he spoke up again. "Mom took it pretty hard, I gotta say. I was only twelve and there I was all of a sudden, the head of a family. Pissed me off, man. The old man taught me how to shoot pool, though. I'll give him that. It's come in handy down the line."

I bet. The kid's hustled more than his fare share of games, no doubt. But before he could quiz the kid further Boober pushed away from the bar and stood up.

"Let's hit it, boys. We still have a ways to go for D.C."

Sean hadn't really been paying any attention, wrapped up as he still was in how Dwight's pool playing career might have gone—but once they were back in the day light he flashed on what Boober had said.

"D.C.? What's in D.C.?"

"A friend of mine," Boober said. "I haven't seen him like in five years. Seeing as how we've got to go right by there I thought it'd be cool to stop in. Maybe crash there for the night, get all refreshed, and in the morning make the final push to Boston. That a problem for you?"

"No." And it wasn't. "I've got time. You dig? Before I have to be back in Lauderdale and head off to Tuscaloosa." But he was curious if this friend of Boober's in D.C. was one in particular. "You're not talking about Unger, are you?"

"The same."

"Interesting."

"Not to worry, Tonto. How 'bout we walk off some of that grub before we hit it again?"

Leaving the car where it was, they exited the alley to walk down toward the Savannah River. The sun, high in the summer sky, made the day warm and humid. The ancient walls and streets, all that red brick and stone seemed to hold the heat in, and it wasn't long before the three travelers were drenched with sweat, their T shirts soaked, their hair plastered down on their heads.

It was better down along the river, where the three of them stood on the seawall and caught the breeze coming off the water. The river itself was a big swath of brown water, flowing east just then on the outgoing tide. On the north side of the river were smokestacks just like the ones outside of Brunswick, belching gray, stinking smoke. People moved up and down the sidewalk lining the river: tourists snapping photos, street vendors hawking postcards and trashy souvenirs of all kinds, others selling snacks and cold drinks. There were businessmen in suits and ties hustling to get back to their dead-end jobs. Sean was grateful he wasn't one of them—swore again to himself he would never be one of them. *No freaking way, and thank all the gods for that.*

Breaking up this moving scenery were more than a few sweet looking females floating about, some of them secretaries, perhaps, or girls who worked in the fancy shops along the riverfront. Four of these girls were sitting at an outdoor café the three travelers strolled by. These girls were enjoying what had to be a late lunch, their Georgia Peach milky complexions shining fresh and clean in the early afternoon sunlight.

He was digging all of it, taking in everything around him, the food and cold beer having revitalized him—that and the cool breeze coming off the river.

But it was time to roll. Boober took the lead, making the decision for the three of them when he turned suddenly back the way they had come. North. To D.C. And whatever was going to happen there.

~9~ I-95 again

By the time they reached Yemassee, some twenty-five miles into the state of South Carolina, the burgers, beer, and after-lunch joint, had settled in. Georgia was left behind, the Cutlass eating up the highway at the steady 75mph. Meanwhile, the food, alcohol, and marijuana, coupled with the constant motion of the speeding car, had created a drowsy, numbing sensation washing over Sean's senses. He began nodding off—over how long a period of time he couldn't say. The vibrations of the big eights beneath the hood would jerk him awake periodically. *It was kind of nice, this riding dozing off thing. Kind of groovy in a moving funky sort of way*—the only downer being that the wheelman was experiencing the same thing.

"Hey Tonto man." His pal's voice jerked him awake from one of those peaceful reveries. "You feel like driving for a bit? Kemosabe here's having a hard time staying awake."

Sean didn't doubt it, judging by Boober's heavy-lidded eyes. "I don't mind, partner. Gotta warn you though, I'm kinda drifting off my own self."

"Hey guys." Dwight piped up from the back seat. "Wanna do some Black Beauties?"

Here was a suggestion warranting Sean's attention, what with his fondness for amphetamines of any sort—even if he had to shoot them, like he did with Pinko at the Cave.

Boober was all ears, too, his dark eyes, as he swiveled around in the driver seat, demanding upon the new guy in the rear. "Pass them over, bud," he said, reaching his hand out, palm up and open across the back rest. "I can't believe you've been holding out on us."

Dwight opened that battered suitcase of his, rooting around in it until he came up with a plastic baggie full of black pills, one of which he slipped into Boober's open palm.

"Shit, guys." He handed one to Sean, keeping one out for himself as well. "All you had to do was ask."

The three adventurers, awake and excited now at the prospect of soon being even more awake and excited, washed the capsules down with beer, purchased at a grocery store on the outskirts of Savannah to replenish the cooler, Boober explaining as he pulled up in front of the store, "Hopefully our Brothers inside have a better price on beer than those thieves out on the highway."

Not that this proved to be the case. In fact, the cost of Budweiser there was higher than they had paid at the packy store in Starke that morning.

"Oh well, even our Black Brothers are falling prey to the evils of capitalism these days, I suppose." Boober, still deep into his goof, added, "But damn it, Tonto, if you'd bought malt liquor you might have gotten a better price. You know, man? Let the bloods know you're one with them. Dig?"

"No way." Dwight had said as he packed the lid down on the now-filled-to-the-brim Styrofoam cooler. "Malt liquor will fuck you up, man."

"Yeah, I know." Boober had nodded in agreement as he gunned the Olds out of the dirt parking lot. "Exactly what I like about it."

By the time the Cutlass blew past the exit for Rosinville, SC, another thirty miles up I-95, the Black Beauties had kicked in. The sleepy time feeling of earlier was gone. In fact it was a whole new ball game inside the Olds, what with the teeth grinding, gum numbing of the amphetamine working on the three travelers. As if to punctuate the new state of affairs, the Stone's *"Monkey Man"* suddenly blasted out of the car radio, courtesy of an FM station in Charleston, the three of them in synch, yelling out with Mick, "All my friends are junkies."

As the song faded out Sean realized the situation called for the retrieval of the travel bag of herb from beneath his seat. "Well then, my boy," he said to the wheelman. "Seeing as how you're so keen on that Black Experience and all, perhaps I should roll us a spliff?"

'Yah, mon." At the same time, never taking his eyes off the road in front of him, Boober reached his long arm over the backrest. "Dwight, mon, hand me a beer."

It was kind of scary, Sean thought, as he began his rolling-a-joint task, the look on his friend's face. Instead of the ever-present sarcastic smirk some kind of horrible looking speed grin had taken its place. The rest of his body, too, seemed frozen in place, his hands holding the wheel in a death grip, except when it was necessary to pry one loose to flick ash from the smoldering Camel hanging in the corner of his mouth. Sean wondered if his features looked the same as Boober's, hoping that wasn't the case. But he could feel the speed ripping through his system, the top of his head tight as if it might explode at any moment. At least the muscles of his face seemed to be working; proof of this the constant swallowing he was doing to cut the edges of the dry mouth. His hands were working as well, seeing as how he managed to roll a fairly decent joint—despite the unexplained trembling in his fingers that scattered pot across his lap.

Sean fired up the fresh-rolled joint, that first long inhale bringing everything back into place. Strangely enough, unlike just a few minutes before when the Stones were blasting from the car speaker, they seemed to be suddenly traveling in a radio dead zone. The good tunes had faded out, replaced by crackling static, the occasional faint voice, or a high-pitched whistle no amount of Boober's fiddling with the dial could change. They still had a way to go to get to D.C., probably seven hours or more, a long haul without good radio tunes to help them on their way.

In the meantime the highway had pulled away from the coast to curve inland. Now, instead of flat, coastal plain and pine tree scrub, they were cruising up and down rolling hills. There were still pine trees here and there, but also oaks of various sorts, and plenty of kudzu as well, the roadside foliage lush, green, and looking clean and sharp through the speed constricted slits of his eyes.

"Thanks, partner." Sean turned to Dwight in the back seat, radiant with his new insights. "For the Beauties, man. Just what the doctor ordered if you ask me."

"You're welcome," Dwight said. "Shit, they didn't cost me anything."

"Oh?" Sean raised an eyebrow at this interesting fact. "I'm sure there's a good story behind that little tidbit."

"Yeah, there is. How good it is I can't say."

And then, with the speed finally loosening the tongue of their-up-until-now quiet passenger in the back seat, Dwight launched into the story behind the Beauties: of how a year or so back, when he was seventeen and the end of his junior year in high. There was no denying it, no nice way to look at it, he guessed. But he just wasn't cutting it in school. And maybe it was because he had to work at the garage after school. You know? Help his mom out with the bills and all, now that his old man had run off. Between school and the garage, he was fucking fed up. Fed up with his shitty grades because he didn't have time to study, or do homework by the time he got home after work. Fed up with the smell of grease he couldn't wash away, no matter how hard he scrubbed. Fed up, too, with the little row house he and his mom lived in on the edge of Bean Town.

One day on his way to work after school, he said to hell with it. Left his mom a goodbye note, grabbed his sixteen year old girlfriend, Joey and loaded up their stuff in his '64 Volkswagen van, and rolled out of Boston, heading south to Miami, where Joey's older sister was hanging out in some kind of commune in Coconut Grove. It seemed like a good idea to him and his girl, the two of them not knowing anything their whole lives up to that day other than Boston, snow, grease and the stuck-up kids at the high school. So yeah, it was a good idea all the way around.

Except, the van blew a rod, the engine seizing up on the south end of Jacksonville, this happening in the middle of the night. Dwight managed to get the clanging bus off the highway onto the shoulder.They laid in the back of the van until dawn when he climbed out to ascertain the damage in the light of day. There wasn't much to see in that he didn't already suspect. The van was fucked. Actually, the Volks was quite fixable. If they'd had the cash. Which they didn't. So squeezing what was totally necessary into one suitcase, they thumbed the rest of the way down to Miami. Dwight discovered it was pretty easy when you had a chick traveling with you—even if the looks, and comments about Joey from the middle-aged salesman types who gave them rides made him uneasy. Enough of an unease that he kept one hand close to the black handled switchblade he always carried in his right pocket—the knife a present from his older cousin in the Marines who had sent it as a Christmas present to Dwight from Saigon when he was on leave. The knife was also the only thing Dwight had left of his cousin, who had bought it one morning in a firefight outside of Da Nang.

But they made it down to Miami without incident, the Vietnam shiv never having to be brought into play. Though they were safely out of Boston, in Florida and all, it didn't take Dwight long to see how Miami was pretty much the same as any other big city: crowded, dirty, noisy, and constantly on the move. But the beaches were nice, there were plenty of palm trees like he'd seen in the movies and magazines, and the ocean warm enough to swim in *year round,* unlike the beaches in his native New England.

The commune Joey's older sister was involved with was okay. At first. There were twelve or so members, the comings and goings of a few of them making it hard for an accurate count. Most of the boys, and the few female members, possessed long, usually unwashed hair. Both sexes dressed in similar apparel, bellbottom jeans, tie-dyed T shirts, and the like. The living space consisted of two small apartments side by side in a one story complex, where most of the time, they stayed stoned on one thing or another, a state of mind suiting Dwight just fine.

The leader of the commune was cool enough. Older than the others, maybe thirty or so, tall and muscular with wispy brown hair hanging down to his shoulders. He went by the name of James. What with the weather mild most of the time, James went about bare-chested, making visible the Service tattoos and scars running down his back and along his arms—scars and tattoos, mementos from a Nam scene of his own. But now he was all peace and love, just doing his thing with his brothers and sisters in the Grove, writing songs, playing his guitar, selling a little dope, supplementing this income with a government disability check for injuries received in the service of his "grateful" nation.

But he was a good leader, one who never hassled any of the other commune members or tried to force his issues on them. Occasionally, one of the girls did a grope scene with him; scenes he never demanded from them—at least not in Dwight's presence. All James ever asked for was that the members contribute what they could to the food, rent, and dope stashes. The rest of it was just a good groove.

So that life for Dwight and Joey in the Grove was rather fine, a stoned gas all the way around. Until what little cash they'd arrived with ran out. It wasn't like Dwight, or Joey for that matter, could write home for cash since they were runaways, underage and all. But then Joey managed to score a job at the McDonalds where her sister worked on Le Juene road, doing the three to eleven shift which wasn't so bad. Except that Dwight came to hate the way she smelled when she came home at night, the stench of fried beef and stale cooking oil lingering in her hair and clothes. But after a shower and a change of clothes, they were kicking back with a joint and getting it on.

He found work of his own after a while when one late morning he drifted into a funky pool hall off Old Dixie Highway. Pretty soon he was hustling games on a regular basis. He kept his profile low by letting the old timers win on occasion—an important lesson he'd learned from his old man before the bastard ran off. Besides, Dwight liked those old timers. Liked how they bought him beers while he listened to their tales of how it was back when they were young and handsome and making their way in a tough world—Dwight thinking how there might be a tip or two to be gleaned from listening to his elder's wisdom.

The owner of the pool hall, one Studs, reminded Dwight a little of his dad, back when it was still good. Studs was even from Boston, though according to him he left Bean Town just before the Big One and hadn't been back. Studs admitted to Dwight once that his first inclination had been to run the obviously underage Dwight out of there. Instead, Studs decided to let him stay, and hadn't found any reason to change his decision, adding a stern, "Yet," before pouring him another draft.

So yeah, life was cool there in that Coconut Grove.

Until James started handing out Black Beauties. The pills were courtesy of both a script pad one of the commune girls had lifted from the doctor's office where she was working temp, and a drugstore down the street that asked no questions as long as cash was the method of payment. The Beauties weren't bad, mind you, and everyone in the crew was happy to have them. Except, unlike the others, they seemed to turn James into a big ball of tension, a walking rack of constrained energy ready to just burst out. He ate Beauties for days on end and then crash, disappearing into his room, only to emerge a day or so later, pale and emaciated, but somehow sort of back to his old smiling guitar playing self. It wasn't long, though, before he wrote a new script, sent the girl off to the drugstore, and the cycle began all over.

On a warm, balmy morning the week before Dwight found himself on the side of the highway thumbing for a ride, Joey had an unexpected day off. Dwight snuck out early while she was still sleeping, his plan to head over to the pool hall and rustle up some bucks, come back and take Joey out to lunch, maybe to one of those beachside cafes she liked so much. He made the money all right, but when he got back to the apartment Joey was gone. Not only was she gone, but the room was a mess, clothes thrown everywhere, the books Joey brought with her, on the floor, their mattress thrown up against the wall. And no Joey. Just a bare-chested James in a fucking Speedo strolling into the room with a tight Black Beauty grin on his face.

"Wow, man," were his first words to a very startled Dwight, followed by, "that Joey of yours is a real tigress. I see why you stay with that scrawny little chick."

Dwight exploded, slamming punches at the older man's face with one hand while clawing for the knife in his pocket with the other. Before he could bring the switchblade into play, Jame's jungle training kicked in. When Dwight came to he was bleeding from his mouth and nose, and was sore all over. For days afterwards he walked the streets of the Grove looking for Joey and not finding her.

One night he said, "Fuck it," and went into Jame's room where the vet lay crashed out from his latest speed binge. Grabbing one of the bricks that served as bookends on a funky stand James had made, Dwight smashed it into the side of the sleeping man's head. James let out a soft groan, and then, except for the spastic twitching of one leg, lay still. Dwight ransacked the room, coming up with the stash of Beauties and a wad of cash. With the goods in hand he fled, not knowing if James was alive or dead, and damn sure not caring one way or the other. Throwing the wad of cash, the Beauties, and the rest of his things into the suitcase he and Joey had been sharing, Dwight stuck his thumb out on the highway, letting it take him to that desolate spot on the interstate outside of Brunswick, Georgia, where Sean, Boober, and the black Olds came along.

"So that's how I got the Beauties," he said, wrapping his sad tale up. "Pure, clean pharmaceuticals. What d'ya think?"

Sean—looking at the kid with a respect almost bordering on awe, images of Dwight's story ripping through his brain on the currents of the amphetamine—said the only thing he could think of. "Cool."

"Yeah," Boober said. "Pretty fucking cool."

~10~ Highway 301 (Sort of)

And it was cool: that chilling sensation rushing through Sean's blood from his heart pumping at a faster than normal rate courtesy of the Black Beauties. With Dwight's sad tale over, Sean leaned back in the seat, savoring the rush—a rush mellowed by the bomber that, despite his trembling fingers, Sean had managed to both roll and fire up in celebration of the lift Dwight had unexpectedly brought to the day. The joint had gone a long way toward cutting the initial teeth grinding of the speed. The joint had even managed to loosen Boober's tight grip on the steering wheel. His black eyes were still constricted, though, like tight little beads focused on the road in front of them.

So yes, no doubt, it was all cool. All of it would be even cooler if it stayed just as it was—Sean knowing in an equally fast moment that it could not. He remembered a similar event he had experienced in the past. A night when he was first getting to know Luellen who had invited him to hang out with her at the Rock, the stone house she and her roommate Kat were living in at the time. The three of them dropped some acid, powdered Owsley. Sean was a little nervous about doing so, what with him and Luellen so new to one another. But hey, the acid was a gift from Kat. Not only that, but he'd been raised that it was wrong to refuse a gift—especially one of such loving kindness as Owsley LSD.

The first intense rush of the drug pushed Sean out of the house and onto the front porch. The stone columns holding up the roof of the porch seemed like symbols of solidness to him—and maybe because the rest of his world was melting before his eyes. Lost in the rush, he didn't know where he was but only that he was caught up in a stream of light rushing away from him. A light trapping him, and the life still ahead of him, in its brilliance as it took him all the way to the end. *The end?* He couldn't imagine an end. Knew only that he was right there—when out of nowhere, he could hear Luellen crying inside the house. *Luellen. She needed him.* Sean rushed away from the stream of light and back into the house. Where yes, Luellen was crying as she sat on the floor in front of the stereo, head in her hands, her brown hair falling over her shoulders while Dave Mason's *"World in Changes"* flowed out of the record player.

Lifting her face to stare at Sean, her green eyes shining and undulating with some fast-melting insight all her own, she cried out, "It's true! All true, Sean. We've got so much to learn."

And it was true. The truth of it synching into his brain as he sat down next to her and took her in his arms, the two of them holding on tight as they swayed to the music—swayed to the simple truth of what Dave Mason was singing; how they had a lot to learn about one another. And Sean wanted to learn. *Oh yes he did.* For he loved this woman he barely knew—another simple truth. This insight, along with the drug, took the both of them, as they sat in the living room and into the future, Luellen bowing her head to the music, saying every so often, and so softly Sean could barely hear her, "So much to learn. So much."

All the rest of that tripping night into the future Sean was totally lost in the colors and the flashing trails, of how cool it was that it might never end.

Yet, it did end. And now Luellen was far away, somewhere outside of Cairo digging for history in the Egyptian dust. Their love was dust as well. While he was in a speeding car, high on a different drug, moving on without her to whatever future it was awaiting him. But as he looked out the window, there it was: the green exit sign for Hwy 301, Yemassee, SC—a sign that reminded him of another time. A time he needed to remind Boober of before it slipped away in the rush of the Beauties.

***

"Hey Bobby. Remember 301?"

"How could I forget?" Boober groaned a little through the tight grin on his lips. "Freaking nightmare like that? No way to forget."

"That's right Kemosabe. Freaking nightmare, indeed. Man, you gotta hear this one." Sean turned to Dwight in the backseat. "I think you might dig it."

"The kid's too young," Boober said before Sean could launch into the tale of what happened to Boober and him on a remote stretch of 301 two years back. "Might scare him, man. Don't want him freaking out in our car. Dig?"

He couldn't tell if Boober was kidding, or serious. But he went ahead anyway and left off on rehashing that particular road memory; busied himself with rolling another joint instead—the end result, Sean, astride the amphetamine, began a long rap. One mostly about bands, girls he had lusted after, weird drug deals he had been involved in; touching once on the bust at the Cave, his freaked out-ness over watching the cops lead Will and Tommy out of the house; his narrow escape afterwards; his midnight ride to Lauderdale—pretty much his whole recently past history leading up to Boober showing up at the Party Palace. This talk of dope rolled into remembrances of the good old days. "You dig," he asked no one in particular. Back when one could buy a nickel bag that was truly a quarter of an ounce, turning to Dwight in the backseat to ask if he had ever bought a matchbox of weed. Not bothering to wait for the kid's answer he turned back around to carry on with his drift. "Hey, what about when oz's only cost twenty bucks? And then out of nowhere the price jumped up to twenty five, and what the hell, man, what's capitalism doing in something so sacred as marijuana, huh?"

This long discourse on weed suddenly reminded Sean of something else, and breaking off this long ramble he asked the Wheelman, "You ever get your dad to smoke pot with you? You said you were going to. I always thought your old man was pretty cool. Just didn't know if Lew man was that cool."

"Yeah," and Boober's sardonic grin pasted to his lips spread a little. "I got him to give it a try one night at the airport when we were on break, having a beer in the hanger with the other guys. This one cat, Herb, a longhair, though a little sketchy I always thought, broke out a joint and fired it up. Shit, my dad, you know, he was the crew boss, so I had to wonder just what the fuck Herb was thinking, but you know, when he handed the J to me after I took a good poke, just sort of kidding around, dig? I passed it to my old man and damned if he didn't take it and give it a try."

"Wow," Sean said, nodding his head up and down. "See, I knew he would. Given a chance, yeah, I figured Lew'd go for it."

"Well now, Tonto, can't say I ever shared your confidence about that. So to put it bluntly I was surprised. Think Herb was, too, not that he ever said anything about it afterwards. Lew's reaction to it was sort of like Dwight's, you know? He busted out in one of those spewing coughs, spluttering and hacking, his face all red, and me and Herb couldn't help but laugh, and man, you know, I figured that was the end of my old man and pot, but damned if he didn't grab that joint on the next go around and have at it again. By the time break was over, the three of us were pretty mellow, the only bummer being that suddenly, the sirens at the fire station went off and the next thing you know, fire trucks are racing out to runway 5, and here coming out of the freaking sky was a little Cessna with its engine on fire and all hell breaking loose on the ground, sirens and lights and men running around to get ready for the Cessna. I looked over at my dad and shit he was laughing like a maniac. Everyone else is fucking freaking out over this plane getting ready to crash on the runway and burn up and I'm like holy shit what the fuck, Dad? You're in a laughing frenzy? So I pushed him back into the hanger and into the men's room, he's just giggling the whole time and asking me if we could smoke another of those 'funny cigarettes' and then he starts singing that song, *Don't Bogart that joint my friend*, and where the freak did he hear that one I ask? You know the only music I ever heard him listening to was hokey old country and western crap. But that was it, man, let me tell you. I said sure, sure, dad, knowing all the time, not on my watch, no way, man, dig? No fucking way. Fortunately, that Cessna came in okay, nobody hurt or killed, everything cool except for the superintendent coming around when the shift was over that morning and asking Dad where the hell was he during the madness. Dad. with a stone cold face, told him, 'I was in the bathroom taking a dump.' The super just giving him a look as he walked away, and man, now that made me laugh, let me tell you."

'Wow." This from Dwight in the back seat. "Now that's a rap, Boober man, that's a rap."

Sean had to agree with Dwight's take on the Boober/Dad pot thing—the only downer being that all this talk about Boober's dad being game for weed was a not so subtle reminder for him of his dad. Sean Sr., who uptight and all would have never done such a cool thing. *No way, no how, as in never happen.* This sad truth suddenly started him down a memory lane he always did his best to avoid. But now, wrapped up in the Beauties, weed, beer, the Cutlass eating up the highway—there it was, his father coming back from the grave to haunt him when he was in the midst of one truly fine trip.

Because if there was ever a total suit, it was Sean Morgan, Sr. Going to that workaday forty hours, sometimes more, gig at the insurance agency in the Sweet building downtown. Coming home religiously at five o'clock to sit down with the first of three martinis before dinner, newspaper in hands, quiet, never a word to either son or wife, his only utterances being to blame the ills of the country on the fact that Nixon was defeated by that "Catholic bastard, Kennedy." And then, according to Sean Sr., driving the final nail into the coffin of America: the defeat of Goldwater at the hands of that "criminal hick from Texas." Meaning Lyndon B. Johnson, who surer than anything, was plunging America into the bowels of socialism.

Following Sean's father's three martinis, came dinner, where the three members of the Morgan family sat quietly at the table as they ate—quiet except for the usual questions from Sean's mom to her husband about, "How did you day go, dear? Everything all right?" Questions sometimes answered by rants about contracts lost, or the ineptitude of those above him on the insurance business ladder. If not this, then a smirking gloating over contracts he had successfully secured. Contracts that would make both the firm and Sean Sr plenty of money, mainly at the expense of the client, who invariably Sean Sr would label, "Dumber than a post."

The smile of satisfaction on his father's face at his small victories was usually enough for Sean to request to be excused—requests always granted by his mom, never by his dad who couldn't be bothered. And then it was upstairs to his bedroom where he could let go of his dull home life, via the Beatle's "Rubber Soul," Camus', "The Stranger," and more often his salvation at these times? Kerouac's "On the Road," and its promise of another way of life, one full of adventures and kicks and that sure enough, just as soon as he was able to, Sean was going to jump into with both feet and take off running. *And no one, no fucking one, was going to stop him until he had found what he was looking for.* His first foray into this life was the summer when, like Dewey and Harv, Sean began to let his hair grow out. A foray that led his father to quit talking to him for months. All the way up, in fact, until the day he died in the car crash.

And yes, it was sad news Sean supposed—as well as sort of weird, mainly because he did not miss his dad—mourned this loss only because his mother did.

While Sean was lost in this reverie of days long past the Cutlass devoured the Southern states: South Carolina, North Carolina, amd Virginia. *Huh? How did that happen?*

Even more perplexing? Boober coasting to a stop in front of a fairly un-assuming two-story house on a quiet, dark street in the suburbs of D.C, around ten or so, and shutting the engine off.

"Whoa. We're here?"

"Yep," Boober said.

And just like that there were at Unger's.

~11~ Unger's House

With the cessation of the throaty growl of the big eights, the quiet street in Alexandra, Va, along with the Unger domicile they were parked in front of, took on a surreal quality—one intensified by the hooded streetlights lining both, their circles of illumination dotting the sidewalk all up and down the working class neighborhood. This, and the fact no lights were on inside of the pretty-much-the-same looking houses—because of the lateness of the hour and it being a week night.

"Well, Kemosabe man." It was the best Sean could up with at the moment as he surveyed the darkness surrounding Unger's house. "What now?"

"I don't know." The Wheelman did one of his shoulder shrugs. "I haven't gotten that far."

"Don't you just go up and ring the doorbell?" Dwight suggested from the back seat.

"Yeah. Maybe. Let me think a minute." Boober got out of the Cutlass, his lanky body uncoiling from the seat. Once outside the confines of the automobile the Wheelman stood up fully, stretching his long arms over his head towards the night sky hovering above the dark street. "I'm pretty sure Will's room is around back. I'll go check it out. See if I can roust him without bothering his folks."

"Yeah?" Sean looked again at the darkened house sitting forebodingly on the quiet nighttime street. "What're you gonna do, man? Throw pebbles at his window?"

"I guess."

"What if you hit the wrong one and Daddy Unger comes running out of the front door with a shotgun?"

"That's unlikely. They're fucking Quakers, man." Leaning down Boober stuck his head through the driver's side window, a recently lit cigarette hanging from the side of his mouth. "You got a better idea … I'm all ears, Tonto."

"The freaking nut's your pal." It was Sean's turn to shrug. "Go wake his ass, man."

Dwight and he watched as Boober vanished in the dark around the side of the Unger house. The Wheelman's a pretty suspicious looking character, Sean thought. That is, if someone were to see. Hopefully no one would, Sean prayed—prayed no neighbor would wake at the unusual sound of the Cutlass prowling up the street before shutting down in front of Unger's pad. Their curiosity aroused by this un-neighborhood sound and the suspicious looking Boober making his way around the back of Unger's house. A sudden police presence would be a most unwelcome scene. What with the cooler of beer in the back, cargo of contraband in the trunk, and three longhairs with no good explanation as to what they were up to in Alexandria.

But no police cars came screaming down the streets with their obnoxious flashing lights—just Boober, back from the darkness to slide into his seat.

"All cool, guys." The Wheelman fumbled in his shirt pocket for another smoke. "He's coming."

And indeed, the porch light winked on above the front steps of the house, and Will Unger stepped out of the front door. He was tall, like Boober, Sean could see in the faint light from the porch as he came down the walkway. Unlike Boober's, Unger's face was fuller and pale of complexion.

"Why, hello Sean." Unger extended a bony hand through the open car window for Sean. "It's good we finally meet. I've heard from Bob so much about you."

Sean couldn't help but be disarmed by the sudden appearance of the famed apparition so close at hand—disarmed even further by the soft, carefully modulated cadence of Unger's voice. From what Boober had told him in the past, Sean expected a ranting madman of some sort. Instead, Unger had the look of a tall cherub, what with the locks of brown hair wisping just below the tops of his ears, the dimples blushing a faint red in his otherwise pale face.

"Back at you, man." Sean finally accepted the hand. "Yeah, it's good to meet you, too. And likewise, Bobby's told me a lot about you."

"I bet he has." For some reason Unger's soft chuckle sent a chill down Sean's spine.

While Boober was busy opening the trunk to rummage around inside for his bag, Dwight stumbled out of the backseat, battered suitcase banging at his knees, to introduce himself. "Hey man, I'm Dwight."

"Yes, yes," Unger told him. "Nice to meet any friend of Bob's. But let's get inside fellows. Not good really, standing out here on the street like this." He took Boober's bag, and after Sean crawled out, Unger headed off for the house. "Just be quiet. Don't want to wake the folks, you know."

Instead of falling in behind Unger and Dwight, Sean went around to the back of the Olds and grabbed Boober's arm as he was about to close the trunk.

"Hold on a sec, there, Kemosabe." He pulled his bag out of the trunk, hesitated for a moment, then making up his mind reached into the dope duffel to find the plastic bag of 714's he'd copped from Kat while they were kicking back at her place. "These might come in handy, dig?"

"You bet," Boober grunted in approval as he headed off toward the others. Sean watched him go for a second, not exactly sure yet, as he was, about the end of this leg of the journey north. Deciding it wasn't the time, or place, he hefted his bag to his shoulder and fell in behind the Wheelman.

Soon they were all hunkered down in Unger's bedroom, where at Boober's suggestion, Sean rolled a fat joint and passed it around. Unger opened his bedroom window and lit a stick of incense to mask the odor of the weed. It was nice, even sort of cool, actually, being able to sit back in a peaceful bedroom and stretch his legs out on the carpeted floor. Unger was perched cross legged on his bed, while Boober leaned back in the chair occupying one corner of the room. Dwight plopped down on the floor next to Sean and stretched his legs out, too, the two of them listening as Boober and Unger rapped on about their old hometown, school buddies, girls they used to know, and so on.

None of their rap made much sense to Sean and he suspected the same could be said of Dwight. Not that Sean really cared. It was just so damn good to be out of the steadily moving car and let his amphetamine frayed senses wind down. A crash was imminent, he knew, and to forestall said crash he passed 714's all around, it being decided before the nod set in, that in the morning Unger would show them around D.C.

Just as a curtain of sleep was slipping down, Sean overheard Unger telling Boober, "By the way, Bob, I happen to know of a reputable topless bar in Georgetown you and your friends may enjoy." *Now here's an interesting tidbit of info.* And then the Quaalude sleep over rode everything else.

Come morning, the three adventurers, along with Unger, were awakened by Mrs. Unger barging into the room.

"Willy? Do you know who the car parked in front of the house belongs to?" she managed to get out, before coming to a stop in the open door at the sight of the unknown young men sleeping on her son's bedroom floor.

"Yes, mother, its fine." Unger, lifted up from his bed on one arm to reassure his mom. "These are friends of mine. You remember Bobby, I'm sure."

Boober, stretched out on the floor by Unger's bed, groaned as he looked at Mrs. Unger standing. But despite the groan he was able to croak out a cheerful, "Hi Mrs. Unger," before rolling over on his side to escape the light streaming in through the window.

"Bobby? Bobby Wilcox? Well, isn't this a nice surprise." Sean had to give her credit for not forgetting her proper New England manners for even a moment. But, they were wasted on the crashed-out dope fiends who had mysteriously found their way into her house. "Now Willy, you and your friends get up and get dressed. I'll be downstairs fixing you boys a nice breakfast. I'm sure everyone has quite the appetite on such a fine morning. Hurry up, now."

Mrs. Unger departed from the open doorway as suddenly as she had appeared—leaving Sean wondering if maybe it all hadn't just been a dream. That maybe he was still asleep on Unger's bedroom floor. That before he knew it, Boober, Dwight, and he, would all be back in the Olds, speeding their way north. Just it had been. Just as it should be now.

But the sound of her footsteps receding down the stairs convinced him that it was real all right. Not only that, and just as quickly, the idea of a home cooked breakfast turned into all the enticement he needed to do as Mrs. Unger asked. Real, or not, as he struggled into his jeans and dusty boots, he couldn't help but wonder how the woman could be so cheerful to her son and the pack of strange looking longhairs crashed out on his bedroom floor. Especially if one were to consider the fact that not more than a year before, Mrs. Unger's son came creeping up the stairs, his brain fired up with madness beneath a big harvest moon, butcher knife in hand, and all the intent in the world to commit the most grievous harm possible upon her and his sleeping father.

Yet none of that past seemed to bother Mrs. Unger as she bustled about making scrambled eggs, pancakes, and pouring hot coffee into big mugs for the boys a half hour later as they sat hungrily waiting at the table in the nook set off from the wide open kitchen. On the table lay a copy of the morning paper, left there by the Mr. Unger before he went off to work. While sipping at the hot coffee, Sean picked it up and scanned the headlines. In a flash of déjà vu he happened to notice a small column at the bottom of the page—a column similar to one he'd read at Hap's diner in G'ville *When damn, just yesterday morning. How did that happen?* This story, too, was about the break-in at the Democratic HQ in D.C. Apparently new information had come to light: a reliable source was linking the crime to the president's re-election committee, CREEP. *A suitable name all right. Considering who the current president is.* Before he could ponder this any further, Mrs. Unger was setting plates of hot food down in front of her son's friends, the smell, and sight, more than enough to drive any ponderings of what was going on in D.C. with the creepy president, far away.

Sitting in Mrs. Unger's kitchen wolfing down the hot breakfast with his pals, a strange sense of *home* enveloped Sean. Perhaps it was just a numbing residue from the beer and the drugs of the day before. The hours spent on the road. Dwight suddenly appearing in the life he was leading—Sean didn't know. But this sense washing over him as he ate reminded him of an old longing he sometimes had, not really having such a thing as home anymore. The last four years of his life had been spent in a variety of different apartments and houses with a variety of different roommates. And none of those places, or people, had seemed like home. He knew that well. They were just places, and people, he had stopped with for a time.

Well, Sean thought, after the food had been consumed and he, and his fellow adventurers, were doing their part for Mrs. Unger by rinsing and stacking the empty dishes in the sink, he wasn't anywhere close to a home now. That was for damn sure. When the dishes were done, Sean followed Boober out the kitchen door into the back yard. The sunlight seemed to flow around Boober's tousled hair, making it shine even brighter in the morning light as the Wheelman rummaged around in his top pocket for a pack of smokes.

"C'mon Will." Boober turned to Unger who had come out the door behind Sean. "Let's hit it."

A wreath of grey tobacco smoke, like a faint halo, hung just above the Wheelman's head—at least it looked like a halo to Sean. Not for long, though—his next thought being, *That's rich. Boober with a halo. Never happen.*

"C'mon, man," Boober repeated. "Let's hit it, pal."

~12~ D.C.

An hour later the four adventurers trooped down to the Olds, all of them showered, in clean t-shirts, and freshly fed. Unger had to clear things first with his mom who was peppering him with questions while the others waited. Yes, it was true he wouldn't be attending classes that day. And no, it wasn't a big deal. He would make up the work. There were no tests scheduled that day, so it was a good day to skip and show his friends around the nation's capital. The classes he would miss, as he explained to Boober while they were pulling away from the house, were Psych and Behavioral Science. Sean, hearing this from his new position in the back seat with Dwight, wondered if it was Unger's hope those two classes might help him stay abreast of his schizoid condition.

Strangely enough, and unexpected, before they were to head for the city Boober had drawn Sean off to the side.

"Hey man, Will and I were talking last night."

"Yeah, I heard you."

"We came up with an idea I need to run by you first."

"Oh?" Sean's curiosity perked up at the serious look on the Wheelman's face. "Do tell. I'm all ears."

It was true he was all ears—but he was eager, too. Eager to get into town and see what was happening in Nixon land, for one thing. Eager as well to get with the day, the morning shiny and warm with June rising over the houses and streets of Alexandria, the slight breeze ruffling the flowers Mrs. Unger had planted along the front of the house. But pushing his hair back from his face he waited as patiently as he could for Boober to fill him in.

Because come on, man, get it over with, man. There's something's happening down the road, I just know it. If we don't get to it, it will do it without us. This D.C. thing crazy ass Unger wants to show us, where who knows? Maybe I'll find that my theory of bad vibes, floating like a diseased miasma over the capital city courtesy of the crook in the White House isn't true at all. That maybe those Yippie cats did levitate the Pentagon and chanted all that evil crap away while they were doing so. That just because I wasn't there to see and be a part of it, just because the corporate news folks claimed it didn't happen, damn it all, man, that doesn't mean it didn't.

None of which he shared with Boober just then—asked instead, "So what's this grand idea of yours?"

As it turned out the idea wasn't totally Boober's alone. In fact, it had been Unger who mentioned it first, when towards the end of their rambling conversation, he asked out of nowhere if Boober could leave him, say a pound, certainly no more, of the weed they were carrying north to Red in Boston. If so, then Unger could easily unload it and have the money waiting there, not only for Boober, but Sean, as well. A safety net, if you will. Unger's only interest in all this, besides wanting to help his old friend Bob, being he would keep a little out for his own personal use. Which would help him out, the prices of weed having skyrocketed lately. Without a job he had no money—and hey, like anybody, he enjoyed a toke or two here and there. So what do you say, Bob? Or so Unger had asked Boober.

"I'll tell you what I say, Bobby old boy: forget it." It didn't take Sean long to come up with this opinion. "We told Red we'd have ten keys for him and that's what we're going to give him. I don't really know Red, but if this works out then who knows? We may be able to help one another out in the future. Ripping him for a pound first time around is no way to secure a solid business partner. If you can catch my drift."

"I hear you." Boober leaned up against the side of the Cutlass, lighting up a Camel as he mulled over Sean's take on Unger's idea. "Yeah, I hear you. But look. It's no big deal. We'll skim it off the tops of the bricks and no one will miss it."

"Bob—"

"Look, man, I owe Will. Big time. He took the heat for me back in high school before my folks moved us down to Florida. Let me stash a pound of reef in his locker until I could get rid of it. Some little fucker dimed him out and Will got sent to Juvie. Being closed in like that didn't sit too well with him and he ended up in the psych ward." Despite the fact he wasn't behind the wheel of the Olds, Boober did that wheel shrug thing of his. "Kind of feel like maybe it's my fault, dig? That he turned stoned cold whacked."

And there it was. Sean turned away to pace a little up and down the sidewalk, trying to sort out this thing he wanted no part of. He wanted to do right by Red, a guy he didn't know. He knew nothing about Red at all—other than he was a pal of Boober's and was going to help him get to Canada to avoid being shot to pieces in Southeast Asia. *If* Boober brought him some decent weed. Which is where Sean came in, drawn by the idea of helping his pal, true. But hey, the money looked good too. Now Boober wanted to right a wrong he had done in the past—a wrong that might have turned Unger schizoid. Not that Sean knew if that were possible or not. Had no idea, in fact—knew only that as crazy as he had ever gone, personally, was due to some downright nasty acid he bought in Coconut Grove at a love-in. Certainly his times in Juvie had sucked. But it hadn't pushed him over some nutjob edge.

"Okay, man." Sean turned back to Boober. The brightness in Boober's eyes, when he realized Sean was going to agree, made it a little easier. "But if Red gets hip to the load being light it's all you, Kemosabe. All you."

"That's cool, man. He'll never know. Trust me."

"That's asking a lot, Bobby."

They messed around with the dope duffel in the trunk, Sean hoping the open trunk lid would shield his actions from prying eyes until they managed to come up with an amount of weed Unger could pass off as a pound.

"I sure hope your man Red doesn't bring out the scales." Sean had just finished stuffing the makeshift pound into the garbage bag Unger brought out to them. "And that's the last I'm going to say about it."

Any uneasiness left over from his recent moral dilemma vanished for Sean once he was inside the Olds, Boober at the wheel spinning the big car around on the quiet street to head it in the general direction of D.C. He was just happy to be back in the car, looking forward to a great day of stoned kicks in the nation's capital.

Boober seemed to be back in his groove as well, as he wheeled along the streets of Alexandria, sardonic grin on his face, lit cigarette dangling from the corner of his mouth. At the first red light they encountered he turned to Dwight in the back seat where Sean was busy rolling a joint. "Hey bud," Boober asked. "Can you see if any of those beers in the cooler are still cold?" He paused, thought of something, then added over his shoulder as the light turned green, "Hot or cold I don't care, just pass me one."

The beers indeed *were* still cold, as Dwight passed one over the seat. The kid waved one invitingly at Sean and Unger, an offer Sean declined. But Unger took one from the kid, gulping the beer down with an urgency Sean didn't expect from such a laconic individual. He was a little surprised he hadn't taken one himself—surprised as well at how good he was feeling that morning, considering what he had put his mind and body through the day before. But that day was in the past. Now he was savoring the sun-shining overhead and the lingering effect of the good food cooked by Mrs. Unger.

"I knew you were gonna wimp out on me sooner or later." The Wheelman had noticed Sean taking a pass on a beer. "That's okay, man. Like I always say: means more for me."

"I figured you'd be pleased," Sean said. "And like *I* always say: drive."

Boober did just that—eventually steering onto the Beltway, that mass of confusing interstate running the circumference of D.C. The Beltway that morning was a constant flow of heading-to-work traffic. Boober zipped the Olds in and out of this traffic as if it were some smaller foreign make, instead of the beast of Detroit auto making it actually was, the Wheelman laying on the horn at every slower moving car in his way. Yelling out the window as he passed. Giving the finger to the cautious drivers who did not yield the right of way as quickly as he would have preferred—all the while looking ahead for the next gap in the wall of steady moving automobiles, pumping the gas, or hitting the brakes, as needed, beer can nestled in his lap between his legs, Camel smoldering in the corner of his mouth. Occasionally he turned to Unger, sitting in Sean's normal place in the front seat, for directions, asking stuff like, "This exit? No? How much further then?"

Once, exasperated when he missed the exit Unger suggested Boober snapped. "What the fuck, man? You've got to speak up quicker. Can't you see what I've got to deal with here?" Sardonic grin gone he angrily flipped the cigarette butt out the window, while reaching at the same time with his other hand into his shirt pocket for another one— suddenly changing tack to follow this outburst with something that may, or may not have been, on his mind for who knows how long. He turned to Dwight in the back seat, sitting quietly looking out his window. "What the fuck's with you, kid? You only talk when you've got a head full of Beauties going on?"

"C'mon, Bobby." Sean spoke up in the kid's defense. "Lay off him."

It being his feeling that Dwight, quiet as he was right then, might be pondering his impending homecoming up in Boston, where all of them, minus Unger, would ride into on the morrow. Who knows? *That homey scene in Mrs. Unger's kitchen earlier may have had the same effect on Dwight as it'd had on him.* The one difference between Sean and Dwight being that Dwight *was* going home. Back to that rundown row house he had split from a year before with his girlfriend. The two runaways leaving their mothers to worry about where their children were. To worry if they were okay out in that very wild world no decent parent wanted their children to get beat up in. Now, one of those children was coming home, alone, the other one who knows where.

Dwight's worries aside, at the moment what Sean was really curious about was the animated version of Boober, a madman now at the wheel of the Olds, as opposed to the usual laid back cat he normally was when driving. Could it be that just like he was, Boober, too, was simply jazzed to be alive on such a brilliant summer morning. Not only alive, but a thousand odd miles from the problems he'd left behind in Lauderdale: the draft, money, parents on his case about being a longhaired ne'er-do-well with no future in sight. Pretty much the same problems a lot of young dudes their age were looking at that summer. He wondered if those cats felt the same as he did right then, perhaps lifting up to the world a communal, *Hey, well fuck it. I'm just gonna do it. Get out on that ol' highway, let 'er rip and take it from there.*

It was a wonderful thought coming at him in the back seat of the car running at 70 mph on the Beltway towards the capital—an epiphany that made Sean say out loud, "Yeah, that's right. Fuck it." Uttered out of nowhere like that it got Boober's attention, the quizzical look on his face turning to one of approval as Sean dragged the travel bag out and began rolling another joint.

By the time Boober pulled the Olds off the Beltway toward Pennsylvania Avenue, all inside were fairly stoned as the Wheelman cruised slowly along the famous avenue past hulking government buildings like the Federal Trade Commission, Justice Department, District Court, the National Archives, and such.

Inside the drab interiors of these gray buildings, Sean could imagine the legions of faceless workers, at their desks, walking the endless halls of bureaucracy. All of these workers dressed the same, all of them engaged in boring, menial tasks that fine summer morning. Tasks directly concerning the welfare of the country, perhaps, but that meant nothing to Sean, who was picturing the endless hallways and faceless workers as being some kind of nightmare scene straight out of Kafka: flat-headed men and women hurrying to and fro, carrying armloads of word-covered papers that all said the same thing. These men and women rushing papers down twisting corridors leading into nowhere, while those in positions of authority barked out instructions that made no sense. Sean shuddered, sad, but also amazed, that one could get caught up in such work, when outside a whole big wondrous world flowed all around those bureaucratic halls. This revelation followed by the thought of how everything he'd just imagined was likely due to the fat bomber they just smoked.

The White House came up on the right, the morning sun, higher now in the sky, lighting up the presidential home and the tourists milling around in front of the iron gates hoping to catch a glimpse of their Fearless Leader. Unger picked that moment to surprise everyone in the car by launching into an incredible narrative pertaining to his recent dream. In this dream, extra-terrestrials came down and kidnapped Nixon and his old lady, holding them for ransom in long glass tubes in their spaceship where they did experiments on the helpless First Man and Lady after the ransom wasn't paid. Unger went on and on with minute details about the space creatures and the planet they inhabited until Boober had heard enough.

"So, Will, this dream you had? Was that on one of those days you forgot to take your morning Lithium? And don't tell me, 'No.' If you do, that's it for you and this excellent reefer we've been smoking."

Unger grinned a goofy little cherub type smile but shut up. Boober turned down 17th Street, cutting across Constitution Avenue to where it flowed into Independence Avenue. The Lincoln Memorial rose up in front of them, white and shining. In another moment Sean could see the statue of Honest Abe sitting tall and forlorn looking as he stared out over the wide Potomac River, the president, carved out of stone, maybe waiting for hordes of mad dog Confederates to finally come storming across the water. As the Olds passed by, Sean flipped the monument off.

"You fucking Rebs." Boober laughed at Sean's finger, still waving out the window at the statue. "You lost, man. It's over."

It was getting late in the morning—both the passage of time since breakfast, and the recently smoked joint bringing on hunger pains. When Boober asked for suggestions, Unger directed him down a side street behind George Washington University to a little bar tucked away there. The Wheelman squeezed the big car into a narrow parking space in front of the bar, grunting as he manhandled the steering wheel to get it in there. *A job well done,* and Sean told his friend so.

"Ah now, nothing to it, Sean." Boober shut the engine down. "But seeing as how you think I did such a fine job you can buy me a beer. And quickly."

With Unger leading the way, the four adventurers strolled into the bar, where in the darkened interior workers on noontime break drank beer and wolfed down big sandwiches stacked neatly in wicker baskets. There were pages, secretaries, clerks, men and women in coats and ties and neat dresses, some of whom turned to stare at Sean and his pals entering the bar; taking in the three hippies in their dusty jeans and tee shirts, one of them wearing a flashy Hawaiian shirt.

Dwight, having noticed the pool table in the back corner, perked out of the quiet slump he'd been going through. "Get me a beer, man, will you?" he asked Sean, while pointing at the green felt waiting for him. "If you don't mind? I'll be back. Hopefully with the cash to pay for it."

"You got it, pal." Sean didn't doubt for a minute that the gangly, pockmarked kid would do just that.

Having a better than average day on the pool table, apparently, Dwight surprised everyone but Sean by paying for the beers and sandwiches they wolfed down. Then it was out of the bar and back into the Olds where Unger gave the Wheelman directions to a place he called the "Great Falls." Just below these falls, Boober turned the car off of the highway winding along next to the Potomac, onto a dirt road leading down to the river. After parking in a pull over roughed out in the scraggly oaks lining the dirt road, the four of them trekked down a narrow path to a bluff overlooking the flowing stretch of water. The waterfall was just north of where they ended up standing on the rocky bluff next to a lone, majestic, oak growing out of the rock, its leafy branches spreading out over the river. A rope swing hung from one of the oak tree's branches, the swing swaying in the breeze coming off of the water.

They sat down on the hard ground beneath the mighty oak, and it being such a mellow scene, Sean fired up a joint. Dwight got into the act, reaching into his jeans pocket to pull out a handful of Beauties. As the weed, and the Beauties, began working their chemical magic on Sean's system, he happened to look up towards the sky. A flock of white birds were wheeling across the city to the east, the birds seeming like nothing more than tiny white specks in the blue sky above the tops of those far away buildings. For one strange second he felt as if he were rising up with those birds. *Rising up to float in the wind over the capital of the nation. Maybe going with those birds into the past. Into that place where all the history of the surrounding countryside and that city on the far away hill was constant. Never-ending.* All of it flowing in, and through him, as he drifted on the wind with those white birds in the distance.

But just like that he was back, Dwight having come to life all suddenly—his loud, "Aiyee!" as he stripped down to his Jockeys, grabbed hold of the rope swing and sailed way out over the Potomac— snapping Sean out of his pleasant reverie about birds, blue skies, and history, to watch stunned, yet admiringly, as the lanky kid let go of the rope, his plummeting body making a loud splash when it hit the water below and disappearing from sight. After what seemed longer than possible the kid's head cleared the water, his long hair slicked back from his face, his angular, pockmarked features glowing in the sunlight streaming down.

"Goddamn." Dwight had a wild grin on his face as he clambered up the bluff. "What a fucking rush, guys. That water's freakin' cold."

Soon, all of them were taking turns with the rope swing, digging the freaky rush of letting go, the jolting shock of hitting the cold water, the fight back up to the surface, and that first big gulp of air back into the lungs. The summer afternoon waned as they swam, Sean wondering once as he was rolling up another joint if the others felt like he did right then. *You know, just being completely free on the banks of the river, the sounds of the city only a faint rumble.* He decided it didn't matter if they did. He was just happy he felt that way.

~13~ Georgetown

As the afternoon sun began its descent it became too cold to swim. Instead, they hung out on the bluff above the river, letting the fading light of the sun and the warm afternoon breezes dry them off. Once sufficiently dry, they clambered into their clothes and walked back up the dirt path to where the Cutlass sat waiting for them.

Flying high on everything he'd consumed on the river bluff, the Wheelman smoothed the Olds into Georgetown, where following Unger's directions to a side street off of MacArthur Boulevard, he slipped the car into one of the narrow parking spaces lining the street. "Damn." A smug grin of success creased Boober's face as he shut the engine down. "Good thing I didn't fail parallel parking in Driver's Ed, wouldn't you say Tonto m'boy?"

"Yep, Kemosabe. You're a freaking genius behind the wheel."

"First true thing you've said today."

It was a good goof to hit the streets with, Sean thought, as he crawled out of the back seat and stood on the sidewalk before heading after the others following Unger up the street, past funky bookstores, head shops, and underground record stores that appeared to be the main type of commerce in that particular area of Georgetown. Strolling along just behind the rest of the crew, Sean couldn't help but notice the hordes of sweet looking hippie chicks hanging out on the late Friday afternoon. *Man, there are girls everywhere. Bra-less underneath tie dyed tee shirts, maybe panty-less, too.* They wandered along the sidewalks, ducked in and out of the various shops. Though all these chicks kind of looked the same, with each one of them there was some sort of difference. Some sort of trademark to separate them from the others: an exotic peace sign necklace, an ornamental leather headband holding long hair back from their face, and the like. One of them really stood out to Sean because of the glittering third eye pasted in the center of her forehead. But alike, or different, it didn't matter any to him. Not with the sudden stirring in his groin, this stirring intensified by the steady body rushes washing over him as he walked.

In one of those funky head shops, Boober bought a pipe. The "Octopus," as it was billed, appeared to be constructed out of a four barrel carburetor, one probably damn near identical to what lay beneath the hood of the Olds. Four lengths of surgical tubing hung from the jets of the carb, and all in all Sean had to admit, it was one hell of a design—not to mention very fitting for the ride they were currently cruising in.

Still, as he watched Boober examining the exotic pipe, and then, having made up his mind to buy, counting the wad of bills jammed in his wallet, he couldn't help but have reservations about the practical use of such a pipe. Especially when one considered the duffel bag of dope stashed in the trunk of the Cutlass.

"Hey, man." Boober frowned at the curious look Sean threw his way while the longhair behind the desk was bagging up the pipe. "How can I say no to this thing? It's a freaking work of art."

"Art, yeah. But discreet? Definitely not."

"Since when has discretion been my style?"

But it was all cool, Sean decided, indiscreet crazy pipe or not, this cruising along on the streets of Georgetown as evening was falling. A groove, emanating out of the head shops, bookstores, and coffee houses strung out on the sidewalks, flowed through him as he walked; this groove magnified by the substances in his body and the steady stream of loud rock music coming out of the above-named establishments. The hippie girls, and guys, stoned smiles on their faces as they strolled along the avenue, were all part of this groove. *Yes indeed, dig those stoned smiles.* For everybody was stoned in Georgetown that late afternoon. How could they not be, what with the smell of marijuana drifting out of alleys, and the red brick townhouses here and there interrupting the line of stores and such. All of it: the smell of reefer, the smiles on the young faces flowing by him, the smile he knew was on his face, the rock music carrying the message. Man. You know it's happening now. Right here. The Movement, baby! And by god, when this mission of his and Boober's was over, well then, this cat, one Sean Morgan, was heading to Tuscaloosa, his next mission in what was left of his life.

And if you didn't think he was going to make that scene, and every scene possible after, well then, you did not know Sean Morgan. And that was all there was to it.

"C'mon Spaceboy." Boober, up ahead with the others, yelled at Sean who had fallen back, lost in his reverie of everything going on around him. "Let's go, man."

He picked up the pace, catching up with his pals just as Boober was opening the door to a seedy looking bar and waving them in. As he was going through the door, Sean looked up to catch the name of the joint: "The Dharma Den." The sign was written in elegant calligraphy bordered by scenes of a Japanese garden. Once inside, after casually checking out the pictures of mandalas, yogis, and other mystical type figures hanging on the walls, he ordered a pitcher of beer. Sean pondered what Buddhism and beer might have in common—deciding as he sat down at the table and poured out glasses all around, that it probably didn't matter.

The beer was ice cold though and just in time to wash down the Beauties Dwight was passing out again. A wise move on the kid's part, Sean figured. A second wind could come in handy for the night of wild kicks Unger had been promising all day. Speaking of Unger, he seemed to be a tad on edge. Judging by the way he sat quietly, tight grin on his face, the grin broken by the occasional off the wall comment concerning schizophrenia, his long bony hands lifted up out in front of him as he tried to drive his points home.

But when Sean leaned over to Boober and suggested it might be best to start limiting the drugs going Unger's way, Boober waved him off.

"Ah now, Tonto, he's just having a good time. You can see he doesn't get out much."

"Yeah, I see that. Easy enough to see why, too."

Suddenly Unger jumped up from his seat, knocking it over backwards as he declared it was time to hit the topless bar. He was out the door before the others could react. Sean, Dwight, and Boober hurried out after him — finding him by the Olds pacing back and forth on the sidewalk, rubbing his hands together and muttering over and over, "C'mon, c'mon." Sean shot Boober a look, but the Wheelman just shook his head as he slid into the driver's seat.

Barely able to swing the car around on the narrow street, Boober headed her back to the capital city, to what Unger swore was the absolute best strip joint in all of D.C. The lights of the government buildings and monuments sparking up the night in the distance seemed to beckon them on. Splashing sprays of water jetting up from fountains created rainbows in the fluorescent light. Until finally the Wheelman brought the car to a stop in front of a two story, neon lit up building in among some warehouses on the edge of D.C. This building, painted a kind of weird hot pink, proudly displayed the club's name in winking lights above the door: *"APHRODITES."*

"Well my friends." Unger surveyed his fellow passengers from the front seat. "Inside yon building are some of the loveliest naked ladies you have ever set eyes on."

Sean couldn't help but be skeptical, having a hard time by now believing anything the twitching kid in the front seat might say. To his surprise, though, after entering the place through tinted glass double doors, he found out that Unger was correct. For indeed, beautiful, half-naked women were everywhere inside of the softly lit club. Some of these girls were dancing on a garish stage in the front of the room, spotlights shining on their pale, naked breasts as they gyrated to the music blaring from speakers hidden somewhere behind them. In between songs a polka-dotted suited MC, an old-timey burlesque straw boater of a hat perched at a jaunty angle on his head, made feeble jokes as he introduced the dancers. Girls with names such as Ruby, Billie Jo, Debbie Sue, and other such nonsense, Sean figuring for a fact that these names were not their real ones.

Other girls sat at the little round tables surrounding the stage, business types in suits and ties, buying them drinks while doing their best to flirt with them. The girls, sipping from champagne glasses, wore only G-strings, their breasts exposed to the hungry eyes of the businessmen sitting with them. At other tables, blue collar guys, some still in their Dickie work clothes, chugged beers, leered at the dancers on the stage, and when they had the chance, stashed dollar bills in their garters.

All in all, Sean found it a fairly decadent scene, though fascinating in a campy, garish sort of way. He'd seen his share of naked breasts in his young life—just never in such a setting, and he wasn't sure if it was a turn on, or just stupid. While he was sorting this out Unger led them to a table right up by the stage where they ordered beers from the topless waitress who magically appeared at their table. She returned, a big smile on her heavily made-up face as she set the absurdly expensive beers down in front of them, bending over low as she did so they could see her hard nipples, just out of reach of any potentially groping hand.

None of which Unger paid any attention to, Sean noticed. Unger, instead, stared at the dancers onstage writhing lewdly on the lit up platform, his face twitching with each suggestive movement the girls made, his hands seemingly flying between the beer in front of him on the table and his lap. The longer Sean watched the clearer it became to him, that right there before his eyes, Unger had evolved into a human batch of exposed nerves, the beer, reefer, and Black Beauties having finally caught up to his mentally unbalanced brain and in the process removing the proper use of his faculties.

What also became clear to Sean was the fact it was time to split. That is, if they wanted to make it out of "Aphrodite's" in one piece. Any chance for escape would only be possible if Unger didn't make some sort of radical move on one of those dancers he was so hungrily eyeing. And by doing so, giving just cause to the burly bouncer by the door to pounce. Yep, Sean figured splitting the scene immediately was their only hope. If it worked, well, once back safely at the Unger homestead, a 714 or two for Will would probably do wonders for his damaged psyche. As it would for his.

Shortly, though, maybe sometime after midnight, and before Unger could do any sudden damage, the revelry had grown tiresome, it was mutually decided by all at the table. The novelty of being surrounded by lovely women displaying their charms while nursing three-dollar beers had worn off. Boober led the way out of the joint, back to the sanctuary of the Olds. Tomorrow, Sean thought, as the Wheelman cruised them down the dark streets of D.C. towards Alexandria and the safety of Unger's bedroom—tomorrow would bring the last leg of the trip to Boston. Dwight would be gone. Sean and Boober would hook up with Red, and complete the mission they had set out on three short days before. *Yes, tomorrow they would be on the road again. Everything would be different. Everything would be good.*

Once back at the quiet house, the four of them crept up the stairs to Unger's bedroom, where Sean and Dwight immediately swallowed one of those 714's. Strangely enough, Boober and Unger passed on the 714's, heading instead back down to the kitchen to hang out and talk. Sean didn't see how it could be much of a conversation. Not with the way Unger had been going on all the way back to the house, rapping on and on about aliens, space travel, and time transference, a utilization of which Unger claimed to be working on, and that would make him rich beyond his wildest dreams.

But that was on Boober and Unger to deal with. Not Sean—and as the Quaalude began to come on, and with just the faintest whisper of Boober and Unger downstairs talking coming up to him, Sean thought that, Yes. It's time to go.

And indeed it was. Though that departure came sooner than expected, with Boober shaking Sean awake in the early hours of the morning. "No, man, you've got to get up," Boober yelled when Sean brushed his hands away. "We've got to leave. Now!"

"What's going on, Bobby?" Sean sat up on the floor, groggy and confused from the 714. "We've got to leave?"

"No questions. Just get up."

He did, helping Boober to wake Dwight up, too. In the darkness of the bedroom Sean suddenly realized Unger was nowhere in sight—a fact he mentioned to Boober as they were grabbing up their things.

"He's gone, Seano. Way gone! Now let's hit it."

Once they were back in the Olds and on the move, the Wheelman clued Sean and Dwight into what had happened. It seemed that Willy boy had flipped his lid, as Boober put it. On top of the beer, speed, and reefer, Unger had forgotten to take his daily dose of Lithium that morning. A "forgetting" Unger was prone to. While he and Boober were talking in the kitchen Unger suddenly became agitated, informing Boober how he realized now that Sean and Dwight were actually agents from the hospital. Not only that, but agents on a mission: bring Unger back. Dead or alive. Neither possibility that Unger approved of. Before Boober could get him settled down Unger jumped up from the kitchen table to run out the back door into the night, screaming as he ran down the streets.

"So, we're out of here. There's no telling what that maniac might do. No way we can stop him, either."

For just a flash, Sean had the terrible thought that maybe, just maybe, Poco's spell might be behind this current situation. Thankfully, this paranoid thought disappeared just as quickly as it had come, when the stop light turned green. The Wheelman stepped on the gas, the Cutlass carrying the now three adventurers far from anyone's—except Dwight's—home.

~14~ I-95 North–again

As Boober wheeled through Alexandria, Sean kept an occasional eye out for Unger, thinking he wouldn't be surprised to see that rampaging dude screaming through the neighborhood, butcher knife in hand, mayhem running amuck in his brain. He couldn't help either, try as he might, those random thoughts of Poco, and her evil spell. *Was Unger's freak out an isolated happening—or worse, Poco's spell finally kicking in?* Boober and he would have to stay on their toes if somehow Poco's spell was behind Unger's sudden madness. Of that, Sean had no doubt.

No rampaging Unger was to be seen, though, and as the Wheelman ran them up on the Beltway to skirt D.C. proper and eventually merge in once again with I-95 running north, Sean let out a mild sigh of relief. They were moving again. Beginning the last leg of the journey to Red in Boston where they would deliver the drive away car. Deliver, as well the dope in the trunk, and for their efforts receive a nice wad of cash.

But before that? For Dwight, a homecoming. Followed by, hopefully for him, once the hellos were said and the recriminations from his mom dealt with, a successful search for Joey, his girlfriend who, raped by James, had done what she thought best at the time and fled the scene.

As for Boober, if all went well, the next stage of the road for the intrepid Wheelman would take him to Montreal. To that peaceful commune of others like him. Guys who'd had no choice but to flee the draft. And Nixon's damnable war in a country none of them had ever heard of before until it burst into the headlines of every newspaper in the country, becoming just about the only news the TV networks reported come dinner time in America.

And for Sean? Bus, train, or airplane, whatever conveyance would best get him back to the 650 Bonneville motorcycle parked out in front of Dewey's Party Palace in good old Ft. Lauderdale. From there, next stop Tuscaloosa and the Stone's concert. And when the concert was over, west, to that shining beacon on the other side of the continent, where whatever dreams he had left waited for him.

Other than the Top 40 tunes from the only radio station Sean could find, it was quiet in the car. Dwight had fallen back to sleep, head leaning against the top of the seat where it met the window, his long legs stretched out as best he could manage in the cramped space. Boober, at the wheel, staring straight ahead at the highway, grunted occasionally in exasperation when he had to go around a slower moving car in front of them, rolling his eyes at Sean when he did as if to say, Look at that asshole. He never said this out loud, just did that shrugging snort thing of his. The shrug was sometimes punctuated with a spent Camel out the window—the sparks of the cigarette, when it struck the roadbed, flashing up for just a moment before the tailwinds of the Cutlass blew them away.

Meanwhile, the morning commute was picking up, Sean watching as the headlights of the cars heading the other way on the highway towards D.C. disappeared in the rising light of dawn. Cars, he figured, filled with men and women on the way to their anonymous jobs in the nation's capital. He shuddered for a moment, thinking of those gray, lifeless, government buildings they had passed by the day before, glad once again he wasn't trapped inside one.

His spirits lifted somewhat when D.C. and its urban mess were behind them. Instead, as the Olds growled along on its way north, the Maryland countryside was unfolding in the building light of the June morning. No more congested streets of D.C., Alexandria, or Georgetown. But green fields that stretched away on both sides of the interstate to far off stands of trees standing atop rolling hills. The further away they got from the city, Dwight's soft snoring in the backseat became a strange counterpart, not only to what Sean was seeing but to the jumbled thoughts racing inside his head.

Spirits lifted or not, he was definitely still dealing with the aftershocks of the day and night before. And how quickly everything had changed. How in its own different way the whole mess was reminiscent of that night in G'ville with Pinko, the eruption at the protest march, Poco's sudden appearance, followed by her just as sudden disappearance. His flight back to the Cave where a different sort of hell was breaking loose—leading to Sean's flight to Lauderdale on Tommy's bike. All of which led him to where he was now. Riding with Boober and Dwight toward whatever was coming next.

Concerning Unger, the more awake, and aware, he became, Sean realized it couldn't have gone any other way. Unger slipped further from reality with each toke of reefer, with each Beauty he swallowed. Boober should have put an end to it. Unger was his pal, after all. Hell, Sean should have tried to stop it. At least he had warned Boober. Saw it coming and tried to say something. The best he could do at the time he supposed. But they were out of there alive. That went a long way in Sean's book. A long way. Still, as the little Maryland towns slipped past, Oxon Hill, Morningside, Forest View, he couldn't help but wonder, just what Unger might be up to. Was he still chasing his demons through the streets of Alexandria? Or had he simply settled for killing his mom and dad like he had wanted to the year before?

Questions he decided to put away for now. It was a new and sunny morning, and they were doing what they should be: hauling north on the interstate to complete their mission.

As for that interstate, now that they were well past D.C. the highway seemed almost devoid of traffic. Boober had no trouble keeping the Cutlass at his preferred 75 mph. In the distance as they ripped along a military jet could be heard taking off from an airbase somewhere out of sight and with the sound of it suddenly roaring overhead Dwight sat up in the back seat. "What the fuck was that?" His eyes were all fogged out looking, the kid obviously still half asleep. "Where the fuck are we?"

Boober laughed as he lit up a smoke. "Relax kid." Turning to Sean, he exhaled a thick stream of gray cigarette smoke. "We're just fixing to drop you off at the base, here. So you can report to duty. Cool?"

"Yeah man," Dwight mumbled before sinking back in the seat. "It's cool."

"Fucking kid," Sean said, grinning back at the Wheelman. "He doesn't know what the hell is going on."

"Yeah? You think?" Boober shook his head. "Do you?"

More questions. Out of nowhere, too. Ones Sean had no answer for. Maybe never would have.

The Wheelman made a sudden decision. Hitting the brakes he veered off the interstate at the exit for a place called Randolph Village, the Cutlass just making the off ramp in a squealing rush of burning tires and brake pads. It was a move Sean couldn't quite wrap his head around. As best he could tell, when they came to a stop at the light at the end of the ramp, Randolph Village wasn't much of a town. "Village" was a stretch for sure. The only thing visible, other than more of that rolling farmland, was a truck-stop complex atop a hill to the right of the ramp where semis, and other rigs, puffed in and out of the gas station, streams of diesel smoke wafting up from their smokestacks.

But indeed, the truck stop was exactly what the Wheelman had in mind.

"Buddy, I really need some coffee before we go any further."

"I can dig it. Some grub to go with it," Sean said.

"Yeah." Boober nodded as he turned the Cutlass into the truck stop. "Maybe that, too."

In the morning light coming in through the car windows, Sean suddenly saw how pale and sunk in his pal's face was, his hands trembling as he turned the key in the ignition to shut down.

"Jesus, Bobby. You all right, man?"

"I guess." Boober did that shrug thing of his. "Considering I was up all night with the nut job I guess I'm okay. Don't know if I can handle food, yet, but coffee is damn sure needed. Or a beer." A sheepish look on his drawn out face replaced the sardonic Boober grin. "Not sure I could handle one of those right now, though."

"That's very un-Boober-like."

"I know. Don't tell anyone, okay?"

He assumed this was a joke as he followed the Wheelman into the diner. At least he hoped it was a joke. They had tried to rouse Dwight, but it was a no-go and they left him where he was, snoring softly in the backseat. The diner was just like any other dotting the highways of America, Sean supposed. Dimly lit, the shades pulled down to keep the harsh sunlight from blasting in through the plate glass windows fronting the building, the place reeked of stale coffee and cigarettes. Two waitresses, in pink uniforms hustled back and forth serving coffee and breakfast to the travelers and truck drivers. Patsy Cline and George Jones songs wailed out of little individual jukeboxes on the end of the tabletops in the booths, the mournful tunes setting the pace for the waitresses as they worked.

After grabbing seats at the counter, one of the bleary eyed waitresses came over and poured steaming java into cups for them. Boober drained half of his in one long swallow, his empty hand rooting around in his shirt pocket for the pack of Camels. Lighting up he downed what was left of his coffee and slid the cup across the counter for a refill. Halfway through this second cup, Sean noticed a little color returning to the Wheelman's features. Satisfied his pal was going to live, Sean took another look around the diner, thinking that a better feel for their new surroundings might be in order.

During this process he couldn't help but notice how some of the old boys, dressed in overalls, and John Deere caps plastered to their heads, were giving him and Boober the eye. Truck drivers, was Sean's guess, maybe local farmers, fueling up both truck and body for the haul or work still ahead of them. The Wheelman and he were fueling up for their haul, too. The only difference between them being their line of work and the longhair hanging down their backs—this difference exactly why some of those old boys were giving them the eye. And not just any eye. An evil eye.

He did his best to ignore those looks as he dug into his fried eggs and watery grits. He'd seen those kind of looks before. Figured to see them again somewhere down the line.

Finishing up his breakfast well before Boober, Sean mentioned in passing how sooner or later he was going to come across a good serving of grits in a roadside restaurant.

"Jesus!" Boober made like he was choking on his coffee. "Grits? Only you Rebs eat that garbage. Up north grits is dog food."

One of the John Deere caps down the counter from them must have overheard Boober's comments—or at least enough of them to make him turn to what could have been his identical twin sitting next to him and say something Sean couldn't catch.

"C'mon Kemosabe." Whether or not he could hear what the John Deere caps were saying, Sean stood up from the counter. "Let's pay up and blow this scene. We've got too much riding in the car to have one of those old boys pull an "Easy Rider" on us.

Boober, nodding in agreement as he stood up, laid some bills down on the counter to cover the food and tip, and headed for the door, Sean right behind him.

"Hey Bobby," Sean said, once they were out in the parking lot. "I think that gentleman kind of digs you, man." He pointed back to the diner where one of those grizzled old Caps stood in the doorway glaring at them.

Opening the door of the Cutlass, Boober flipped the Cap the finger. The sunlight streaming down on the diner's parking lot lit up the grin back on the Wheelman's face. In that sunlight, Boober looked to Sean like some drug-crazed reincarnation of Lord Byron.

"Man," Sean yelled as he jumped into the car. "That's exactly the sort of thing that got Captain America killed. You dig?"

"Fuck 'em," Boober said, cranking the engine over. "That's what I dig. Fuck 'em all." He gunned the Olds out of the parking lot back towards the interstate.

~15~ Jersey Turnpike

Paranoid, even with the diner several miles behind them, for a while Sean kept an eye glued to the passenger side rearview mirror, worried that any minute a redneck pickup truck would come roaring up out of nowhere with some old boy leveling a shotgun at them. But no death-bearing pickup arrived and just outside of Wilmington, DE they took the dogleg over the Delaware River to pick up the New Jersey Turnpike. It was mid-morning and Dwight finally woke up, yawning and stretching as best he could in the backseat as he asked, "Where are we?" Boober, busy pulling the Olds into the parking lot of a convenience store just before the turnpike entrance, told the kid not to worry about it, but instead to make himself useful.

Dwight fell in behind Sean already heading into the store. Once inside, Dwight mumbled something about the need to pick up some deodorant and disappeared in the aisles. Before getting out of the Cutlass he had rummaged through his battered suitcase, shocking both Sean and the Wheelman, when he retrieved a clean white shirt from the depths of the jumbled mess inside. Sean could understand the kid wanting to make a decent impression on his mom, and the clean shirt made sense. But after a year of being gone he didn't think his mother was going to notice her son's BO.

Shortly after the mission into the convenience store the three travelers were back on the road, where the Wheelman seemed to be back in the groove. The bomber Sean fired up probably helped as well. No matter the cause, Sean was relieved color had returned to his pal's face, that his hands didn't tremble anymore when he lit up a smoke. Some of this re-acquired groove of the Wheelman's could likely be attributed to the beer he was nursing as well.

Sean was back into the groove, too and happy for it. With that Unger bad trip thing behind them, he was able to once again quietly dig the world unrolling outside. Lit up by the mid-morning sun, the New Jersey countryside was all lush green with early summer new growth. Grass fields trailed off to distant farms where red barns, silos, and grazing cattle hung out peacefully. But this pastoral scene, sooner than Sean would have liked, began to change the closer they got to Newark, the green fields replaced by smokestacks, and the smog-colored structures of the Northeastern Corridor. Even the light of the morning sun seemed to fade away, discolored and hidden away in the industrial waste spewing into the skies above the sprawling city. Along with the dingy looking buildings, the smog coming through the open windows of the Cutlass, came the smell of what Sean figured to be hard times.

"So it's true, Kemosabe," Sean said as they ripped by the Newark's city limits sign. "They call this scene the 'Garden State'?"

"True indeed, Tonto me boy."

"Why?"

"What'd you think they were going to call it?" Boober tossed his empty beer can out the window. "The 'Armpit of the Nation'? Who the fuck would want to live here?"

It was a dismal fact, one Sean had to agree with—had to agree, as well, with the Wheelman's casual tossing of his empty beer can out the window. *In a place like that, what could it hurt?*

As the turnpike took them further into the outskirts of Newark, Sean fired up another joint. The occasional mileage signs about how much further to New York, and beyond, gave him hope they would soon be out of the Jersey mess. Even if they would only be trading one urban mess for another. But they were moving, inching closer and closer to the end of the mission. Pleasantly stoned, he drifted into a reverie of what he was going to do with the money Red forked over to him and Boober. The same old dream: Tuscaloosa, a great Stone's concert, then heading west, maybe that vision of a woman and true love sliding in to the mix. And who could say? Perhaps some sort of possible enlightenment once he reached the western shore to gaze upon the Pacific Ocean. So yes indeed, the same old dream that never failed to give him hope.

The sensation of the big car slowing down, and then coming to a complete stop, snapped him from his pleasant reverie. In front of them on the expressway was a line of barely moving cars. For as far as his stoned eyes could see, stalled cars as the Wheelman pounded the dash with an angry hand and yelled out, "Goddamn."

~16~ Traffic Jam and more

At that moment, "Hey Jude, don't bring me down," came blasting out of the car speakers. "Fuck that noise." Boober, in angry disgust, turned off the radio.

So many cars, Sean thought as the Wheelman slammed the dashboard again in frustration at the holdup. *So many cars, none of them really going anywhere as they crept forward at 5, maybe 10mph.* Outside of the Cutlass it was heating up, shimmering mirages wafting up from the pavement and the roofs of the stalled cars in the seemingly endless line stretching off toward the city. It was only pushing the end of June. *What would this place be like come August?* He didn't want to know. Couldn't see how any place could be hotter than where they were now, trapped on the turnpike outside of New York City.

"Maybe the Sahara?" He said this out loud. "Hey, man, I like that song," and he turned the radio back on, Paul's voice singing, "Take a sad song and make it better," reverberating inside the unmoving car.

"What the fuck is wrong with you, man?' Boober slapped the steering wheel this time. *Giving the dashboard a break?* "Screw that. What's wrong with these people?' The Wheelman pointed at the cars motionless in front of them. "Can't they see I have somewhere to be?"

A fine bead of sweat lined the Wheelman's upper lip, pearling up on his forehead as well, now that the cooling rushes of air coming in through the open windows had come to stop. They didn't dare turn on the AC—not with the car already reeking of reefer, stale beer, and sweat seeping out from the pores of the three of them. The Cutlass would be back with its rightful owner soon. How that unknown individual wouldn't figure out that a long, intense, dope party had been going on in his automobile, was beyond Sean's comprehension. Besides the smell, there was spilled Budweiser on the floor mats, scattered pop tabs that hadn't cleared the open windows—not to mention the raft of random pot seeds lying here and there. Probably be for the best, Sean decided, to just run into the drive-away car office in Boston and throw the keys to the clerk and split before any questions could be asked. *Now there's a plan, for sure.* Feeling better about everything, even with being stuck in the godawful traffic jam, Sean joined in as Paul's voice went, "Na, na, na,na, na."

"Anybody want one of these?" Dwight was opening his first beer of the day. "What's the holdup, anyways?"

"Damned if I know, bud." Boober gave the wheel another slap before taking the peace offering from Dwight. "Can't see nothing up ahead except cars. And more cars. At this rate we might make Boston by tomorrow. Maybe later if nothing changes."

The other two adventurers could only nod in agreement as the Olds inched along with the rest of the traffic jam. The smell of over-heating engines and exhaust fumes became a constant, drifting in through the open windows. A white, Chevy Nova came creeping up in the emergency lane, the middle-aged lady inside of the little car asking Boober with her hands in driver's sign language, if he would let her cut in. The Wheelman gave her a sweet smile, raising his hand to politely wave her in. Just as she was pulling in front of the Olds Boober laid on the horn, the loud blaring startling Sean and Dwight from whatever stoned thoughts they were rolling with. Frantic from the unexpected blaring, Nova Lady jerked her car back into the emergency lane, almost plowing into the guardrail in her haste to escape the black Cutlass and the horn-blowing maniac at its wheel.

As they crept past her, Boober turned to look at the lady in the Nova, now stopped completely on the side of the road, mouthing silently as they rolled by, Fuck you. Sean didn't know what to think of all this—until Dwight cracked up laughing, his laughter infectious enough that Sean couldn't help but to join in. Boober looking at the both of them, an innocent grin on his face, asked, "What? What'd I do?"

In that moment it all made sense. There was nothing to it anymore. The traffic jam they were snarled up in just a simple fact of life on that NYC highway and nothing more.

"Kemosabe," Sean said as he passed the smoking bomber to Boober. "You're some kind of asshole. Do you know that?"

"I do, Tonto. Have known it for a long time, now."

An hour or so later they were finally clear of the reason for the jam-up: an overturned semi-trailer in the southbound lane. The big rig had jack-knifed across two lanes, spilling its cargo on the road, boxes upon boxes the police and firemen on the scene were busy gathering up. Clear of the hurdle the Wheelman stepped on the gas, the three adventurers digging the cool breeze blowing through the open windows once more.

Not much later the city, and the traffic jam had been left behind, the groove of moving was back, the traffic hassles of the city a thing of the past. Feeling relieved, Sean rolled another joint, a slim-Jim. When he handed it to the kid, a shy smile came on Dwight's face as he mentioned how he was kind of looking forward to seeing his mother again.

"You know, man," and he passed the J back to Sean. "Now that it's looking fairly inevitable and all."

"Yeah, I can see your point." Sean exhaled his own toke as he handed the joint to Boober. "She'll probably be mad at first, I bet. Won't be long before she starts crying, though, and then it'll all be just like before you split."

"Oh man." Dwight laughed. "That's what I'm scared of."

"Look on the bright side," Boober broke in. "Maybe that Joey chick of yours made it back."

Dwight fell silent.

"What the fuck?" Boober tightened up on the wheel when Sean punched him in the shoulder. "Now what'd I say?"

Some seven hours after leaving Unger's house in the rear-view mirror they, reached the outskirts of Boston. Boober pulled off of I-95 and onto the Mass Pike, and it wasn't long before they rolled into Boston proper, the Wheelman following Dwight's directions to his mother's house. Just as Dwight had said, the house was one of those little row affairs, one of many all up and down a street in Roxbury. Kids of all ages played ball and other games in front of the grungy brick buildings, the summer afternoon shining down upon the street while mothers, grandmothers, and other adults, watched from stoops and open windows. This city neighborhood scene appeared to Sean like it was in simple black and whites, his stoned synapses flashing on images from the Bowery Boys and Father Flanagan's Boys Town movies of his youth.

"Wow, man." Boober came to a stop at the curb in front of what Dwight said was his house. "You ever go over to the Combat Zone? You know, to party? You're so close and all."

"No way, man," and he laughed—his first vocal expression other than giving directions since Boober had mentioned Joey. Grabbing his battered suitcase, he exited the car and stood out on the street in his old neighborhood to stretch his legs. "I've seen what happens to white kids who hang too long after dark over there."

"I always knew you were a wimp." Boober was doing his own stretching thing, now that he was on non-moving terra firma.

"So thanks for the ride, guys. It was cool. "Dwight took hold of Sean's hand, pressing the baggie with what was left of the Black Beauties into his palm. "I won't be needing these anymore, but you guys have some road still in the front of you. I've got that Jame's cash, though. That fucker. Gonna use it, too. Set myself up here again. Help Mom out some, too."

"Sounds righteous, man." The kid's okay, Sean thought as he stared into Dwight's eyes, their color lost in the glare of the sun lighting up his narrow face. "It was a stone blast riding with you, pal. That's for sure. I ever get by this way again I'll be sure to look you up. Maybe you can teach me how to shoot good pool. You know? The way you do."

"That's a deal, man. Anytime, man. Any freaking time."

"Hey bud, listen to me." Boober, back behind the wheel of the Cutlass, reached out through the window to grab Dwight by the shirt tail. "Be cool, kid. It was real."

At the top of the steps to his mom's house Dwight turned on the stoop to wave goodbye. *Just another kid.* The Olds pulled away from the curb. *A forlorn kid alone in this crazy damn America, hiding underneath his old Army jacket the clean white shirt he was wearing for his mom. Not knowing what's coming his way next. Or where he might be headed. For now just waving goodbye to two guys he had ridden with briefly. And then would probably never see again.*

As the Cutlass was picking up speed, the Wheelman intent on the road in front of him, screaming kids playing in the street scattering out of the way of the black car, Sean remembered something.

"Hey Dwight." He stuck his head out of the Olds to yell back at Dwight still waving goodbye. "You find that Joey, you dig?"

Dwight turned on the steps, one hand on the doorknob, a half-smile on his thin lips as he nodded his head. In another second he had opened the door of the house and disappeared inside.

~17~ Boston

A Mobil station stood on the corner down the street from Dwight's house where the Wheelman suddenly whipped the Olds to a stop in front of a phone booth on the side of the building. "I better give Red a call, Tonto." Boober slid out of the driver's seat. "Let him know we're here." Flicking his cigarette butt away he stepped into the booth and pulled the glass door shut behind him.

The gas station—quaint looking was Sean's first thought, all built out of New England red brick—was busy, its two pump jockeys in their blue and white striped uniforms taking care of the needs of those waiting on their fill-ups. Suddenly thrown into this workaday Boston gas station scene came a beat up Volkswagen van, rock music blasting out upon the world from inside it. Sean had no problem recognizing the tune. *Wow! Street Fighting Man by the Stones. Cosmic?* Yes, and he could dig it. And hey, there was that message again. Just for him, courtesy of the Stones. *Yessir, now you're talking*—all of this rushing through Sean's mind as he watched one of the occupants of the van tapping his hand against the side of the vehicle, his head leaning comfortably out of the open passenger window, his brown hair hanging down on his shoulders, letting his freak flag fly to the beat of the tunes; Sean thinking, *Oh yeah, my man, I'm here with you too.* Just waiting on the day. A day somewhere in the future. A day that would just have to wait. For at that moment and time in space, he had something to do first.

While the Wheelman was busy plunking change into the pay phone, Sean went around to the back of the Cutlass and popped the trunk lid open to check on the items stashed inside. He squared his and Boober's duffels away, making them ready for a quick transfer to Red's ride when the time came. Finished, he opened the hatch to the crude compartment Dewey had cut into the bottom of the trunk and dragged the dope duffel out. He couldn't help but wonder what the look on the car owner's face would be like if he ever discovered the hole carved into his Oldsmobile. Not that it mattered any. Boober and he would be long gone by then.

Checking to make sure all was cool behind him, using the open trunk lid for further security, he opened up the dope duffel. The rush of rich aroma from the weed inside almost made him choke. Stepping back he fanned the air around his face in a feeble attempt to dissipate the odor. Reaching in the duffel he rummaged around until he found the smaller baggie of 714's tucked inside and stashed what was left of the Black Beauties in with the Quaaludes. Staring at the open duffel, the baggy of pills in his hand, he marveled for a second at his good fortune: this chemical cornucopia there at his disposal. He toyed briefly with the idea of popping a Beauty. *To add an extra dimension to the whole thing, maybe chuck half a 714 down with it. To cut the edge a little.* But he held off, aware of the pressing business still to take care of.

Shaking his head, he closed the lid of the trunk and headed for the Mobil station's men's room. He must be really slipping, was his thought. A few months back he wouldn't have hesitated at popping the Beauty and 714. Of course he *was* already pretty high. A functioning high, really, with no need to take it further. He didn't know Red — whatever business discussion to take place between the two of them would require his full attention. Then there was the slight matter of the weed they had skimmed off. An act Sean wasn't comfortable with. Did it only for Boober, actually. He had a feeling he might to live to regret it. But what was done was done.

As Sean was finishing up, Boober came into the men's room. "Everything's set," he said as he bent over the sink and splashed some cold water on his face. "Red said it'll take him an hour or so but he'll be here. We're to meet him at a bar he knows of by the Commons."

"Cool," was the best Sean could come up with and that seemed okay with the Wheelman.

"Shake it off, pal, and let's hit it."

Shortly after Boober, parked in front of a little tavern with the unassuming name of "Earl's Place." Adding to the unassuming quality of the tavern was the flashing neon sign above the window proudly stating that Rheingold's On Tap was served inside—a beer Sean couldn't remember ever having consumed. Judging by the neighborhood, consisting of more of that row house scene where they'd dropped Dwight off, along with the squat little tavern, he had a feeling he wouldn't be tasting that beer any time soon—no matter the proud boast above the bay window.

"Now what, Kemosabe?"

"I don't know." Busy lighting up a Camel, Boober did that wheel shrug thing of his. "I guess we just wait."

But Sean had been in the car way too long to just sit still for the hour or so Red claimed it would take him to get there.

"Think I'll get out and stretch my legs. Take a walk or something."

"Suit yourself. Just don't get lost." But in the next minute Boober had opened the car door and climbed out. "Think I'll join you after all."

A rush of warm, garbage smelling air greeted Sean as he stood on the sidewalk lining the narrow street, courtesy of an alley right next to the tavern. At the far end of this alley a grubby looking old man rooted around in a trash bin set out behind the door of some nameless establishment. A garbage truck, the exhaust pipe running up the back side of the cab spitting out puffs of grey fumes, turned into the other end of the alley, two men jumping off the back of the truck to grab up the waste bins put out for disposal.

"Jesus, Bobby, your man couldn't' come up with a classier place than this to meet?"

"He did say it was pretty discreet."

"I'll give him that, I guess." Realizing he had never been to this city before Sean had to ask, "Surely there's more to Boston than this dumpy scene?"

"C'mon, Tonto." Boober laughed as he pushed black curls back off his face. "Let's go find out if, as you say, there's more to Bean Town than this dumpy crap."

"Right behind you, Kemosabe."

Two blocks up from "Earls" the Wheelman hung a left, his lanky legs setting a pace that at first Sean, still cramped from the long drive of the day, had a struggle keeping up with. But by the time they walked a couple more blocks he began to unwind and soon he was striding along next to his pal. Not only that, but he was starting to dig the walk—the walk getting even better when they came to a much wider thoroughfare, crossed over it, and just like that, were in the Boston Commons.

The smell of freshly mown grass rose up to meet the two adventurers as they left the sidewalk and set off across the green. Breathing in a deep lungful of the clean air, Sean stopped where he was for a second to take in the whole of the park, all sparkling green with summer. Everywhere, it seemed, tourists strolled the hallowed grounds, cameras dangling from cords around their necks, or held loosely in their hands. Some of these tourists were younger, couples walking along hand in hand, some pushing baby strollers. Elderly folks were out, too, enjoying the sun as they sat on stone benches scattered throughout the park, watching the younger folks.

More to Sean's liking were the young cats and chicks laid out on blankets on the grass. The girls were in various combinations of shorts, loose halter tops, or tie-dyed tee shirts; the guys, in jeans or cutoffs, some of them bare-chested. All of them, male and female, had long hair that swayed and shone in the light of the afternoon sun as they tossed Frisbees, or flew kites overhead. The kites, colorful birds made out of cloth stretched tight on balsa wood, cruised along on almost invisible strings via the equally invisible winds blowing across the park. *Also carried along on that invisible wind:* the sweet, pungent smell of marijuana, drifting into his nostrils as he walked along next to Boober. Once again, here it was. All around him. Proof of how the scene was happening everywhere now. Here to stay. Not even the occasional cop on horseback riding through the park, able to put a stop to it.

"Gotta tell you, man," Boober said at one point as they walked. "I'll be glad when this business with Red gets done."

"Bobby, man, you need to relax." For Sean could almost feel, see, the tension flowing from Boober as they walked through the Commons. "Just dig this beautiful day, man. All these chicks hanging out!"

"Yeah, yeah. If you say so."

"Ah, man, I'm serious. Give it a try, maybe start by digging this wind." Taking Boober by the shoulders he turned him into the breeze coming off the pond on the edge of the park—the same breeze carrying those kites higher and higher into the New England summer sky . "Yeah, man. Just dig this breeze."

But the Wheelman wasn't into it—was, in fact, already on his way out of the "Commons," Sean watching as Boober crossed the street on the back side of it, into what looked to be another public park. Cooling wind, or not, Sean followed after him, losing sight of him for a minute as he rounded a corner; but then, there he was, sitting on a bench, and lighting up a smoke as he gazed up at a bronze statue of, Sean realized when he got closer, Paul Revere. Just as he was sitting down next to his pal, a middle-aged couple appeared out of nowhere, snapping photos of the famous statue from every angle as they walked slowly around it. The female half of this couple, a fairly nondescript looking lady with a shy smile and thinning brown hair, asked Sean if he wouldn't mind taking a picture of her and husband in front of the statue.

"No problem, ma'am." He stood up from the bench to take the little Kodak the lady held out for him. "It would be my pleasure."

"Well aren't you just the polite young man," Boober said when Sean sat back down and the couple had continued on their way—the couple happily satisfied, Sean hoped, that a photograph existed to commemorate their time in Boston honoring one of their nation's founding heroes.

"Yeah? You think? At least one of us was raised with some semblance of manners. No surprise it wasn't you."

But Boober wasn't listening—staring instead across the gardens reaching out behind Paul Revere, while tapping one booted foot on the sidewalk to the beat of a song Sean couldn't hear.

"Fuck that, pal. I just want to get out of here. Get this thing done."

Sean could sort of relate to this. Everything they had done since leaving Lauderdale had been punctuated by the roaring eights of the big Olds. The eventual end of the run may, or may not, have really factored into the Wheelman's thinking as he drove. Yet here it was. Close at hand when Boober may have just wanted it all just to continue.

"C'mon, man. Not to worry. Red's on his way." Sean hoped this was true. "When he gets here we'll take care of things. Until then, maybe we ought to just go back to the car and burn one."

"I need a break from that shit, Seano man." The Wheelman stood up and stretched his long arms over his head, the white skin exposed at the end of the short sleeves of the Hawaiian shirt. "Let's go check the river out," and he set off across the gardens.

They walked the few blocks down to the Charles River, the steady noise of city traffic, industry, and people living their lives, following them, muffling what Sean liked to think was the sound of their boot heels ringing out on the sidewalk. Down by the river the two adventurers jumped up on the seawall to watch as boats plied up and down the waterway. All the while seagulls dipped and dove, flying low over the river in search of food. It reminded Sean of that Savannah River scene—where he, Boober, and Dwight hung out after beers and burgers at "Mickey's Pub." The only difference being that they were eight hundred or so miles further up the east coast—and minus Dwight. The rest was pretty much the same.

"Hey Bobby,man." Something had just come to Sean. *Something important.* "You remember that song by, ah man, I think it was the "Standells" maybe? You know man? Love that dirty water … Boston you're my home?"

And then Boober was laughing again, smiling—maybe, just maybe, letting some of that road slip away from his shoulders.

"Jesus, Tonto, but you're the only one who'd remember that tune'"

The wind coming off the river blew steadily on Sean's face as he stood on the seawall, taking in truly for the first time since leaving the parked Cutlass, all that was around him. Digging the fact of just *being* there. And the *knowing* that he was young. And free. And so was that Boober. In harmony with, in celebration of knowing this, he started to dance on the seawall by the River Charles, crouching low over an imaginary keyboard as he sang out, "Down by the river/ by the banks of the River Charles…."

Boober, getting into it, began strumming his air guitar, the two adventurers singing out at the top of their lungs, "Oh! I love that dirty water …," An older couple stopped to gape at the two goofs rockin' and rollin' on the seawall and it didn't matter. The sun was way up high over the old New England city—where, on that day, at that moment, Sean and Boober were alive, and nothing could touch them.

~18~ Mass Pike

Though that turned out not to be all that true—that nothing could touch them. For Sean, at any rate. And sooner than he'd have wished.

After Red arrived they drank a couple of drafts at Earl's Place before dropping off the Olds at the drive-away car office by South Station. The scene there went pretty much as Sean had imagined it would. The two adventurers strolled into the office, dropped the keys off at the front desk, and then fled the joint, the startled clerk behind the counter yelling at their backs, "Wait a minute, what car?" Followed by, "Hey, I have to clear it first, you know!"

But it was too late. By that time, they were in Red's bright yellow Volkswagen Bug, personal and dope duffels already stashed in the trunk back at "Earl's." Red at the wheel pulled them away from the drive-away-car joint for the Mass Pike, next stop Amherst, where he lived in a little apartment by the U of Mass with his wife Freya. Or so he told them once they were safely away from the South Station area. All of this happened faster than Sean had thought it would, leaving him to wonder if that were a good, or a bad, thing—before deciding it didn't matter.

While Red and Boober sat up front Sean tried to get comfortable in the cramped confines of the Volkswagen's back seat, now that the luxurious space of the Cutlass was a thing of the past. Also a thing of the past was that Boober was no longer the Wheelman. Red occupied that position now. And differences there were. Red was tall and pale skinned like Boober, but they were the only features he shared with him. Thin and freckle faced, with a shock of red hair drifting down the back of his neck, Red appeared to be a couple of years older. Besides, Red was pretty much just plain goofy looking—not to mention the Howdy Doody smile when Red asked out of nowhere, "So tell me, Sean, are you ready to party?"

Not bothering to wait for an answer, he turned back to Boober and the non-stop conversation the two of them had been engaged in since leaving South Station. This conversation was all about people, places, things they had done as kids in Bramford, the town in Western Mass where the two of them had grown up. None of which had anything to do with Sean—until Red mentioned that Ron and Teddie had moved back to Bramford. Sean knew Ron and Teddie. From G'ville, in fact, through Boober, who had introduced them to him. After Boober disappeared from G'ville, Sean took to hanging out with Ron and Teddie, happy to have them as friends in that otherwise lonely town. They drifted apart after he met Luellen and she became his main focus.

But other than that, the steady rap had nothing to do with Sean at all. But then Red pulled a slim joint out of nowhere, fired it up, and passed it to Boober. As Boober was taking a toke, Red instructed him to make sure Sean got some—almost as if Red had realized suddenly Sean was in the car. That it wasn't just him and Boober rolling along, catching up on old times.

Paranoia perhaps. Sean wasn't sure. What he was sure of, though, was how everything had changed. Now here he was, starting a leg of the journey he had known was coming. Everything before had simply been the reality of moving headlong down the road, just a few basic facts to roll with, the rest of it depending solely on karma, good luck, and whatever the winds of fate had in store for him.

But as Sean passed the slim J back over the seat to Boober, Red's question about partying stuck in his head—an innocent question that began swirling around in a wave of sudden loneliness Sean hadn't seen coming and didn't know what to do with. So that just west of Brighton, where Red headed up the ramp onto the Mass Pike, what he really wanted to do at that moment was scream.

As if by screaming he could let it all out. The end of one part of the trip. The leaving behind of Dwight. The loss of the Olds. And beyond that, perhaps, the leaving behind of a life he had lived—even if sometimes it didn't seem he had. Those long-gone childhood days with his mom and dad in the big house at the end of the street that always seemed so safe. Until it wasn't. And mainly because of his dad. That cold, aloof, un-accepting shell of a man who made a point of looking away when Sean needed him most. The relief he felt when he heard that man was dead. The shame he felt at being relieved. The sadness in his mother he couldn't understand. The judge she worked for who started coming around to comfort her. That comforting that turned into something else. A something else that at fourteen he was just beginning to understand—revealed by the murmurings coming from behind her closed bedroom door late at night when Sean was supposed to be asleep and wasn't. His wanting to be angry at her then. And yet, how could he be? *How could he be?*

So how could any of it have been his fault later? When tired of being suffocated by what he was feeling, he began to run. Beginning with that first girlfriend. The afternoons spent at her house after school, listening to the Beach Boy's "Wouldn't it be Nice," while dry-humping in her mother's bed. Afternoons that ended with him walking home, alone, the sun going down, but not taking with it the un-relieved ache in his groin.

The un-relieved ache in his mind. Until finally the neighbor girl he had never paid any attention to waved him over one afternoon. Into her bedroom. Where, with a sly grin, she took him in her hand and jerked him off, Sean more excited by her nasty touch than he ever thought possible as semen spewed out of him. And nowhere near old enough at the time to make any sense of it.

All of it, now—death, loneliness, desire—rising up within him like a nauseating wave as he sat in the back of Red's Volkswagen heading west out of Boston. Knowing as they went that it was only the toll of the last four days catching up to him, streaming out of him in the beads of sweat slicked across his forehead and rolling down his cheeks. All of it coming out of him to the sound of Red's voice, asking over and over, "Do you want to party, Sean?"

And that other voice, the one always in his head, no matter where he was or what he was doing, answering, *Ah fuck, man, everything I've ever done in my life since turning fifteen has been done on the edge of someone's party. I never said no. It had always been: Hey, man, let's do this drug. Or, let's break into this house. Take that old bastard's loot he's hiding there. Steal his car while we're at it. Or, Man, can you help me unload this? Maybe just let me stash it with you? C'mon, man. I'll make it worth your while. You know I will. Dig?*

Those long-gone voices were jamming in his head—rocking along on a blast of coming down paranoia—remembering as he was, all those times he could have said, No. And did not. Losing himself in the process. Except that "self" thing was something he'd never been sure of. Not since a long acid trip at Crow's house one weekend when he was seventeen, and on the third day of eating Orange Wedges, he witnessed whatever it was that was Sean, float out of his navel to vanish into the night tripping sky.

But hold on. Didn't that "self" thing come back to him? Returning on that cold night in Gainesville when he was wrapped tight in Luellen's arms, both of them spent as he slowly slipped out of her, and looking into her eyes, for what it seemed like the very first time, he told her he loved her. *Remember?* How when she said, yes, it was like his soul had come back. In the process shattering his pretenses, his illusions of cool. All of this simply by merging with a woman he truly loved. *Didn't he remember that night?*

But he wasn't sure, as Red at the wheel steered them along the Mass Pike into the green foothills surrounding Amherst. Wasn't sure if he was remembering properly how that night had gone down.

Was only aware, really, of those moribund feelings he'd thought were hidden away since Luellen left for Egypt, flooding back into his thoughts—rising up in the blink of the hesitating, "Yes," he gave to

Red's question about being ready to party. Thoughts that, after his answer of "Yes," disappeared. Like a rapidly deflating balloon punctured accidentally, that blinding, intense moment of paranoia and self-doubt went whooshing out of him—leaving him there in the cramped backseat of the bright yellow Volkswagen, holding the half-smoked joint Boober had handed to him without Sean even knowing he had.

Suddenly aware of the joint in his hand, and that it had gone out—and also knowing what had to be done—he leaned forward in his seat and asked, "Bobby? You got a light, man?"

~19~ Route 32

Just then Blind Faith's "Can't Find My Way Home" came on the radio, the song confirming for Sean just about everything he had felt and known about himself for the last five years. Home, no home, it didn't matter anymore. For now, he was where he needed to be. Back in the groove. Heading on towards the next scene. Just like it was meant to be.

With the windows in the little car down, the fresh, evening breezes coming in gave cooling relief. By the time Red pulled off the Pike for Palmer, Sean felt like he was 100% back. The road sign at the end of the exit ramp read, Rt. 32. Ware 10m and Red turned off to follow the arrow pointing toward Ware. Now, instead of four lane highway, they were on a two-lane country road cutting through rolling hill country where, off in the distance, Sean could see the dark tops of small mountains. Oaks and other trees dotted the sides of the hills and mountains in the distance. Below the mountains meadows stretched away from the road. The occasional house sat just below the slopes, the lawns in front of these houses freshly mowed, the pastoral houses, and lawns, protected by field stone walls. These ancient walls were erected in the past by New England farmers. Weathered men who had strained their backs and hearts plowing those stones out of the dirt; the reward for their efforts being the security and pride being able to make a home on that unforgiving ground.

At the junction of Routes 9 and 12, another of those green road signs mentioned the town of Ware again. "Hey Tonto." Boober turned to Sean in the backseat. "Where are we?"

"Coming up on Ware, Kemosabe. I guess. Whatever the fuck that is."

Boober's eyes flickered for a moment and he grinned. *A good sign.* That grin. The anxious Wheelman of Bean Town a few hours back gone—replaced by a Boober in high spirits.

"Where, you say?" Boober repeated as he turned to face front again, adding over his shoulder, "That where you said we were? Ware?"

It was a weak joke for sure—but the laughter coming from the front of the Volks helped to fuel his new hope of how everything just might turn out okay. Apparently, more fuel was on the way, for just outside of Ware, Red pulled into the parking lot of a Cumberland Farms, its flashing neon lights advertising, *Cigs, Cold Beer, Snacks!*

"Now you're talking, Red m'boy." Boober had already opened his car door and was stepping out. "Definitely time for a cold one."

While Red and Boober were in the Cumby stocking up, Sean went around the front of the Volks to pop open the trunk and drag out the faithful travel cooler. He liked the idea of a cold beer, not having one since leaving the dingy tavern a couple hours back, his mouth all cottony from the last joint they'd smoked. He wasn't thrilled with having to share his already cramped quarters in the back seat with the bulky cooler. But he figured it was a small price to pay for the wet relief of a beer. With the trunk open and cooler out, he reached into the dope duffel for the baggie of pills, taking out three Beauties that he dropped in his jean's pocket. *What the fuck. Good as time as any to re-up the rush.*

As an afterthought, and because the night coming on was turning cooler, Sean rummaged around in his bag until he found the fringe jacket he'd bought at the head shop in Ojus. As soon as he put it on he felt better. For whatever reason, he wasn't sure. It was true he was no Billy to Boober's Wyatt. But the little trick he and Dewey had borrowed from Easy Rider, had worked well for him in his dealings with Hector and the heroin thing. Seeing as how he was at the end of another dope run, he figured any karma he could generate might be a help.

When Boober and Red came back to the car, Sean took the much needed supplies from Boober and stashed them in the cooler. He then handed Boober and Red, each, a black capsule, getting a kick out of the new wheelman's eyes when he realized what had been given him.

"Ah ha!" Red wasted no time in washing his Beauty down with a long pull of Budweiser. "Looks like Seano *does* want to party."

The Volks barreled west on Rt. 9 toward Belchertown, twilight falling over New England as they rolled along the country road. The fields and lawns were only faintly visible in the dusky light, and porch lights were popping on in the houses. Red kept up a non-stop narrative as he wheeled the Volks through the approaching dark—a narrative fueled by the onrush of the Black Beauty—consisting of stories about his college days at Cornell before dropping out. His childhood days with Boober, the pranks they pulled, separately and together, mishaps at school and such.

And that was fine with Sean. He was content to hang quiet in the back of the Volks, nursing a beer, digging the FM station out of Boston spinning out a steady stream of Hendrix and The Doors, the DJ even playing some local New England bands Sean had never heard of. It was all good music—especially the local groups, their mix of rock and country fitting in perfectly with the New England evening as they swung north past Belchertown on Rt. 202, making good time to Amherst.

Shortly before eight they pulled into the little college town, another community of quiet streets and shake roof homes sitting all quaint. Everywhere Sean looked were the buildings of higher learning, rising up to take precedence over whatever else the town may have to offer.

"Now listen, Seano, man," Red said over his shoulder while they were waiting on the light in the center of the town. "We'll drop off your bags, and the most important bag, if you get my drift, at my place." Red laughed, continuing on after the light turned and they were scooting down the street. "That done we can kick back a little bit. And then I'll show you and my man Boober the finer aspects of Amherst night life."

This sounded good to Sean, who looked forward to getting out of the car, and work on putting the miles covered that day behind him. In another minute or so they were pulling up in front of where Red lived, one out of a row of similar looking apartment buildings not far from the college. Red and his wife occupied one of those apartments, a one-bedroom affair. His wife was sitting inside on the couch in the tiny living room as the three of them trooped in. A glass of red wine was in her hand, the stereo playing "Tapestry," and a quizzical grin on her elfin like features as her husband and his pals came in the front door.

"Freya, baby, I'm home." He grabbed his wife up in a big bear hug and kissed her hard. "Look who I brought with me. Bob—you remember Bob? And his buddy Sean. What you think about that?"

Freeing herself from the hug she resumed her seat on the couch without saying a word—leading Sean to believe she didn't have any thoughts about them at all. If she did, he was willing to bet, they would be along the lines of wishing her husband and his pals were someplace other than her apartment. But then she smiled, a wide-open smile, proving him wrong as she waved her husband off. "Get away from me you goof," and then told Boober and Sean to go ahead and make themselves comfortable. Could she get them anything? A question Boober declined by flashing the open Budweiser he held in his hand. Sean nodded, No, followed by Freya saying how nice it was to meet them. That any friend of Red's was immediately her friend—and the ice was broken, ice that apparently only existed inside Sean's head it seemed. She lit up a joint she took from a little tray on the coffee table in front of the couch, and passed it around.

Joint smoked, Red, picked up the dope duffel, laying by the front door where he'd dropped it on the way in, and waved at the two adventurers to follow him into the bedroom.

"Let's see what we have here," he said, once they were inside the small room. Sitting on the bed with the duffel at his feet, , Red took out one of the bricks and opened it up on newspaper he had spread out on the floor. When he broke open the key the weed spilling out on the paper smothered the room with its lush odor. "Oh man," Red said, "but doesn't that smell good?" Looking up at Sean he added, "Do I need to weigh these bricks, Seano? Or can I take your word for it? Boober swears by you. Is that enough for me?"

"Well, man." With the fact of the pound skimmed off for Unger back in D.C. suddenly right there in front of him, Sean fought the urge to duck his head or shuffle his feet like he was prone to do when nervous. "It doesn't matter to me one way or the other. You wanted ten keys and it's ten keys we brought you."

Cool bluffs had worked for him in the past. Hopefully one would now. A pair of scales sat on top of the desk over by the wall. Sitting there just waiting for Red to put them to use. *Fucking Boober. It's on him if Red goes ahead and weighs those bricks. All on him. And up to him and his pal to sort it out. All on him.*

"Well then fuck it." Red put the opened brick back into the duffel and stood up from the bed, his features hidden somewhat in the soft glow of the little lamp by the head of the bed. "I don't need to weigh it. The bozos I've got lined up aren't going to. I'll bag it up into eleven bags tomorrow and get rid of it."

So now ten was going to become eleven. Cool. Guess it's true about that old "honor among thieves" thing. Or lack of it, which was certainly happening here. All the way around. This proved when he looked over at Boober standing by Red and Boober winked at him. *Yep. Happening all the way around.*

But, "Hey, man," is what he said to Red. "Whatever you want to do is cool by me."

"What I want to do my friends is hit it. There's a great band playing at the Quicksilver and we've got time to be there for their second set. And trust me, boys, you don't want to miss it."

Before heading out, though, Sean thought of something. The reef and beer they had been consuming, along with the Black Beauty, had settled him out some from the long day—he figured it had probably had the same effect on his companions. But the amphetamine was cutting through the mellow and to ease that oncoming edge he took a Quaalude out of the pill baggie, and splitting it in half, offering the other half to whoever might want it. Red jumped on this offer, but Boober had something else in mind.

"Fuck that half thing, Tonto. I'll take a whole one, thank you very much. Between the speed Dwight forced down our throats yesterday, and then having to deal with that madman Unger, by my calculations I've been up over twenty four hours. I can't see me surviving another night like that."

"Suit yourself." Sean handed him one of the 714's. "But I don't recall Dwight forcing those Beauties on us. Seems like you were pretty eager. Least that's how I recall it."

"That's always been one of your problems, buster. Not seeing the facts."

Boober was laughing as he washed the lude down with what was left of his beer. Red, satisfied that everyone was on board asked politely, "Now that's settled can we leave now?" All of it pretty much just a stoned goof at the end of a very long day—a day with the ending of it promising some good music at a local scene Red swore by—all in all, now that Sean thought of it, just what the doctor ordered.

~20~ The Quicksilver Lounge

Red hugged his wife goodbye, told her that he and the boys were heading down to the Quicksilver, they would be back later so don't wait up, and just like that they were back in the Volks, Red at the wheel heading them out into Amherst.

Where the evening had gone to, Sean had no idea, for it was pushing eleven o'clock by the time Red had parked in the alley behind a noisy bar and led the three of them through a back door opening into the alley. The bar, "The Quicksilver Lounge, Your Place for Music," as the poster tacked to the door proclaimed, appeared to be pretty much like any college town bar Sean had visited. A strobe light flickering wildly from the ceiling framed the band playing on the stage set up against one wall, and the people dancing to the beat laid out by the band. Red knew the place well, though, leading Sean and Boober through the noise, strobing light, and tobacco smoke to what he called, "my table," in the back of the rocking room. In another quick moment a barmaid appeared with a pitcher of beer and a "Hi Red, good to see you," as she set it down on the table.

Not long after the waitress disappeared, a girl appeared to take her place by Red at the table. Tall, lean, kind of winsome, with long red hair falling down past her shoulders, the girl possessed a face that looked vaguely familiar to Sean. Funny, but she was wearing a fringe jacket sort of like what he had on.

"Hey, Red," she said, this faintly heard over the music. "You have anything for me?"

The band launched into a cover of the Stone's "Street Fighting Man," their version minus Mick's antics of course, but still a solid cover. When the music started the winsome looking girl began marching in step to the beat, leading Sean to ponder his next mission—*Tuscaloosa, man! Oh yeah. Just as soon as he got back to Florida, squared away a few things. And hey, who knows? Maybe that chick right there, the one in the fringe jacket sort of like his, grooving to "Street Fighting Man?" Yeah brother, maybe she'd be on the back of that 650 roaring off to Alabama, and the possible mayhem and madness, to be found there when the Stones took the stage*—a great vision, one that vanished as soon as Red answered the girl's question.

"Tomorrow, Angel," Red told her.

"Cool." Still sort of marching to the beat of the song, the girl went to walk away. Until Red reached with one long arm and grabbed her.

"Hold on there, Sis. Sit down, meet my pals here, and I'll explain about why it has to be tomorrow." The girl sat down in the empty chair next to Sean, a fact he did not mind at all. "The cat you're sitting next to is Sean, come all the way up here from Florida with Bob on a mission of mercy that will be beneficial to both Bob and us pot-starved boys and girls here in town languishing away from lack of good reefer. You remember, Bob from Bramford don't you?" Before she could answer Red continued. "Oh yeah, this is my sister, Angel. Short for Angelina." Flashing that goofy Howdy Doody smile of his Red added, "Sadly enough she doesn't live up to her nickname. But we still love her."

She smiled along with what Sean imagined was a tired joke of her brother's before nodding her head at Boober and telling him that, yes, she remembered him. And then—as if they were attending some sort of society function, and not sitting in a bar where most of those there, including her brother, Boober, and Sean, and probably her, were stoned to the gills on one substance or another—she took Sean's hand and said, "Nice to meet you, Sean. And thanks for coming all the way up here to stuffy old New England to ease our suffering."

"And ease it will," Red jumped in, "as I can attest from personally tasting it." Red got serious. "I have to run the boys over to Bramford tomorrow morning, Sis, and when I get back, say, noon time or so, I'll give you a buzz and we can take care of things."

"Cool," Angel said again as she stood up from the table. "I'll see you tomorrow then," and then she disappeared back into the crowd as quickly as she had appeared. Sean, to his wonder, was kind of sad to see her go.

He turned to Red. "What's this about Bramford? First I heard, man. I've got places to go, Red, and Bramford wasn't on the list, if you can dig that."

"Not to worry, Sean." Red waved his long arms over the table, reminiscent, Sean thought suddenly, of Unger back in D.C. The thought of Unger sent a chill through him. "It's all cool, my man, and Bramford won't interfere with your schedule any." He took a long pull off the fresh beer the waitress had brought when she saw their pitcher was empty. "We'll party some tonight, and in the morning I'll run you and Bobby over to Bramford to Ron and Teddie's place, okay? Ron's the man with the Montreal connections." Again, one of those long arms pointed over at Boober, sitting quietly in his chair sucking on his beer like a desperate man.. "He'll set things up for Bob. While Ron's doing that you can make your arrangements to get back to Florida and from there wherever you're headed next. While your friend Red," and he tapped his chest, "will distribute the goods you two were kind enough to bring me. Soon, life, as they like to say, will return to normal and all will be as it should. Dig?"

Sean supposed he did—decided to just go with the flow for now—when Angel returned out of the crowd and tapped him on the shoulder. "Feel like dancing, Sean?"

Her brother, seeing Sean's hesitation, said, "Hey man, you might as well do it. She won't leave you alone until you do."

Leaning in close to him like she was he could smell the earthy perfume she was wearing as she told her brother, "Fuck off, Red." Laughing, she added, "But he's right, Sean. I won't back off." As if that settled the matter she took her fringe jacket off and after draping it over the empty chair next to his, took his hand and led him into the gyrating crowd.

The band launched into "Gimme Some Lovin'" by the Spencer Davis Group and as if a switch had been thrown, the people dancing kicked into overdrive. Sean and Angel kicked in right along with them, rocking to the driving beat. Angel moved in a frenzy of arms, legs, and hips that Sean, lousy dancer that he was, did his best to keep up with. And it didn't matter. He felt too good for it to matter. Stoned, in a good groove, moving to the music with a good-looking chick in a rocking little bar on a Friday night in a town oh so far from home—*Hell no it didn't matter.*

The band segued into "I'm a Man" also by Spencer Davis, and when that song ended, slid into "Magnolia" by J.J. Cale, the ballad kicked up just a notch by the band's electric guitars and drums, adding an element to the song that sounded just right to Sean. Angel, without missing a beat, was in his arms, holding him tight as they swayed slowly on the floor, her lithe body pressed closed to his. With her in his arms like that he realized that, she was indeed all girl—one with breasts beneath the thin shirt, and womanly hips that fit just right up against him.

And again, that feeling of being right where he was supposed to be, all the wacky issues of the trip that brought him to this college town in New England—when she leaned her face up from his shoulder and kissed him hard on his mouth, he did what came naturally, and kissed her back.

Later, with the band on break, the dancers taking the time to catch their breath before the next assault on their senses, Sean and Angel sat at the table, Angel holding his hand in her lap while they drank beer from the fresh pitcher. Across from them, Red sat talking with Boober—though in fact, Boober didn't seem to be paying much attention to him. Boober seemed focused instead on wolfing down as much beer as he could and occasionally acknowledging whatever Red was saying to him.

The last set of the night started up and once again Sean and Angel were back on the dance floor, this time to "Good Lovin'" by the Young Rascals. He was amazed he was able to keep up--figured that maybe whatever edge of the Beauties not dulled by the half of Quaalude he had ingested earlier, had given him a second wind. Enough so that when the band grooved into "How Can I be Sure," her softly swaying body up tight on his, he didn't want any of it to end.

It was just as the band was starting into "My Generation," that the end Sean didn't want to come, appeared. Coming, much as Sean hated to see, in the form of a loud voice echoing across the bar and the dance floor—this voice so loud that it overrode the band as it yelled out, "Tonto, where the fuck are you Tonto?"

He broke away from Angel—all of it happening in slow motion, the look on Angel's face, even the band seemed to pause at this interruption into their last set of the evening—and saw Boober staggering through the crowd yelling as he came, "Goddamn it Tonto, where the fuck are you?"

Pushing people out of the way Boober continued his stumbling charge across the floor until finally he saw who he was looking for. In a wild leap of arms, legs, and body, he jumped. Sean, on pure instinct, pulled Angel out of harm's way, just in time, as Boober, missing by a good two feet, crashed to the floor of the bar. The music stopped, the dancing stopped, the only movement being the strobes still flashing, catching the astonished looks on the faces of all those around them. Sean didn't move, didn't even want to watch, disgusted as he was by the incredible lack of cool Boober had managed to attain.

Not only that, he was disgusted by the reality that whatever was going to happen with Angel when the bar closed was not going to happen. All because everything had caught up to Boober, the former Wheelman, soon to be an expatriate in Canada waiting out Nixon's war. The dope, the beer, the driving, the events of the last four days, finally driving him to his knees on the floor of the Quicksilver Lounge, a comatose, mumbling, wreck as he finally gave up, stretched out prone and passed out.

Sean and Red picked him up from the floor, and then holding him between them, dragged him towards the exit, Sean thinking as they went, it's over all right. All over.

~21~ Route 20

Not quite all over yet, though—at least for the road part. Another short jog had to be made the next day, from Amherst to Bramford, Red driving Sean, and a quietly hungover Boober, there to stay with Ron and Teddie. How long he, or Boober, for that matter, would be staying in Bramford, Sean wasn't sure. Neither was Boober.

"You know, Tonto," Boober said over his shoulder as they were leaving Amherst, "Ron and Teddie are super cool. You'll be fine to stay there for a bit. You know, man, maybe keep me some company until I split for Montreal?"

Unsettled a bit by the desperation he heard in Boober's voice, Sean was non-committal.

"We'll see, bud." Boober nodded his head in acceptance to this, while Sean, almost finished with the joint he was rolling in the backseat, licked the papers, sealed them tight, and then using Boober's Zippo, fired it up, a little surprised when Boober passed the joint to Red without taking a hit. "You know, Bobby, a little medicinal toke might soothe your brain. If you can dig that."

"The only thing that will soothe my brain is a cold beer, Seano."

Judging by the face Boober turned to Sean as he spoke, Sean felt like he might need to retract his helpful suggestion—led him to wonder instead if a long stay in a quiet little hospital in the woods somewhere might better serve his old pal right then.

"But I'm afraid if I try to drink one I'll puke."

"We'll have no more of that, mister." Red laughed as he passed the joint back to Sean. "Especially not in my car, you maniac. It was bad enough what I had to clean up on the steps this morning."

True enough that was, Sean had to agree. He and Red had managed to drag Boober out of the club and shove him into the back of the little Volks. Angel followed behind them, asking if there was something she could do to help. Sean could think of a way she could definitely help *him*—but said nothing. Other than to tell her as he was getting into the front seat that maybe he would see her tomorrow. Maybe, she said, as Red was pulling away from the curb—a 'maybe' Sean was willing to bet, would not happen.

By the time they reached Red and Freya's apartment, Boober had sort of come to—even if he was still barely able to walk when he tried to stand. At least the retching had stopped, and that was a plus. The sound of it inside the cab of the small car had almost made Sean *want* to puke. But if he couldn't walk, Boober could talk. Wouldn't shut up in fact, carrying on a mumbling conversation with himself, consisting mainly of the phrases, "Fuc' t'is, Asshol's, and Go t' hell." It was irritating to Sean, and probably because he was bummed by how Boober had ruined a perfectly promising evening for him. But Red was laughing, repeating here and there, "C'mon, Boober man, let's get you inside," as they reached the door of his apartment.

Boober wasn't having it, though, opting instead to flail his arms about wildly in the air and take drunken swings at Red and Sean, until he finally collapsed in front of the apartment, silent except for the ragged snoring seeping from between his closed lips.

"Well, pardner." Sean gave up. "Looks like Bobby's done for the night."

"So what're we going to do with him?" Red looked perplexed—whether he was concerned about Boober, or just worried about his wife or neighbors who might have witnessed Boober's drunken antics, Sean had no idea.

"Leave him. When he comes to he'll find his way inside."

Sean slept on the sofa in the living room of the small apartment, a restless sleep at that, despite the other half of 714 he retrieved from the pill baggie and swallowed down. For the longest time he couldn't escape from thoughts of all that had happened over the last five days.

To make this restless attempt at sleep even worse, he had to jam a cushion over his head for at least an hour, maybe longer, to drown out Freya's loud moans coming from the other room where Red, apparently fueled by the Black Beauty, was having his way with her. Freya's moans and Red's loud grunts were a painful reminder of what might have gone down with Sean and Angel had Boober not come charging across the club in a fit of a drunken mission to ... well, who knows what kind of drunken trip he was up to at that moment.

The sun coming through the open blinds of the window above the sofa woke him earlier than he would have liked. Coming further awake he did his best to ignore the godawful ache in his head, the slight trembling in his hands as he pulled his boots on, and then grabbing up his fringe jacket from the floor where he must have tossed it, stood up. *Oh yeah. There was certainly a wild joy in the consumption of drugs and liquor. But sometimes, damn. At what cost?* Realizing the living room was empty he went to the front door and cracked it open. Surprised, but only a little, he saw Boober laying where they had left him last night. Curious if he was even alive he went out and nudged his shoulder with the toe of his boot. Getting no response he nudged him again, this time harder.

"Jesus, man." Boober groaned, and then rolling over, drew his legs up into a semi-fetal position while covering his head with both hands. "You don't have to kick me. Can't you see I'm down already? What the fuck?" Groaning again he sat up. His eyes were so red Sean wondered if he could even see out of them. "God, Sean, is that you kicking me, man?"

"Yeah. It's me all right."

"Well, Christ, man if you're gonna continue kicking me can you at least tell me where my smokes are? I need one, badly. As any idiot could see."

Angry as he was for the night before, there was no way he couldn't help but feel for Boober in his sorrowful condition. "Lucky for you, I do know where your smokes are." Reaching down he pulled a crumpled pack out of the top pocket of Boober's Hawaiian shirt, the shirt no less crumpled than the pack of Camels. Helping Boober to his feet he handed him a cigarette. "C'mon, Kemosabe, get your ass inside before Red's neighbors start debating just what kind of fools he's running with these days."

'Won't be much of a debate." Scrabbling his Zippo out of his jean's pocket Boober lit up the cigarette, exhaling a long stream of smoke from nose and mouth in the process. "Sad to say, Tonto."

"You got that right." Sean turned back toward the apartment. "Very sad to say."

Boober slept most of the way to Bramford. He woke up once in Belchertown demanding they stop for a beer that once procured at the local Cumberland Farms, he gulped down and then promptly fell back asleep. He woke up again when Red brought the Volks to a crunching stop in the dirt and gravel driveway of a two-story frame house on Springfield Street in Bramford. It had to be pushing four thirty or so, Sean guessed, on another warm, sunny afternoon in New England. Behind the house a long, green meadow stretched out towards some red brick buildings in the distance. The grass had grown high in the field, a soft wind caressing the tops, making it sway. He felt for a moment, after crawling out of the cramped backseat of the Bug, as if he were swaying, too—like that windblown field, adrift on currents he didn't understand. A gang of kids were kicking a soccer ball around by the brick buildings, their shouts and laughter faintly reaching his straining ears. A rush of sudden loneliness washed over him. *For what?* He knew. And again, did not.

"This is it, guys." Red was helping Sean with the two duffels of his and Boober's stashed in the trunk. Over by a solitary oak tree rising up next to a stand-alone garage at the end of the driveway, Boober was taking a long piss. "It was a great scam we pulled off," Red continued. "Maybe we can do it again sometime."

"You bet."

Sean wasn't as sure as he hoped he sounded. The wind and the children playing in the field had him spooked. That and the fact of Boober casually urinating in what was basically the side yard of someone's house.

"Yeah, man, you bet," he repeated. "I've got solid contacts down south. I get back from Tuscaloosa, you know? From wherever I head to after that, then maybe I'll look you up. See what we can put together."

"Now that's what I like to hear." The Howdy Doody grin stretched Red's freckled face as he pumped Sean's hand up and down. The slight wind blowing across the field pushed Red's straw-like hair away from his forehead, his goofy grin spreading even wider when he realized what Boober was doing by the garage. "C'mon Boober man. Quit watering Mrs. Wahl's bushes and come get your shit."

In another moment Red was gone, backing the Volks out of the driveway and speeding away up Springfield Street on his way back to Amherst.

'Well, Kemosabe, now what?"

"Damned if I know, Tonto." Shaking his head he picked up the duffel at his feet. "Guess we go see if Ron and Teddie are home. Maybe we'll get lucky, and he'll have some beer in the fridge."

Absent of any other viable plan, Sean had no choice but to agree as he followed Boober up to the house, preparing himself once again to rely on that proverbial kindness of strangers thing.

Part 2: Up North/down South

1972-1974

~22~ Alligator Alley

On a hot weekday morning in mid-May of 1974 they drove west out of Lauderdale on SR84, Harv at the wheel of his '62 Anglia coupe, and Sean riding shotgun—two young men in their mid-twenties just looking to do something, anything, to make them feel alive; to make them feel it was worth it to be so.

At least that was how Sean felt. He couldn't speak for Harv. He was pretty sure if he were to ask, Harv would give him a funny look, probably followed by something along the lines of, "What? You fucking nuts or something?"

They had been friends since junior high. Blond , blue-eyed boys, letting their hair grow long like the Beatles, sporting cords, Gantz shirts, and Bass Wegian loafers, the horn-rimmed glasses they wore, being nearsighted, the only studious aspect about them. Sean actually was studious, luckily born with the ability to make A's and B's without much effort. Harv found that goal to be basically impossible, happy if he got a C on a report card, a failing not because of any mental lack on his part, but simply because, as he put it, "I don't give a fucking rat's ass about school." To prove his point, as soon as he turned sixteen Harv dropped out and went to work for his older brother Rob setting tile. Once Harv dropped out the two of them drifted apart, reconnecting again unexpectedly after almost five years when they bumped into one another one late afternoon at the Parrot Lounge on the Strip. They had been hanging together ever since—at least when Harv wasn't working or after the day's work was done and he was ready to have a beer, maybe two or three with his old pal.

As they came up on the yellow flashing caution light at the intersection of 84 and US27, Harv slowed down, turning left after a semi rumbled by in the northbound lane and the highway was clear.

"Thought we were going out on the alley?"

"We are." A tight grin stretched Harv's thin lips. "Gotta hit Andytown first, buster. Get some shiners and beer."

"Yeah, that's a definite on the beer." It had warned up fast outside as they drove, the hot wind coming through the open car windows doing little to cool the temps down. "Always need beer."

"Damn straight." Harv tilted the beaver skin Stetson he wore everywhere back on his head. "By the way, you didn't happen to shit your pants, did you?"

"Not today."

Harv was skeptical—crinkling his nose he asked, "You sure?"

"I did yesterday."

They both laughed as Harv wheeled them south down the highway towards Andytown, the old joke never failing to amuse them.

Andytown wasn't much of a town. A truck stop actually that the owner—Andy, of course—had built up over the years, adding a bait shop/convenience store, a bar, and hot showers for the truckers. Even at nine o'clock in the morning the bar looked full, and trucks were lined up to get diesel. Harv grabbed the last empty spot in front of the bait shop and got out.

Harv bent down and leaned his head into the window before he went inside the store. "Need anything other than the beer and shiners? Maybe you've got to run in and take a dump?"

"No man." Sean laughed. "I told you I shit yesterday. Just get the stuff and let's hit it." He flipped a tenner at Harv. "Here's my share. I'll wait here."

"I guess you will."

Harv had that right. Still on crutches Sean was comfortable where he was on the front seat of the Anglia. Unless he absolutely had to, he had no intention of getting out of the car until they pulled over to where they planned to fish. The cast had been removed from his left leg a month ago, but he still couldn't walk on it. Not shriveled up and muscleless like it was he couldn't.

The car that plowed into him and his motorcycle last October had done a job on him all right. The only good thing about it? Drunk as he was the accident wasn't his fault. With the 650 totaled and Sean lucky as well he hadn't lost his left leg, the months since the accident had been spent recuperating at his mother's condo by the Port Everglades inlet.

Today with Harv, was only the second time, other than going to the doctor, he had been out of the house. Crutches, shriveled leg or not, he was going to hang with his pal, drink beer, catch fish, and enjoy it. The doctor, when he removed the cast, had told him to do his exercises every day, and within a couple of months he would be walking on a cane. From there the rest would be up to him.

Damn straight, Sean had thought, as he hobbled out of the doctor's office to his mother's car where she waited to take him back to the condo, drop him off, and then continue on to work. *And when I get the insurance settlement I'm going to buy some wheels and put this town as far back in the rear view mirror as I can.*

But all that was yet to come as he waited for Harv to return. A semi pulled in, going past the gas pumps and over to the side of the building. As Sean watched, the truck came to a stop, the passenger door opened, and a woman, brunette, looking a little worse for wear in a pink mini skirt and some kind of tight top, hopped down from the truck, turned to blow the driver a kiss and made her way to the bar where she disappeared into what Sean knew was air-conditioned darkness.

Yeah, he thought as he watched the truck continue on to the truck parking lot behind the building. *Maybe get me a woman too, while I'm at it.*

"I saw you, buddy. Yes I did."

Harv was back, opening the driver's door of the car to put a Styrofoam cooler and a bait bucket, water slopping over its metal rim on the back seat.

"Saw me doing what?"

"Eyeballing that little hottie strolling into the bar. You want me to leave you here? Pick you up on my way in?"

"Jesus, man, that's fucking sick. I wouldn't fuck her with your dick. Even if you were paying I wouldn't."

"Just trying to make your day as bright as I can my boy. That's all."

"One of those cold beers would help."

"Sure thing." Harv grabbed two beers out of the cooler, handing one to Sean as he slid into the driver's seat and cranked the engine over. "You're gonna miss me if I have to go, ain't you? All these nice things I do for you."

Having received his official Welcome letter from the United States Army, Harv had to report for his physical at 8am sharp the following Friday. And he was right. Sean would miss him if he had to go. Not that he was about to say so and didn't.

"Fuck, no. It'll be peaceful. I'm looking forward to it, in fact."

"Aw that's bullshit, and you know it."

"Besides, no way they're going to take a drug crazed moron like you into the army."

"Man, what're you yapping about? I'm in the flower of my manhood. And check out my belly? Ain't no one, not in any branch of the military, got such a fine beer belly as your ol' buddy Harv."

Lifting his white T shirt up Harv puffed his already impressive gut out even more, the pale white skin of his stomach shining in the morning light.

"Huh? What you got to say for yourself, now," he asked as he pulled his t-shirt back down.

"The same, pretty much. But you might have a point with that gut of yours. Probably scare the Viet Cong to death they take a look at that. More likely they'll die from laughing so hard."

"Now see? There you go. That's a bright idea you have there. I bet I mention it to the head honchos they'll put me in a special unit to carry it out. I'll be like the Dirty Harry of the beer belly division."

"Yeah, yeah, okay then. Quit admiring your gut and let's go."

~23~ Bramford

Reminiscent of that night at the Cave back in May, though not quite as unnerving, for him at least, Sean's plans for the future began to unravel the next day while he was drinking beers with Boober and Ron on the front stoop at Ron and Teddie's place. Other than some wispy clouds hanging over the ridgeline of Bramford Mountain — just visible beyond the roofs of the brick buildings across the field where the kids had been banging a soccer ball around the afternoon before — the sky was clear and blue. The day was pleasantly warm and Springfield Street, running in front of the apartment building, was pretty much quiet except for the occasional car or delivery truck. Sean, and he figured Boober, too, judging by the healthier look on his face, were rested and feeling better after a good night's sleep in Ron and Teddie's spare bedroom where they crashed.

All in all, the day to that point was peaceful, something sorely needed Sean believed, after the last few days on the road. Just then a Volkswagen Van, the Stones song, "Happy," blasting pulled in the driveway.

"Wonder what she's doing here," Ron said as he stood up to go greet the new visitor.

Sean was wondering, as well, his hopes rising beyond his wonder, when he realized the person at the wheel of the van was Angel. *Red's sister come all the way over from Amherst because she just had to see him again?*

But, as Angel explained when she climbed out of the cab, gave Ron a hug, and then joined the boys on the stoop, something more pressing than Sean had brought her to Bramford.

"Hi guys." She sat down next to Sean on the stoop and said, "Got another of those cold ones, Ron? I could use one. Considering the heavy shit I went through last night."

"Sure thing, kid." Ron disappeared inside the apartment, returning shortly with a Budweiser which she drank long and hard from before she explained what the "heavy shit" she had been through was.

Just before midnight the night before, Amherst's Finest had come barging through the door of Red's apartment to catch him red-handed with the goods. They arrested him, Freya, who was tripping at the time, and a black cat by the name of Irving who was there to buy one of the keys Red was weighing up at the time. The picture of Red sitting at the scales making up what he considered to be a kilo of reefer, made Sean wince for a minute—made him wonder if before all of that had gone down Red had figured out the product Boober and Sean had delivered was off by a pound or so. Though of course, with the cops on top of him like that, whether or not Boober and Sean had burned him a tad was probably the last thing on Red's mind.

"Funny thing." Angel paused here to finish off the beer, giving Ron a quizzical look when she was finished, and that Ron interpreted correctly by retrieving another cold one from the kitchen. "The pigs weren't really there for Red. They were after Irving, who, and whether or not my brother even knew this I don't have a clue, but this Irving dude is apparently a honcho in the local Black Panthers." She gave them a minute to let this possibly disturbing info sink in—a bit of info Sean didn't find disturbing, his reaction in fact being, *Well right on, Red, Power to the people I guess, helping that cat Irving like that.*

"But," Angel continued, acting on a tip phoned in to the station earlier, "when the cops, who were following Irving anyway, saw him go into Red's holding a duffel bag, they thought they might get him in the act of buying illegal guns or some shit like that. "So my brother was collateral damage. Meanwhile, poor Freya, flying high on some Sunshine I gave her the other day, which," and here was that smaller version of Red's Howdy Doody smile, "I know for a fact is some very good shit. Anyway, she was out of her gourd and God knows what went through her brains with all that chaos in her apartment going down and then ending up in the jail like the others. Jesus..." Trailing off in her own thoughts Angel stopped.

And yes, Sean agreed, that pretty much said it all, picturing as he could the look on Red's face when the cops came busting in. Not to mention the look on this Irving cat's face. Or Freya's for that matter, off in another dimension of her own. So yeah, a quiet "Jesus" seemed appropriate indeed.

What he said though, was, "Damn, that sucks."

"Yeah, no shit. You guys are lucky you weren't there, that's for sure. Of course," and she cracked a smile at Boober, "a drug bust might have helped you. You know? With your draft issue?"

"Fuck that." Boober opened up one of the fresh Buds Ron brought out for all of them. "I'd rather take my chances with the army."

Neither jail nor the army would work well for Boober was Sean's guess. Didn't think either of those choices would work well for him either, come to think of it. *But wait—was a message being sent?* People he knew recently being brought low by the forces of the law? Will and Tommy in Gainesville. Hector's cousin in Key Largo. Now Red in Amherst. Common denominator being—*Me.*

A message he didn't want to consider too long just then—saved from doing so when, responding to Angel's statement of how she needed to get out of town for a while and could she crash there for a few days, Ron told her, "No problem. Make yourself at home. What can I do to help out?"

Angel said, "Cool, and I'll just crash in my van. Got plenty of room. Been wanting to hit the road anyways before my internship starts in the fall, so thanks Ron," and then poking Sean on the shoulder, adding, "bet you didn't think you'd be seeing me again so soon, did ya?"

"No, I didn't." He stopped before he almost blurted out, But I'm glad you're here—glad he stopped before saying something so godawful uncool, especially considering the circumstances that had brought her there. "But I'm sorry, though, to hear about Red and Freya. Anything I can do to help, just ask."

"Nothing you can do, Seano. He's got a good lawyer and knowing Red he's already out and back home. Hopefully Freya's with him, that poor chick. Getting arrested like that kind of gives the word 'bummer' a new meaning." With those green eyes boring right into his, she added, "But thanks, man. I appreciate it."

Feeling a need he got up to head inside, Boober right behind him, and stopping him before he closed the bathroom door. "Man, are you bad luck or something? Your past history makes me wonder."

"You'd better be joking, Kemosabe." Sean was in no mood to admit he had just been wondering the same thing. That he *was* bad luck, and all because of his leaving Poco high and dry in G'ville the night of the bust at the Cave. She had warned him about breaking her spell. Had said that breaking one of her spells was not a good thing.

But it hadn't been his fault. He never meant to lose her in the flowing mass of people retreating from the cops at the protest march and afterwards at the Cave where more cops were swarming all over the place. He had no choice but to flee if he wanted to save his own, admittedly, sometimes sorry ass—and to do it quickly. And in the process leaving Poco without a ride to Key West like they had planned. He had no choice at all. And surely that had to count for something.

"Yeah, Tonto, just a joke," Boober reassured him, breaking, fortunately, Sean's train of thought regarding Poco. "Now hurry up, man. I've got to piss like a racehorse. I'd use Mrs. Wahl's bushes again but don't want to frighten Angel. You know? She sees what I'm packing."

"Anyone ever tell you you're a fucking idiot?"

"Maybe. Once or twice."

"More than that I imagine."

He shut the door behind him and that was that for that day.

38 Roads

~24~ Alligator Alley

Between the beer, the hum of the tires on the highway, and the hot wind coming through the open windows, Sean seemed to drift in and out of consciousness as they headed west on the Alley. Harv had the radio tuned to WQAM out of Miami and the drone of Top 40 picks added to his drifting. He kept going back to the idea of Harv in the army—something he just couldn't picture. Harv, hair cut short and in fatigues marching through the jungles and rice paddies of Vietnam, rifle in hand searching out those who wanted to kill him. Hard to picture as well Harv wanting to kill them. The Harv he knew would rather smoke a joint with them, drink their native brew, and make goo-goo eyes at their women. Once, over beer and a fat joint, when Harv was wondering if he would be receiving that official government notice any time soon, Sean had brought up Boober. How he had gone to Canada and last Sean heard, doing okay in Montreal. He even had a girlfriend and a job in an architect's office doing drafting work. Maybe that would be something for Harv to consider? Harv's response had been a flat, Hell no, I ain't running.

So there it was, plain and simple. And no, it didn't make sense. Not to Sean. But what did anymore? Damned if he knew—knew only that Harv was right about one thing. He would miss him if he had to go.

After how long a time drifting, as he had been while they drove, they came up to a bridge spanning a canal going north and south. On the other side of the bridge, a gravel road ran along the edge of the canal. Just past the bridge a green road sign informed them they were entering Collier County. Without the sign, Sean had the sudden thought: how would one know? Collier, Broward? This far west it all looked the same,once the urban concrete had been left behind. Just vast swaths of sawgrass on both sides of the highway, the tops of it swaying in the hot wind. The grass itself looked almost golden in the sunlight, the swaying expanse broken here and there by hummocks of trees. But the hummocks seemed to promise shelter from the watery sawgrass flowing by them.

"Pretty soon we'll be there buster. Mile marker 27, home of the biggest bass in the whole state of Florida." Laughing, Harv chucked his empty beer can out the window. "Maybe those bass ain't all that big. What d'ya think numb nuts?"

"I think I have to piss. That's what I think. I'll worry about the size of the bass afterwards."

"You're such a profound man, Seano. One of the many things I like about you. Now you just hold onto your little weenie and we'll be there directly."

"I hope directly will be soon enough."

Harv pushed the accelerator down as he shook his head at Sean. "There will be no wetting of one's britches in my ride. No sir. Not on my watch."

Just past the bridge they came up on a slower moving semi. As Harv pulled around to pass Sean pumped his arm up and down for the driver to blow his air horn. The driver, a red-faced older man with a beaten up ball cap jammed down on his head, gave Sean the finger instead.

"Jesus! Did you see that?"

"I did." Harv was laughing so hard he almost dumped the beer can held between his legs. "I certainly did see that. Guess that old boy don't like longhairs like you and me."

"Well fuck him then."

Yes sir. Fuck 'em if they can't take a joke."

~25~ Mountain Road

By the end of the following week Sean had come to believe the last two weeks were the best two weeks he'd spent in a long time. Part of it had to do with the mission being completed, despite Red's being busted—on his and Boober's end successfully completed at that. What happened afterward in Amherst sucked, and that was for certain. Still, that was on Red's end. Besides, sad as it all was, her brother's arrest had sent Angel to Bramford, her presence there turning into a nice break from being with Boober and all that had led them to New England in the first place.

As for Boober, when he was heading north to sanctuary in Montreal was anyone's guess. Sean certainly didn't know, and Boober wasn't saying. For the most part the former Wheelman spent his time with Ron drinking beer and smoking cigarettes on the front stoop carrying on conversations about the past. For the most part those conversations were boring. Making it even worse was the fact that the drunker Ron got the more he tended to ramble on about his college days with Red at Cornell—when they were both active in the anti-war movement. So active that they took Tom Hayden and Abbie Hoffman's advice and went to Chicago for the infamous Democratic convention of 1968, the shining hour of Ron's existence apparently being clubbed to his knees by one of those Chicago pigs.

Sean was all for activism, he supposed. After all, he had joined in with his vet pals to march in G'ville just a few months backs. And what did that accomplish? Pinko being dead was one answer. Poco's perhaps spell another. And yet Nixon's war still raged on with no end in sight. Ron was three years older than Sean and Boober, and that may have figured into his bitterness over the whole thing. Being older like that, Ron had been involved in the heyday of what he called The Movement when success seemed to be in their grasp. And yet was not. It was Sean's belief that the chaos at Chicago should have been a clue of how things were going to go. That and the failure of the Yippies to levitate the Pentagon—a failure Sean had chided himself for thinking it might actually happen.

I mean, Come on, he wanted to say when yet again, Ron started in about how he and Hayden had drafted the Port Huron statement. How the two of them had worked together every day after to affect the desperately needed change. Irritating to Sean was how any schoolboy could do the math, and quickly. And by doing so see that Ron, when that famous statement was drafted, was only fourteen years old. Not only that, he was nowhere near Ann Arbor but finishing up junior high in Bramford.

So Angel showing up after the debacle in Amherst turned into a pleasant change of scenery all the way around—a pleasant change she initiated on the third day of her arrival, when returning from an overnighter with some pals in Springfield, her van rolled back into the driveway at Ron and Teddie's around noon, and once again, while Boober, Sean, and Ron were having beers on the stoop.

Angel, barely out of the van, called out, "Hey Seano, want to go for a ride?

And what was he going to say, bored as he was doing the same old thing, but, "Sure." Eager as he was at the invitation he had to—once again—stop from almost blurting out, "God fucking yes!"

"So, Sean." They were waiting on the one red light in town at the intersection of Bramford Road and Mountain Road. "Any place you have to be? Maybe some exciting plans with Boober and Ron?"

The look in her bright green eyes told Sean she pretty much knew the answers already. But feeling like he should at least confirm her suspicions he answered her in the negative.

"Good." The rush going through him at the smile she flashed him as the light turned was like a jolt of energy ripping at his nerve endings. "There's a place I'd like to turn you on to."

"Count me down m'lady," Sean said, feeling that the day was about to go from being pretty damn boring to something else altogether. "Not that I'm a knight by any stretch. But again, count me down as being all for it."

"Good," she repeated, then added, "But bag the m'lady stuff. It doesn't sound right coming from you."

She smiled that little version of her brother's Howdy Doody smile—the one that didn't look bad on her. It was pretty much quiet then as they continued up Mountain Road. Sean wondered as they went why his 'm'lady' goof didn't sound right coming from him.

"Care for one of these?" Angel had just turned to follow the arrow on the sign saying Mountain Road—in her hand were two reddish gelatin capsules. "Mescaline."

"Sure," Sean said, washing one down with the beer he'd brought along with him from Ron and Teddie's.

"It's a slow go at first," she told him, using his beer to chase hers down. "Then it get's faster."

"I can do slow. And when it happens, yeah, faster, too."

"I thought you might."

The place Angel wanted to turn him onto was a large rock bluff jutting out from the side of Bramford Mountain just below its peak. Parking the van in a little pull over off the side of the road, saying, "C'mon, Seano," she led him along a trail cut through the underbrush that emerged out on the bluff. The day had started off cool but now, pushing one o'clock and the sun way up blasting through an almost cloudless sky, it was downright warm out on the big rock. Sean shed his fringe jacket and standing out on the rock in just his t-shirt and jeans, he held his arms out, face up, just wanting to allow the light of that sun to envelope him in its welcoming warmth.

"You like?"

Angel, standing beside him, held her arms out as well, the light on her freckled face, green eyes, the red hair falling down around that elfin face, seeming to blend in with her smiling features.

"Like it very much." He let her take his hand as she sat down on the rock. "Very much."

"Yeah, me too." Taking a joint from her jacket, Angel fired it up. "Feel like I'm kind of one with all of it when I'm up here. If you can dig that?"

"I can." He took a long drag off the joint and passed it back, saying, Very much so."

He was happy just sitting there on that rock overlook, amazed at the warmth of the sun overhead, the world stretching out below—and oh yes, there was something else and he said so.

"I believe," and he turned to Angel sitting next to him. "The mesc is kicking in."

"Yeah?" And then she was laughing, almost doubled over with that laughter, holding her sides, her face in her lap not enough to muffle the laughter flowing out of her and surrounding him. Finally, she lifted her face up to look at him. "I believe you're right."

What was there in that simple statement that was even remotely funny? Nothing—except the fact that it was. Enough so that the next thing he knew, like her he was doubled over with laughter. Laughter that felt good. That felt like a release. That, despite the fact it was enhanced by both the mescaline and the reefer, felt real.

When it happened Sean had no idea, lost as he was for a while in his own thoughts drifting away from him over the valley below—but when he looked over to check on Angel, he discovered that she had stripped her fringe jacket off, her tie dyed tee shirt, and jeans, and was laying on the jacket she had spread out on the rock, eyes closed, her arms and hands reaching up to the sky as if to gather in everything shining down. And though he didn't move, or say anything to disturb her, she opened her eyes right then, and with a slight wave of her hand indicated he should do what he already knew he was going to. Not very long after he lay naked next to her on the rock.

It wasn't sexual at first. Not with all the colors, trails, and sounds flowing all around him like they were. Looking at his naked body stretched out on the rock in the full light of the sun he saw how his Florida tan had faded, leaving him almost white. This was a minor thing for sure—but for a while of great interest to him, this visible change in a body he took pretty much for granted. He started to say something to Angel about his new discovery, but seeing how very white she was, realized how silly it all was. In fact, he forgot all about what he had discovered—caught up as he became in the way her red hair, ablaze with the mescaline, highlighted the paleness of her face as it flowed down around her shoulders—highlighted those green eyes, all of her.

And then she smiled. Pulling him down on top of her, she removed his glasses, saying as she did, "You don't need these to see me." And how true that was. He felt as if he could see all the way through her— through her skin, bones, right down to the bare rock she lay on. It was a frightening seeing at first, until she laughed and pulled him back down on top of her. And just like that he was inside her. Not only inside her, but wrapped up with her in the body as they moved together. It wasn't just sex, wasn't even love in a way. But words were not enough—*could never be enough right then*—to describe what Angel and he were doing. And that was okay. Better than okay. Perfect, he thought for a minute. And then that too was lost in this different world he had found himself in.

Later, as evening was coming on, the mescaline wearing off, the two of them giggling for some reason as they dressed, she led him back up the trail to the van and drove them back down the mountain. All of it felt like a little loss as they went. This feeling was replaced when she pulled up in front of a little grinder joint off of Bramford Road, and he realized how hungry he was—glad she had known this as well, and was hungry, too. Food, after all that had happened up on the mountain, suddenly became the only thing on his mind—the importance of getting something to eat and drink that would not get him high.

Though there was something else on his mind. The effects of the drug were pretty much gone, though the walls, overhead lighting, the window, the booth they sat in, seemed to move just a little as they sat there. But that was okay by him. The little after effects were a good reminder of what had gone down just a few hours back—until he realized again there was something on his mind needing to be said.

"I better start getting serious about heading south," he told her over the straw in his mouth after taking a long pull of the cold root beer he'd ordered. "Very serious."

"Yeah?" He wasn't sure if he would ever get enough of those green eyes flashing at him as she sipped her lemonade. "What's happening down south?"

"Just some stuff I need to square away before I head to Tuscaloosa."

"Tuscaloosa? Why would you go to some redneck dump like Tuscaloosa?"

"The Stones." He had to laugh at the look on her face, the way she'd said what she had said. "They're playing a big gig there. Going to be huge and I need to be there."

"You better get going then." Now it was Angel who was laughing. "That concert's in three days."

"What're you talking about? It's set for July 6th."

"Oh Sean, Sean, whoever told you that was dead wrong. The concert's on the 28th of this month. Three days from now."

"Whoa."

The girl brought their order just then and for a while it was quiet at the booth while they ate, the Italian sub, or grinder as they're called up north, just what the doctor ordered. But as focused on the grinder as he was, he couldn't ignore the hammer Angel had just dropped on him—her phrase about whoever had told him the concert was on the 6th of July had been dead wrong, being closer to the truth than she knew. But as he was finishing up the grinder, taking his last sip of the root beer, a solution came to him.

"In that case maybe I'll hang out here for a while."

"Yeah? That'd be cool. Be fun."

His thought exactly. Staying on in Bramford, hanging out with Angel, digging whatever came his, *No, their, way*—could indeed be cool.

~26~ Alligator Alley

Shortly after the middle finger thing Harv slowed down, looked at the green mile marker on the side of the road, said, "I believe this be the place," and pulled off on the shoulder of the highway.

"You *believe* this is the place?" Sean finished the beer he was drinking and tossed it out of the window. "I thought you knew where we were going."

"Jesus, buddy, I haven't been here since I was a kid. Used to come out here with Pops and Rob and camp on the weekends. That's been a while. So to answer your question, Yes, I believe this is it. Can I swear to it absolutely? No, but hey, it looks as good as any we've passed so far. Now get your crippled ass out of my car and lend me a hand."

Just then the semi they had passed came by, the driver, when he saw who they were, leaning over to yell something out of the window. Sean couldn't make out what the driver yelled, but Harv was laughing as he gave him the finger

"What'd that fucker say," Sean asked.

"I believe he called us, and I quote, 'hippie queers'."

"I'll be damned. How impolite of that fine gentleman. 'Course he *is* partly right. There is one queer here. But it ain't me."

"Yeah, yeah," Harv said. "You're a regular Bob Hope. Now, let me get the cooler and bait bucket out of the car. We got some fishing and drinking to do. As much fun as this little repartee between you and me might be, I believe that'll be funner."

It was around one o'clock, Sean figured—neither he or Harv wore watches so he couldn't be sure—and they had just finished the PB&J sandwiches Harv had made at home, , and tossed in the cooler, when a kid came rolling into their spot on a beat up red Honda 90.

"How you guys doing?" The kid turned the motor off, put the little bike up the kickstand and came sauntering over to where Sean and Harv were sitting in lawn chairs on the bank of the canal. "Catching any?"

"Nah." Harv tossed his empty beer can into the crude fire pit behind them. "It's been pretty slow. Who the fuck are you, anyways?"

"Jaimie. I live around here."

Sean couldn't imagine such a thing and said so. "Where the hell exactly is 'around here'?"

"On the other side of the road." The kid pointed with one hand behind him. "Off of mile marker 25, that dirt road there."

"No shit?" Harv asked. "Human beings live around here?"

"Sure. Me and my dad. Got a trailer back there, now, the last five years or so."

"No shit," Harv said again. "I'll be damned. Who'd of thunk it?"

He was looking at Sean when he said this, who, no less surprised than Harv with the new arrival, and the fact he was from 'around here,' just shook his head.

Harv was right about the fishing—it had been slow. The canal certainly looked promising enough. There were patches of lily pads here and there. Cypress trees growing up out of the water on the north side of it offered shade from the sun. Plenty of bugs frizzed above the water, and pods of minnows swam along the edges of the bank. One nice fish had taken his shiner with a wild splash and gulp before promptly breaking him off in some lily pads. The rest of the few fish caught had been small bass, maybe a half pound or so, if that.

But the beer was good and cold out of the cooler. He was away from the condo where his entertainment had been reading, the Watergate Hearings on the television, more reading, followed by martinis before dinner when his mom got home from work, and that had been it. Slow fishing or not, hanging out with Harv on the edge of the Alley, slinging shiners into the water on the end of his fishing line and drinking beer—well, so far it had been just about the best time he'd had since the accident. Not only that, but with this new arrival, the day might get even more interesting.

~27~ Unexpectedly home

Fort Lauderdale could be a trap for Sean. The town had proven this to be so a few years back when over Christmas break he fell in love with Krista, and instead of going back to school had stayed. Working that mind-numbing job at the gas station. Saving up his money so that Krista, her young daughter, and he, could make the trip west to that Promised Land of California. Instead; Krista had broken his heart. Leaving him stuck in his hometown until Boober sent a postcard, and the next thing Sean knew he was heading north to Massachusetts, vowing to never come back.

And yet he had. Recently, when that nightmare scene at the Cave sent him flying south to seek sanctuary in the only place he knew he to go—Fort Lauderdale. And though he had every intention of going to Tuscaloosa, and from there all the way to California, Boober's showing up at the Party Palace that morning saved him yet again from his hometown. The fact that Sean, not even knowing it, was wallowing in the trap by telling himself every day that soon *he was going to be on the road*. He only realized this on the plane back to Lauderdale—realized by staying at Dewey's apartment, when he should have been on his way to Alabama, he had stacked the odds against himself. Instead, he had just hung out, enjoying the easy living, usually somewhat high, and all the time blissfully unaware that the longer he stayed, the sooner the time would come when it was too late. And just like that, once again he would be trapped in Lauderdale, with no way out.

But even knowing all that to be true, he was going back. He had no real choice in the matter, courtesy of the phone call home he made the night after his tripping, love-making time with Angel on the bluff overlooking Bramford valley. Sean, as he walked off the plane at the Fort Lauderdale airport two days after that phone call, was painfully aware that the day was the 28th of June—aware that had Pinko not been so misinformed, he would have been rocking out with the Rolling Stones in Tuscaloosa—instead of Fort Lauderdale, and the jaws of the trap waiting to clamp shut on him if he stayed there too long.

But he had made the phone call home and none of that was to be. As if to drive this fact home there was his Aunt Helen waiting for him outside when he exited the main entrance of the airport with a big smile on her face below the huge sunglasses, like the ones Jackie Kennedy used to wear.

"Oh, Sean," his aunt told him as she wrapped him in a hug. "So good to see you again and I just know your mother's going to be thrilled you're home as well." She paused and released him from the hug to straighten her dress. "Especially at a time like this when she really needs her son to be with her."

Well, he hoped so, uncertain really what, or how much, he could do for her. Other than when his father died it had never been Sean's job to offer comfort of any kind. *He was fourteen, for chissakes!* Close to a decade had passed. Changes had gone down inside him—either because of his guilt over being relieved at his father's death, or the troubles he had gotten into, he just didn't know. Only knew that when he called home to check in, instead of his mom on the other end it had been his Aunt Helen.

"Oh my God, Sean, oh thank you for calling. Where are you? It doesn't matter. We've been so worried. Haven't known how to get hold of you to tell you but you've got to come home at once, please, you've got to."

She continued on like this, not allowing him to get a word in until finally he practically yelled into the phone, "For freak's sakes Aunt Helen tell me what's going on!"

His mother had to have surgery. "A touch of cancer," Aunt Helen said, leaving Sean to wonder how someone had just a 'touch' of a disease like cancer. "Involving her female parts, Sean, and I think you're old enough now I can say that to you." He was relieved when Aunt Helen got to the point, not wanting at all to hear any details about his mother's female parts. "But the main thing is your mother's going to be okay. Going to be just fine. I'm bringing her home tomorrow." And here Aunt Helen went again, off on a tangent. "But you know how my sister can be, I mean your mother, though of course she is my sister, but she can get so dramatic over nothing really. So I had to tell her about my friend Carol Ann who had it much worse, they had to remove—"

Again, not wanting to hear about what they had to remove from this Carol Ann person, he broke in. "Are you sure she's going to be all right?"

And relieved once more when Aunt Helen said, "Well of course, honey. But she has to heal. So please come home. You know I can't do it all myself."

So there were to be no more good high times with Angel, grooving in the New England summer, causally making his way back to Lauderdale on his own terms before hopping on the bike and making tracks for the west, or wherever the whim took him. *Nope, none of that.* Instead, just a noon flight out of Hartford two days later and there he was, back in town.

The upshot of it all being that some six months later, at eight-thirty on the first Wednesday morning of the new year, 1973, Sean finished getting dressed for the job he had to be at by nine. After donning jean cutoffs, he pulled an official white "Roland's Cheapest Bike Rentals on the Beach" tee shirt down over his head, slid into the pair of Keds on the floor by his bed, shut the apartment door behind him, and walked down the green carpeted hallway to the the parking garage where the 650 awaited him.*How in the hell did any of this come to pass?* he wondered

~28~ Alligator Alley

"No school today?" Harv had put his spinning rod down on the grass next to his lawn chair and gone to the cooler for beers for him and Sean. "You sick, or something? You don't look sick to me."

"No sir, I ain't sick." Jamie, after taking the collapsible spinning rod strapped to his bike, and setting it up, carried both the rod and a small bucket down to the water. "I missed the bus this morning."

"For real … you missed the bus?" Harv wouldn't let it go Sean knew well from past experience. "Or on purpose missed the bus?"

The kid was maybe fifteen or sixteen, wearing jeans, white t-shirt, and sneakers, like Sean and Harv, broke into a big smile.

"On purpose, but please don't tell my pop. I wanted to go fishing and skipping school is the only way I can do it. Pop has me working at his hot dog stand with him on the weekends."

"In the first place, I don't know your pop." Harv slapped the kid on the back. "In the second place, even if I did know him, I wouldn't squeal on you. I skipped many a school day in my time. Didn't I, Sean?"

"I'd say you skipped more than you attended."

"Damn straight I did."

The kid looked relieved, and Sean could see he was starting to warm up to Harv, and his goofing ways

Meanwhile Jamie had popped the lid on the plastic bait bucket, and reaching inside, pulled out a squirming, wet, shrimp looking creature, though bigger than any shrimp Sean had ever seen.

"Hey now." Harv's face and eyes went all wide open like they did when he came upon something new." What you got there, buddy?"

"It's a crawdad. You ain't ever seen a crawdad before."

"Well no, I have not."

"Then watch." He hooked the crawdad on the hook, running the barb through behind its bulging eyes, and with a smooth cast slung it to the water on the other side of the canal beneath some overhanging cypress. "Crawdads are like candy to bass, sir. They can't resist 'em."

"You don't say? And bag that 'sir' crap. Do I look like your grandpa? My name's Harv and my pal over there is Sean."

Right then the line on the kid's rod went tight and the rod started to bend. Jerking back hard on the rod the kid set the hook. When he did a big bass came flying up in a water shaking jump, before falling back in to race up the canal, the kid running along on the bank chasing it, Harv running along right behind the kid, yelling as he went, "Goddamn but ain't you something, kid? Crawdads! We got to get some crawdads, Seano."

Sean went to go after them, realized that because of the crutches he would never catch up to them, and instead, stayed put in the comfortable lawn chair, deciding that watching the fray was his best bet. Harv tripped over something just then, a root, or pothole of some sort. Harv stumbled and his hat came off. When he bent to grab it he missed, let it go, straightened up, and then kept on after the kid racing down the bank. Watching Harv go like that, once again Sean couldn't imagine his pal in the jungles of Nam, gun in hand looking to kill or be killed—couldn't imagine Harv anywhere but where he was right then, chasing after some kid he'd just met, who was trying to reel in a huge bass in the middle of nowhere.

The two of them disappeared around a curve in the canal—only to reappear a few minutes later, Jamie holding the fish by its mouth.

"Looky here, Sean man," Harv said as they came up. "Look at what this fine young man pulled out of yon water!"

Harv looked as proud of the kid's accomplishment as if he had caught the fish himself, smiling and laughing and slapping Jamie on the back, before taking the fish from the kid to hold it out closer for Sean to admire.

Sean struggled to his feet to go congratulate the kid. The fish was a beauty, probably five or six pounds of largemouth bass, its gills moving in and out grasping for the oxygen it wasn't getting. "Damn kid, you done good for sure. Looks like you'll be eating pretty fine tonight."

"I wish, but I can't keep it," he said. "Pop'll know I skipped school and went fishing if I do. He won't like that." His face brightened. "Why don't you guys take it? I'll clean it for you no problem."

""That's a damn generous offer, Jamie, me boy," Harv said. "And I am happy to accept. We'll stop and get some rice and beans on the way in, Seano, and I'll cook up a feast for us when we get back to my place."

While Jamie laid the fish out on the grass off from the clearing and started to scale and gut it, Harv went over to the cooler to get another beer for him and Sean. "Shit." He plopped the lid back down on the cooler. "Hells bells, Sean, man, but we are flat out of brew."

Before Sean could say anything Jamie piped up. "Pop's got beer back at the house. He won't be home until dark so you're welcome to come and get some."

"That sounds absolutely wonderful," Harv said. "Wouldn't you agree, Seano?"

"Fucking A."

"Fucking A my pal says. I couldn't agree more. But heck, Jamie, don't you want to stay and fish some more?"

"I don't mind. That was my only crawdad anyways, so I'm good."

"Now there you have it, Sean." Harv leaned over and patted the kid on his back as he was busy scaling the bass. "This young man, and others like him, are the future of our country by God. And a fine future it looks to be in their hands."

~29~ More Fort Lauderdale

Not that it was all bad, mind you, being in his old hometown. By mid-September, after he had been home a little over two months, his mom was back on her feet, a few gray hairs in her otherwise jet black mane, the only signs she'd had major surgery. Despite his aunt never saying so, and that his mom only confessed to him one night when she'd had three, instead of her usual two martinis, she had come very close to dying. This fact bothered Sean more than he cared to admit. Yes, his father had died, and despite his guilt over being relieved by that death, Sean pretty much carried on as if losing his father was a good thing.

But losing his mother—no, that was unsettling to the extreme. She had always been there for him. Always on his side when his father was acting the jerk. Encouraging him when he needed it. Reprimanding him when that was needed as well; but without the blunt force his father felt to be the proper way to go. And because of this, her love for him had meant more to him than he was ever able to put into words.

So to see a smile back on her face, after two months of tending to her the best he could, was just great. He made simple meals for her, helped her out of the bed to the bathroom, cleaned up around the place, ran errands for her, to the store, the post office, driving her big gold Chrysler Imperial, the one her boyfriend had given her two Christmases back, around town—enjoying the hell out of driving that big beast. He helped his mother because it was the right thing to do. And because the smile on her face when he came back from these errands made him feel good.

There was one time he realized that if he allowed it, his mother could be part of the trap his hometown was capable of being. She had finally been allowed to get out of bed and move around some and have a few martinis while watching the evening news. Out of nowhere once when Cronkite broke for a commercial, his mother told him, "It looks like it's just you and me now, son." The simple little sentence cut through him like the proverbial knife. *Because, yes he was there for her now and happy to be so—even if it got pretty damn boring at times.* But being there for her was destined to change.

As soon as she was back on her feet, young Sean Morgan was out of there. Nope, no way that plan had changed any. Not at all.

Not long after that night, when his mom was back to work for the judge at the courthouse, he had another of those realizations: he was pretty much spinning his wheels. If he was going to get those wheels going again in the right direction, he was going to need some money. His earnings from the run with Boober up north had dwindled away. Because of this, and as much as he hated to do it, one morning after his mom left for work, instead of hopping on the bike and taking a ride down by the beach, and he picked up the morning paper and started to cruise the want ads—something he had never, ever, done before. He'd had enough of his former mode of earning money. Red getting busted like that had gotten his attention. Yes, it was nice to think one was immune to such things. But in the real world that just wasn't so—that scene at the Cave, and then not long after, a similar scene going down with Red, was proof enough of that.

Or was Boober's caustic suggestion that maybe he was bad luck, true? Up until then he had always considered himself one downright lucky guy. Had that luck of his run out? Starting that night at the Cave and then further, at Red's pad in Amherst? Or could he blame it all on that evil spell Poco had threatened him with? After all, ditching her like that with no explanation in G'ville probably pissed her off. Actually, no probably about it. But did he believe in spells? Yes, and no, and maybe. What he did believe in as he picked up the classified section that mid-week morning in September of 1972, was that he wasn't going back to dealing dope. That party was over. And if he had no intention of starting a career or any capitalist American madness like that, he still needed money. Perhaps the morning paper had the answer.

Skipping the pages of ads for restaurants and hotels, he browsed the listings for construction laborers, carpenters, apprentice carpenters, electricians and so on. It didn't take him long to see that construction laboring was going to be a bit more work than he cared to do. Dewey, earlier that summer, had told Sean he basically felt like he was too good for menial labor and there was a lot of truth in what Dewey had said. Why that was true, Sean had no idea—though it may have been due to his experiences in the drug trade. No matter now, but after ten minutes or so he was about to ditch the want ads and give Kat in Gainesville a call and see if there was anything going.

He was saved from making that call when his eyes fell on a listing at the bottom of the last page of the classifieds. Roland's Beach Bicycle Rentals had positions, both full, and part time, available. *How hard could renting bicycles be*? he asked himself. Followed by, *I wonder if doing just part time will be enough to cover my freight.* Looking for the answers to these two questions he left the paper on the kitchen table for his mom to read later and headed out th to Roland's Beach Bicycle Rentals to find out.

It turned out that Sean was right: renting bicycles wasn't that hard at all. The bossman, Roland, a stocky, gruff looking bleach blond surfer type always in baggies and an official Rolands Beach Bicycle Rentals, Best Bikes on the Beach! Tee shirt, seemed to like him, and he liked him. He also took to heart the sage advice Roland gave him his first day on the job: the customer was not always right. If they gave you a hard time, even after you had gone out of your way to make them happy, then fuck 'em. The best part of being gainfully employed at the bike rental shop was working the four days a week Roland assigned him. Wednesday through Saturday, with his cash wages, along with tips from grateful customers, was more than enough to keep gas in the 650, buy beers after work at the Parrot Lounge, purchase whatever reefers needed—and even stash some bucks away for when it was time to cut loose of that mortal coil Lauderdale represented for him, and get the hell out of Dodge.

His mom liked the fact that Sean was working, and so far, not acting like he was going to split the scene any time soon—a liking proved one day when she mentioned she had spoken to the judge about that little problem Sean had with his motorcycle. This 'little problem' Sean revealed to her one night when he mentioned how he couldn't get the Bonneville registered in his name because of not having a title, or bill of sale. The judge, when Sean's mom brought it up at work that day, said he could work it out. Sure enough, after giving his mom an old registration slip Tommy had stashed under the seat, she came home from work one afternoon with a new registration in Sean's name. Not only that, but she handed over to him a title issued by the State of Florida stating that one Sean Morgan was the proud owner of a 1970 Triumph Bonneville 650cc motorcycle. What, and how, Tommy might think of or do about this Sean wasn't too worried about. He and Will had pulled five years up at Raiford. When he was released then that would be the time to set things right. Meanwhile, Sean was eternally grateful, not only to his mom, but to the judge for going out of his way to help him—something Sean's own father had never bothered to do.

So that yes, it wasn't all bad by a long shot being back home. He had legit money that he didn't have to bust a nut for. A free place to stay, his mom not asking for rent or anything. A decent set of wheels. And for once, after a pretty long while, he didn't have to be constantly looking over his shoulder to see who, or what, might be catching up to him. All of which got even better one October Friday when after work at the bike shop he strolled down to the Parrot, bellied up to the bar, ordered his seven drafts for a buck, and was just putting that first draft up to his lips when someone slapped him on the back. A voice rang out behind him,

"Well shit, Christ, howdy but I do believe it's Sean Morgan, his own self, living and breathing and drinking beer like a regular human being."

~30~ Alligator Alley

Just as the kid said, the trailer he and his dad lived in was at the end of the dirt road running south from the highway just west of the bridge and the Collier County line. The road ended in a crude cul-de-sac, the kid's home off to one side. As trailers went, this one was a pretty ramshackle affair. A dilapidated pickup truck sat rusting away on one end of it, along with a junked washing machine and a couple of engine blocks that had seen better days. An old pit-bull chained to a pine tree in what was the front yard, looked up when the kid, leading the way on his Honda 90 pulled in, and then went back to sleeping in the dirt under the tree.

"C'mon in guys, and I'll get you that beer," Jamie yelled over his shoulder as he put the bike on the kickstand and headed for the front door of the trailer. Harv, already out of the Anglia, was right behind him, while Sean struggled to get himself and his crutches out of the low slung car. Stopping before he opened the door to let them in the kid added, "I'll have to charge you fifty cents apiece, though. That's what Pop gets for them at the stand."

"That the stand by the boat ramp on the Miami Canal?" Harv turned to grin at Sean behind him on the front stoop. "Shit, I've bought beer and hot dogs from your old man, before. Lots of times. Back when Rob and I had that big tile job in Naples and had to run back and forth between there and Lauderdale. A tall, mean looking dude with one crossed eye—that your Pop?"

"That's him." By then Jamie had the door open and the three of them were standing in the living room of the trailer. "He's mean all right. When my mom left him I wanted to go with her but he wouldn't let me. Said he needed me to help around here."

Jesus, kid, that's a shame." Sean was trying to ignore the smell of the place, some sort of combo of stale air, dirty dishes in the sink, and a pile of dirty clothes lying on the floor in the hallway in front of a recess where the washing machine had to be. "Bet you miss your mom, huh?" *Bet he missed her cleaning up the joint.* But he let that thought go.

"Not so much anymore," the kid said as he headed into the kitchen. "All they did was fight anyways when she was here. Grab a seat and I'll get you those beers."

"Right nice of you Jamie boy." Harv had found a comfortable spot in the middle of a ratty looking couch. "Right nice of you for sure."

Leaning over he whispered to Sean, who had decided on an old armchair next to the couch as being a safe enough seat for him, "That hot dog stand of the kid's Pop's? He doesn't have a license to sell beer. Some sort of a mix-up related to felony charges in his past. That's what Rob told me. But the old man don't give a shit. Even though he's been popped a couple of times. Pretty wild, huh? You and me being here like this?"

"Pretty wild all right." Pretty stupid, being what he wanted to say. "Let's just drink our beers and get out of here."

"Aww now, Seano, that's no way to be."

Harv was enjoying himself, it was plain to see, all settled back on the couch, his legs splayed out on the floor in front of him, Stetson pushed back on his head, and ready to play his country boy hick part to the hilt.

"Here you go guys." Jamie came out of the kitchen holding cans of Old Milwaukee in his hands. "Just like I promised, two cold beers for you. I looked for the Budweisers, but Pop must have taken them when he left this morning. Hope these'll be okay."

It was the second time that day Sean felt bad for the kid—the first time being when he heard about his mom leaving, and now this, having to bring out Old Milwaukee to the newfound pals he was trying so hard to impress.

"No problem, Jamie boy." Harv pulled the ring tab off, took a long gulp from the open can, looking up when he was done with a satisfied grin on his lips. "Yes sir, but that sure hits the spot. Doesn't it Sean?"

Sean did his best to be polite and not frown at the bitter taste of the beer, wondering as always how such a brew could be the one that made Milwaukee famous.

"Yeah, kid, this hits the spot all right." Looking over at Harv he added, "We ought to be heading back pretty soon, don't you think?"

"You don't have to worry about Pop, if that's what you're thinking."

Jamie had a beer of his own, and Sean would have laughed at the look on the kid's face as he drank from it, if it wasn't so obvious he just wanted them to hang out with him for a while. *He probably feels pretty cool, grooving with a couple of older dudes. Not to mention it must be godawful lousy living out here with his mom gone and a mean ass dad to top it all off.*

"He won't be home until dark, after he closes the stand up."

"Yeah, Sean," Harv said, coming to the kid's rescue. "What's your rush?"

"No rush. Just don't want to get anyone in trouble is all."

"We'll be fine, buddy. Don't you worry." Harv turned to Jamie. "So it's just you and the old man out here, huh? Must get pretty lonely for you."

"It's not so bad. Pop's girlfriend lives here, too. She works at the Winn Dixie over in Naples. Usually comes home right around the same time as Pop. She's a good cook, too!"

"A good cook comes in handy, all right." Harv winked at Sean. "She good looking? Pop's girlfriend?"

"She's okay, I guess." The kid seemed a little nervous suddenly with the questions. "Not as good looking as my mom."

Sean, though not nervous, was curious where Harv was going with these questions, if anywhere—though Harv as Sean well knew, was always going somewhere. He didn't have long to wait to find out.

"Well Jamie, let's hope your old man's new girlfriend don't end up like your mom."

"I told you my mom left, Harv, and that's all to it. Pop kicked her out."

"What the fuck are you babbling about, Harv?" It didn't sound to Sean like Harv was kidding right then. "You know something I don't know, or what?"

"Ah, just some shit my brother picked up here and there when we were doing that job in Naples. You know, the usual, a man's wife leaves suddenly, no one sees her around anymore, you know, people say shit, is all."

"That's right, Harv," Jamie blurted out. "Just shit people were saying because they don't like my old man. None of its true and I know that for a fact!"

"All right, Harv, lay off the kid." Sean didn't really care one way or the other, only wanted to finish the beer and get out of there. "Let's hit it, man."

"Now, now, Seano." Harv turned to Jamie, his hands out in front of him in supplication. "You see, Jamie, my lad, Sean knows I'm a curious man. I just figured you would know the skinny, that's all. Didn't mean to upset anyone, no sir, didn't mean to do that at all. We still pals, kid?"

"Yeah, still pals," the kid grudgingly conceded. *He wanted to be friends so bad, and Harv had pushed too hard*—well, Sean had seen this sort of scene happen more than once with Harv, and people he wanted to mess with. "It just bothers me when people—especially people I like—start up with that crap again."

"I'm sorry I hurt your feelings. It won't happen again. I promise." Harv winked again at Sean—a wink, that considering what had just gone down, didn't make him feel much better. "What about this new girlfriend of Pop's? You think the old man might have some naked pictures of her?"

31~ A1A and the Tunnel Bar

Just like that, after an absence of five some years since he had dropped out of high school to work with his older brother Rob, Harv was back in Sean's life. Older and with a bit of a beer belly—odd, considering how lean and tough he'd been when the three of them, Sean, Dewey, and Harv, used to hang out together. But beer belly or not. he was the same old Harv. A shit-eating grin on his face, his blond hair grown longer once free of high school restrictions, tied back in a ponytail. Unlike when he was in high school, his appetite for any drugs that came his way appeared to have been replaced by a constant thirst for cold beer.

It was Harv who turned Sean on to the Tunnel Bar that afternoon by explaining, with a serious look on his face, how the Parrot had become completely not cool these days, filled as it usually was by visiting Yankees wearing loud Bermuda shorts and Hawaiian shirts while looking for some local color. Harv went on to say that the last few months the old gang had been hanging out at the Tunnel Bar. "You know? That dumpy little joint over by the tunnel?" Sean knew of the place—figured it to be one those bars where bums and serious alcoholics went to cure their ills. "You remember Belinda from high school, right? That big titted gal, sort of Italian maybe, kind of loud, yeah, but pretty good for a laugh here and there, dig?"

Apparently, after Belinda took over the afternoon/evening shifts at the place all the old crew began hanging out there, drinking that funky Pabst draft beer for a quarter a pop and just going with the groove. "Hells bells, man," Harv said. "The only reason I'm here at the Parrot now is because of a repair job me and Rob are doing at the old Bonnet House down the street. You know, man, but Jesus, Seano, that old house has no air conditioning. The place's been closed up for years, man, the only people ever in there are the caretaker and the ghosts, and I guess neither one of those guys give a damn about getting some fresh air in the place. So fuck, man, its hotter than a sonofabitch inside there, and shit, buddy, but when I finished up there today and Rob was going home to his old lady, I'm like dying for a cold beer, this lame joint being the closest place I could get to before passing out from thirst, if you can catch my drift?"

This had to be the longest rap Sean had ever heard from Harv over the years. But he was glad to hear it—filled as it was with pertinent information that could possibly upgrade his social scene. Especially seeing as how the only social scene he'd enjoyed of late was the seven drafts for a buck at the Parrot after work, then going home to have a couple of martinis with his mom, eat dinner, watch stupid-ass TV, and go to bed, then do it all over again the next day—point being, that he thanked Harv for the turn on about the Tunnel Bar and he would see him there soon.

And he did; by getting into the habit of riding down there after work. Technically, the Tunnel Bar was out of his way—seeing as how Roland's bike shop was on A1A, his mom's place only a mile or so south of there, and the Tunnel Bar was off of Federal Highway, tucked in behind the south entrance to the New River Tunnel. But going out of his way was just fine with Sean. Belinda was happy to see him and remembered him from high school, even though they had never hung out together. She even turned him onto a free draft the first time he came in. "For old time's sake," she said, though there had been no old times he could remember sharing with her.

And just like Harv had said, there were plenty of familiar faces there. Dewey was one of them, who Sean hadn't seen since picking up the 650 from where he had stashed it at the Party Palace, and for whatever reason, had not hung out with since. So it was good getting that particular groove back. Harv was there, of course, just like he said he would be, and others from high school, like Belinda, that Sean had never run with. But now they all seemed to be long lost pals, everyone off work for the day, knocking back beers, listening to the tunes Belinda played on the juke. Tunes like *Crocodile Rock, Tiny Dancer, Me and Mrs., Jones,* the usual top 40 stuff, but plenty of Frank Sinatra too. Sinatra was apparently a favorite of Belinda's—so much so that whenever *My Way,* or *New York, New York, Summer Wind,* and the like came on, she would crank the juke all the way up and sing along. All in all Sean found the whole scene at that bar to be a very good one indeed.

The fall of 1972, for Sean passed by in a dream: four days a week doing his shift at Roland's Bike Rentals then going to the Tunnel Bar when he got off, usually until closing time. The dingy, dark, little bar in a part of town that always seemed to him like it was lost in time, became a second home to him. A thought that sort of bothered him. But he was putting some money away—even if he spent more than he put away on those Pabst drafts. And that was okay. It would all work out, he kept telling himself. Summer would be there before he knew it. And then, with his mother all better now, he would be out of there. *Oh yes he would.*

Suddenly, there was a girl. A hippie-like chick he met one Sunday afternoon when he was nursing a draft at a pretty much empty Tunnel Bar. Bored, he ordered another beer and took it with him to the pool table in the back of the bar and began setting up different shots. Most of these shots, because he wasn't very good, he missed. One errant shot when Sean stroked it, sent the cue ball flying off the table. Landing on the floor the ball rolled towards the back door and stopped by a girl walking in. Leaning over she picked the ball up, and with the brightest smile he had seen since being with Angel on Bramford Mountain, asked, "This yours?"

Beth was her name, twenty three years old with dirty blonde hair she wore long down to her shoulders, bright blue eyes that shined, with an aquiline kind of nose and mouth, she was dressed in a loose, long flowing skirt with nothing on underneath, as evidenced by the points of her nipples pushing against the cotton fabric Sean couldn't help but notice. In other words, your average hippie type girl — the type he was always attracted to. Down from New York, she was taking a semester off from Juilliard where she studied music. She shared an apartment with some other girls in a run-down, two story wood frame house on the banks of New River two blocks away from the bar. Bored that gray January afternoon, she decided to take a walk through the neighborhood and check out her new surroundings. Hearing the Led Zeppelin tunes on the jukebox coming from inside the bar, she decided to check it out.

Afterward, when things were over between Sean and her, and Beth having returned to New York for school, every time he heard *Babe, I'm Gonna Leave you,* he thought of her. But until then, things were pretty good between the two of them. He downright dug having a steady girlfriend — maybe because he knew it wouldn't last, what with that school thing of hers. The two of them took to riding the 650 down to the beach on Sunday afternoons, swimming in the ocean if it was warm enough, and then drying off in the Elbo Room over cold beers and maybe a bite to eat. One Sunday afternoon they cruised down to the Grove in Miami to check out a jazz festival. *Digging different scenes, the kind he hadn't been involved in since his time with Luellen back in Gvile.* He liked having her arms wrapped tight around him on the back of the 650 as they rode, the wind blowing their long hair back and feeling free as they rode. One time — when they had been hanging together for almost three months and after making love in her bedroom, he considered asking if she wanted to go with him out west that summer.

But he considered this only for a moment because he knew it was a silly thought. He had been with her long enough by that time to know her commitment to Juilliard. Her dream was not his dream. And that was cool. He was beginning to grasp the concept by then that nothing lasted. It all changed, and the only thing he could do was enjoy the time now, that time with her. And afterwards, when she was gone and it was all like before, he would just carry on.

Funny, but after she left for school the first part of April, he got a letter from Luellen. He hadn't heard from her since she had gone to Egypt over a year ago. Yet here was a letter from her, saying she hoped he received it, that she wrote to his mother's address, figuring if he wasn't there she would forward it to him wherever he might be. Even more important, she was in Tampa now, going to the U of South Florida to work on her masters in anthropology. That was all well and just fine—but the most important info in the letter was the fact she had two tickets to the upcoming Led Zeppelin concert May 5th at the Tampa stadium and would he like to go with her? Well, yes, he did want to go with her. And wrote her back to tell her so.

For the next few weeks he played mind games with himself— mulling over what he wanted more. To see Luellen again or to see Led Zeppelin live? By the time he saddled up the 650 and headed out Alligator Alley on his way to Tampa, he still had no answer, other than the belief that he would find out when he got there.

The answer to his question was that both were equally good—even if perhaps he leaned a tad more towards Led Zeppelin. Behind this answer might have been the acid they took before leaving her apartment and going to the stadium in Luellen's Volkswagen Bug. The ride there was just long enough for the Blue Barrels to start kicking in—which made finding a parking spot and then their way across the seemingly vast parking lot and entrance up to their seats in what appeared to be the farthest bleacher away from the stage, an adventure all its own. The band, on the stage so far away, looked like stick figures and this had nothing to do with the drug fragmenting his brain. Huge video screens were set up around the stadium, so they at least had visuals of the group, the band awash in otherworldly colors and slashed by trails, courtesy of the acid. But the music blasting out of the stack of speakers behind the band, was larger than any life—even if it was coming from shimmering matchstick men somewhere to the front of him in the strange zone the acid had taken him.

On the way back to Lauderdale on the Sunday morning after the concert, Sean was sure of one thing. He and Luellen had no future—a hope he realized he had carried with him all the way to Tampa. If he were to be honest with himself, he had held that hope way before that. But much like Beth leaving to back go north, that was okay. Carry on was his new mantra. *Carry on.*

And carry on he did. Enough so that the last week in July he told Roland at the bike shop, Adios, and began making his preparations to head west. He had managed to save up almost two grand—a sum he felt comfortable with and believed would surely last him until he ended up where he wanted to be and was settled. In that vein of thought he bought saddle bags for the 650, started putting necessities into a small duffel bag that would fit inside one of the saddle bags, leaving the other bag for things like maps, clean jeans and tee shirts for easy access. When he had all this doped out to his satisfaction, he told his mom his plans, holding resolute when she did what he figured she would—this being a lot of sobbing and hugging and asking, "Are you sure this is what you want to do, Sean?" Her distress made him feel bad—but not quite bad enough. Holding her in his arms he told her that he loved her, would stay in touch more frequently than he was prone to do, that everything will be all right. Mom, I've got to do this, I love you, thanks for everything. I'm sorry but I've got to do this.

His last day at the bike shop was a Saturday and that night Harv threw a going away party for Sean. Belinda had made up some Good Luck and We'll Miss You type banners she strung across the walls and beer for him was on the bar all night. It wasn't Sean's plan to get loaded that night. He planned to hit the road early the next morning—figuring if he made it to Cedar Key on the Gulf coast by evening his first day on the road, he would be doing all right. But plan or not, when he left the bar around midnight he had a pretty good rolling buzz going on. So much so that it took him two attempts to get the 650 off the kickstand. Not only that, but he narrowly avoided going all the way over when he pulled a wheelie in the parking lot to impress Harv and Dewey and Belinda yelling and waving goodbye to him.

By the time he reached the red light at the intersection of 17th and Federal he was feeling more in control, the wind on his face having sobered him up a little. After crossing the 17th street bridge over New River, he was on the home stretch to his mom's condo. He began thinking how great it was going to be in the morning and finally on his way. Yes, and finally, after a good night's sleep, Sunday morning breakfast with his mom, a shower after, get into some clean jeans and tee shirt, put on his boots, grab his duffle, hug his mom goodbye, take the elevator down to the garage for the last time, kick that Bonneville off the stand, turn the key, start her up—and by all the gods, o yeah, Sean Morgan would be on the road. First stop that day would be Cedar Key and the next day he would run across the panhandle and into Alabama.

And fuck Alabama. He wouldn't go too far into the interior of that state. No sir, there'd be none of that Easy Rider shit for him. He'd just run along the gulf coast into Texas, probably take two days or so, judging by what he'd read in his Rand McNally. Just take the southern route all the way to Cal, no need to be too high up in the Rockies, it being maybe too late in the year for that, potential snowstorms and all, lousy place to be on a motorcycle. But no matter—the main thing was the fact that he would be on the road.

All of this running through his head as he just happened to notice what looked to be a Cadillac, the big model they put out that year, pull out of a darkened driveway. He had just enough time to swerve around the Caddy's rear end, thinking he would be all right, he could do it. He almost did, free and easy—except for the sound, followed by the feel of his left leg whacking the rear end of the car. Whacking it hard enough, actually, to send Sean and the 650 spinning into a slide across the little space of road between the sidewalk and the pavement, the exhaust pipe hot against his right leg as he and the bike went over and came to a stop under a streetlight. The driver of the Caddy must not have been aware something had hit the rear end of his car, because he just kept going on his merry way—leaving Sean lying there on the road, as he watched the Caddy finally come to a stop, its backup lights on as it made its way back to where he was. Sean, by that time, was trying to get himself and the bike right side up and do some damage control. Only to discover when he tried to put weight on his left leg that it was swinging freely all on its own—so that when he put his left foot down on the pavement the leg just crumpled up. Down Sean and the bike went once again.

He lay there for a bit—gave up actually, it being so freaking obvious that the trap he always knew his hometown to be was still in effect. That just as he thought he was going to escape, damned if the jaws of that trap didn't clamp down on him yet again.

~32~ Alligator Alley for the last time

"Jesus Christ, Harv, that's enough." Sean was out of the armchair and on his crutches. "Time to go, buddy."

"Sure he does," Jamie said, surprising both Sean and Harv. "Let me go get them."

Before Sean could make it to the door, the kid was chasing down the hallway, while Harv, that shit eating grin on his face, was waving at Sean to sit back down.

"Wow," Harv said. "Gotta say, I didn't expect that answer. No sir, I did not. But like my Grandpa used to say, it never hurts to ask."

"Your grandpa died before you were born, asshole."

"True. Maybe it was my mom who used to say that."

"C'mon, dude, let's blow this scene."

But it was too late—Jamie had returned, holding what looked to be a couple of Polaroids in his hand.

"See? I told you he had 'em."

He handed the photographs to Harv, who looked them over as if they were rare artifacts, going over first one, then the other, then back to the first one, then to the second, before passing them to Sean, who didn't really want to look, spared from looking by the sound of a vehicle rumbling into the yard and coming to a stop.

"Shit," The kid yelled, grabbing for the photographs in Sean's hands. "It's Pop. He's home early."

Polaroids in hand the kid disappeared back down the hallway, the front door opened, Sean, and Harv left behind to greet Jamie's dad as he came in.

"Where's Jamie?"

Just as Harv had said earlier the kid's pop was mean looking all right—Sean wouldn't argue with that. Tall, red hair like his son's, cut in a military crew, muscular arms coming out of a sweat soaked tank top, the crossed eye Harv had mentioned, looking the other way, his steel toed boots rang across the floor of the trailer as he came inside, right up to where Sean and Harv were.

"And who are you guys?"

"Harv, sir, or as my mother calls me, Harvey." Harv reached his hand out for the other man to shake, dropping it to his side when this offer was refused. "This here's my good pal, Sean. We had the pleasure of making your son's acquaintance earlier this morning where we were fishing, and when the sun just got too unbearable to stand anymore, Jamie offered to bring us back here for some cool relief, good boy that he is."

"No one's allowed here when I'm not home. Jamie knows that."

With a 'fuck you' look Pop brushed by Sean and Harv, just as Jamie was coming down the hallway.

"Hey, Pop. You're home early."

The minute Jamie came into the living room Sean knew they were screwed, what with the guilt written all over the kid's face.

"You gave them my beer?"

"I didn't give it to 'em, Pop. Charged 'em fifty cents just like you do at the stand."

A weak defense all the way, Sean thought. But Pop had something else on his mind.

"What were you doing in my room?"

"Nothing Pop, I swear. Wasn't doing anything."

But the kid's face said otherwise, and his father knew it.

"You boys better get," Pop said over his shoulder, his eyes never leaving the now frightened kid's face. "I need to have a little talk with my boy here."

"Yes sir." Harv started for the door. "We understand and thank you for your hospitality."

Sean, already at the door and holding it open, waved for Harv to come on before he could do any more damage.

'See you, Jamie," he said over his shoulder as he followed Harv down the stoop and headed for the Anglia. God but he wished some good luck for the kid right then. Even if he knew, and was certain Jamie knew as well, there wasn't enough luck in the world to help him at that moment.

As they were getting into the car they heard the kid yelling from inside. "No Pop. I didn't do anything wrong." This was followed by the sound of what had to be Jamie being slammed against the wall of the living room.

"Damn, bud." Harv started the car up and went to back out of the yard. "I do believe our young friend is in for a world of hurt."

"Yeah? You think we had anything to do with that 'world of hurt?'

"Do you?"

"Hell yes. I tried to get you to leave, but oh no, God forbid we get out while the getting was good."

"But we were having such a good time."

"Why don't you go back in there and ask Jamie how much fun he's having now?"

"No." They were on the dirt road, the dust kicking up behind them as Harv headed them for the highway. "No, I don't think that's advisable under the current situation."

"Yeah, I figured that's what you'd say."

It was quiet then inside the Anglia, Harv driving, Sean on the seat next to him trying not to think of what was happening to the kid right then—trying not to be mad at his good friend, who more than anything, had caused it all.

But the kid had been a part of it, for sure. He had fucked up and was paying the price for it. That happened sometimes. Had happened to Sean. Look at the accident that possibly ruined his leg for life. If he had just left the Tunnel Bar earlier. If he hadn't been drunk. If he had just seen the car coming out of the blackened driveway a moment sooner, swerved a little more to the right to avoid the collision. Too many 'if's.' Too damn many.

It had been a good day, though. No question about that. Getting away from the condo. On the road with Harv. Drinking beer. Catching a couple of fish. Losing that big one in the lily pads. The kid on his Honda rolling in and changing everything up. Sadly for the kid, not in a good way for him. But Harv and Sean were on their way to Harv's place. Unscathed by all of what was going on with the kid and his pop. Once back at the apartment, Harv would cook the fish Jamie had given them. They would drink Jim Beam, clown around, and when it was over for the night, go to sleep, or pass out more like it. The next day would be a new one. One day closer to his leg getting better. One day closer to getting his insurance settlement. Buying a truck. Hitting the road. Going west—*all the way to fucking California.* Maybe Harv would ride with him. If he wasn't in the army by then, getting shot at in Nam, Sean was sure he would. Hell yes Harv would come with him. They had come this far as pals. Didn't see how anything could change that.

So too bad, for the kid. He would survive. Maybe learn a lesson. In the meantime, Harv was okay. Sean was okay. They were getting it. Would continue on that way if they were lucky. Yes, if they were lucky they would get it.

"I need me a cold one." They were once again at the yellow caution light at US27. "How 'bout you, pardner?"

"Can always use a cold one," Sean said.

"That's the spirit" Harv turned right onto the highway, headed for Andytown where the day had started. "Knew I could count on you, Seano. Always know I can count on you."

"Fucking A."

38 Roads

Part 3: Out West & Back
1975

~33~ Main Street

A year or so later, on a cold July morning that was pushing towards noon, Sean was nursing an Olympia draft in a rundown bar just off of Main Street in Dillon, Colorado. During the passing of that year things had gone very different—even if he didn't really know it as such at the time. But he could feel it. A bleakness, similar to the unease hovering over Gainesville back in 1972, seemed to cover the country. The 20th century was three quarters of the way over and of those seventy-five years he had been around for twenty-four of them. Perhaps because of that bleakness he felt none of the excitement he believed he should be enjoying at that time in his life. The war in Vietnam was over, the Nixon era now history, having fallen apart around the wreckage of Watergate and said war in Southeast Asia. Now there was nothing left to protest against. No radical ideology to embrace. No rallies and love-ins to attend. There were no street fairs to participate in. A peanut farmer in Georgia was gearing up for a run at the presidency, fueled, oddly enough by the music and the fundraising of the Allman Brother's band. Strange days—as Morrison had wailed about—strange days indeed.

All of which he was doing his best to ignore as he sat that morning in the Old Dillon Inn, nursing his beer and watching Harv shoot pool. "Inn" was probably too refined a word for the place—at least in its current state of existence—for it was actually just a bar and grill some seventy miles west of Denver, straight up in the High Country. The joint had certainly seen better days; the aged drabness of its furnishings proof enough of the Old Dillon Inn's time of being the main stopping point for travelers coming through the area, long gone.

But in the dimness of its interior one could nurse a cold beer, stare out the windows at the snow-covered mountains off in the distance, listen to the C&W tunes playing on the jukebox, or wonder at the sadness of the old gal with the beehive hairdo sitting at the far end of the bar. If one was in the right frame of mind, they might also wonder at the changes and vagaries of a life that had brought them there—exactly what Sean was doing that dreary morning.

Changes there had been, at least physically. Harv, for instance, and right before they left Fort Lauderdale, had gone to the barber and got a crew cut. The extremely short haircut made his round face look even rounder, while somehow heightening the blueness of his eyes. Sean, too, had gone to the barber, but not for any crew cut, opting instead to leave his hair hanging down to his collar line. A look that with the sideburns he had grown out, gave him sort of a Stephen Stills look. Or so he hoped. Like Harv, he still wore jeans and a tee shirt. Unlike Harv's solid white tees, which Sean had certainly carried along with him on this journey, he liked to wear his official "Rolands, Cheapest Bike Rentals on the Beach" work tee shirt. And unlike Harv's work boots, now that he was off the crutches and the sneakers he had worn for their stability while he was hobbling about, he had gone back to his snakeskin boots. Boots that along with the Stephen Stills haircut, long sideburns, and his fringe jacket, gave him what he felt was an appropriately hip sort of aura—one perfectly suited for the journey he was embarked on. Even if that journey was momentarily stalled in a very unhip place like the Old Dillon Inn, leaving him to ponder the bleakness of the times and his age.

Not that his traveling partner seemed to share that frame of mind. He was too busy shooting pool with a young cowboy who had come in with his girlfriend not long after Sean and Harv had. The girlfriend had promptly plunked herself down at one of the little round tables scattered throughout the large room, and in between slipping quarters into the jukebox and cheering her boyfriend on, she sipped at a Bud Light.

The girl's cheering wasn't doing the trick, though, as Sean observed from his quiet post at the bar, for Harv beat the young cowboy every time. This was beginning to suit the young man not at all. The fact they were playing for a buck a game instead of the standard beer bet—at Harv's insistence—did nothing to improve the cowboy's mood. Not judging by the cue stick he slammed against the side of the pool table after his latest defeat. Yet the cowboy kept putting quarters into the slot and racking the balls for another go.

"Hot damn, Buck." Harv had come up to the bar for a refill; his round face stretched in as big a smile as Sean had seen there in a long time. "This keeps up I'll be set for the rest of the summer."

"Don't go spendin' that money quite yet," the cowboy said as he was racking the balls. "I aim to win some of it back."

"Yes, yes, that's what I like," Harv told the cowboy. "A positive attitude."

"No attitude about it. Jus' cold, hard fact."

"You might want to ease up on him some," Sean whispered when Harv grabbed his fresh beer up from the bar. "Your buddy there's not having quite as much fun as you are."

"Ah Buck, now that's no way to be. Spoiling my good time. Fuck 'em if he can't take a joke."

"That's what I'm afraid of. His failure to see the humor here."

Harv left the bar for the pool table and the scowling cowboy. Watching him go, Sean suddenly flashed on Dwight—the pool shark pockmarked youth fleeing disaster in Miami who Boober and Sean had picked up from the roadside back in '72. Sean wondered if Dwight had ever found his girlfriend. *Joey? Wasn't that her name?* He thought it was. Hoped that things had turned out okay for Dwight and her. If he indeed ended up finding her. Everything had been falling apart that summer. Falling apart and then evolving into something else altogether. Or so it had it had appeared at the time.

Funny, but on this run he was making with Harv, Massachusetts had been their first port of call. Spurred on by spring fever and fueled by Sean's insurance money, and riding in the used Jeep pickup truck he had bought with some of that money, they left Ft. Lauderdale the end of April. While initially planning this run, laid up with his broken leg and just biding his time, he hadn't factored a return to New England as being part of the plan. Until out of nowhere he received a letter from Teddie.

Apparently, still up in Montreal and doing good by all accounts, Boober had told Ron and Teddie about Sean's misfortunes regarding the motorcycle accident. This inspired Teddie to write Sean a letter to cheer him up. The letter, written in a neat feminine script that filled up three pages, was actually full of nothing much of importance—just casual mentions of Red and how he was doing well. Of Angel, too, and how she was doing good. Everything fine up there in Bramford, the letter ending, though, with something that did catch his eye. If Sean was ever up that way again when he was back on his feet, just give her and Ron a call. *He was welcome anytime, so good luck Sean, hope you get better soon, and that sort of thing.* As he was reading it, his spirits were lifted.

So when formalizing his road plans, making a date to leave and such, Harv fully on board having managed to beat the draft and comfortably on unemployment for the next six months after he and his brother were laid off —*well then, why not make a stop in Bramford on their way west?* They had nothing but time after all.

They ended up staying almost three weeks in Bramford at Ron and Teddie's place. Sean had mixed emotions about being there, but Harv jumped right in, with Ron at least. When Harv discovered Ron liked to drink hard every bit as much as he did, the two of them became running buddies, hitting all the bars Ron knew in the area. Sean sometimes tagged along, but more often did not. He was a little disappointed Angel wasn't still around—but down in Mexico with her boyfriend. In Manzanillo to be exact, where they had hooked up with some Pranksters who'd stayed behind when Kesey returned to the States to face the music. Now Angel, her boyfriend, and those ex-Pranksters, were thriving in the Michoacán pot trade. *All was well and so it goes,* was Sean's thought when he heard this news.

Good for her. Hell, good for them. Very good, in fact, to know that someone, somewhere, was still carrying that particular torch on. As for him? Not his gig anymore. If it ever really was.

But the whole Bramford scene started to go stale, that old *let's get back on the road thing* beginning to eat at Sean. Enough so that one night, when Harv came in from getting plastered with Ron, Sean told him to be ready in the morning. They were going. And they did. Leaving Bramford in the dust and ripping up the highway ever since, drinking beer and laughing as they went, camping out at night along the way when they just couldn't make another mile. The whole time he kept the nose of the truck pointed west, and as the wheels of the Jeep ate up the asphalt a steady refrain, in the back of his mind sang to him: *This is it.*

There in the Old Dillon Inn it didn't take too much longer for Sean's fear to come true. When Harv raised both hands over his head in triumph after yet another victory, the young cowboy snapped. The next thing Sean knew he jumped over the table and grabbed Harv by the throat, apparently planning to choke the life out of his tormentor with his bare hands. While Harv was gesturing wildly with one hand for Sean to come and help him, with his other hand he worked at prying loose the cowboy's grip from his throat. The whole time this one-sided battle was going on Harv never lost that little shit-eating grin—the one that came on his lips whenever he found something even remotely amusing. Sean wondered briefly if his buddy would be smiling like that when the Grim Reaper came to claim his sorry ass—then he was on the cowboy's back, doing his best to drag him off his pal.

"Goddamn it, Carl," the burly bartender's voice rang out in the Inn. The bartender had let ride the cue stick the young cowboy had smashed against the side of the table earlier. But it seemed that starting a fight in his otherwise quiet bar was the last straw. Now he was leveling a double barrel shotgun at the three combatants struggling on the pool table. "I've warned you before, Carl, about causin' trouble in my bar. Now get outta here. All of you."

"Geez, Buck," Harv said a little later as he was tilting a cold Budweiser to his mouth. They were in the Jeep heading west on 91 out of Dillon, Sean not real sure where they were going. "Who'd have thought folks would get so testy back there? Talk about a sore loser."

And there was that shit-eating grin again.

~34~ Highway 32

An hour later they were driving through Leadville, an old mining town that somehow, and just barely, had survived the times. The air grew colder and the sky grayer the higher they rode up into the Rockies in the advancing afternoon. The buildings looked lifeless in the gray light of the day and no people were out and about on the solitary street running through the town. A light burning in the window of what turned out to be the Post Office/General Store was the only sign of human life. *The name suits the place* was Sean's thought as they waited on the one traffic light. Perhaps Deadville was more like it, though, and he smiled at his little joke.

Wheeling out of Dillon, Harv had asked where they were headed. Sean's answer had been, "Up." It seemed as good a destination as any, now it was clear their sojourn in Dillon had come to an end. According to the Rand McNally road atlas Sean had bought for the trip, the Continental Divide lay not too far ahead of them. He suddenly felt it important to get to the other side. If pressed for a reason he might have answered, "We're traveling west, aren't we? We won't truly be in the West until we cross the Divide."

He might have added, if asked—might have tried to explain how the whole time they had been driving west he'd felt like he was going against the current. Fighting his way upstream it seemed. Once across the Divide the rivers would flow west, and he would be like those rivers. Finally a part of their flow. But the only one with him was Harv. A detailed explanation wasn't necessary. "Up" had been plenty enough for him.

Ten miles out of Leadville they turned onto 82, the green highway sign at the junction proclaiming in bold white letters, Independence Pass 15 m. Aspen 30m. Camped beneath the road sign were two hippies, a man and a woman wrapped tight in matching buckskin jackets against the cold. What appeared to be all of their worldly possessions bulged out against the side of a canvas sea bag at their feet. The woman held a cardboard sign across her chest that said, Aspen. Without putting any thought into it— the only place to put the hippies would be in the cab of the Jeep, what with the truck bed loaded with his and Harv's things and covered by a canvas tarp, Sean downshifted and pulled off on the side of the road. It was starting to rain, a cold steady drizzle, and he knew he wouldn't want to be stranded out on the road in dismal weather like that. *Not in the middle of nowhere.*

The hippies ran up to the Jeep and tossed the bulging sea bag under the tarp. Then, over Harv's, "What the hell you thinking, Buck?" they squeezed into the cab. The musty, earthy smell of dirt and marijuana suddenly enveloped the small space. Along with the smell, there was the pressure of the hippie girl's thigh against his.

The hippie couple wasn't as old as they first looked. Youthful dark eyes peered out from under the dirty black hair falling over the guy's forehead, the rest of that hair tied back in a ponytail. The bushy black beard was what made him look older than the early 20's he probably was, Sean realized. As for the woman, she was actually just a girl—if out of her teens, then just barely so. Despite her weather-beaten look under her floppy hat, she had a pair of bright green eyes and wispy blonde hair leaking out from beneath the hat.

She was also pregnant. They were on the road that day—the guy told them when he saw the quizzical look on Sean's face—hitching from their hometown of Colorado Springs to Aspen and a commune located near there. A woman in that commune was known as the best midwife in the "Free Zone," and they wanted their child to have the best entry into the world possible. Word was that the Aspen commune was a very happening scene, made up of men and women who had *really* dropped out.These men and women were busy with raising the crops and the structures the commune would need to survive.

"Man, they're putting up domes," the guy said, his dark eyes glowing. "You dig? Geodesic, man. Just like that ol' Fuller cat said."

Man, Sean thought, looking at the gray swirling mist and skies outside the cab of the truck as they rode up the two-lane road higher into the mountains. They're going to need those domes, all right. It's only July. He couldn't imagine the winter there. Not coming from sub-tropical Florida as he had, where a cold winter day was maybe 70 degrees. He had read stories about the harshness of winter in the western ranges, the Donner Party saga being one that stayed with him. When the snows settled in and the temps were way past zero, domes or not, he figured it could be a rough time for that commune—a rough time for a newborn for sure.

"A commune, huh? In … what'd you call it? The'Free Zone'?" He took one of the beers Harv was handing out from the travel cooler stashed on the floorboards. "So the Revolution is still on?"

"Revolution's over, man. They already won." The hippie looked sorrowfully at the beer in his hand while his woman sipped quietly at hers. One of her hands cradled her stomach, her eyes looking ahead at the road. "Nope, those fuckers won all right."

"Who won?" Harv looked over the top of the couple's heads at Sean, a genuinely puzzled look on his face. "Wasn't aware there was a freakin' war going on. I miss something or what?"

"No man. Not that. The fuckin' straights won. Dig?" The hippie swiveled his head back and forth from Sean to Harv, his dark eyes shining. With righteous anger, was Sean's guess. "Man, Morrison was flat wrong. He had it down about them havin' the guns and all. But we sure as hell didn't have the fuckin' numbers. You know, man? Fuckin' *five to one*, man?"

"Yeah, I hear you all right," Sean said softly.

"Ah man." Harv popped the top on his beer. "Not that old shit again, huh boys and girls?" That grin was back on his face. "Fuck that noise, man. I just want to get high and have some fun. Nothing's gonna change in this old fucked up world."

"I dig that my brother," the hippie said. "Getting high's all that's left." He patted his woman's stomach. "That, and my old lady here," and the two of them smiled at one another.

"That's right," Harv said. "Fuck all that Revolution crap. "It's nowhere, man."

Sean said nothing—just kept his eyes on the road and drove. There was nothing to say. Not that he could think of.

The last long grade up into the range began to level out and just on the outskirts of a small town nestled up against the drab rock cliffs, they came upon a gravel pullover where a Colorado Park Service sign announced: Independence Pass, elev. 12,095 ft. Below this in bolder letters: **The Continental Divide**. Sean parked in the designated area, and everyone piled out of the truck to stretch their cramped limbs in the cold air blowing down from the mountains.

July, Sean remembered, as he stood next to a low brick wall bordering the designated scenic spot. *It's only July.* At that elevation, July or not, there wasn't much summer to be seen. On the other side of the low brick wall was apparently the Great Divide. It didn't look any different from the rest of the landscape—looked the same as the rest of the brown, barren ground and scraggly trees reaching up towards the surrounding peaks. Snow covered the very tops of those far off peaks— snow Sean was willing to bet covered those peaks year round. Gray swirling clouds, blowing across the sky on the cold wind currents, added to the starkness of the day. A small pond, gray as well because of the overcast, lay on the other side of the brick wall, the cold winds ripping down from the mountains pushing the surface of the water.

It certainly wasn't the roaring river he had imagined would be there, flowing east on one side of the divide, miraculously enough, west on the other. He laughed at his foolish image—turned back then for the Jeep and the beer he'd left perched on the dashboard.

"Sean. Hey, Seano!" Harv's loud voice rang out. "Look at me, Buck. Look at me." He was standing out in the road, his legs astraddle an unseen line in a grossly exaggerated manner, face contorted in a goofy smile, his arms raised to the sky. "I'm a split personality, man." He held a can of Budweiser in one hand, the joint the hippie guy had fired up once free of the crowded truck, dangling from Harv's mouth. "Part of me's in the east, and part of me's in the west. I'm a freakin' schizoid, Buck."

"You are, Bro, you are," the hippie cried out as he and his old lady danced around Harv. In the spirit of that dance, Harv launched into one of his own, stomping his legs up and down within the moving circle created by the hippie and his woman. "You're wild, man, but I dig you," the hippie yelled before prying the joint out of Harv's fingers and putting it to his lips. A cloud of reefer smoke drifted in the cold air above the road as a horn blowing tractor-trailer rig came chugging up the grade, scattering the dancers to safety on the side of the road.

"You're something all right," Sean said as he started back again for the Jeep. "No doubt about that."

But something about the whole scene wasn't right. He hadn't expected the Continental Divide to be so ordinary—hadn't expected it to be a letdown. Yet it was. There, way up in Independence Pass, with snow covered mighty Mt. Elbert glowering down, the Great Divide was just another road sign along the highway.

A half hour later they dropped the hippie couple off in the middle of Aspen and rode on. It was getting close to the end of the afternoon and Sean wanted to make Glenwood Springs, the campsite there, before night came all the way on. A soak in the hot springs sounded like a good way to end the day. Then in the morning, back into the truck and out on I-70 again, west towards Utah. He had heard Utah was wild. Had heard it was truly beautiful. Perhaps something was there.

~35~ Las Vegas

Sean parted ways with Harv in Las Vegas, the Lucky 7 Campground in the desert outside of the glittering town being the last stop on the journey the two travelers shared. On a scorching August morning, clad only in cutoff Levis, they sat on the steps in the shallow end of the pool at the desolate campground drinking beer. Both of them were hungover from their adventures in Vegas the last three days. Not a breath of wind was available, making the hot morning even hotter. Way off across the desert valley, Sean could see the skyline of Vegas, shimmering like a mirage in the heat rising up from the desert floor. Hell, he thought. *It is a mirage.*

"Well now this is it for me, Buck." Harv took a long gulping pull off his beer, grimacing as the brew went down. It was a grimace Sean could relate to as he stared at the just-opened Bud in his own hand. "I ain't going on with you."

"Say what?" He almost choked on his first, tentative, drink of beer—whether from surprise at his traveling partner's statement, or the roaring hangover clawing at his senses, he couldn't say. "We're almost there, man. California can't be but another few hour's drive. Half a day, fucking tops."

"Nope. I'm sorry, Buck, but I'll be hanging on here for a while. With Caroline."

Caroline was the big-breasted, heavily dyed blonde barmaid Harv picked up, though more likely it was the other way around, their first drunken evening on the Strip. She was considerably older than Harv—at least in her mid-40's Sean figured—but now, three even drunker days later apparently Harv was planning to spend the rest of his immediate future with her.

"You've got to be kidding me, man." He took another sip of beer, glad it was beginning to taste a little better. "Jesus, buddy. You'd have been better off taking me up on my hooker offer. No offense," he added, seeing the frown come over Harv's face. He smiled at the memory of his first ever paid-for sex at the hotel room the hooker had taken him to that night in town. Ignoring the frown on his pal's face he repeated, "You'd have been a lot better off."

The hooker had cost him yet another of those crisp fifty-dollar bills from the traveling fund stashed in his money belt, those bills courtesy of the insurance settlement. But she had been well worth it. Especially after the last few days of hot, dusty, driving down from the mountains of Colorado and into the desert. He hadn't liked the desert. The bleak surroundings, cactus and prickly pear, the Martian looking red landscapes at dusk, the sandstorm that blew up on them outside of Albuquerque, filling their mouth, noses, and eyes with grit before they could get the windows of the Jeep rolled up. It was truly a land suitable only for "Horney toads and Ahab the A-rab," as Harv wryly pointed out after washing the sandstorm from his system with beer. When Sean informed him that Arabs didn't live in the deserts of America, Harv wasn't concerned. "Hell's bells, Sean, there you have it! How you and me're gonna make our fortune. We'll start importin' 'em. Charge 'em a hundred bucks a head, plus one night with the best-lookin' woman in their harems. To make it seem more like home to these newcomers, we'll throw in a free camel. What d 'ya say? Sound good?"

The redheaded hooker had a friend she told Sean. A friend for his friend. She had sidled up next to him at the Longhorn Saloon & Casino where he and Harv were drinking whiskey shots and beer. The western motif of the joint didn't really mesh with the rest of Vegas. But if the proprietors of the place felt that saddles, lariats, pictures of cowboys and rodeos, the boots and spurs the dealers wore, the Western style clothes the waitresses had on, were viable, then who was he to say? He was just happy to be out of the Jeep and in an air-conditioned place where the beer was cold, the music loud, and the women pretty. "You're new around here," the hooker told him.

"Don't you know it." For some reason she thought that was hilarious.

As if it were just a natural progression of the evening, the next thing he knew she was sitting next to him at the bar, drinking the watery-looking drinks he bought her as she listened to his tales of traveling with Harv. She was good looking, no doubt, around thirty with strawberry blonde hair and high cheeks above a sultry lipstick painted mouth. Sean was somewhat naïve, maybe—but not so much that he didn't know where she was coming from. But he liked her looks right away—liked the way her thighs in her tight jeans melded into the denim. He liked even better how she pressed her soft breasts against his arm when she leaned over to tell him about her friend being available for Harv.

But by that time Harv was spoken for. Caroline, who had been tending the bar when Harv and Sean sat down and ordered their first beers, had finished her shift. After freshening up in the ladies' room, and just as she had promised Harv, who had been drunkenly flirting with the chubby, bleary looking woman all evening, she came and sat with him.

"C'mon, sweetie," she urged, draping a fleshy arm possessively around Harv's neck. "Drink up and then we can dance."

"Jesus, Buck." That damn grin was all over his face. "I do believe I'm in love."

"That's right, sweetie. You and me are going to be great lovers," Caroline said, before giving Harv a long, sloppy kiss right there at the bar.

The last he saw of Harv that night he and Caroline were locked in a drunken embrace at the bar. Then Sean was out the door of the bar, into all the lights and noise of the Strip, while Renee, pressed tight against his side, whispered in his ear all the naughty things the two of them were going to do.

But that had been then. Now, in the hot daylight pounding down on the campground, the pleasures he had enjoyed with Renee were long past. All Sean wanted to do right then was to finish his beer, load up the truck and head out. California was right up ahead. Once they were down the road a bit, away from Vegas and hopefully in a greener clime, he would pull over, take a look at the Rand McNally, and decide on the best route to get there.

"No, Buck, I ain't kiddin'." Harv set his beer down on the pool deck and walked out into the water until only his neck and head were visible. In the bright sunlight he looked disembodied, just a talking head in the glare coming off the concrete pool deck. "I'm stayin' on with my baby. She's coming to get me this morning, as a matter of fact. Indeed, I do believe that's her a-comin' right now."

He came back to the shallower water where he stood up and pointed across the desert towards Vegas. Sure enough, when Sean turned to where his pal was pointing, he could see a long dust trail blowing up above the graded road leading to campground. In front of the dust was Caroline's purple 1962 El Dorado.

"Wow buddy." Sean drained what was left of his beer. "I just can't believe you sometimes."

"Ah now, Seano. Ain't nothin' but a thing. You know that."

"I guess. I guess I should know that by now."

"That's exactly right, Seano."

Two hours later, after the new lovebirds had loaded Harv's things in Caroline's Cadillac and headed back off across the desert, to Vegas and whatever awaited them there, Sean was moving west, alone now in his Jeep, away from the fabled city. His head throbbed a little less than it had been, but was still crowded with frayed thoughts—mainly centered around: *Just what in the hell was going on?*

What in the hell?

~36~ I-15 South

Sean drove all that day, long hours across more desert. With Harv no longer a part of the journey things didn't seem quite so innocent anymore. He was a far way from home. If the shit were to hit the fan it would be just him to clean it up. He wasn't sure if he liked this new going-it-alone thing, but it looked to be what he had.

He kept the truck radio turned way up, listening to a mélange of C&W, some underground rock from a pirate station god knows where and that didn't last long, a black, gospel station for a little while, Top 40, whatever he could tune in that created sound—anything to override the droning noise of the tires on the asphalt threatening to bore right through him. He bought a six pack before getting on the interstate, and as he wheeled across the last stretch of Nevada desert, he nursed those beers steadily; well past the point when his hangover had ceased. Keeping him company, along with the beer and the music were his thoughts. He much preferred the cold beer and the crackling radio. Some of his thoughts scared him—consisting as they did of a long, rambling narrative apparently centered on fear. These thoughts were as desolate as the land he rode across.

Once over the state line into California he began to feel better. He stayed well west of Los Angeles, giving that smog covered metropolis as wide a berth as possible and still keep on course for the coast. He stopped for something to eat in a little town on the edge of a national forest. Over a greasy burger and fries at a quick stop joint he studied the Rand McNally, looking for back roads around LA.

According to the road atlas if he pressed on he could make the coast before nightfall, to a black spot on the map called Ventura. Looking at the black spot, circled by various colored lines indicating highways and such, he seemed to recall a song mentioning that town. He couldn't remember the tune, or the words, and it didn't matter. Visions of a semi-decent motel, a hot shower, something better than a greasy burger to eat, and a bottle of bourbon, flooded his consciousness. With that image for a dangling carrot, he wheeled the Jeep back onto the highway.

The next morning—refreshed by a good night's sleep on clean sheets, several strong drinks, an okay dinner at a family run steak house not far from the beach at Ventura—he was back on the road. His intent was to make San Francisco that day, another long haul. But he was rested, his belly full, the two days' long hangover accrued in Vegas, finally gone. He felt good, and it was a good day for a long ride, what with the western sun as he ran up the coastal highway, sparkling down out of an amazingly blue sky.

The Pacific Ocean on his left as he drove seemed so different, so unlike the Atlantic he knew from home. Bigger waves, for one thing, crashed upon the shoreline. He came upon, and passed, busy surfer beaches that were like scenes straight out of a Beach Boys' song— though with a leaner, hipper look. Blonde and tanned longhaired girls and boys wearing bikinis and baggies hung out in the sun. In the water beyond the break, surfers sat on their boards, bobbing up and down in the swell as they waited for a good wave.

Outside of Grover Beach he pulled into a parking lot at one of those beaches. It was almost noon and between his legs, bought at the last convenience store he passed, nestled a cold tall boy wrapped tight in a brown paper bag. Sitting in the cab of the truck, he watched a couple of hot doggers do their thing—zipping gracefully down the faces of high crashing waves on their boards, the sunlight creating rainbows in the spray blowing off the waves. One of the hot doggers either lost his balance or miscalculated. Either way he disappeared beneath a wildly breaking wave. Meanwhile, his partner blasted under the curl, riding the long tube until the wave began to die and he glided on the foamy crest up to the beach where his wiped-out buddy stood waiting for him. The two surfers laughed, punched one another on the shoulders, and gesturing at the ocean yelled something Sean couldn't hear. Then they were back in the water, paddling out through the break to do it all over again.

He reached San Francisco in the late afternoon and spent that night in a funky motel on a side street off of Grant. It was cool that night and wanting to breathe fresh air he left the window open. From outside came the night sounds of city traffic going by on Grant, this sound mingled with the murmur of people's voices lifting up from the sidewalk. Sometime in the night a throbbing in his left leg, a residual from the accident and the metal plate holding the bones together, woke him. It was very cold in the room and getting up from the bed he went to close the window he had forgotten about and left open. But standing there by the open window he could hear the soft, far away moan of a foghorn somewhere out in the bay—could see how the street lights were muted by a thick fog that had rolled in while he was sleeping.

The throbbing in his leg reminded him again how the accident had taught him for the first time that he was not invincible. A rude awakening no doubt. But one he had a funny feeling other young men his age had gone through—or were going to before it was all over. It could have been worse. The doctor told him so more than once. Told him during the many examinations following the surgery that he was lucky not to have lost the leg. This was a sobering fact, no matter how much he tried to take it lightly—telling himself every time he left the doctor's office that once again his luck had come through for him. Yet, there had been nights, after the accident, in his bedroom at his mother's condo on the inlet, when the moaning of the whistle buoy out past the jetties, sounding much like that distant foghorn coming through the open motel window, would wake him. The muted sound of that buoy, for whatever reason, seemed to bring home the fact that not only was he not invincible—but alone. No matter how much he chose to believe that wasn't so.

Well, he was certainly all by himself now, Sean thought as he closed the motel window. No Harv riding with him. Or Boober, like they had done that summer three years back when everything had been so different. *No, he was on his own all right.* No traveling partners, no roommates, no girlfriend, no mom sleeping in her bedroom down the hall in the condo—no one at all anywhere close. It was just good old lucky Sean Morgan. Twenty-four years old now and finally on that quest he had envisioned that long ago night in the living room of the Cave in G'ville.

And now here he was. It had just taken him a little longer than planned to get there. That was all. And now that he was there, the throbbing in his leg and the fog enveloping the city, would be gone by morning. Yes, come morning it would all be different and he would be okay.

Except come daylight the fog was still there. And window finally closed or not, it was damp and cold in the motel room. Pulling on his jeans and boots he dragged a sweatshirt down over his tee shirt and headed out to see what was up. He found a diner on the corner down the street stuck in amidst the brownstones and Victorian style houses. He ate a hot breakfast there: over-easy eggs, crisp bacon, and whole wheat toast. After his breakfast he lingered over several cups of hot coffee in the comfortable little diner, enjoying the sounds of the people—blue and white collar workers, a boy and a girl with book bags on their backs, a couple of older, most likely retired, men—talking at the counter next to him or at the tables by the wall—enjoying how their voices seemed to blend in all together with the smells of the cooking coming from the kitchen on the other side of the counter.

Sitting in the busy diner he felt he was part of this new community he'd found himself in. But once the diner began to thin out, the collared men off to their jobs, the boy and girl off to school, the retired men off to wherever they went, that feeling of being a part of began to fade. With nothing left to gain by being there, he paid his bill and followed the others out the door and on to the sidewalk, where the morning sun was doing its best to break through the fog.

~37~ The Hashbury

The high point of his first morning in San Francisco was the time he spent in the City Lights Book Store. And what a bookstore it was. Racks and racks of books to get lost in. Books, magazines, newspapers, local and foreign, there just to be picked up, thumbed through, read, and maybe bought. Many of them were by obscure writers and poets he had never known existed, along with many by those he did know and had read. He picked up a copy of *On the Road* and immediately remembered how he'd stolen a copy of that book from the drugstore on Federal Highway when he was fifteen. Remembered again how after finishing it he ran away from home the next day, bound and determined to do what the book suggested: get on the road, find your kicks, and just dig all that life had to offer, the joys, and the sorrows. *LIFE.*

All the while he was there a steady stream of people came in and out of the store. Some of these were shaggy haired hippies, their eyes a-glitter with the drug of the day. Others were cool beatnik types, most of them somewhat older than the hippies, dressed in black, their eyes serious with the moment, books of poetry and essays tucked under their arms. Also in the mix were Middle American tourists, bundled up against the damp morning coming off the bay, faces agog with the wonders already seen on the streets of the city—now inside this wild and intelligent place so unlike their local library back at home, staring at book covers with photos of dangerous looking people on the covers. Music from Jefferson Airplane, the Grateful Dead, Moby Grape, filled the room with sound—unlike the libraries back home where silence was the rule. And downstairs in his office? Ferlinghetti, cool architect of the scene, Protector of the Flame as some would have it.

He bought four books, two by Kerouac he hadn't read, *Naked Lunch* by Burroughs, and *Howl*, by Ginsburg. One of the Kerouac books was *Big Sur*, which Sean thought might be sort of karmic since he was so close to that place and intended exploring it even further. *Desolation Angels* was the other one, bought mainly because of the title seeming so cool. With his books in the plastic bag, he left the store and headed toward the Wharf, figuring somewhere along the line he would find the bus for Haight Ashbury.

Walking through North Beach towards the bay he was glad he left the truck back at the motel and decided to hoof it, or make use of public transportation. Trapped behind the wheel, navigating unfamiliar streets, would have been a pain in the ass. Not only that, but he wouldn't have been able to pay attention to what he was going by, hear the talking of the people around him, or breathe the air of the city. The exhaust fumes from the buses and big trucks rumbling by, were noxious, yes, but fortunately blown away quickly in the clean, salt-laden breeze coming up from the water. And really, when he thought about it, those noxious fumes were just part and parcel of any big city anywhere.

After getting off the bus at the corner of Haight and Ashbury he wasn't prepared for what he found there. It was true that years ago, like many his age hearing the message, he had made the move to get high, let his freak flag fly, turn the world on, and do his best to affect the change. Now, judging by what he saw on the streets of the "Hashbury," it was clear no real and lasting positive change had been made. He had suspected as much before he even made it there. Still, the evidence up close like that was hard to take in. Proof that the Summer of Love was long over everywhere in the casualties littered along the sidewalks. Thin, pale, refuges from homes and lives they'd known elsewhere, dressed in Salvation Army duds and whatever else they could scrounge up, hung out on the stoops of the old Victorian apartment houses lining the street, or shambled listlessly among the crowds on the sidewalk. Flower Children past their prime, he thought as he walked with them. *Past their prime and stuck in nowhere.*

For a moment, in his bland Levis, boots, and sweatshirt, which after all were somewhat clean, he felt out of place again—just as he had in the diner earlier. But he only felt like that for a moment, what with Harv's comment at the campground outside of Vegas, "It ain't nothing but a thing, Seano." *Boy, wasn't that the truth?* What he was witnessing was nothing but a thing. And nothing he could do about it either. Other than being glad right then and there, that he had never boarded the proverbial Bus bringing those children here when it was taking on passengers. Glad that instead of joining in with the herd he had struck out on whatever his own might be.

On a wild whim he bought a nickel bag from a lean, black, dude in a camouflaged jacket who appeared out of nowhere at Sean's side The transaction took place in an alley way off the street where the black dude opened up his jacket to reveal inner pockets bulging with bags of weed. "Lids're twenty-five, man," the dealer said in a low, hurried voice. "I got dimes and nickels and some pre-rolled, too. So c'mon now and makes up your min', man. We gots to be quick here." He swiveled his head, looking up and down the alley. "The Man's been everywhere this week. Heat's somethin' furious on the street, no lie." Sean bought a tin foil packet of five joints for five dollars. "Some righteous weed there, man," the black dude said over his shoulder as he walked out of the alley toward the main drag. "You won't be bummed, my brother."

Sean waited a minute or two before following him out of the alley, the tin foil packet in his pocket made suddenly heavier when he considered the dealer's comment about the heat being furious lately. He had no idea if this sudden paranoia was justified. The black cat's hurried comments could have been just a jive to get him to buy without thinking. It was possible, he supposed, that any of the nameless faces pushing by him on the sidewalk could be an undercover narc. But seeing as how the only thing the people on the street appeared to share was a certain look of resignation, he didn't think that was the case.

He flashed on the hippie couple on their way to Aspen and "the best midwife in the Free Zone." *At least they still had a dream.* A hope of living life their way. Even if they already looked old before their time. Even if the male half of the couple had said the Revolution was over.

He could hear Harv's voice loud and clear. "C'mon now boys and girls. Fuck that revolution crap and let's get high." Getting high ,even if he was planning on doing just that in the near future, didn't seem to be much of a replacement for a once glorious Movement. But the hippie had said it was all that was left. On the damp, gray streets of the Haight Asbury that morning he didn't see anything to prove the hippie wrong.

He grabbed a trolley car down to Golden Gate Park, bumping along with the other tourists on board as the car bounced and clanged on the old rails as it made its way. It was a little after noon and the fog was finally lifting, the morning sun having broken through the gray clouds to burn the moisture away. As the sun rose higher he felt he could detect a change in those sharing the bouncing trolley car with him. The tourists began talking in a more animated fashion about their plans for the day, where they were going to go, what they were going to see. The locals were checking their packages or looking at their watches—but with smiles on their faces where there hadn't been before. He could feel his own mood lifting with theirs as the blue skies unveiled themselves, and when the trolley disgorged its passengers at the park, out beyond the green expanse he could see blue wave tips sparkling in the light streaming down on the Pacific Ocean.

After walking through the park for a while, letting his disappointment of earlier clear all the way out, he sat on one of the benches scattered throughout the area. Even with the warmth of the early afternoon sun, there was still a chill in the air. It felt good, though, and he took his sweatshirt off, enjoying the breeze from the ocean and the sunlight on the skin of his bare arms and face. Observing some longhairs on a blanket not far from his bench smoking a joint, he retrieved the foil packet from his jean's pocket and fired one up. *When in Rome.*

The park wasn't all that crowded: a few tourist couples snapping pictures as they strolled. The hippies getting stoned on their blanket. Some college students reading textbooks on the grass. And Sean on his bench. That was it. He smoked less than half of the joint, putting it out when the first head rush enveloped his body. He rarely smoked the stuff anymore, prone to get more paranoid than high whenever he did. But that afternoon—on a bench in the Golden Gate Park with the afternoon, indeed the summer, waning all around him, he felt secure. There was nowhere he had to go, and the rest of his life to do so, if and when he finally figured out just where it was he wanted to go.

Taking the copy of *Howl* out of the paper bag, he read the long poem all the way through. He wondered, as he read, who the Carl Soloman cat was Ginsberg had dedicated the poem to—wondered as well if he could say the same as Ginsberg had twenty some years earlier: "I saw the best minds of my generation destroyed by madness."

He wasn't all that sure who the best minds of his generation were. Wasn't sure if he even cared anymore. It felt good, though, being where he was right then, close to the edge of America, not far from where the land stopped and the mighty Pacific took over. His fears of two days before were gone. The disappointment washing over him as he walked the streets of the Haight? It was gone, too. He might not have found the IT that had Sung to him when he and Harv finally left the east coast behind and headed west. But if he hadn't, then surely it couldn't be too much further off. Not feeling like he did right then it couldn't be.

He dozed off a little in the sunlight, the warmth of the afternoon and the reefer making him drowsy. He didn't know how long he dozed but when he snapped out of it his head was in a fog and his fingers numb from holding the book he'd been reading. There was no one around him in his part of the park. The hippies getting stoned on the blanket must have cleared out while he nodded off, the tourists strolling the grounds, gone elsewhere as well. The Ginsberg book lay on the ground and when he picked it up the pages flew open in the breeze coming off the ocean. The half a joint he hadn't finished fell out of the flapping pages, and on instinct more than anything else, he grabbed it, stuck it in his mouth and fired it up.

"Care to share?"

A girl stood on the sidewalk in front of him, her features hidden in the shadows created by the sun at her back.

"It smells so good, dude, and I haven't been high all day." She paused for a moment, one hand stroking her chin in an exaggerated reflective gesture. "Come to think of it I haven't been high in … several days. Oh no!" Her trilling laugh floated off in the air as she stepped out of the shadows, that laughter vanishing in the breeze like the reefer smoke he'd exhaled as she spoke.

She was pretty, he realized, dressed in a loose, tie-dyed shift, and a Levi jacket. The blonde hair falling around her shoulders was held back from her face by a leather band, two colorful feathers of some kind jammed down in the band. Rounding off her semi-Native American look were brown suede moccasins. Her bright green eyes wide and alive in the afternoon light, her mouth partly open in a Mona Lisa like smile, she could just easily have been a stoned daydream.

Real, or not, he answered, "Sure," and handed what was left of the joint to her. Sitting down next to him on the bench, her soft body leaning against his as if she had known him all her life, she put the joint to her lips.

He closed his eyes as another rush washed over him, enjoying the feel of it and her body next to his. With his eyes still shut he listened as she took a long toke off the joint. After what seemed a very long time he heard her letting that toke out—could feel her body gone tight, then relax. Then it was like he was lost in a cloud of moke, a pungent smelling low hanging mass that covered his senses. Opening his eyes, he found that indeed, he was lost, in a massive pot cloud, the girl having taken another of those long hits and then blown it out all around his face.

"Wow," she said softly as she leaned again into his side. His arm had been lying across the top rail of the bench, and as if they were familiar lovers she pulled that arm down around her shoulder. "I needed that, dude. Got any more?" Then she let loose with that trilling laugh of hers, seeing, he was sure, the surprised look he knew was all over his face. "Now, don't worry, man. I'm not a narc or anything like that. And I'm pretty sure you're cool. I can tell by your aura. My name's Janie. What's yours?"

She collapsed again into laughter, her rush of words drifting off across the park in the breeze. He was laughing, too, as he rummaged in his pocket for the foil packet. Finally he was able to drag it out and offer one of the joints to the still laughing girl.

"Yeah, I've got more. There's three left after this one." When her laughter finally stopped, she extended her hand to him, and he took it—again from instinct more than anything else. "I'm Sean. Pleased to meet you."

"Likewise, I'm sure." She pumped his hand rapidly up and down, the half-smile back on her face. "Shall we get high?"

'Yes, lets," he said—the day, and the girl changed everything.

~38~ Pacific Coast Highway

Late that night, with the windows of the motel room left wide open again, Sean and the girl lay naked on the bed, their bodies covered in a fine sheen of sweat. The outside sounds of the city were the same as they had been the night before—even the moaning fog horn from far out in the bay. Sean knew if he were to go to the window and look out he would see the streetlights covered again with fog. All was the same. Except the naked girl lying beside him.

They had spent the rest of the day together, eventually winding up back at his place after a meal in a little Italian joint she knew of in North Beach. There was no hustle to the girl. She was simply the free spirit she claimed to be. Having fled her parent's house, the suffocating life they provided in Ohio, when she was fifteen, she made her way to the free Mecca of San Francisco. That was many years ago, she told him. A lot had happened.

Somehow she survived the perils of the aftermath of the Summer of Love. Survived even when others around her were succumbing to the crystal meth and other drugs biker gangs were importing into the Haight. Removing herself from the scene, she found a waitress job at a joint that asked no questions. She still worked there, almost ten years later. Art school was a part of her life now. Music, too, along with the small apartment she shared with another girl from school. Occasional love affairs were another aspect of her life. She was twenty-five and free, she said. Free to follow her impulses. As long as she did no harm. Do no harm was her motto. Her impulses had brought her many a good adventure—had kept her sane and alive. She hoped, she told him, as she leaned across the checkered tablecloth covered table in the Italian restaurant, that he would be one of those good adventures. He hoped so as well.

In the darkness of the motel room after all was said and done, they made love. She was wet and open to his touch, and the sounds of the streets outside coming through the open window provided a driving beat for what they did, Sean marveling all the while at the whims of life. Of how things, people, appeared when nothing like that seemed remotely possible. Something was there, too, between him and the girl. Not love—but different somehow from the drunken, groping he had experienced outside of the two relationships he'd been in before. Thrusting into her he looked down into Janie's half-open eyes, her legs wrapped around him urging him on, that slight smile on her face. Then she was moaning. "Uh, uh, uh," as her body strained beneath his. And though he wanted to hold off just a little longer—*it felt so damn good, so necessary he do so*—he couldn't. And he came, the girl pulling him into her deeper than he thought he could go.

Opening her eyes fully she looked into his. "Oh yeah," she said.

"Yeah." It seemed like the right thing to say. Whether it was or not, he didn't know. .

After spending the next day roaming the city together, on the following morning they headed out of Frisco, southbound on Highway 1 to Big Sur to camp for a couple of days. Janie knew of a place below Carmel on the edge of a state park there. A good place to camp, she said. All of this brought forth when he mentioned how he wanted to check out the Big Sur and she said, "Let's go, I have a few days before school starts."

Her going with him hadn't been something he thought about beforehand—but like that afternoon in the park when she suggested they get high, he said, "Sure. Sounds good."

They left the city early the next morning not long after daybreak with take-out cups of hot coffee from the diner down the street in their hands. When they were below Palo Alto the fog began to lift, and he could see the ocean off to the west. In the leftover mist from the fog he could just make out the water stretching off in the distance. To where, he wondered. Infinity, he supposed.

Neither of them seemed to have much to say as they drove along the coast. Sitting next to him Janie rested one hand lightly on his thigh, the other reaching out occasionally to change the radio dial. He was content with this, the wild ocean against the rocks below the highway as he drove barely heard above the whine of the truck's tires on the fog wet road—content with the feel of her body next to his.

They pulled off once just before Carmel to turn into Big Basin Park south of Saratoga. After refilling their coffee at a roadside stand he wheeled the Jeep down a graded road to where the big redwoods grew. The ancient trees reaching up to the sky amazed him. It amazed him as well that man had ever been able to bring something so magnificent crashing down to earth.

"I'm hungry, man," she said as they rolled into Carmel, her first words since they had made love in the dark hours of the morning. "Too much caffeine. Has me all lost in my head. Some food might cut the edge, if you can dig that." She smiled.

Her moods were infectious. He had learned this in the short amount of time they'd been together. Like her, he had been swirling along in his own thoughts as he drove, not all of them as pretty as the country they moved through. It was good to see her smiling. It gave him hope for a good day.

After Carmel and a hot breakfast they were in the Big Sur proper, where cliff faces dropped away suddenly from the highway down to the ocean below. Equally, sheer cliffs rose up on the landward side of the road, the rock overhangs reminding him of the grades up into the Rockies. Not quite as severe, perhaps, but still impressive.

Traffic was light that morning and for the most part he and the girl were alone, traveling the man-built highway through primordial wilderness. On a sudden whim he whipped the truck into a scenic pullover where they stood on the brink looking out, and down, at the sea. The pullover was above a cove rounding into the shoreline, and with the wind off the ocean blowing Janie and his hair back from their faces, he watched the waves crashing into the cut over two gnarly rock formations rising up like ancient sentinels at the opening of the cove. Sea birds wheeled in the sky, their shrill cries echoing off the rocks and scraggly trees growing out from the sides of the cliffs. It was pushing towards noon, and the fog had completely disappeared. In the clear noon light he could see how it was going to be another glorious day. Like the day before last—when he was bouncing along on the crowded trolley through the streets of San Francisco—he felt his spirits lift up with the sunlight.

From the pullover they drove another ten miles, the highway curving inland away from the coast through what a brown park's sign said was the Andrew Molera State Park. On the southern boundary of this park they came upon a little two-track heading west back towards the ocean. "Quick, turn here." Janie had been dozing but now sat up straight and alert. "That's the road we want, dude."

Taking her word for it he turned off. The track cut through dense underbrush before opening up into a green, sloping valley where trees lined the far edges, the track finally dead-ending at a stand of small trees and brush. A small hiking trail led away through the trees and brush, another of those brown Park Service signs at the entrance stating: Cooper's Point. They left the truck and walked down the trail, a quarter of a mile later coming out to the point. And there was the ocean again, battering the shoreline as it had been for millennia upon millennia.

It was overwhelming—all that raw beauty. The Rockies had scared him at times, with their tremendous heights, and then, just inches away from the road, their fearsome depths. But the western ocean had called to him for a long time and from very far away. Now he was there, and from what he could tell of the Pacific's blue vastness it was never ending.

Returning to the truck they headed back up the two-track to the edge of the valley. Following Janie's directions he wheeled off the road and across the grass covered valley floor to a tiny copse of trees. It wasn't exactly a legal camp site, she explained. But it was out of season now, and she and some friends had camped there before.

'It's perfectly fine, man." She cut him off when he started to question where her finger pointed. "Believe me, it's cool." The smile on her face was enough to convince him and he said, "All right."

Whether it was cool or not the spot was a great place to set up camp. Behind the group of trees a small creek ran toward the sea. Standing in the shade of the trees he could hear the steady sound of the water following its course. Sunlight filtered down through bare spaces in the treetops so that the surface of the creek was a mix of dark and sparkling blue flashing a sunlight prism into his eyes.

She was no stranger to camping and as they worked together at pitching the nylon two man tent he thought how she was actually a better hand at it than Harv had been. She hammered the stakes in confidently, secured the proper lines, and managed her end of the poles capably as they raised the tent up. While he was unloading the camp stove, lantern, cooler, and other needed items from the bed of the truck, she opened the window flaps, erected the doorway awning, and swept out the inside of the tent. When that was done she spread out the sleeping bags and blankets he handed her, creating a cozy bed for the two of them in the center of the tent.

As he started back to the truck, thinking to check and make sure he hadn't forgotten anything, he turned and saw her standing in the doorway of the tent observing her handiwork. She was wearing the same cotton dress she had on the afternoon they met, the sunlight pouring into the nylon enclosure lighting up her loose, blonde hair. The light also made the material of her dress nearly transparent. Seeing the swell of her breasts against the cotton, a sudden rush of pure lust washed over him. Just then she turned in his direction, her green eyes boring into his. Smiling, she crooked a finger his way, beckoning him on.

It was a quick and furious love they made. Lying down on the sleeping bag she simply pulled the cotton dress up past her naval, while Sean, dropping his jeans, fell between her open thighs and was inside of her. She grunted beneath his sudden weight and then—as he saw it—they rutted like the wild animals he imagined to be watching them from the shade of the trees surrounding the campsite. When it was over they lay panting on the sleeping bags. A shaft of late afternoon sun came through the open side window flap, lighting up the blonde pubis of her sex. He rolled over on his side, following the shaft of light with his eyes to where it shone on the matted hair between her thighs.

"God," he said. "I wish I knew what was happening here."

She turned away from him for a second and suddenly it seemed as if he were alone in the tent. But when she turned back to look in his eyes the small Mona Lisa smile was back. Wherever she had gone in that moment of time, she had returned.

"Don't worry about what's happening. Just let it." Untangling from his embrace, after stretching out her limbs she got up. "C'mon, dude. There's still work to be done."

For the next three days they hung out in the valley. In the mornings they hiked the trails along the creek and up into the hills. One sunrise they walked quietly down to where the creek fed into the sea. It was low tide, the winds out of the west had not yet risen, so that instead of pounding the shoreline there were only gentle swells rolling in. They watched wading birds feeding on the exposed flats, scooping up crabs and the other crustaceans making up their diet. Everywhere he looked it was raw, primeval, and with no sight of man. With the sun growing higher they made their way back up the creek toward the camp and the breakfast of eggs and bacon he planned to make on the camp stove. Walking with her at his side he thought of how alive he felt—thought of how he had truly, and finally, come to a Garden of Earthly Delights.

If the mornings were for exploring, the afternoons were for kicking back. He liked the quiet reading they did together on a blanket spread out in the sun away from the tent. He started the Kerouac book, *Big Sur*, but found it too depressing and put it down. Where he was at that moment in his life was no place to be reading about endless drinking and mental breakdowns. *Desolation Angels* was better he thought. He enjoyed the stuff about Kerouac gearing up and then heading off for his three-month tour as a fire lookout in the forests above Seattle. The Buddhism references in the books were sort of new to him, but interesting, and something he thought he might look into down the road.

Janie was reading "Leaves of Grass," for the "umpteenth time," she told him. She read aloud some of the long poems as he lay beside her, her voice strong, the expressions of her face giving emphasis to what she read. "I sing the body electric," he heard the voice of the old Poet Father say through her. And for the first time—unlike all those times in school when he had struggled to—he understood the joy the long dead graybeard had written about.

The best part of this afternoon reading, he felt, was when they dozed off together on the blanket in the sun, her body next to his when they did.

At night they sat around the fire, talking of where they had been, where they might be going, what it was like where they were, and what it was going to be like when they reached where they needed to be. Afterward, after dinner, wine, and marijuana, they would make love in the silent darkness of the tent. And then sleep.

They were both quiet around the fire the last night of the trip. He had found a bottle of whiskey behind the seat of the truck that Harv must have left behind. Keeping an eye on the veggie packs he'd placed in the hot coals, he sipped from the cup of whiskey on ice he had made for himself. Janie, even though there was still some red wine left, wasn't drinking. Instead, she sat next to him on the log he had pulled by the fire without saying anything.

"It's been nice," he finally said, tired on the silence hanging in the air between them. "These last few days and all. Too bad we have to go back."

It seemed pretty lame to him, but it was true, and he didn't know what else to say.

"Yeah, it has been nice." Her green eyes glowed in the light from the fire. "I hate the end of things."

"Maybe it doesn't have to end."

But he knew the answer to that one—had felt it in her as the day grew on.

"School starts up the day after next, Sean." Raising her eyes up past him and the fire she wrapped both arms around him. "Nothing ever lasts with me. I'm sorry but I'm just not like that. This has been real, you, me, all this. Yet, it's not. It's just another part of my big dream."

And there was that trilling laugh of hers he hadn't heard all day.

"I know it probably doesn't make any sense to you. And I can dig that. But it's how it is for me."

"Makes sense, I guess." He hesitated, looking into her eyes reflecting the light from the fire. "I was going to head south, you know? Down the coast into Mexico, maybe. But maybe I could stay on in Frisco. Get a job, you know? See what happens, you know, between you and me?"

He had a quick flash of how it might go: nice homelike scene, he, working at some mundane daily gig, bringing home the paycheck and all. Janie doing her art and music scene. In between that making their pad all domestic like and such.

"It's not like I really have to be anywhere, you know," is what he told her.

"Oh, dude. That's not true at all. You're just passing through, Sean. I saw it all over you in the park that afternoon."

She kissed him quickly on the mouth, and when she drew back from him the half smile was there on her face.

"That's what drew me to you in the first place."

~39~ Big Sur

She said she was tired, and disappeared into the tent to crash, while Sean stayed out on the log in front of the fire. The coals in the fire pit made a popping sound as they dwindled down. He wished he had some sort of constant—a reason for his coming and going. Janie had told him he was just passing through. While she took things as they were. It was as simple as that. Not that she had said so. But she had seen a cute guy smoking dope in the park one afternoon and curious as to what might happen had forced the issue. It was her way. She had her life and his part in it was coming to an end. Even if he had offered to stay on. Even if he wanted to stay. But she said no. Said school was starting soon and she had to be there. Leaving him to be wherever he was.

He hadn't figured on the girl, despite that other part of his vague vision—the part where somewhere along the way he finds "The One." *The other half of him. The one who will travel with him, both of them sharing in his golden dream of the West.* Despite that vision he hadn't figured on Janie. Probably even knew from the first she wasn't the face of his vision. Look at Harv. He hadn't figured on a girl either. And then Caroline came along. A woman, true, and not exactly a girl, but still. Harv had ridden a way with him, the two of them adrift in a big country, following that long held vision of Sean's. That vision didn't matter to Harv. The ride was the thing, and it had been a good one. As long as there was beer and some laughs, Harv was okay with it. But they hit Vegas, Harv found Caroline, and that was as far west as he needed to go. "Ain't nothing but a thing," he said. And that was that.

The wind picked up, coming down into the valley from the high ground off from the camp site. He could easily picture that wind meeting the ocean in the dark—two un-stoppable forces, a frightful cataclysm of sound and foam and breaking water. All of it coming and going. Always on, never off.

Out of nowhere he thought about his mother. Wondered how she was doing back home in the condo. That inlet just more water coming and going without end. He hoped his mother was doing okay. Hoped the judge was taking care of her. He was a good man, that judge. A kindly, but also stern at times looking man in his 50's, who not only helped Sean's mother out when necessary, but had also pushed Sean's insurance claim through after the accident, in the process securing a bigger sum than the insurance company wanted to pay. Did more for

Sean than his own father ever had was how Sean saw it. Took him seriously, listened to him on the rare times the two of them were alone and talking. Like they had the night before Sean left town, the judge asking him where he was planning on going, and when Sean said, "West," the judge had asked, "Taking Horace Greely's advice, I take it?"

Smiling when Sean told him, "Something like that."

Still smiling the judge had wished him luck, and then added, "Listen, if you get in a jam out there, or simply need some advice, just call me. I'll do my best to help." And then surprising Sean even more said "I love your mom, Sean. I hope you know that. I want more than anything in this world to marry her. But my wife, being the good Catholic she thinks she is, won't divorce me. So there you have it, son. I'm stuck. And so is your mother, God bless her. God bless her, too, for understanding and not making me feel like a jerk about the whole thing."

Sean didn't know what to think about these revelations—other than that they were grownup problems. His next flash being: *Hell, I'm a grownup. Right?* That night with the judge seemed like a long time ago now as he sat in front of the fire. Seemed like a long way away, too, when he thought about the miles that lay between him and his mother's condo on the inlet. There had been a time not so long ago when he thought the more miles between him and his hometown the better. Now, he wasn't so sure.

It sounded like the surf was picking up, driven by that wind, the sound of it almost screaming in his head as he sat drinking. The whiskey, like the fire in front of him, burned its way down his throat, lighting up a fire in his gut and making him drunk when he wasn't sure being drunk was a good thing. Deciding it wasn't, he tossed the bottle in the fire, his eyes glued to it, hoping to see it melt back into the sand it once had been. *Just more of that coming and going thing, dig?* Bottle into sand. His father. His mother. Even the judge. Those students protesting in Gainesville the night Pinko was killed. The cowboy and his girlfriend at the Old Dillon Inn—a cowboy who couldn't win a game of pool if his life depended on it. Harv had known that and drank free because of it. The hippie couple on their way to Aspen. The big letdown of the Continental Divide. Harv meeting Caroline, the last Sean saw of him being the back of his head in her Caddy as they roared down the road towards Vegas. And now Janie, sleeping in the tent. People coming and going in his life, seemingly with a purpose he could not understand.

It was all just too much to think about. The fire went out and in the dark all around him he suddenly wanted to cry. Instead, he stumbled his way into the tent and went to sleep.

~40~ I-80 East

It was a long haul east and there were times on the road he wasn't sure if he had made the right call. Voices without faces whispered to him during the silences between radio stations on some of the long stretches between towns. Sometimes, getting on, or off of the interstate east, feelings of déjà vu would wash over him. He didn't know if it was because he had been at that particular place with Harv in their travels—or did the faint feelings of being there before came from something deeper? Cracking open a fresh beer one late afternoon as he pulled into a KOA campground in desolate nowhere Wyoming, he decided his sad thoughts and questions of that drunken evening by the fire while Janie slept in the tent didn't mean much. They just were. He might be stuck with them but that wouldn't last.

Bustling about the KOA campsite the next morning as he prepared to hit the road, it struck him suddenly how glad he was to be alive. Alive, awake, and getting ready for another day of eating up miles—glad to still be on the planet as another summer was slowly coming to an end.

He was still young, after all. Somewhere out where it could all happen for him if he gave it a chance. He had seen the west coast of America. Heard and smelled the mighty Pacific as it crashed into the coast. Smoked marijuana in Golden Gate Park with the sun shining down and wrapping him in all the grace it had to offer. Part of that grace had been Janie. The time they spent together, getting high, talking, making love as if they had been doing so for a very long time. He had accomplished a big chunk of what he had set out to do—a fact he kept reminding himself of as he drove the unfolding miles back east.

He thought about her often—especially during those radio silences when he couldn't find a decent station to drown out his thoughts. Their goodbye had been awkward, mainly because of how he felt about it. Out on the sidewalk in front of her place, the noise and hustle of San Francisco an enveloping background he was only dimly aware of, Janie told him, "Thanks, Sean. For all of it."

"Yeah, that's cool. You're welcome." What else could he say? She knew what he really wanted—and wanted no part of it.

"Maybe I'll see you around again, dude." Her green eyes were lit up, that Mona Lisa smile across her lips, her mind probably focused on the next aspect of her life. "You know, sometime?"

"Maybe, huh?"

"You never know!" Then she was gone, up the steps of the old brown building where she lived, turning once at the top of the stoop to flash him a big smile. "Be good to yourself, Sean." The depths of the building took her then, the long blonde hair bouncing down her back the last he saw of her.

And yet, days later, she stayed with him, the thoughts of her and how he felt when he was with her. The clean, natural way she smelled. The urgency she exerted when they made love. Her easy smile and song-like laugh. And beyond all that, her pure acceptance of life—how one morning on the mud flat at the mouth of that river in Big Sur she had scooped up a handful of mud and water, letting it run out between her fingers as she laughed in the early sunlight.

"Oh, man," she'd told him as she wiped her now empty hands on her jeans. "Buddha was right, you know. We are all one. Every little bit of it. All the same."

He hadn't understood her then—did not understand her now. But he sure missed her as he drove.

It hadn't been Sean's intention as he rolled out of Frisco to go back east. As best he knew when he crossed the Golden Gate looking for the exit to Highway 1 he was on his way to Mexico. He had an idea of maybe hooking up with Angel, and her Prankster friends down in Puerto Vallarta. Could be cool, he figured, hanging with her and those cats on the beach in Old Mejico. Smoke some good reefer, maybe trip again with Angel and see where the vibes took them. That was his vague intention, at least, as he hooked up with the Pacific Coast Highway and headed south.

But as he was sitting in a booth in the back corner of a Jack In The Box outside of Monterey eating a greasy burger and some equally greasy fries, out of nowhere he realized he didn't really want to do that. Angel and he were a thing of the past, and hanging on a beach with a bunch of hipsters probably past their prime struck him as potentially being old news. A diner before him had left the day's newspaper on the table and picking it up and seeing that the day's date was August 15th, a Friday, was sort of the catalyst for his wake-up call on Mexico. Time was racing forward, and here he was, thinking about getting together with a girl he had known three years before, along with some people he did not know, all of them still lost in a scene that was gone. What he had seen on the sidewalks and streets of the Haight had convinced him of that. Convinced him all the way, in fact.

The day's headlines weren't very reassuring, and maybe that added to his sense of unease about where he might go be going and how time was racing along. Ronald Reagan was exploring the idea of a run for the presidency. Ronald Raygun as president? Nixon had been bad enough. A mediocre actor sounded even less promising for the country's prospects in the days ahead. Pakistan had accomplished a coup d'état in Bangladesh, a ceasefire in the Philippines between the ruling government and the Morro Liberation Front had been signed, and Betty Ford, apparently had sat down on 60 Minutes to shock the world with her views on marijuana and making abortion legal, while her husband was out and about on a tour of Europe, boring everyone he encountered.

The same old nowhere shit he thought as he folded the paper and left it where he found it on his way out of the fast-food joint. Nothing was new. Despite what people might think—this little insight more than enough to convince him that Mexico wasn't really where he should be heading. Without really thinking about it, he backed the truck out of the parking lot and turned away from the coast.

One morning, four days out of San Francisco, he awoke shivering after a fitful night inside the nylon tent. He was camped on the Platte River not far from Fremont, Nebraska. When he crawled out of the tent into the cold dawn he saw the broad river smothered in a low hanging fog. A plaque at a rest stop back on the highway had informed him he was following the trail of Lewis and Clark. Because of this unexpected information he had gotten off at the next exit and turned down a dirt road leading to the river, thinking to get closer to where those explorers had actually been.

Now, in the cool morning, he wondered if they had seen this river at daybreak as he was right then—the riparian banks shaded with cottonwoods and willows. Away from the bank on the other side, were hickory stands where deer, and other wild creatures hidden in the protective cover of those trees, might very well be staring back at the stranger on the other shore. He bet those men had indeed seen this river like that, and then some. While taking a long, draining leak at the river's edge, he thought of what the day ahead might hold for him. Thought suddenly again of how he was twenty-four years old and a long way from anywhere. Thought, for maybe the first time in a long time, of how very fine that was.

Zipping up, he turned from the river and headed back to the tent. "So be it." He spoke this aloud. There was no reply. No one there. Only the river hidden in the fog.

An hour later he broke camp and was back on the road.

~41~ Bramford again

"So tell me two things, O Wanderer," Teddie asked. "Where have you been and what are your plans now?"

"Not sure," Sean told her. "And no idea." And this was true—but aware of the silence suddenly between them he added, "Been a lot of places. Saw some things, too."

He had slept well the night before, the night of his arrival back in Bramford after almost two weeks on the road. Teddie had offered him the fold-out in the living room but he declined, unrolling his sleeping bag on the floor in the spare bedroom instead. He was used to the sleeping bag and except for the few times in motels during his recent travels it had been a while since he'd slept in a real bed. Sooner or later he figured to make sleeping in a real bed a regular thing. *When the time was right.* When he was somewhere more permanent he figured.

Now, some twelve hours after showing up at their front door, night coming on and cool air blowing in earnest down off Bramford Mountain, Teddie and he were sitting at the rickety metal dining table in the kitchen drinking coffee. Ron had been passed out when Sean arrived—when he got up that morning he was already gone to work. Teddie's shift at Friendlys didn't start until eleven and when she offered him coffee he jumped on the offer. Behind him, in the apartment's narrow living room, he could hear the TV, an unseen voice announcing that the "Mid-Morning Movie" was coming next. "'The Seven Year Itch' starring Marilyn Monroe and Tom Elwell." The TV announcer's voice faded out, rising up in its place was Anita Bryant singing a bouncy jingle extolling the benefits of drinking orange juice from Florida. For a moment, upon hearing the word Florida, Sean felt a rush of homesickness—that old, and familiar longing for something he was never sure he'd had.

"Well, I guess that answers my questions." Teddie's voice snapped him out of that homesickness thing. "Though instead of Wanderer perhaps I should call you Man of Few Words. Yes?"

She laughed, her eyes shining. With a start he realized it had been a long time since he had heard her laugh—probably not since that night in late April when he and Harv had first shown up at their place.

"But seriously, Sean, I hope I don't have to remind you that you're welcome to stay here for as long as you like. Or need. Ron and I don't mind. You know that, yes?"

'Yeah, I think I do. And thanks."

"Of course." She reached across the table and placed her hand on his. "But you need to lighten up around me. I was lonely that night is all. You've seen how Ron is."

"I've seen." He removed his hand from under hers—picking up his coffee mug to take a sip his excuse to do so. "It's cool."

It was silent again in the small kitchen, the wall clock above the stove ticking away in the uneasy stillness. She was a good-looking girl, he thought, no way around it. With sort of a Rubenesque type figure and dark hair falling down on her shoulders to frame her oval, almost Asiatic face and her deep, dark eyes—*yeah, she was good looking all right.* How she ever ended up with Ron was certainly a mystery. Ron, just a tall, lanky dude content now to work in the stock department at Bradleys over on Springfield Road. His nights and weekends spent drinking beer upon beer. Whatever fire once in him gone. That loss even more evident back in the spring when Sean and Harv had showed up, than it had been in the summer of 1972 when Red dropped him and Boober off on their doorstep. So, yes, how a beauty like Teddie had ever ended up with Ron was a question Sean could not answer—though there was a question he could. One asked by Teddie just a few minutes back.

"Hey, you know I finally saw that Pacific Ocean. Man, but it was nothing but amazing."

"Oh really?" As an afterthought, "Where's that buddy of yours? Harv?"

He didn't answer these two questions, enjoying as he did the curious look on her face. It reminded him of that 'night' she had mentioned earlier. A similar look had been on her face then. A night when Ron was passed out in the bedroom, Harv off God knows where, and Teddie and he were sitting out on the stoop, talking as they watched the tops of the oak trees on the other side of the driveway blowing with the gentle breeze. Sean surprised himself and kissed her. Even more surprising was the way she kissed him back, hard and, eager—until one of them, he wasn't sure who came to their senses and pulled away.

Whoever it was that pulled away, perhaps did so because they suddenly remembered another time. This was in G'ville, that summer Sean was on his own, Boober having mysteriously disappeared and Curly called home for the semester to work with his dad. Adrift, Sean had gravitated towards Ron and Teddie, the only others he knew in town at that time. One warm spring day they made the run over to Crescent Beach where they dropped some mescaline. While Ron was body surfing Sean and Teddie hung out on the beach, just going with the flow of the crystalline world they had found themselves in—when out of nowhere Teddie started kissing him. The kissing ended when Ron, coming out of the water and up on the beach, spied them and laughing yelled out, "Hey now, that's my old lady." Because of the good vibes from the mesc, and the lack of real malice behind what Ron had said, Sean started laughing too—before running down into the water and that was all. Now, sitting in Ron and Teddies kitchen, miles and years away from that day on the beach, and more recently, that night, he was reminded of how much he liked her—and of how very careful he needed to be around her.

Not only reminded of all that, but relieved when he remembered he had more to tell her. Much more.

"Hell yes, really." Having answered her first question, he moved on to the second one. "And Harv's a long story. He bailed on me in Vegas. For a strange chick he met at the casino. But I made it all the way to Frisco, and it was pretty damn cool."

"Oh man, I think I'm envious. Ron and I never go anywhere anymore."

"I checked out the Haight Asbury scene. Pretty fucking dead, nothing happening there at all except for a bunch of burn-outs." And now he was speeding up with his words, eager to tell it to *someone* after the last two weeks on the road by himself. "I went to the City Lights bookstore. Even saw Ferlinghetti there. Scored some good weed from a paranoid black cat and got very stoned in the Golden Gate Park. Made it down to Big Sur, too."

"Wow," she sighed. "I *am* envious."

"Met a pretty cool chick in Frisco."

"Should I be jealous?" She arched her eyebrows in a goofy way. "Even just a little bit?"

"I don't think so."

"Geez, Sean. There you go again being a drag. Lighten up, dude."

The way she said, 'dude' suddenly brought Janie into the small kitchen with them, and he was surprised at how quickly, how much, he missed her.

"It was her who took me down to the Big Sur. We camped in a very neat spot there by a river and the ocean for several days. Very cool."

"Do tell."

And he did. Decided to tell her all of it, beginning with: Vegas, the redheaded hooker, Harv meeting Caroline at the casino, the morning at the RV campground outside of Vegas and the dust kicked up by the wheels of Caroline's Caddy as she sped across the desert to get to Harv. He told Teddie of the loneliness he felt crossing the Nevada desert after Harv was gone. Of how he didn't know what he wanted or where he was going. That his head hurt from the three days of beer and whiskey drunk in Vegas. How the cold beer he nursed as he drove across the desert all the way to the California shoreline finally eased that hurt. He told her of how it was before all that—how he hadn't known really where he was going, other than a vague vision of West. But he had made it that far, to the showdown with Harv in Vegas, and well, after that, after Harv was out of the picture, he had no choice but to finish the ride. To see that other ocean. The fabled City. So he had kept on going and Janie was the payoff. He guessed. Had seemed so at the time for sure.

This rush of words didn't seem stoppable just then and he didn't try—went on to tell Teddie how everything with Janie seemed so right. Even told her how intense the sex with her was. And how lonely and small he felt after leaving Janie at her doorstep, the Big Sur behind them and only uncertainty in the front of him. And how he moped around the city for a few days afterwards, drinking beer in Kerouac's old bar, the "Vesuvius" next to City Lights. Told her of how he took to hanging around Golden Gate Park in hopes of running into Janie. Hoped beyond hope that if they ran into one another she might have a change of heart.

Then one morning he gave up on that, checked out of the motel off Grant, threw his duffel bag in the back of the truck and that was it. He was back on the road, as best he knew heading for Mexico, thinking to hang out in the sun with Angel and her Prankster pals, getting high, finding the groove and letting it all flow. But he changed his mind at the Jack in the Box outside of Monterey, struck as he was by the possibility that Angel and her pals, were probably living in a scene that wasn't even real—just a continuation of a past long gone. So leaving the Jack in the Box, instead of going south he turned east.

He told her how after that morning by the Platte River in Nebraska he headed into Michigan, camping in a state forest for a few days in the UP before going further north, into Canada. How after crossing over out of Detroit, he ran along the edge of the two countries, stopping here and there to camp where possible, sometimes staying in a motel for a shower and some real food, other than the hot dogs and beans he made at camp. Finally. he crossed back into the US at Niagara Falls. And from there— well from there, why here he was. Back where his journey west had begun almost four months before. How long he was going to stay was up to them. And that was it. He was done. Done talking. Exhausted suddenly from this he shrugged his shoulders as he looked up again into Teddies eyes.

"So, that's the all of it. What do you think?"

'Well, Sean." She stubbed out what was left of the cigarette she'd been smoking while he rambled on. The spiral of smoke from the cigarette lingered over their heads in the tiny confines of the kitchen, lit up in the muted beams of sunlight coming in through the back door window. "What I think is that you just had one fantastic journey and I'm happy for you that you have."

"Cool." And then, embarrassed for reasons he couldn't put a finger on, he added, "Thanks, Teddie."

"I know something else, Sean. I can relate to that Janie chick."

"Yeah?"

"Yeah. I could have been that girl. Damn, but I should be that girl. Living in a happening city. Having those 'adventures' as she called them. Doing something with my life. Instead of this," and she waved her hand around the room.

"Then change it. If you're so unhappy with it."

"What makes you think I can?"

"You and Ron used to talk about changing everything."

'Yeah, we did. But that was then. I don't know how to do that anymore." She stood up from the table, "It was all talk, back then, anyway. Right now, though, I've got to get ready for work. That much I *can* do."

She brushed past him on her way into the living room, where halfway across the narrow space she stopped and turned back to him, her face set in as serious an expression he had ever seen there.

"Things just never turn out how you envision them. Do they?"

"Jesus, Teddie. That's pretty damn grim. You really think that?"

"I do, my Wanderer. I'm the living truth of it."

She disappeared into the bedroom, and a few minutes later, while he sat on the sofa in the living room trying to tune into the Mid-Morning Movie, he could hear the rattle and banging of drawers being opened and shut, the stream of running water in the bathroom—all the mundane noises of a woman preparing for another day of work rising up to merge in with the sound of the TV and that of the outside world drifting in through the open window as he sat.

~42~ Boston Road

On an unseasonably warm Monday morning in late September he sat out in the front yard of the old apartment building watching the traffic go by on Boston Road. Most of the cars traveling the thoroughfare that morning seemed to be headed for Springfield. To work, or school, or wherever, he figured. Boston might be the destination for some of that traffic. If so, they were taking the long way to get there. Faster ways to get to "Bean Town" existed, he knew, the old post road running by the apartment in reality no longer serving the purpose it was designed for in the past.

Not that it mattered to him. He was comfortable where he was. Lounging in a lawn chair with a mug of fresh coffee the jeans and tee shirt he wore were plenty enough clothes for the seventy-five-degree temperature. The temps would climb into the mid-eighties by afternoon, if the last few days were any indication. But for now, the skies were a clear blue and a mild breeze blew down from Bramford Mountain. The leaves of the trees on the mountain had started to turn the week before when a short-lived cold front ripped through. Now, with the warmer days back, the once bright leaves lay scattered on the ground. Indian summer, Teddie called the mild days. Don't get used to it, she said. It won't last.

A Spiderman comic book, along with the current issue of Creem, lay on the ground next to his chair, courtesy of Ron. Apparently those two were the depths of Ron's magazine reading these days. Unlike before, when he first met Ron and Teddie, and Ron seemed to have in his possession every radical mag known to exist. Sean enjoyed reading Rolling Stone, like most people he knew—besides Harv, who was proud of avoiding any reading whenever possible—but he had never checked out Creem, which billed itself, according to the cover, as "America's Only Rock 'n' Roll Magazine!"

The cover was certainly interesting enough, displaying as it did a shot of a teenage girl in a cheerleading outfit upending a bottle of whiskey to her wide open mouth, hair and uniform in total disarray, and scattered around her on the ground she sat spread-eagled on, empty beer cans and bottles. Across her crotch area was stamped in a red-lined box: Special Report. The Booze Revolution. *A cover to catch one's eye, especially a red-blooded lad such as himself.* Above and beyond the revelations on today's youth's booze consumption, as opposed to the rampant drug use of the 60's and early 70's, the issue also contained articles about the Stones, Alice Cooper, Pete Townshend, and others making noise in the current rock music scene. He liked most of these musicians and looked forward to reading all about them once he finished with Spiderman.

Issue #49 of The Amazing Spiderman, according to the black boxed caption on the bottom of the cover, proclaimed to be "The astonishing climax of the Spidey-Jackal war! Even if I live ... I die!" The brightly inked cover, all reds, blues, golds, and greens, depicted two Spidermen swinging by their web shooters as they fought across the side of a skyscraper. Hanging by his wrists, chained to a bundle of dynamite lashed to a window ledge above the grappling Webslingers, was a man in a business suit. Hovering above him, a green, scaly looking creature, the Jackal, was in the process of lighting the fuse to the dynamite, saying as he did so: "The Jackal will have his Revenge!"

Sean figured the identity of the man chained to the dynamite, along with the reason for there being two Spidermen, would be revealed once he read the comic. He had been a fan of Marvel Comics ever since he was eleven and his eyes were drawn to the likes of "Kid Colt" and "The Rawhide Kid" next to the usual DC comic books on the swiveling rack at Whitey's Five & Dime. He soon plunged into the adventures of "Sergeant Fury and the Howling Commandos," and "The X-Men." His favorite, though, when it came out, quickly became "The Silver Surfer." There was a night when he was seventeen, tripping on a tab of Blue Barrel acid Tommy turned him on to, when he read over and over the very first issue of the "Surfer" series.

The comic was one he had already read several times before. But when Tommy tossed it to him and said "Hey check this out," well then, Sean didn't see how he could say no. With the Airplane's "Crown of Creation" playing on the stereo in the corner of Tommy's bedroom while colors exploded in his head Sean was drawn deeper and deeper into the Cosmos the silver hero surfed in an endless quest for identity as he rode the Waves of the Universe. The comic and its hero all made perfect sense to Sean that night. For days afterwards, too, when he was theoretically down from the acid. Though, what with all the pot he was smoking at the time, he never felt like he wasn't high.

But on this balmy, early fall morning in New England, the far reaching cosmos was long gone. The Spiderman comic would probably occupy him until noon, when it would be time for a beer, cold out of the icebox. If he so desired he might crack open the issue of Creem and look it over while he drank. Afterward, he planned to run over to Friendly's and have lunch with Teddie on her break. His possibilities for the day were simple. He didn't have to do one single thing that didn't agree with him. There was no doubt, he decided as he pondered all of this: It was a good way to live. He hoped to do so for as long as possible.

"Seano!"

A lone figure stood in the glare of sunlight at the end of the driveway, clad in dusty jeans and boots, an equally dusty jean jacket draped over his upper torso. A battered looking brown Stetson perched atop his head while on the ground at his feet lay a faded duffel bag. What Sean found strange about this sudden apparition at the end of Ron and Teddies driveway though, was the little white statue tucked under the dusty figure's left arm.

"Goddamn Buck man, am I happy to see you!"

Sean got up from the lawn chair, letting the comic book fall to the grass, and met his old pal coming up the drive. Almost two months had passed, he thought. And yet, it was just like old times.

"Where the hell did you come from?" Sean asked as they met halfway up the gravel drive and shook hands. "Or do I want to know?"

"Jesus, Sean. That's it? No, 'how ya doin', Harv? No, 'good to see ya, buddy?'"

Also like old times? That shit-eating grin on his long time friend's face—so that suddenly he found himself shaking Harv's hand again, the two of them staring at each other in the driveway of an old two story wooden apartment building in a Massachusetts neighborhood very far away from the Nevada desert.

"Who's your friend?" He let go of Harv's hand to point at the little statue tucked under his pal's arm.

"This here's the Buddha, Buck'" Harv held the statue out in front of him for Sean to inspect. "He's been traveling with me."

"Yeah, I see that."

The little Buddha was some sort of garden ornament, was Sean's guess. It was a good likeness of the holy figure, serene face, chubby belly, stubby legs akimbo in a full Lotus, his hands joined together at the palms and fingers in a classic mudra, his eyes half shut, a beatific smile stretching his lips.

"I brought him for you, man," Harv said after a minute. "Sort of a spur of the moment thing, if you can dig that. I figured you might get a kick out of him."

"I do. From Caroline?"

"You know it'"

"She aware that the Buddha's traveling with you?"

"By now she probably is."

"Could be bad luck, Harv. You know? Bad karma and all. Stealing the Buddha."

"You think?"

"Maybe."

"Well damn, Buck. Too late now."

And there was that grin of his, spread even wider if such a thing were possible.

"Yeah. So it is."

~43~ How Harv Got There

Harv's tale of his recent adventures unfolded over a six pack the next hour or so out in Ron and Teddie's front yard. Like Sean, he was in a lawn chair, carefully setting the little Buddha down on the grass before sitting down. He complimented Sean on the quality of the lawn furniture they were using, grinning as he remarked on how his pal was, "Certainly coming up in the world." Sean answered this unwarranted charge by explaining he had nothing to do with the lawn chairs—said that the chairs actually belonged to the older couple living in the apartment above Ron and Teddie. He wasn't sure the couple would approve of their chairs being used by such ruffians as he and Harv—a moot point since said neighbors weren't home.

"Well now, Buck, I don't hear 'em saying anything." Harv took a long pull off his beer. "Do you?"

"Not a word."

"I say fuck 'em then. If they can't take a joke. Ain't that right, Seano?"

"I'd say that's exactly right."

It was an old goof between them. That 'fuck them if they couldn't take a joke' thing. Now, sitting together once again after a time apart, it was a good reminder of how they had spent some of the long hours when traveling together—a good reminder of how he had missed the company of his longtime friend.

At Harv's insistence, Sean went first, explaining how, and what, had happened since they parted ways at the Lucky 7 Campground. Harv grunted here and there as he listened, his eyes lighting up again when the dope and Janie came into play.

"You're such a stud, Buck man." This comment was followed by, "Hey, was she a *real* blonde, man?"

This wasn't exactly how Sean had looked at his time with Janie, and for a moment he wondered if Harv didn't have the better idea of how it should be between a man and a woman: raw, carnal, and to the point. When he wrapped up the chronology of recent events in his life, Harv grunted again. "Yes, yes, truly great, man, it sounds like. Any more beer inside? I'm really thirsty today, Buck."

By twelve thirty both the six-pack and Harv's version of his last two months were almost done. Daylight Savings time still had two weeks left to go and the noon sun wasn't quite at its pinnacle. If it wasn't for the steady breeze coming off the mountain, Sean knew it would be downright hot in the wide open yard.

Harv knew it wouldn't last between him and Caroline as they drove away from the Lucky 7 campground. "You saw that gal's boosums, didn't you Buck? Shit, Christ, howdy, man, it wasn't like I had a choice in the matter." Harv rode the "matter" and Caroline's "boosums" for as long as he could, and for a while it was fun. The nights she worked at the casino bar he had the run of the place as long as he stayed out of the bouncer's way. All the booze and food he wanted, plenty of chicks to eyeball, and three pool tables where he quickly made some friends, along with a couple of not-so friends. During the day they slept late, and when awake, ate and fucked at their leisure in the coolness of Caroline's air-conditioned apartment before she went to work. On her nights off ,they zoomed around Vegas in the purple Cadillac, Harv at the wheel, an arm around Caroline at his side, a cold beer nestled between his legs, one hand on the wheel. Sometimes, during the day, they drove up into the mountains surrounding the valley for picnics on the shores of cool, high country lakes, where they drank beer and fucked in the sunlight on the blanket Caroline made sure to bring along. It was an easy life and Harv liked it.

"I was a fuckin' gigilo, Buck! Can you dig it, man?"

The bloom faded quickly, though, when Caroline's ex entered the picture. Jack, a big, burly biker dude, was fresh on the streets after a five year layover for armed robbery and various other offenses against the good citizens of the state of Nevada. There was a whole litany of crime Caroline reeled off to Harv the evening she learned of Jack's release. Some of these crimes she had been a part of; crimes that Jack, being the stand-up guy he was, had shielded her from being implicated in. But Caroline was scared for Harv because her good friend Denise, who had been the bearer of the bad news concerning Jack's release, had gleefully related, along with the rest of the sad tidings, how Jack had heard Caroline was seeing someone—a fact he was none too happy about.

"I didn't put a whole lot of credence into it, Buck. Jack, smack. Fuck 'em. You know how chicks make a big deal out of nothing."

This turned out to be a mistake. One Harv discovered the night Jack came strolling into the casino. Caroline was working up at the bar, while Harv was earning money at the pool table, when he felt the room go silent. "Jesus fuckin' Jones, Seano, but that sonofabitch was a big boy. You know me, man, I ain't really afraid of anyone. But there have been a few guys here and there who caused me to rethink that some. This Jack fucker was definitely in that category." Harv watched from the pool table as Jack strode across the room up to the bar where Caroline was setting down a round of drinks for a suit and his pickup. Jack, in one swift sweep of his arm, sent the drinks flying, then using his other hand he yanked Caroline over the bar. In the next second he had her squashed up against his barrel of a chest and was screaming in her face.

"I was gonna help her out, Buck. I swear I was. Even kept my cue stick with me, though I was hatin' the thought of breaking such a fine stick over that big gorilla's head. But man, Caroline peeked around that dude's chest when she saw me comin and pointed me out to the fucker. Pointed me right out to the big galoot. Suddenly I realized man how true love ain't all it's cracked up to be. I boogied, man. If you can dig that?"

Sean assured his longtime pal that he could indeed dig that, enjoying the turn the day had taken, the cold beer they were drinking, and the fact of Harv sitting there like he'd never been elsewhere.

"I had the keys to that Caddy of hers and I just said, screw it. Jack was breathin' hard down my neck I'm here to tell ya, Sean. But I beat his big ass out the door, hopped in that Caddy, which thank freakin' God I'd been able to park at the curb for once, and I was gone, man. I mean fuckin' flat out gone. I booked back to her place and snatched up my stuff in a major hurry. On the way out to the car I seen the Buddha sittin' there in her little flower garden and I snatched him up, too."

He kept the Cadillac for a day and a half, driving it all the way to Springfield, Missouri. Thinking better of holding onto a hot car for too much longer, he parked it behind a bar in the downtown section of the city and ambled over to the Greyhound Station. "I purely hated to give up that car, Buck. You know I did. But it seemed like the best move at the time." The money he had on hand from his pool winnings took him as far as Pittsburgh. From there he relied on his thumb, "And the generosity of my fellow man," to get him to Bramford. When Sean asked why he hadn't gone south, back to Florida, Harv gave him a quizzical look.

"Hell, man, I wanted to find you. I didn't think you'd be headed home. Not the way you were talking when last I saw you. Here," and he swung his arm around in a wide arc covering Boston Road, the apartment building, and Bramford Mountain looking down on all of it, "is where I figured I'd find you. Turns out, as usual, I was right. Didn't it, Buck, me boy?"

"Yep," Sean said, hoping the grin on his face was as big as the one staring back at him.

It was quiet for a bit between them, the noon sun warm on Sean's face, a mild, soothing buzz from the beer creeping over his senses. He thought for a minute, his eyes closed, the easy sound of cars rolling by drifting into his ears, how nice it might be to just stay like he was. To stay where he was. Time, life, wasn't like that, though—Harv's sudden arrival proof of that.

"So tell me, Seano man, what's been keeping you amused around here?"

"Pretty much what you see."

"Reading comic books and sipping coffee? I know you better than that, Buck. You've got something going on. Might as well tell me now."

"Nothing to tell. I've been kicking back, buddy. Enjoying the peace and quiet while I figure out what comes next. It's been nice."

"Well you can cut out all that 'figuring out' stuff, now that Ol' Harv's back in town. Man, it's time to kiss that quiet crap goodbye."

"Are you suggesting I'd best prepare myself?"

"Fuckin' A. You know I get bored real easy."

"Yeah. I know that. I was hoping traveling with your man, Buddha, there, might have settled you down some."

"Nah." Harv upended his beer and drained what was left, holding the can out from his lips and letting the beer flow into his open mouth. Sean had to laugh—at Harv, and the strangeness of the Buddha statue sitting on the ground between them. "Besides," Harv said when his beer was gone, one hand pointing at the garden figure. "He never says nothin'. Unlike some people I've traveled with. Any more of these in the refrigerator?" He rattled the empty can he was holding, burped loudly, and then tossed it on the ground. "A packy store anywhere close by?"

Sean saw how the day was headed now. Even had a flash of what it might be later, the two of them staggering into the apartment trying to be quiet and not wake Ron and Teddie. Failing at that when one of them, it didn't matter who, banged into something as they stumbled through the door into the kitchen, maybe knocking a glass off the counter, or tripping over a chair while laughing about something one of them had said, or done earlier, wherever it was they had wound up, a place Sean had no idea of where, or what, it would be. Everything would seem hilarious in the lateness and the drunkenness of the hour, and with any luck Sean's spirits would soar again in the liquid, golden haze.

And who knows? Maybe Harv would have an idea of where they might head, or what they might do. God knows Sean was tired of making the decisions. Hell, he was fine right where he was. Had told Harv that. But Sean knew it wasn't going to last now. Harv was back. Just as he had said. Something was bound to happen. It always did with Harv. It would probably be a good thing. Though there was certainly no guarantee of that. Sean knew that well enough, too. Had in fact witnessed some of the bad things. Didn't really want to witness any more of those. But if he had to then he guessed he would. It was all out of his hands for the time being.

"There's a state store in Palmer. Got all the beer you want to drink. In this lifetime, or the next, as your friend the Buddha would say."

"Now you're talkin'." Harv stood up from the lawn chair, kicking it over in the process. "Best idea you've had all day, Buck."

They headed over to Sean's truck parked under the towering oak bordering the edge of the property. Just as Sean was climbing into the driver's seat he thought of something.

"What about the Buddha? You going to leave him there?"

"Huh? Oh Yeah."

Harv ran back to scoop on the little statue, on his return placing it carefully atop the spare tire in the bed of the truck.

"He'll be all right, now, Buck. The little feller don't drink much and that's a good thing for us. Let's get it, man. Beer's a-wastin'."

Sean could feel their laughter drifting out of the truck and over Boston Road as they pulled out of the driveway, entering the afternoon traffic going anywhere but where he'd been.

~44~ Route 20

They drank seriously for the next few days. Teddie had quit her job at Friendly's over a dispute with the manager and was working at a bar behind the mall on Springfield Street. This bar, Cocktail Time! Any time is Cocktail Time, is where serious drinking began. Instead of driving over to Palmer and the packy, Sean took them there. While Teddie worked her shift they sat at the bar in the rear of the dimly lit room. Behind them, businessmen in suits and ties, lounging at the little round tables scattered around the room, drank their way to the end of three martini lunches. Husbands of lady shoppers at the mall ducked in for a quick one, and later on in the afternoon, construction workers done for the day came in to drink beer and play pool.

Teddie was happy to see them when they strolled in. She even gave Harv a big hug that made him grin as he held on tight. "Whoa, darlin'. If I'd known a hug that delightful was waiting for me I'd've come back to Bramford a hell of a lot sooner."

Flashing Sean a knowing smile she pushed Harv away and after setting up their Budweisers, went back to waiting on those at the tables. For a brief moment after she left, Sean caught his reflection beaming back at him from the mirror running the length of the wall behind the bar, the bottom part of his face hidden by a Rheingold display perched on a shelf holding rows and rows of neatly arranged liquor bottles. But his eyes were plain and clear in the glass, and for some reason his reflection bothered him—made him feel as if that reflection wasn't really his, but of some stranger staring out at him.

The drinking ended the first night at The Happy Luau, a squat, flame red structure sitting off of Route 20 just after it crossed over into Connecticut. Being flame red made the building stand out. But adding to the bizarre concept of the joint were the tall, wooden totems flanking the ornate entranceway. Once past these doors the place opened up into a cavernous room. Wooden torches blazed in the corners, and plastic tropical flowers decorated the typical round bar tables scattered about. Topping it all off were the colorful murals covering the walls depicting various scenes of Polynesian life.

Hidden lights flickered against the murals and the blue walls of the room, creating a wavering effect as if the lights were reflecting off water. Dreamy steel guitars and rhythmic drums music played softly out of speakers set in the ceiling, music raining down gently on the waitresses in grass skirts with bikini tops, unlike the native girls in the murals on the walls, moving amongst the tables to serve the customers. The whole scene was totally beyond the pale of anything Sean had yet encountered in the New England he had grown accustomed to over the last few weeks. The few couples with their dinners set before them, frond ovals loaded with heaping portions of what looked to be pretty exotic fare, gave the place a sense of legitimacy.

"Damn near perfect, wouldn't you say, Buck?"

Harv doffed his battered Stetson to a waitress passing by. The loose grass skirt slung low on her hips, the lei around her neck looked foreign against the girl's white New England skin and freckled face. But looking past the waitress Harv found the bar in the rear of the building.

"Let's belly up, Seano, and see what happens."

"I think we should just split." He was tired and half drunk. "What the fuck are we doing here?"

"Shit, man, if we leave we won't find out."

The long days and night of drinking were way past its time, as far as Sean could figure . Anything in life can happen, he had thought earlier, out of nowhere. *Given enough time*. Now the long river of time had brought him to a Hawaiian oasis in the hinterlands of Connecticut, where somehow, past its time or not, the longer he stood in the doorway the more it seemed strangely right. How weird, he thought, as he followed Harv up to the bar.

But it was all anticlimactic. After an hour of drinking , the only thing that happened in The Happy Luau was the emptying out of its customers. Finally, the steady drone of Polynesian music ended and the house lights came on. In the glare of the overhead, all trace of the South Pacific faded away, and the waitresses in their costumes no longer looked exotic. They only looked tired and ready to go home.

Harv seemed a little disappointed as he drained the last of the beer he'd been drinking. A row of empty shot glasses sat on the bar between him and Sean. "Guess I was wrong, huh Buck?" He fiddled with one of the empty glasses as if he was considering maybe one more. "Gotta be a first time for everything, though. Right? Least we can say we've been here."

"Who in the hell would we ever tell?"

"I don't know. Somebody, I imagine."

On their way out two guys roughly their age going into the lounge brushed past Sean and Harv. There wasn't a whole lot of light outside to break the dark of the late hour, just that given off by the two harsh bulbs on the far corners of the roof. But the two guys pushing their way into The Happy Luau looked to be bikers. At least the Harley-Davidson jackets and motorcycle boots they wore indicated that. The first guy brushing by looked lean and sinister, a jagged scar running down below his left eye.

"Don't bother boys," Harv said as they went by. "Joint's shutting down."

"Fuck."

It was the sinister looking one who spoke, his voice lean and low much like he was. Sean had the feeling this guy wouldn't be one to mess with. If anything, you'd want him on your side. Then he and Harv were in the Jeep heading back to Bramford.

The new day turned out to be more of the same, this time at a more regular type joint in Palmer, the Nine Mile Pub. A body of water known as Nine Mile Pond glimmered in the noon light not far from the pub.

But no matter—the place was more to his liking, cozy, a well-polished wooden bar top running the length of a side wall, a shiny, lit up juke box in one corner, some rickety little tables set off from the glitzy Wurlitzer, two pool tables, soft overhead lights, other lights, actually neon signs advertising the various brews offered. Rounding off this familiar scene was the grizzled looking, balding, pot-bellied older gent behind the bar wearing a chest high apron, and who Sean expected at any minute to call out, "Hey Craze! Got a minute?" a la the Jackie Gleason variety show he used to watch with his mom on Saturday night. This bartender had stronger arms and shoulders than the famous comedian. A black and white framed group photo of young men in Navy whites on the wall behind the bar testified to a long gone youth.

The wide grin on Harv's face as he took his first long pull of Black Label draft indicated that he, too, was pleased with their new surroundings, leading Sean to figure that they would be spending some time in the Nine Mile Pub that day. Looking out the front bay window at the leaf-less trees under a gray sky lining the two lane road into Palmer, he could see how Indian summer appeared to be gone. Fall was coming and a promise of rain hung in those gray skies overhead. But looking out on this gray scene, the new surroundings were as good as any. *For the time being. Hopefully no longer than that.*

Ignoring Harv's request to rack the balls on one of the empty pool tables he wandered over to the silent jukebox, Black Label draft in hand as he scanned the play list. There was the usual smattering of Top 40 hits. His eyes hit on a title at the bottom of the fold-over page, "Babe, I'm Gonna Leave You" by Led Zeppelin." Dropping a quarter in the slot he punched up the numbers for that song, along with the numbers for "Wildfire" and "Come To Boston," and only because he knew Harv hated them.

The other two tunes played first, and Sean was back at the bar when the first lonely guitar chords of the Zeppelin song began. He found himself thinking of Janie as he listened to the ballad build, Robert Plant's wailing voice rising and falling with the beat of the song. The gray skies, visible through the big bay window, seemed to blend in with the music and reminding him of how the fog was just lifting that morning when he said goodbye to her. She had left him, though. Even if he did the walking away. *Had he loved her? Who could say?* They weren't together that long. But that afternoon in Big Sur when they made that furious love in the tent had seemed like love. To him. If it were, it sure hadn't lasted.

Funny, but suddenly, as the plaintive song came to its end it was Teddie's face he flashed on. *Could she possibly be The One? Was she the real reason he had returned to Bramford?* Too many questions he decided. The last gentle guitar chords of the song faded away, the jukebox, the bar, falling silent. It was a good song, and he'd wasted it. Clouding it up with questions and sadness.

They ran into the biker with the scar again on the last day of the bender. Neither of them had said as much but Sean, at least, knew it was time to back off. His body and head were telling him so. A certain, haggard look on Harv's face suggested that he, too, was coming to that same conclusion. These things ran in cycles. It was pleasant enough to begin the day's drinking at the lounge where Teddie worked and after a few beers there make the run up to Palmer and the Nine Mile Pub. Cheeseburgers and fries from the grill at the pub served for their daily sustenance. When Harv grew tired of shooting pool, they would head over to Boston Road and the lit-up nightclubs on the edge of Springfield.

It was fun to hang in those clubs late at night, drinking beer and whiskey shots, listening to the bar bands, watching the chicks watching them, just generally being with people they didn't know. At the end of those long nights, they drove back to Bramford, where, safely at the duplex, they crashed in their sleeping bags on the floor—only to wake the next morning and before long start it all over again. So yes, it was a fun time. Three days, four, a week, the length of time didn't matter, wasn't always the same, and Sean and Harv had done this sort of thing all over the country after leaving Florida. The steady drinking days just seemed to end on their own, by a mutual agreement rarely reached by spoken words. For a while they did other things. But sooner or later the cycle would start again. Of that Sean was certain. As long as he was hanging with Harv he could be sure of it.

The day this most recent bender ended, the promise of rain in the air the last few days finally came true. The day this most recent bender ended and they ran into the The tires of the Jeep had hissed on the rain-slick road as they wheeled into Palmer in the early afternoon, the wet and bare branches of the oak and maple trees lining Route 20 looking forlorn in the steady drizzle coming down. Even the evergreens looked like they'd rather be somewhere else. Only a ratty old Dodge pickup sat in the dirt parking lot as they pulled in and Sean could feel the emptiness of the bar.

The biker cat was sitting at the bar alone, his thinning black hair drifting down over the collar of his leather jacket. A shiny, chrome chain ran from just below his right collar, under his armpit, and up again on the other side, the Harley-Davidson emblazoned in red on the back of the dark jacket standing out, even in the dim light of the bar. Though his back was turned to them Sean knew it was him—had known somehow that night at The Happy Luau it was only a question of time before they crossed paths again.

Harv, of course, ended up playing pool with Wade, as it turned out the biker's name was. Wade Parker, from right there in Palmer. All his life, except for the two tours of duty he pulled in 'Nam. The scar on his face was a shrapnel wound from his first tour. The dope, Asian women, and the killing, according to him, had been so much fun he volunteered for another stint "in country" when the first tour ended. Fortunately, or not, depending on how you looked at it, he'd been wounded badly enough in a firefight the next go-round to warrant an early discharge with full disability. Now he spent his days amusing himself by riding around the countryside looking for kicks and, "A few extra bucks here and there."

"Ain't that right, Hammond?" The grizzled bartender shook his head, Yes, as the two shared a smile—a secret one, Sean thought, concerning something he probably didn't want to know.

A chill had run down Sean's spine when Wade mentioned fun and killing in the same sentence. But he tried to keep in mind that he didn't know Wade. In fact, he didn't know a whole lot about what happened to the guys who'd gone to Nam. The vets he had run with in G'ville never spoke about it and he never asked. Sean's uncle had been an Army colonel with a plushy job at the Pentagon, when at the age of fifty he decided to go see for himself what he was busy sending troops off to. A year later he was recovering at Walter Reed, lucky his family hadn't had to avail themselves of a free burial for him in Arlington. A year or so after being back on his feet the uncle had counseled Sean to do whatever he had to do to stay out of the military until the war was over. The fact of the matter, as his uncle explained, was that the US had no business being in Vietnam, should never have been there to begin with, and it was not worth the shedding of any more American blood.

Now the war was over, his uncle retired from the Army with a Silver Star and selling real estate in Alexandria. And Sean? He was sitting in a little dive on the outskirts of a dying New England town listening to a different vet recalling fondly his days in the jungle.

Harv and Wade played for several hours and it was pleasant enough for Sean to wile away the time that gray, rainy afternoon, nursing his hangover while the clack of pool balls on the table and the wisps of talk coming from Harv and Wade filled his consciousness. It was also good to see that Harv wasn't doing anything stupid. Like wanting to play for money. Sean didn't figure the scar-faced Wade for one to put up with Harv's Country Rube bullshit hustle very long. There was no hustle by either party, actually, Wade turning out to be a pretty good pool shot in his own right. After watching a couple of their games, Sean came to the conclusion that Wade was actually the better hand with a cue stick. Both of them moved around the table with an easy sureness, though Wade was hampered a little by a slight hitching in his gait Sean figured to be courtesy of Viet Nam. But they were damn near an even match, and it wasn't long before they were laughing, or cursing loudly at one another when a shot was made or missed.

"Man, this sonofabuck is good," Harv exclaimed once as he came up to the bar and signaled to Hammond for two more rounds, one for himself and one for his new pal. "Shit, Christ, howdy, Seano, I hate to say it but he's maybe even better'n me."

"You think?"

Harv's face scrunched up in a slight frown. "No, you're right, Buck. He's not better'n me. Close. But not better."

By mid-afternoon Sean felt no different than he had when he walked through the door of the bar. It was still raining, he wasn't drunk, or even close to it, and he didn't care. It seemed to be one of those days—a dreary fall day when no amount of drinking was going to change the world around him. Harv and Wade had gone out back of the bar to smoke a joint earlier, and now Harv was all giggles and goofy grins as he moved between the bar and the pool table.

Two workers from the day shift at the tampon factory down the road came in when their day was done, dressed in identical gray work pants and shirts, the factory name stitched over one breast pocket, their name on the other. Sean could see the dark, smoking structure of the factory rising up from the banks of Nine Mile Pond in his mind's eye, wondering for a moment at the world's needs for tampons that the factory could run non-stop seven days a week. Other than that he paid no attention to the new arrivals, trying instead to get engrossed in a local hockey game Hammond had tuned in on the portable radio he kept behind the bar.

Over the muffled broadcast Sean heard Harv's voice rise up behind him. "Well, well, why sure. I suppose it's all right. You say you want to play partners, is it? Uh huh. Sounds good to me. How 'bout you, pard?" It wasn't much, and maybe he was only imagining it—but without even turning around to see he knew it was all going to change.

For a while it was okay. The factory guys took turns buying the beers they kept losing to Harv and Wade. As long as it stayed just for beer Sean thought there was a chance. He found out sooner than he'd have liked, that wasn't going to be, when he realized it had been a bit since anyone came up to the bar for fresh brews. Turning away from the game on the radio he checked out what was happening at the pool table—only to see a wad of crumpled bills laid up on one of the rails and a determined look on the two worker's faces as they waited, cue sticks in hand, for their turn. Sean wasn't surprised at any of this. He wasn't happy. But he was not surprised.

Just as he turned back to his beer and the hockey game he heard Harv say, "Hot damn but I do believe that's the game, boys. Eight ball side pocket, gents." Sean could hear the excited nervousness in his pal's voice—could hear how Harv knew, too, how everything was right on the edge. Sean didn't bother to look, but he could plainly hear behind him the clacking sound of two pool balls engaging, followed by the quiet thud of one of those balls dropping into the pocket—this sound followed by, "Yes sir, yes sir, that's all she wrote."

Except one of the factory guys didn't like the end of the story as Harv had written it.

"I don't appreciate being made fun of, buddy."

The worker was tall and wiry, maybe in his late thirties, Sean couldn't really tell, with thinning hair, and big hands. Maker of feminine napkins or not, Sean thought, he could do some damage with those hands.

"In fact, I've had about as much of your bullshitting as I can take. Me and Ralph here played you and Wade in good faith. Wade seems to understand that. But you don't and I want my money back."

Though Wade stayed quiet at the mention of his name he did move a little closer to where Harv was standing.

"I don't think so." That come-and-get-it grin was spread all over Harv's blond face. "No sir, that ain't the way it's done where I come from. My partner and I won fair and square. You're just gonna have to take your lumps and learn to live with it."

"That's right, Melvin." Wade spoke up, his hands hanging loose at his sides. Like a gunslinger, Sean thought. In one of those Italian westerns popular a few years back.

"This has nothing to do with you, Wade. You've known me and Ralph for a long time. You know how we are. This is just between me and that jackass."

"Jackass is it? Now my feelings're hurt."

"I'm going to hurt more than your feelings little man if you don't give us our money back."

"Not gonna happen." Harv's eyes were all lit up at what might be coming. "You want it, try and get it."

And that was it. Sean didn't blame the worker guy. Harv's shit-eating grin, the way he danced back from the pool table, this would have been enough to piss anyone off. It didn't help when he snatched the pile of money up and wave the greenbacks at Melvin and Ralph. In a flash Melvin lunged, dodging the pool balls Harv grabbed from the table and flung in his direction. The balls missed Melvin but one hit his partner above his right eye. It was all chaos then: pool balls flying, Melvin snorting like an enraged bull as he chased after Harv, who was laughing and dancing around the room, waving the dollar bills with one hand and taunting Melvin with the other. Above this chaos hung a pall of gray cigarette smoke over the pool table, while Dolly Parton's "Jolene" wailing from the jukebox, somehow seemed to set the tone for what was suddenly happening inside the Pub.

Sean got up from his bar stool, waiting to see if he was going to be needed. The bartender paid no attention, the only sign he made that anything different was going on in his bar being to turn the volume up a little on the radio and then pour himself a Black Label draft. Apparently Hammond had seen this sort of thing in his place before. *Probably more than once, too.*

The fun of it came to an end when Melvin finally caught up to Harv and got him in a headlock, his big hands slamming Harv's head into the pool table. Harv didn't let go of the money, but with his free hand kept pulling at the back of Melvin's shirt. Meanwhile Ralph, one hand holding his face where the pool ball had connected, had run over to help his buddy with Harv.

"Fuck that," Sean heard Wade say above Dolly Parton and Harv's laughing. Taking the bottle of Genesee he'd been drinking he smashed it against Ralph's face. This was too much for Ralph. Blood streaming between the fingers holding his face he reeled away from the pool table to stumble out of the bar. But Wade wasn't done, yet. He dragged Melvin off of Harv and began jack hammering his fists into Melvin's body and face, rapid blows that after the first two or three Melvin quit trying to defend himself from. When he was finally able to push away from Wade he fell to the floor, Wade standing quietly over him, his fists still clenched. The jagged scar on his face pulsed a bright red down his neck. What bothered Sean, though, was the smile on his face. He had enjoyed what he had done. It was obvious. *Had enjoyed it a lot.*

"Goddamn. I say Goddamn!" Harv was on his feet, pounding Wade on the back with one hand and waving the wad of bills with the other. "Fuckin-A Tweety, now that's what I call a pool partner!"

Then Sean ran with Harv and Wade out the back door of the bar to his truck in the rear parking lot. The three of them piled in and headed back to Bramford.

~45~ More Boston Road

With the hard drinking over Sean felt like he could breathe again. The first day was a little rough, complete with nausea in the morning that left his mouth and throat raw, tasting bitterly of the alcohol he'd been steadily consuming the last four days. Toward the end of the first day he began to feel better, the resilience of his age kicking in. Ron came home from work at six, happy it was Friday, payday, and a case of Schlitz under his arm to start the weekend. While Teddie worked the night shift at the lounge, Sean, Harv, and Ron drank the beer, Sean nursed his while his two pals slammed the rest of the case down, and watched the National League Championship game on TV. The next morning there was no nausea, and he felt like once again he had made it back to the land of the living. The sun was already up, sending slashes of light through the closed blinds, and though Harv rolled over on his side to escape the light, Sean sat up, ready for whatever might be out there. It was probably just a lull in the chaos that was Harv being in the picture, but he was glad for it.

Harv didn't know anything about *lulls*. Instead, he began running quite a bit with Wade, the two of them having forged a bond that afternoon at the Nine Mile Pub. Wade had a Harley he was in the process of chopping, a process on hold because money was scarce at the moment. "Wrapped up in some investments," Wade said. Still, the beast of a bike ran and he took to coming by the apartment and picking up Harv. The biker and the semi-cowboy were a strange duo as they raced out of the driveway up Boston Road to who-knows-where, Wade in black leathers and greasy motorcycle boots, Harv, in dusty Levis, flannel shirt, Levi jacket, the battered Stetson jammed down on his head with one hand while the other held onto the bike seat. Harv never went into detail about where they went or what they did, other than mentioning once how he was helping Wade keep an eye on those "investments."

That was enough information for Sean, He had a pretty good idea what Wade's investments involved and wanted no part of it. That was Harv's look-out. If it kept him busy and amused—and out of Sean's hair—more power to it.

In the meantime Sean kicked back, relaxing once again. Weather dictated his long-term plans. When it got too cold in Massachusetts he would head south. Or maybe southwest—like to Arizona or New

Mexico. He had heard that Taos was a pretty happening town. Had heard that about Tucson, too. Get a job, save some bucks, and when New England warmed up, head on back. If Harv was around and of a mind to go with him, fine. But any decisions made would be loose and non-binding—just the way Sean liked.

There was a park in the center of Bramford, what Sean supposed could properly be called the village square. A rotary directed traffic from the two roads feeding into the circle and the park sat off from the rotary to the east. Town Hall and the police station flanked the park on both ends. At the end of a sidewalk running along the north end of the park stood another rusted brick building: Bramford's public library. An oak and elm tree grew on each side of the walkway, their height evidence of having been planted before the building was even dreamed of, the two trees sentinels, as well as witness, to those who walked up the recently painted white steps into the library.

In the center of the green was a bronze statue of a Civil War general. An aged plaque at the general's feet revealed his name and the following: Cyrus Bramford, perished from wounds received at Gettysburg while repelling Picket's Charge. According to the plaque, General Bramford was the last scion in a long line of family scions who had come to the area a hundred years or so before 1776 and prospered. Because of their prosperity, the Bramfords had bequeathed their name to the town that grew up around them. Sean took to sitting on the wooden bench in front of the statue with a book, letting all the rest of the New England town behind him move by at its own pace.

He finally finished *Big Sur* while sitting on this bench, disturbed by how that bright spark of the Beat Generation had burned down into a shattered drunk with the DT's on a lonely Pacific coast—a coast Sean had been to. But he could see how being shattered by the world was easily possible. The world could be a frightening place. He had seen some of that frightening potential in G'ville the night of the riots. Above, and beyond that, there were times during the periodic benders he underwent with Harv, when Sean could see the potential for disaster in his own drinking. Men and women with drinking problems were not unknown in his family. After finishing the *Kerouac* book, Sean thought about them—thought about how he was sure he could never become one of them.

In need of fresh reading material when he was done with *Kerouac*, using Ron and Teddies address he secured a card at the library, where browsing one morning he found a dog-eared copy of *Catch-22* and checked it out. Right off the antics of the hero, Yossarian, appealed to him. Yossarian's personal paranoia in the midst of the global conflagration of WW2 struck a chord in him. After Kerouac's DT chronicle, and before that, the bender with Harv, Sean needed some humor in his life. Milo Minderbinder, Major Major, Aarfy, the cold and dying tail gunner, Snowden, Yossarian's wild break for freedom. All of this came to life for him in the little park off from the rotary and center of Bramford. Heller had created a masterpiece of the absurd, Sean thought. He wondered how close to the reality of that war the book was—wondered what the reality of anything might be.

"Well now, Buck, this is gonna be the big one. Yes sirree, partner. When the smoke clears and the dust settles your old pal Harv's gonna be ridin' in the sunshine."

They were sitting at in the Nine Mile Pub on a Thursday afternoon, exactly a week since Sean had last been in that bar. Seems longer, he thought, as he stared at Harv over the rim of the Pilsner glass raised to his mouth. Instead of drizzling rain, like the last time, the day was blue and clear, the wind coming off of the surrounding hills putting a chill in the October air.

Funny, but the last bit of Harv's little speech appealed to him suddenly. The part about "riding in the sunshine." He had a flash of the beach at home on a warm day in early summer, girls in skimpy bikinis lying on the sand, the Atlantic Ocean lapping at the shore. It was a pretty image, and just for a moment, enough to make Sean forget how much he disliked being in his hometown—how trapped he began to feel whenever he was there for any length of time.

"Well, it sounds good. I guess. Hopefully it'll work out."

"It'll do all of that. Don't worry none about that, Seano." Harv's grin vanished as he drained the last of his beer. "Seriously, Buck, this could go a long way toward settin' me up. Finally."

The Country Rube was gone, in its place a well-hidden side of Harv. Sean knew this side. Had, in fact, conversations in the past with his friend where the subject wasn't all about getting high, getting laid, getting by. Harv was like anyone. Even if he rarely showed it. But he had dreams of his own. When he wasn't too unsure of himself, too uncertain of what was going on.

"I'm gonna take my share of this little project, man, and hold onto it. When you get ready to cut out and head home I'm with you. And when we get there, I'm gonna get real intense about opening up my own shop. Like I've been wantin' to."

Harv was an ace tile setter and on the rare occasions he worked legitimately, that's what he did. Other than with his older brother, Rob, he was never good at working for somebody. Instead, when they were between jobs, Harv found it easier to hustle a little pool here and there, or working side jobs when he could. But he had told Sean more than once how someday he'd have his own shop, be his own boss. "There won't be any of that time clock punching crap, either. You can bet the freakin' ranch on that!"

To get there he was going to help Wade deliver two thousand pounds of commercial grade Columbian. Harv's cut was to be substantial. "In the five digits, my man, and that's all I'm gonna say." That was fine with Sean. He didn't want to know the details. In fact, he planned on staying as far away from this venture as possible.

"You know, Seano, there's room for you in this." Harv leaned in closer, his eyes and mouth set tight. "Wade told me to tell you. Fact is we could use your truck. It'd be a big help."

"Thanks. But no thanks." Hammond had placed fresh beers in front of them and Sean took a long pull. "I'm making it fine just the way it is."

"Aww." A goofy, crestfallen grin replaced the conspiratorial look on Harv's face. "That's no way to be, Buck. It'll be a gas. Think of it."

"I am."

And he was. Could picture it all quite clearly. Wade and Harv rendezvousing with who-knows-what kind of shady characters somewhere on the outskirts of Springfield, cigarettes glowing in the dark, murmuring voices drifting on the night air, the engines of the vehicles carrying the payload idling, spewing exhaust fumes into the darkness, the quiet anxiety of paranoia covering all of it in a blanket of potential doom. It wasn't that attractive of a picture. Old news to him. What was the saying? Been there, done that, and bought the T-shirt? Something like that.

"Like I said, Harv. Thanks for the offer. But my cowboy days are over. You know that. I'm not interested in a repeat of Gainesville. Besides, I don't even like smoking the stuff anymore."

"Shit, Chris, howdy, Buck. You don't have to like the crap to make money off it."

He had to laugh at the incredulous smile on Harv's face, but he held firm and shook his head. "No thanks."

"Well, Buck, if that's how you truly feel then okay. Just don't ever say I didn' offer you the chance of a lifetime."

"Oh, I won't, Harv. Trust me."

They drank in silence for a while in the otherwise empty bar, that silence usually a rarity when Harv was around. Sean hated to be that way but he couldn't see how Wade and Harv could pull off a deal of such proportions. Closer to the truth was that he couldn't see how Harv could. Not to mention the fact that Harv, with that kind of money, just didn't register. And yet, according to his easy going, always grinning, friend, the whole thing was in the works and running smoothly. It seemed a long time since the two of them had left Florida. Things had happened in that time he couldn't have imagined. Now it appeared more was on the way.

"If it starts getting funky," he said, a feeling coming over him out of nowhere. "You bail. Right?"

"Fuckin'-A, Buck. You know me, man. I'm like a freakin' cat, dig? Nine lives and always on my feet'"

"You might be getting close to the end of those lives, bud. The way you been going."

"Not a'tall, Buck, my boy. Man, I'm just getting started."

~46~ The Fall Classic

The World Series was starting and in Bramford the upcoming "Fall Classic" was all anyone talked about. The Boston Red Sox, the American League Champions, were going up against the National League's Cincinnati Reds. It seemed to Sean like the whole state of Massachusetts was caught up in a frenzy of hope. With the showdown to commence on Saturday, the 11th at Fenway Park, Red Sox fans were telling anyone willing to listen—and even those who weren't—that this was the year the Curse of the Bambino would finally be shattered and laid to rest. The team from Bean Town was going to win it all.

It was a frenzy that unaffected Sean. At first. Ron was a rabid Sox fan and for his friend's sake Sean hoped they won. If Florida had a team playing in the Series Sean supposed he would be interested in the outcome. But no such team existed, so for Sean it was a moot point. He actually liked Cincinnati's chances, mainly because of Pete Rose. He got a kick out of the third baseman's all-or-nothing brand of play, enjoyed the excitement it brought to the game. "Charley Hustle" was a good nick name for the shaggy haired player, he thought, a name Rose had rightfully earned.

Not that Sean was any kind of real sports fan. He enjoyed football okay, had caught a good case of Dolphin Fever during Miami's '71 and '72 seasons. For baseball, the playoffs and World Series were fun. But he figured he'd have to be plenty bored to hang out and watch a regular season game. There was a bar back home in Lauderdale called Brady's, not far from downtown, one of those old alcoholic bars found on the seedier sides of town that opened at 7a.m. seven days a week, a slew of beat-up cars in the parking lots, and grizzled old timers clustered in front of the door waiting for the joint to open up. The owner had a full kitchen off from the main room where he whipped up down home Southern food served cafeteria style, taking only Sunday off so he could observe the Sabbath. Sometimes Sean, Dewey, and Harv would go there for grub, heap their plates full of fried catfish, collard greens, rice and gravy, and hot cornbread, all for a buck fifty and the best deal in town.

During the World Series, Brady's served free hot dogs, all you could eat. It was a fun place for Sean and his pals to watch the games. Free hot dogs, cheap drafts, surrounded by old boys rooting their teams on, keeping up a running commentary on the game, or telling stories about players of old, how "these new guys" didn't have a clue how to really play the game.

The Nine Mile Pub wasn't close to being comparable to Brady's in Sean's opinion. But it was what he had for now, and Harv and he sat there on the afternoon preceding Game One, soaking up beer and the enthusiasm of the Red Sox fans. Not that Harv was buying into the Red Sox fever—was straightforward about his feelings on the matter, "Fuck a bunch of baseball," being his statement of fact about the issue when a guy sitting next to them at the bar said something concerning the historic series about to begin. At Harv's bold statement, the din created by those gathered at the bar, fell silent.

"Well?"

Harv glared at the stunned faces staring back at him in the soft light of the busy bar. Outside, the afternoon was falling away, night coming on quickly now that it was fall and Daylight Savings Time gone. Sean could feel the cold air of that fall in his bones all the time it seemed now—was beginning to think he'd be headed south pretty soon. His companion's attitude wasn't making the Nine Mile Pub any warmer, Sean thought as he put his beer down to better pay attention to what may be about to happen.

"You want me to say it again?" Harv tilted his Stetson back on his head, drained his beer and then stood up to face the crowd. "Okay then. Here goes. *fuck a bunch of baseball!*"

He waited, swaying slightly on his bowed out legs, for any reaction. None was forthcoming, to Sean's relief. The place was full of factory workers done for the day and local young rowdies, all of them drinking heavily. Things could get ugly in a heartbeat, Sean figured, and Wade wasn't around to help his pal this time, leaving only Sean, always uncomfortable with violence, and in the present situation, none too pleased with the odds against them to back Harv's play if it came to that. It was tense for a minute—then the red, excited, faces of the crowd turned back to their conversations, shrugging off Harv, his manic grin and blasphemous rant. Obviously, the dude was nuts. An outsider to boot, not worth the effort to spoil the good mood they felt as their team stood on the brink of reclaiming its rightful place in baseball history.

"Guess I showed 'em." Harv sat back down and waved to Hammond for another round. "Didn't I, Buck?"

"Oh yeah. They're terrified. Shaking in their boots at the wrath of the Mighty Harv."

"That's right, partner. And don't you ever forget it."

"Oh, I won't man. Have no fear of that."

With Harv off with Wade tending to "business," and Teddie working at Cocktail Time, that left Sean to watch the games with Ron, who glued himself to the TV, ingesting every scene, every tidbit of baseball coming through the flickering screen. Ron knew every player on the Red Sox going back the last twenty years, was able to quote their stats and amazing feats of baseball prowess at will. According to Ron, the current Sox roster might be the best ever assembled. He threw out their names to Sean: Yaz, Carlton Fisk, Dwight Evans, their batting averages that year, .371, .395, .353. His favorite pitcher was El Tiante, aka Luis Tiant, who along with the Spaceman Bill Lee, were damn near unbeatable that year. If it were up to him, Ron assured Sean at the beginning of the Series, he'd just pitch those two, alternating them back and forth, making it a sure thing, nothing to it, four games and out, the Sox sweeping the Series. There was a wild gleam in Ron's eyes as he reeled all this off the Saturday afternoon the Series got underway, both he and Sean popping the tops of the tall-boy Budweisers Ron brought home for the occasion. When the Red Sox won the first game 6-0, El Tiante holding the Reds scoreless, a very drunk Ron felt vindicated.

"Hey man," Sean said as Ron was turning the TV off. "It's only the first game, you know." He was feeling no pain from his half of the case of beer he'd consumed, was happy for Ron that the Sox had won. But he figured it was up to him to keep his friend grounded, what with six more possible games to go. "You'd better take it easy, pal. There's a lot more baseball to go yet."

"Aw fuck. Wha' the hell you know 'bout it anyway?"

Ron had been coherent for most of the game, a surprise to Sean who'd figured he'd be watching the game by himself, what with Ron's propensity for passing out early. But by the end of the seventh inning—time for the "stretch"—the beer began to catch up to Ron. To celebrate the six runs Boston scored, he broke out the bottle of Jim Beam he'd been saving and began belting back shots. Now the game was over, and though Ron wasn't passed out Sean knew it wasn't far away in his future.

"You don' know nuthin' about fuckin' nuthin', Sean." He staggered off into the bedroom, his lanky legs looking like they could give out at any minute. "Nuthin' 'bout nuthin'."

He tried to slam the door shut behind him but missed the knob, lurching instead on his momentum into the room, where a few minutes later the sound of snoring came through the open door.

Teddie came home from work a half hour later, body and face sagging from her shift as she entered the apartment, the vibrant, black haired beauty Sean remembered from their college days, gone—in her place a tattered, tired barmaid dead on her feet.

"What happened here?" she asked Sean, sitting alone on the couch with the last beer from the case. The Jim Beam bottle lay on the rug where Ron had dropped it on his way to the bedroom. Sean had thought about picking it up and taking a pull when he heard Teddie opening the front door. "Where's Ron?"

"Boston won." He pointed toward the open bedroom door. "And Ron's in there." Another set of loud, rasping snoring drifted into the living room."

"I see." She picked up the bourbon bottle. "About what I expected, yes?"

"Pretty much. Yeah, I suppose so."

It was an exciting World Series, though Ron's prediction of Boston sweeping in four didn't hold up. The Big Red Machine took the next two games, one at Fenway and one in Cincinnati. Despite himself, Sean ,got caught up in the flow of the Series, watching the games with Ron who ended up taking vacation time from work for the event. Things looked bleak for Boston when they returned to Fenway, down two games to Cinci's three. Game Six was a must-win situation for the Sox and Ron paced the apartment like a caged animal the day before it was to be played, a travel day for the teams, the weather cold and gray, threatening to rain as October worked its way to a close.

"You need to relax, man," Sean told his friend as Ron lit his umpteenth Camel and chucked yet another empty Bud can into the trash. His tall, lean Ichabod Crane frame was hunched over with worry, the long brown hair he normally kept tied back in a ponytail, hanging loose and unruly on his shoulders. "You're gonna give yourself a heart attack before the game even starts tomorrow."

Might be for the best." Ron's thin face split into a grin, the first smile Sean had seen there since Boston scored those six runs in Game One. "I don't think I can hold up under the strain. Death may preferable, for sure."

But the strain was postponed for a little longer. The next day the gray skies opened up, and rain blanketed the state. Boston particularly, was a wash-out, and for two days the sports announcer on the evening news showed shots of the tarps covering the infield at Fenway, while intoning stats and predictions for the upcoming game, if, and when, it was ever played. Finally, the skies cleared and the first pitch of Game Six was thrown shortly after seven o'clock on a Tuesday evening.

Ron and Sean hunkered down on the sofa in front of the TV with a case of beer, and another bottle of Beam Ron swore he would crack only if the Red Sox won. By this time, Pete Rose, or not, Sean was pulling for the home team, wanting them badly to win, tie it up, and send the series to a winner-take-all seventh game. Teddie had picked up an extra shift at Cocktail Time, and Harv was off with Wade, the two of them making final preps for their big score. It was just Sean, Ron, the case of

Budweiser and the bottle of Jim Beam, to witness the rise, or fall, of Red Sox Nation in the apartment that October night.

The game turned out to be a tense one, even if it started on a high note for Boston who scored three runs in the first inning to take the lead. But the lead didn't last. The Reds tied it up with three runs of their own in the fifth, went ahead with two more in the seventh. For good measure they added another run in the eight to make it 6-3, all of these runs coming off Boston's giant of a pitcher, El Tiante, Ron groaning each time another Cinci played crossed home plate. The bottle of Beam was opened earlier than planned when it was Boston's turn to bat in the bottom of the eight.

"I can't do it, Seano." Ron tilted the bottle to his lips and drank deeply. "These fuckers are killing me."

"I hear you, man. But just remember what Yogi always said."

"Aggh." Ron put his hands up to cover his ears. "Are you insane? Mentioning the Yankees at a time like this?"

But all was not lost. Big Bernie Carbo stepped up to the plate with two men on and two outs, and with an 0-2 count launched a blast into the center field bleachers. Fenway erupted into a frenzy as Carbo took off for first, his homer tying the game up. As Carbo rounded second he yelled something out to Rose the TV couldn't catch, Rose yelling back, the wild grins on the opposing players that the TV could catch, showing no animosity—only the excitement of the moment for them in a tremendous ball game.

"Oh man, oh fuckin' man," Ron groaned as he jumped up and down in the small living room. "That fucking Bernie, oh man, that fucking Bernie."

It took four more innings to decide the outcome. By the time Carlton Fisk hit a leadoff homer in the bottom of the twelfth it was past midnight, the case of beer long gone, the bottle of Beam almost finished. Ron was barely conscious, forcing his eyes to stay open as he watched to see if Fisk's drive down the left field line stayed fair. As Fisk jumped up and down on home plate and the crowd at Fenway poured out on to the field when the ball cleared the foul pole, Ron passed out.

It was all over. Until the next day. Sean left Ron on the couch for Teddie to deal with when she came home, wondering for a second what she would think when she came in, beer cans overflowing the trash, the empty Beam bottle on the coffee table, her husband passed out drunk yet again. It wasn't his problem, Sean supposed. Though he wished she didn't have to come home to such a scene. Supposed if she didn't want to, she wouldn't. He could help her as far as the trash went, though, and did, taking the trash can in the kitchen filled with empty cans, along with the whiskey bottle, and depositing them outside in the garbage bin.

He emptied the overflowing ash tray as well, and spying a can of air freshener on a shelf in the kitchen, sprayed some around the living room, hoping it might help to soften the blow.

Satisfied he had done what he could Sean went into the spare bedroom, stretched out on his sleeping bag on the floor, and went to sleep, faintly hearing the front door open some time later as Teddie came home from work.

~47~ Route 20 again

Sean stayed in his sleeping bag the next morning until he heard the apartment door close behind Teddie as she went out. He'd been aware of her rustling around in the kitchen and the living room before she left, no doubt cleaning up the mess Ron and Sean had made the night before, and that Sean's half-ass cleaning job didn't make right. He had no desire to face her while she was doing that. The spare room was cool from the night air coming through the slightly cracked open window and he was comfortable in the warmth of the sleeping bag. Plainly, the World Series and Ron's drinking weren't sitting well with Teddie and Sean didn't want to be included in her troubles. It was also getting plainer by the day that it was time for Sean to head out. If he managed to stay out of her way until the Series was over and Ron back to his brand of normal, perhaps the friendship the three shared could be preserved. There was a slim chance this was possible, Sean felt, but he wanted it to be so.

Harv never made it back that night—a fact Sean wasn't aware of until he woke once in the early morning to take a leak and noticed his traveling partner wasn't snoring away in his bag. He must have crashed at Wade's place in Palmer which was perfectly fine with Sean. Harv's coming and goings at all hours while going about his transactions with Wade weren't helping any with the scene at Ron and Teddies. With a quick flash of clarity, Sean sat up in his bag. It *was* time to go. No more of that thinking that time was coming soon. That 'soon', was now. The World Series would end that night, one way or the other, and then he would be gone. *With Harv, or without him. Simple as that.* Or as Harv might say, "Ain't nothing but a thing, Buck."

He spent most of the afternoon on a bench at the park. The warmth of the sunlight cutting through the brisk air eased his hangover. There was a time, mid-afternoon or so, when all up and down Route 20 a procession of cars, maybe ten in number, drove slowly up and down the road. The cars strewn with Red Sox streamers and pennants, the drivers blowing their horns loudly and yelling out cheers for their team. Starting the celebration a little early was Sean's thought. Yankee's player, or not, Yogi's admonishment about waiting on the fat lady was hard to dispute. He smiled with this thought; glad his lanky pal wasn't there and able to read his mind. Just then he heard the screeching of a hawk flying overhead. Looking up he saw it going by, the peak of Bramford Mountain a background to the hawk's flight.

Out of nowhere he flashed on a Jefferson Airplane song. The one right after "Lather" on the Crown of Creation album. He could hear in his mind clear as day the opening line about climbing down the mountain. He flashed on Angel as the line faded away in his mind. Of that time they tripped on mescaline on the rocky ledge overlooking the valley below the peak of that mountain. He wasn't sure what colors they saw, but he was sure he had seen a bunch.

He couldn't help wondering then what might have gone down between the two of them had he stayed on in Massachusetts and not gone home like he had. And why had he suddenly gone home? Oh yeah. Because of the phone call. The one where he found out his mother was in a bad way. And he had no choice but to go south back to Lauderdale.

On his way back to the apartment Sean stopped at Center Drugs, bought a case of beer, leaving the Jim Beam to Ron to get, hoping for both their sakes that he did not, and putting the case of beer up on one shoulder he hoofed it back to the apartment. The sun was going down, the procession of cars done. Trudging into the kitchen of the apartment he found a note from Teddie on the table. He must have missed it on his way out earlier, but the little yellow memo sheet held brief instructions from her for the night:

"Boys, I'll be home around eleven, depending on how the game lasts. Good luck to the Red Sox! There are cold cuts and snacks in the fridge. Be good and enjoy the game.

Love, Teddie"

Her signature was a flourishing scrawl, full of the vibrancy he remembered her possessing back in the old days. As he put the note back down on the table, Ron came dragging into the kitchen, obviously just out of the rack. He looked like an un-washed corpse, his skin was all pale and clammy, long tendrils of his stringy hair draped over his shoulders, his eyes dull and lifeless looking.

"That bad, huh," he said.

"You don't look good, that's for sure. Your wife left us a note."

Ron laughed at Sean's honest assessment of his condition—but his eyes narrowed as he read Teddie's note, his hands shaking so badly Sean expected him to drop the note at any minute.

"Wow," Ron said when he was finished reading. "I can't believe she's being this civil. She sure as hell wasn't when she split this morning."

"Hey, that was then. Man, she left us food and said to enjoy the game. I'd say all is forgiven."

"You don't know Teddie very well is what I'd say. 'Enjoy?' Ha! Shows what she knows. How the fuck can I enjoy anything with the Sox down to just tonight?" He snagged a beer from the case Sean had set on the table. "Here's all the food I need, anyway, and thanks buddy for getting it. The "Breakfast of Champions.'"

"Breakfast time is ancient history," Sean said, watching Ron's Adam's apple bobbing as the beer flowed down his throat.

"Who cares?"

Like he had promised himself earlier at the park, Sean called his mom collect from the wall phone in the kitchen around 6:30 that night, giving her plenty of time to talk before the game was to start at 7:30. It was good to hear his mother's voice, annoying as she could be at times with what he felt could be an over-protective manner, one Sean believed should have left her once he was grown. But she was his mom, and it was true what the Judge had told him how a good mother loves her child all the way to the end, no matter what. Ruth Morgan had proved that to her son—many times in fact over the years. And though he rarely thought of it in so many words, he was glad to have her in his life.

So when her bubbly voice answered on the other end, "Morgan residence," he was surprised at how much he missed her right then—almost told her so but for some reason did not. Instead he let her ramble on for a bit, the usual questions, How are you, son? Where are you? Are you eating properly? Not taking those drugs anymore are you? Are you? Questions he answered as a dutiful son would, with honesty, glad for once, he realized, that he had no reason to lie to her about how he was, where he was, was he eating properly, and about the drugs.

Perhaps a first, in a long time. You know? First time he hadn't had to lie.

She stopped halfway through a ramble about the shakeup at the Courthouse, how the judge was retiring, the new sheriff was a jerk, and one of the county commissioners had been caught with a prostitute in a seedy motel down in Dania, saying, Oh, by the way he had a postcard from a girl named Beth. Did I ever meet this girl? Did he want her to read it to him? Or wait until he got home—and when was that going to be, anyway?

The upshot being Sean gave her the go-ahead about telling him what the postcard from Beth had to say. After his mom described the front picture on the card, one of Central Park in the summer, she read on the back that Beth was going to be in Fort Lauderdale over Thanksgiving. If Sean was around maybe they could meet up somewhere? She included a phone number where she could be reached when she arrived. And that was that from Beth. He was both happy, and curious to hear from her—planned to call her, if he was indeed back in Lauderdale for the holiday.

"Thanks, Mom, that's so cool, and yes, I'll let you know my plans," he was saying when Ron yelled out from the living room, "C'mon Seano, the games starting." He told his mom he loved her, and was saying goodbye as Ron yelled out again, "What the fuck, man? You gonna help me through this ordeal or not?"

Putting the phone back in the cradle he grabbed a beer out of the fridge and headed into the living room where on the TV in the corner, Boston's Spaceman Bill Lee was getting ready to throw the first pitch of Game Seven.

~48~ Game 7: It's all over now, Baby Blue

Teddie's instructions or not it didn't turn out to be a game Ron could enjoy. The Spaceman was on point for Boston up until the sixth inning when Cinci's Tony Perez hit a two run shot that cut into the Sox's 3-0 lead. Lee had to leave the mound in the seventh with a blister on his finger after "Charley Hustle" tied it up with an RBI single. The Curse of the Bambino kicked in all the way in the ninth with the game still tied, and the Sox's manager elected to pitch his rookie Jim Burton. When the dust settled Cincinnati was the new World Champion, and while the exuberant Big Red Machine celebrated on the field quiet Boston fans streamed out of Fenway Park.

Ron was quiet as well, the tension and excitement fueling his last ten days vanished. He was also drunk. When he stood up to click the TV off Sean was amazed his pal still had the motor control left to perform that simple function. Having quit the beer in the sixth inning when the game turned hairy, Ron turned instead to the Jim Beam to see him through. Still recovering some from the night before, Sean stuck with the Bud's, nursing them at that. But once he started on the Beam it didn't take long for Ron to cross over into full bore drunk, alternating between rage, laughter, or painful groaning with each twist of the game. Now, after turning off the TV he stood in front of the set, swaying back and forth on his feet as he stared at the blank screen.

"Co'suckers." He turned to Sean, his eyes empty and red. "You see tha'?"

"Unfortunately. Go to bed, buddy, you've had it."

"Co'suckers," Ron repeated as he stumbled towards the bedroom. "And you, you soun' like tha' fuckin' Teddie now. Tellin' me wha' to do." He staggered in front of the open bedroom door and fell face first onto the rug.

"Jesus, man." Sean went to help him up. "C'mon, man, give me your hand. Time to crash."

"Go way, fucker'" Ron lurched to his knees and threw a loopy swing at Sean, his thin features contorted as his arms flailed in the air. "Your fuckin' faul' anyway, fucker. All tha' crap 'bout fuckin' Yogi Berra shit."

Easily ducking Ron's long arms Sean got him up into a bear hug. They wrestled like this through the door into the bedroom and when

Sean flung him down on the bed Ron stayed there, still muttering, "Your faul', all your faul,"" his face down in the covers as Sean closed the door behind him on his way out.

He had straightened up things a little in the living room, thrown the empty beer cans away, and was putting the Beam bottle into the cabinet above the kitchen sink when Teddie came home from work. He started to tell her what happened, but she waved him off. To Sean's surprise, she also stopped him from putting the Beam away, instead taking a long pull off it, and bottle in hand, going into the living room and sinking down on the sofa. Well, Sean thought as he followed her. *When in Rome.* And he sat down next to her.

They sat in silence for a while on the crumpled sofa passing the bottle back and forth. She complained some about the long shift, how the place went crazy when the Red Sox lost, some of the patrons overturning chairs and smashing beer bottles on the floor in their anger. He wanted to tell her about his possible decisions concerning his approaching departure—but before he could she got up, turned the TV on for the late news, and disgusted with what she saw sat back down next to him, took the bottle of Beam from him and drank another long pull.

It was unsettling for him having her sitting so close like that with their thighs touching. She was his good friend's wife, yet all he could think of, with her being so close to him, was how beautiful she was, even beat as she was from her long shift at the funky bar on the outskirts of Springfield where she had to deal with drunken Red Sox fans taking their anger out on the bar and probably on her, too. It wasn't right she had to put up with that. Had to live the life she was living. He didn't like thinking like that. But seeing the sadness, the defeat, on her face as she tilted the bottle back again and drank, he couldn't help it. Apparently, she felt the same.

"This can't go on," she said finally, the bottle held with both hands in her lap as she stared at the blank TV screen. "Ron and me. It's just no good anymore. She looked straight into Sean's eyes. "You must have figured that out by now, huh? A bright guy like you." She punched him lightly on the shoulder, a glimpse of a smile flickering across her lips.

"Geez, Teddie, he's just been boozing it a little more than usual 'cause of the World Series. That's all."

"That's nowhere near the truth, Sean. And you know it."

He supposed he did. Didn't like it. But he knew she was right.

"He doesn't even make love to me anymore." This came out of nowhere after another silence between them. "Not now. You see how he gets at night. And in the morning he just groans, gets up, and goes to work."

Sitting next to him in her cigarette and booze smelling Cocktail Time uniform, her almond-colored skin paler now from the hours she put in at the bar, her face in a discouraged frown as she passed the bottle back to him. Sean—seeing her like this, being with her like this—was at a loss. If there was something he could say to counter her defeat, her sadness, he was damned if he knew what it was.

"Look around, Sean."

She pointed at the shabby walls of the apartment, at the framed Norman Rockwell prints a former tenant had put up. In contrast to the All American look of those prints, on the other wall a poster of Che Guevara Ron must have kept from his college days and tacked up in defiance. The TV on its rickety stand. The overflowing ashtray from Ron's nonstop smoking that Sean had meant to empty and forgot to— all of this blending in to create a sad décor Sean suddenly wouldn't wish on anyone. Least of all a woman like Teddie.

"Do you think this is what I dreamed my life would be? Do you, Sean?" But she didn't give him the time to answer. "Jesus, Sean, I'd be happy if he just fucked me on occasion. The hell with making love. Just fuck me and let me know I'm still alive. Let me know he's still alive."

He put his arms around her, not knowing what else to do, not sure he should even do that. The sad intensity in her voice scared him. There was no talk of Revolution now, no talk of a new order, the new world to come. Woodstock was long over, the supposed Nation it had spawned nowhere in sight. It was just him and a lonely woman in a little apartment on a Wednesday night where everyone there was dying to some degree or another.

"Goddamn it, Sean." She lifted her head from his shoulder. "Goddamn it for how I feel sometimes."

Suddenly she was kissing him, he was kissing her, the two of them falling back on the sofa as he held her body tight to his, thinking that it wasn't right, couldn't be right, but yet—but yet it was happening, somehow the two of them naked on the couch, where their clothes had gone he had no idea, how they had magically disappeared, so it was that he was inside her, groaning with her as she groaned, moving with her as she moved, the idea that none of this was right still somewhere in the back of his thoughts, but unimportant when he was doing something with her he had wanted to for a very long time. Something that she wanted too, had wanted, judging by the way she kept moaning in his ear, 'Yes, oh yes, Sean, about time, about time." And then she shuddered beneath him—and he groaned, knowing, feeling, that what was happening to her was happening to him, as well. He lifted up a little from her and looked into her dark eyes dilated in the dim light But when he went to pull away, to pull out, she clutched his hips with her hands and would not let him.

"Not yet, my Wanderer," she said. "In a little bit. But not now."

The bedroom door opened and Ron stood in the doorway, looking like a ghost. Yes, Sean thought. *Exactly like a ghost.* The way his eyes jerked wildly about, obviously not seeing anything? *Just like a fucking ghost.*

"Teddie!" Hearing her name shouted out like that made her flinch beneath Sean. "Goddamn it, Teddie, I puked. I fucking puked!"

He was too far gone, Sean realized, to see his wife and friend lying naked on the sofa.

"I need you, Teddie. Goddamn it I need you," Ron yelled once more before staggering backward into the bedroom.

'I'd better go to him."

She bent over to retrieve her uniform, her bra and panties, the sadness in her voice, back—its recent departure only a brief moment in her life.

"Yeah." He was already missing her as she sat up. "You'd better."

What else could he have said? Nothing he could think of. *Nothing that would make any sense.*

~49~ I-95 again

If Sean thought the night was over it wasn't. For quite a while the sounds of arguing came from the other room, the arguing one sided, consisting of Ron yelling obscenities and Teddie trying to quiet him down. Whatever joy he had known with Teddie on the couch was like it had never happened, lost in the flood of curses streaming through the walls of the darkened apartment. Part of Sean wished it could all be different. Teddie was a woman he could hang with. He had known this for a long time, having been instantly drawn to her from the moment she held her hand out to him at an anti-war rally one afternoon in G'ville. In her hand was a tab of acid. He could still see the smile on her face as he swallowed the hit—knew then that with a smile like that he would have swallowed anything, followed her anywhere, if she gave him the word.

The noise let off a little in the other room and lying alone in his sleeping bag he thought of how not so very long ago he'd felt the same about the blonde hippie girl in Frisco. Yet Janie was still there, and he was three thousand miles away on the other side of the country. Maybe his emotions were too quick when it came to women. *Too damn fast when it came to a pretty face and an easy smile.* He needed to watch that in the future. Little good seemed to come from it. Holding on to that thought he rolled over on his side, determined, arguing in the other room or not, to go to sleep.

He had no idea of how much later it was when Harv came in. He could have been sleeping for hours, or just a few minutes. How long didn't matter—it was still the feel of ragged breath on his face and Harv bending over him in the dark shaking his shoulder that woke him.

"C'mon, Buck." It was more of a gasp than speech. "We gotta move."

"What the hell?" He felt instantly guilty for being rough like that on his friend—still, after what had gone down earlier he was in no mood for one of Harv's harebrained whims. "Go to sleep, man and we'll hash it out in the morning."

"Can't wait, Seano. We've gotta move. Now."

He could feel Harv sitting down suddenly on the floor next to him, a soft grunt slipping from his mouth as he did. Awake, his eyes open, he saw Harv clutching his one side as he sat—saw as well that instead of Harv's ever present grin, a sickly smile stared back at him in the pale light.

"It all went to hell, Seano," Harv gasped. "We don' have time now to talk about it. Wade started shooting. I think he's dead. I might be, too." He pulled a beat up looking satchel out of the darkness behind him and pushed it towards Sean. "At least I got this, ol' buddy. Worked too hard to leave it behind. No sir, damn sure wasn't gonna do that."

The rest of it was a dream, beginning when Harv pulled his hand away from his side, revealing his shirt soaked with a dark substance Sean understood immediately was blood. Getting up he got a towel from the bathroom in the hall and soaked it in cool water before applying it to Harv's side. He was no doctor, had never seen a gunshot wound before, and now that he had wished he hadn't. The skin all around the little red hole, once cleaned of the wet gore was bruised and blue. When the pressure of the towel was removed dark blood oozed from where the bullet had burrowed in, Harv groaning as Sean pressed the towel to his side again to stop the flow.

"Jesus wept, Buck. Easy, man, you're killin' me."

"Looks like you've done a good job of that on your own. Just hold the towel there and try to keep from bleeding all over Teddie's floor."

"You're worried about Teddie's freakin' floor?"

"I don't know what I'm worried about."

He was out the door then, heart pounding as he raced out to Wade's truck which Harv had stolen, as well. "Christ, Buck, he didn't need it anymore." It was hard for Sean to dispute logic like that. Besides, he didn't see how he could question anything just then.

Wade's old Dodge was parked haphazardly across the driveway and reaching it Sean jerked the door open. There were bloody handprints on the steering wheel and a splotchy stain on the seat. But the keys were in the ignition and ignoring the blood Sean cranked the engine over. Backing out of the driveway and with the lights off, he moved off down Palmer Street. It was eerie, sitting in a truck that smelled of blood and with the headlights off, wheeling down Bramford's other main drag. He expected to be pulled over at any minute, caught in the flashing blue lights and siren of the town's lone police cruiser.

But there were no flashing lights, no siren, and he ditched the truck down the street behind the junior high school. He did his best to wipe any fingerprints he and Harv had left, using another one of Teddie's towels brought along just for that. Finished with that he flung the keys and the towel up on the roof of the school and started on the run back to the apartment. He wasn't any kind of a criminal mastermind—had never thought of his earlier dope running career as being really criminal—but he was doing what he could under the circumstances. With a little luck they just might pull it off. Hadn't the famous Sean Morgan luck always come through for him in the past? This would not be the time for that streak to be broken. Not the time at all.

The next thing he was actively aware of was being in his truck with Harv on I-91 heading towards Boston. There had been no goodbyes back at the apartment. Just a scrawled note on the back of the one Teddie had left for Ron and him earlier—in another lifetime it seemed. But he thanked the both of them for everything. Said it meant a lot to him, and he would explain everything later, adding he hoped to see them down in Florida some time, perhaps in the spring. He signed it "Love, Sean," wondering for a moment if that were true—then he was out the door once again, this time to his own truck where Harv, already inside, was slumped over and asleep.

He drove until dawn, leaving Massachusetts and the rest of New England behind in the dark while Harv wavered in and out of consciousness, his soft groans filling the cab above the whine of the tires against the road. Sean, sort of comatose himself, was doing his best to keep his focus on the driving and not the little hallucinations created by being drunk earlier, his lack of sleep, and the lights of the cars going by the other way on the highway playing across the windshield. As the sun came up they were somewhere in New Jersey, where exactly he could not say. The sleepy-eyed clerk at the aged motel off of the interstate handed him a key, though, with no questions. By this time Sean was feeling sort of like he was an actor in one of those old gangster movies. *You know? Maybe a Jimmy Cagney or Edward G. Robinson flic. Running on the highway late at night. Holing up at daybreak in some cheap dive off the beaten path.* As he helped the moaning Harv out of the truck and into the crappy little room, he was hoping like hell no one saw them—that if they did, they paid no mind. Once safely inside, with Harv laid out on one of the two beds, he pulled the curtains shut, collapsed on the other bed still fully dressed, and fell instantly asleep.

~50~ The Endless Highway

He awoke later, cramped, and his feet sore from his boots he'd forgotten to take off. The motel room was twilight dark with only a crack of sunlight slipping through the drawn curtains. It was still day time. Harv, on the other bed, was sleeping quietly, stretched out on his back, a hand covering the stained hole in his shirt. Sean was startled suddenly by the fresh blood he saw on Harv's pale fingers. *Jesus. Is it ever going to stop?* A man could only lose so much blood and live. With that thought he got up and went to Harv, wondering if he *was* still alive.

"Christ, Buck." Harv's eyes fluttered open. "Man, I was dreamin' my dad was leanin' over me and telling me to c'mon. Only, seein' as how Dad's been dead for the last fifteen years I wasn't real keen on goin'. If you catch my drift. In fact, Seano, I was real happy to see it was you and not him leanin' over me."

"Yeah, I bet you were."

"Damn it all," Harv groaned. "But I sure do hurt."

"I know you do, buddy. I gotta get you to a hospital, man. This is no good."

"No hospitals, Sean. No fuckin' doctors. No fuckin' way. Just get me home. To my brother's place. Rob'll know what to do."

"All right," Sean said, not sure at all if it was right—not sure if Harv's brother would know what to do at all.

But what could he do? There was a code, after all. One that said one had to honor their friend's request. It wasn't a code covered in any classes at school. Never once brought up at home, either, and no surprise, considering what kind of man his father had been. Not only that, but he had already violated that code once before. That night in G'ville as he hid in the pine trees across the road from the Cave and watched the law dogs take his friends away. Not that there was anything he could do about it at the time. *But still.* That night gnawed at him at times. Now, leaning over his friend Harv, who was in about as bad a way as one could get—well then, what choice did Sean have? And here was a question that for once he had an answer to.

When it was dark they set out again. He grabbed a sack of burgers and fries and a cup of soup for Harv at a little diner up the street from the motel. He wolfed down the lukewarm burger and fries as he drove, chasing the greasy meal with long pulls from a large Styrofoam cup of cold Pepsi. He had considered a tall-boy Bud instead but quickly tossed that idea, figuring a little clarity in his head could go a long way for him that night. There was enough caffeine in the soda to keep him moving for now. Later he would stop for coffee. And then keep on rolling until dawn. He supposed that was a good enough plan. For lack of a better one he figured to stay with it.

Harv tried a couple mouthfuls of the soup, but groaning, put it aside. "I never could abide split pea, Buck. I'm sorry. I know you meant well and all, man. But I just can't do it."

The smile on his pal's face lifted Sean's spirits and for a moment he thought they both might be okay.

"Don't worry about it, bud. It didn't look that good to me either. But it was that, or chili, and you fart bad enough as it is."

Harv tried to laugh but couldn't, clutching his side instead. "Hey Seano, you didn't leave the Buddha behind did you?"

"Huh? You're all shot up and that's what you're worried about? The Buddha? That you stole from Caroline, by the way?"

"Yeah, yeah, I know. But I kinda considered the little feller my good luck charm, you dig?"

"Not much of a good luck charm if you ask me. Considering the shape you're in."

"True. But it wasn't all bad luck, that scene with Wade and those Colombian bastards. I walked away with the cash, didn't I?"

"Yeah, there is that, I suppose. But don't worry. The Buddha's in the back of the truck, still sitting on top of the spare tire where he's been since you showed up with him."

"Good, good." Harv sighed, still holding tight to his wounded side. "Thas' real good, Seano. Thanks, man. You've always been there for me. I won't forget it, either." Sighing again he laid his head back against the seat, closed his eyes, and was quiet for a long time after.

With Harv sleeping, radio stations hard to find, and just his thoughts to keep him company, Sean couldn't help but flash back on other times he had traveled the same highway he was on now. Harv and he had come that way back in April. Back when nothing was on their menu but good times and seeing what the country might hold for them. They were outside of Richmond when Harv woke up. Sean wasn't sure what time it was, but it had to be pushing daybreak. Soon it would be time to find another motel. With a little more luck and some hard driving they could be in Florida the next night and damn near home. This sounded better to him than he'd ever thought possible. That being home thing. But he was tired of green place name signs lit up by the truck's headlights flashing by in the dark. The noises of the other cars and trucks he shared the highway with. Tired of this particular journey is what it all boiled down to.

"I feel really, bad, Seano" Harv sat up suddenly, his face drawn and white in the glare of headlights going the other way coming through the truck's windshield. "Pull over, man, if you can. Think I'm gonna throw up."

"Just take it easy for a sec." They were coming up to a rest area on the right and pulling in he drove all the way around to the very back where they would be protected from any prying eyes. "All right," he said, shutting the truck off. "Here we are, bud."

Jumping out of the cab he went around to open Harv's door and help him out. It was cool and moist just before the dawn. In front of him was a bluff running off behind the rest area—beyond the bluff, the taller buildings of Richmond reaching up to meet the day and the sun starting to rise. Holding on to Harv's shoulders he helped him lean forward over the dew wet grass. The dry retching sounds he began to make struck Sean to the quick, the sound going right through him.

"Oh Jesus, man, it hurts," Harv moaned. "Oh God here it comes." He opened his mouth wide and Sean watched as a crimson flow gushed from his stretched lips.

When it was over Sean helped him back into the truck where he slumped up against the seat, his face pale and drawn. "It's better, now, Buck," he said, just a flicker of his old grin back on his lips. "Damn, but I think I'm gonna be okay. It doesn't hurt anymore."

Sean started to say something, started to go around to his side of the truck and get in, when Harv stiffened up. His eyes opened wide as a dry rattle escaped from deep inside of him. It was all too fast. *Too goddamn fast.* A minute later, probably less, Harv's head drooped over his chest, his whole body relaxing.

Empty of everything, Sean stood there beside the truck, staring at what once had been his living, breathing, laughing friend. He could hear the cars and semis roaring by on the highway—could see in the distance beyond the rest area their headlights cutting through the fog drifting over the morning. The bag of money lay next to Harv on the seat of the truck and Sean thought how it was all Harv had in the world. And it wasn't even really his. The fog began to roll in thicker across the bluff, and the little valley below that bluff, as Sean wondered what he had in the world. It wasn't much. A Jeep. Maybe a home to return to. Not much. A little more than Harv, he supposed. The first shafts of real sunlight began to break through the fog. Suddenly Sean felt that terrible aloneness that came over him at times. Felt it coming, said, no to himself, and straightening up said aloud, "Fuck it," and shook it off.

Like the lunch time epiphany he'd had at the Jack-in-the-Box outside of Monterrey, when he realized he didn't want to go to Mexico, it all came to him in a rush, what he had to do flooding over him as he stood looking at the morning fog. And alone or not it was up to him, Sean Morgan, to do it.

First order of business was to find a phone booth and call the judge. The rest area probably had one of those, so finding it shouldn't be hard to do. The judge would know how to help Sean. How to help Harv's brother with what was about to come his way. Hadn't the judge told him in the spring if he ever needed help to just give him a call? Well, he damn sure needed help now, so call the judge it was going to be.

And once that was squared away, and he was back in—well, he didn't know. Had no idea right. Maybe Beth? She might be entering the picture. He hoped so. Maybe Beth would turn out to be just what, or who, he needed right then. Maybe. But thinking that he flashed on Teddie. Flashed on the fact that Beth or not, he didn't think he was finished with Teddie. In fact, once things settled down a bit, he was going to reach out to her. Maybe more than just reach out. But go back to Bramford and take her away with him. Help her find that life she wanted. And why not? They were both young. Married or not, her marriage to Ron didn't have to be written in stone forever. Not if she didn't want it to be. He didn't think she did. Not after what had gone down between them on the couch while Ron lay passed out drunk in their bedroom. The judge could probably help Sean—help Teddie— with that as well.

Wishful thinking? He wondered as he got back in the truck and carefully drove around to the front of the rest area, looking, as he drove, for a blue phone booth sign—telling himself as he did that most importantly of all, he had to keep his cool. Had to play it right. Let the luck that had always been with him, do its thing. Beginning with the phone call to the judge.

And from there? That was the easy part. He would get back on the highway and head south—he would finish the ride.

About the Author

Gene lee has been writing poetry and fiction since he was fifteen. Over the years his poetry has appeared in The Kerouac Connection, Cathartic, The South Florida Poetry Review, and other literary magazines. In his late forties he turned to fiction and began working on the stories and novellas that eventually became the Raines Family Trilogy. The three books that make up this trilogy, Men Without Hate, Raines in the Day, and Emmitt at Love, have been published by All Things That Matter Press. His outdoor stories have appeared in Sporting Classics magazine. An avid outdoorsman Mr. Lee enjoys fly fishing, wingshooting, and a gentlemanly game of golf on occasion. For the last 35 years he has resided with his wife in Sebastian, Florida on the banks of the Indian River Lagoon. When not busy at his desk putting down on paper what his Muse suggest he do, Mr. Lee can be found on the river casting to the snook and redfish that roam its waters.

ALL THINGS THAT MATTER PRESS

FOR MORE INFORMATION ON TITLES AVAILABLE FROM
ALL THINGS THAT MATTER PRESS, GO TO
http://allthingsthatmatterpress.com
or contact us at
allthingsthatmatterpress@gmail.com